MW01131014

The Thirteenth Disciple

Soldier or Saint

Jack Luchsinger

WestBow Press books may be ordered through booksellers or by contacting:

WestBow Press
A Division of Thomas Nelson
1663 Liberty Drive
Bloomington, IN 47403
www.westbowpress.com
1-(866) 928-1240

ISBN: 978-1-4497-1280-8 (sc)
ISBN: 978-1-4497-1281-5 (dj)
ISBN: 978-1-4497-1282-2 (e)

Library of Congress Control Number: 2011922280

Printed in the United States of America

WestBow Press rev. date: 3/7/2011

For Heather, Todd and Brad, insight to life, love, and faith…

And to Pam, my partner in all of the above.

Forward

Jesus' life spanned only thirty-three years. His ministry lasted no more than three years. Yet, his influence on mankind has continued for thousands of years. The New Testament of the Bible has made this possible.

The story of Jesus, his life and his teachings, have been preserved for us in the writings of the gospels of the New Testament. The gospels have been the source of inquiry for many centuries. This book was inspired by such inquiry.

There were more than three hundred disciples of Jesus by the time of his death. Despite this number, the gospels focus on only those that Jesus personally selected as his chosen ones during his three year ministry. Much has been made of the twelve mentioned by name. They are also referred to as apostles for having witnessed the entire ministry of Jesus.

Deeper in the translations of the gospels, there is evidence that Jesus selected another to be a disciple before the end of his ministry. The thirteenth disciple is hardly noticed not having been called by name. He is only identified in the gospels as the 'other disciple.' Even so, his role is as important as any of those mentioned by name. His selection was a necessary part of the plan for human salvation. He is with Jesus in the gardens of Gethsemane. He is with Jesus at his trial. He is with Peter at the tomb. He has a prominent role during the last days of Jesus' life and in the time that follows.

The gospels recognize the thirteenth disciple by his deeds alone. It is the Thirteenth Disciple who is reputed to have authored two of the four gospels that provide the foundation for the Christian faith.

This is the story of the Thirteenth Disciple.

Chapter 1. "Dreams are but fragments of memory."

Lightening struck out violently across the sky. It crashed to the earth and tore gaping holes in the landscape. The dark gray clouds raced in gigantic, swirling circles around each bolt of lightening striking out through the heavy blackening air. The wind whipped at every living thing on the ground below as if to cleanse the soiled earth of the darkening blood that stained each soul.

The lone figure cried out, "My God, my God, why have you forsaken me?" He looked first at the heavens above and then down, down at me. His eyes were piercing. I saw the pain and felt it in my own heart. I saw the fear, the questioning, and the momentary loss of understanding. Finally, with one last gasp for breath, he sighed, "Thy will be done." His eyes dulled as he slowly slipped the bonds of humanity in fulfillment of the prophesies.

I awoke with a start. Sitting up in bed, I realized that it was the same dream that I had had many times over the years.

Why was there nothing that I could do? I had witnessed it all and more. I was a part of it. I guess that I had been a part of it from the day that I was brought into this world. He had told me that it would fall to me to record all that was spoken and unspoken. It is a monumental task but I was born to it. It is my life's work. I shall not rest until it is completed.

I have been known by several names but now I am Mark. I was born in the year of the birth of our Lord, Jesus. My parents were never known to me. At the time of my birth, an edict was proclaimed by Herod the Great, King of Israel, that all male children born to Israel and living in the Town of Bethlehem were to be put to death. My parents, fearing for my safety, placed me in a basket and hid me behind some rocks on a hillside just beyond the town. Roman soldiers sent to support Herod's men found me and carried me to the commander of their watch.

As they approached their commander, they called out, "Hail Marcus. Look at what we have found. A male child hidden among some rocks on the hillside. What do you wish that we do with the child? Should we turn him over to the Jews?"

Marcus approached the soldiers and examined the child. As he reached down to remove the child's blanket, the baby's hand suddenly shot out and grabbed the Centurion's forefinger. Marcus smiled, "This baby has a strong grip for a child of Israel!" He looked more closely at the child. "He has a fairer complexion than those of Israel though there is the touch of this land upon him."

Marcus withdrew his hand releasing the baby's grip. He said to his men, "Turning the child over to the Jews means certain death for this baby boy. Who am I to decide if this child should live or die? That is a decision that only the gods should make." Marcus again looked down at the child. "No, this child will not be turned over to the Jews this day!"

Marcus turned to his most trusted legionnaire. "Quintus, I have a quest for you to undertake. Come walk with me and bring the child."

Quintus took the child in his arms and followed Marcus up the hillside, away from the town. When sufficiently far away from the others, Marcus looked at his friend and fellow soldier. "Quintus, I have a favor to ask of you. I want you to take this baby boy back to Rome. I want you to take him to my old teacher, Flavius. Tell Flavius that I ask a favor of him. I am willing to pay what ever is necessary for him to undertake my request. I want Flavius to take this child and to raise this boy as if he were my son."

Quintus looked long and hard at his commander. This was unheard of for a citizen of Rome and a Centurion. But, Quintus knew that his commander was no ordinary man, no ordinary citizen of Rome. Quintus also understood that the Centurion's military demands were met at the sacrifice of family. "As your son?" Quintus asked.

"Yes." Marcus replied. "Tell Flavius that the boy is to be educated as I was. That when old enough, he is to be taught the use of weapons and trained for the Legions. I will judge the future of this boy on the basis of his success in gaining knowledge and his ability to compete at arms."

Quintus had served with Marcus through many campaigns on the frontier. Each had saved the other's life on more than one occasion. Such experiences create a bond among men that only those who have lived through them can understand. Both men looked down on the child and then at each other. Quintus nodded, "I will see to it that all that you have requested will be done."

Marcus knew that Quintus would do this special task without any hesitation. "I will provide you with a pass and all that you will need for the journey. Come, let's go back to the encampment."

As they walked toward the Roman encampment outside the Town of Bethlehem, Quintus asked, "What shall we call the boy?"

Marcus smiled as a thought crossed his mind. "He shall be called Marcus Titus."

Chapter 2. "The First Journey"

Quintus departed the Roman encampment that night. It was important that the boy be removed from Bethlehem as soon as possible.

Quintus traveled with the baby boy, Marcus Titus, and a nurse procured by his commander to care for the baby. Quintus had his orders under Roman seal. This would provide him a clear passage to Rome.

As he crossed the valley and climbed the ridge, the sound of women wailing filled the night air. King Herod's men had killed all the male children of Bethlehem. The Romans had stood by and done nothing. This was a sovereign matter that by Caesar's decree remained within the province of the King of Israel. The Romans had dismissed the decision as one made by the Gods of Israel. This was confirmed for them when they saw that an unusual light from a brilliant star had singled out Bethlehem for Herod's wrath.

Still, to Quintus and he thought to his commander as well, the decision to punish Bethlehem and kill all male children was unjust and unwarranted. Strangely, the boy, now under his protection, gave him some peace within as he rode away. He guessed that that had played a part in the decision made by Marcus Aurelius as well.

Marcus had directed Quintus to first travel to Jerusalem to pick up provisions for the trip. Perhaps Quintus would be able to join a merchant caravan going west to the Mediterranean. From Jerusalem, Quintus would go into Lydda and finally to the port city of Joppa where he would be able to sail to Rome.

Two days out from Jerusalem, Quintus overtook a man leading a donkey bearing a wife and child. As Quintus approached, the man nodded, smiling and acknowledging what he obviously mistook to be a common bond. Both were traveling with wife and child. Quintus nodded in return.

The encounter would have faded into memory if it were not for the man's wife. Her composure was like no other woman that Quintus had ever seen. There was an inner beauty that shone around her and she was completely absorbed with her new born child. Quintus remembered the mother and her child long after the man's image had vanished from his mind. He would later tell the story to young Marcus Titus describing the woman's beauty as "not of this world."

On the third day of their journey, five soldiers of King Herod's army encountered Quintus and his companions. They commanded him to halt. They asked whom he was and if the woman and child were his. He presented his orders from his commander and explained that the boy was a Roman citizen traveling with his nurse, under Roman protection. As he said this, Quintus placed his hand on the hilt of his sword.

Herod's soldiers looked questioningly at the orders which Quintus had presented to them. It was obvious to Quintus that the soldiers could not read. Quintus looked directly at the soldier who appeared to be in charge and demanded, "Do you not recognize the Seal of Rome? It gives us passage to Joppa and then on to the Great Sea. From there we travel to Rome."

The soldier hesitated. He looked down at the Seal of Rome and then back at Quintus. The fact that Quintus was a physically commanding person and that his large hands now rested on the hilt of his sword, had its effect.

The soldier turned to his men and said, "He has the proper papers for passage." With one last quick look at Quintus, he led the other soldiers away.

Other than a turbulent voyage by sea, the incident with Herod's men was the only time during the journey to Rome that Quintus had any serious concern for the safety of young Marcus Titus. Their galley had sailed from Joppa to Corinthus on the Greek peninsula, then to the port city of Syracusae located at the tip of Sicilia. The weather had not been favorable for the second portion of their journey and the crew spent an extra week at Syracusae to restock their vessel and regain their sea bearing for the final trip to Rome.

Chapter 3. "Teacher"

Quintus found Flavius in his garden tending to his flowers. "Pardon me Teacher. I do not mean to interrupt but I come under orders from my commander, Marcus Aurelius. My name is Quintus."

Flavius stood and turned toward the Roman soldier. "Marcus sent you to me. My former student has done well." Flavius always thought aloud. "What is the purpose of your visit?"

Quintus took note of the steady gaze of the older man. This was a man of power and influence beyond that of a teacher. Quintus spoke, "Marcus entrusted a child, a boy, to my care. It is his wish that you take this boy into your home. He would ask that you educate the boy and instruct him in the use of weapons when he is at the appropriate age. Marcus has provided a nurse and will insure that you are compensated for whatever is needed or required. He said that he would judge the value of this boy based upon how he succeeds with his studies."

Flavius had provided Marcus with his education and had seen to it that Marcus was one of the most accomplished students in the art of self-defense. Flavius knew Marcus well.

"Tell me Quintus, what is this child's background? Is this boy the son of Marcus?"

"No Teacher. This is not a son." Quintus sensed that he could trust this teacher. He explained how the child came into the hands of his commander. He recounted how his commander arrived at the decision to spare the boy and send the child to Rome.

Flavius understood the magnitude of what Marcus was doing. He understood the bond that must exist between Marcus and this soldier,

Quintus. Quintus' use of the familiar reference to Marcus gave additional proof to Flavius about his conclusions. He asked, "Where is this boy?"

Quintus pointed to the outer gate. "He is with the nurse, beyond the outer gate."

Flavius looked in the direction of the gate and said, "Has the boy a name?"

"Marcus Titus." Quintus replied.

Flavius looked harshly at Quintus then a smile slowly crept across Flavius' face. "Bring the young boy and his nurse in. The child should meet Flavius Titus, his Teacher."

Chapter 4. "The Pupil"

Lucius was a strong athletic boy. He could throw the javelin farther than most men of Rome. He was an accomplished horse back rider and had received a number of awards in competitions with the broad sword. He worked hard at everything that he did so that he would excel and be someone that others would look up to. His peers knew not to challenge him and it was with fear that they would compete against him. This gave Lucius an advantage and he recognized this fact. He could see it in their eyes and this made him all the more invincible. His only weakness was in his academic pursuits. There, he struggled to maintain the minimum required scores. Lucius was proud of his physical accomplishments and because of the premium placed upon such achievements, he was a leader by force.

Marcus Titus had been trained in the classics. Flavius had never had a pupil who took to language and mathematics the way that Marcus did. By his teenage years, Marcus had mastered not only Latin and Greek but was well acquainted with History, Religion, and Art. His questions were always probative and his responses were always insightful. To Flavius' amazement, Marcus also seemed to understand how to maximize his physical strength. Although taller than most Roman boys his age, his frame was slight and he seemed years behind his Roman counterparts both in body mass and in muscle. In the competitions though, he always did well. When asked by Flavius, "How do you explain your success in the field today?" Marcus would always respond, "Knowledge is strength!" Both understood.

Marcus and Lucius traveled in different circles. Lucius was the son of a Senator of Rome. His destiny was to serve in the Legions of Rome as an officer and then one day take his father's seat in the Senate. Marcus was the son of a career officer in the Roman Army. His destiny was in the hands of the Gods and more immediately, his teacher, Flavius. Flavius often told Marcus when he would ask, 'What will become of me when I am a man?' "I will provide you with the tools, the Gods will provide you with the way."

During the Roman holidays, competitions took place in the Amphitheater of Statilius Taurus. It was a time for celebration and boys and men would compete with one another in contests of skill, strength, and self defense. Flavius thought that it was time for Marcus Aurelius to return to Rome and learn first hand that a decision made long ago was as the Gods intended.

Flavius informed Marcus Titus that he had been registered by his teacher to compete in the Amphitheater games.

"Do you think that I am ready?" Marcus smiled.

"You are ready for more than the Amphitheater, my pupil. But we will take one step at a time."

Marcus smiled again at Flavius. How often he had heard his teacher and friend say to him, 'We will take one step at a time.'

Marcus was curious about the Amphitheater. "What is the history behind the stadium?"

Flavius was always surprised by the direction that Marcus' mind would take. "Well, my young friend, the Amphitheater of Statilius Taurus is the first stone amphitheater to be built in Rome. Prior to its construction, all amphitheaters were built out of wood.

One of my distant cousins, Statilius Taurus, served Caesar Octavian during the wars and was rewarded by being appointed consul in Rome. During his time in Rome, he promoted sport entertainment for the citizens of Rome and had the Amphitheater constructed as a permanent structure to house the games.

I must admit, it is a beautiful amphitheater and it should last a thousand years. Statilius certainly made the most of his service in the Legions."

"Am I to compete with the Legions of Rome?" Marcus teased.

Flavius frowned, "Never compete with the Legions of Rome. In our world, that is a competition you will never win. Rome is all-powerful. Physically, it will not be beaten."

"Then I will use my mind." Marcus said with finality. He drew a broad sword from its sheath on the wall and measured the length of it with his eye.

Flavius was never quite certain when Marcus was having a joke at his expense or being serious minded with his pronouncements.

"Keep your eye on today, Marcus. Tomorrow will take care of itself."

The pupil and the teacher glanced at one another and in that instant both understood the lesson.

Chapter 5. "Return to Rome"

Marcus Aurelius had received the invitation to come to Rome for the holidays and to bear witness to his son's progress. He arranged with Rome to return with Quintus and his legion for rest and renewal of their bonds with Rome. It was Roman policy to bring their legions back from the frontier posts periodically to reestablish the ties that were essential to Roman control of their broad empire. Marcus received the blessing of Caesar for a brief holiday in Rome with his legion before returning to their post on the frontier.

Marcus had followed his son's progress through regular reports from Flavius. He was anxious to see the boy that Flavius described as tall, slight of frame, agile in mind and body, and touched by the Gods with wisdom far beyond a humble teacher's sphere of knowledge. Flavius had not been known to Marcus to be particularly religious. The phrase 'touched by the Gods' caught Marcus' attention and he was surprised.

Marcus Aurelius' pending arrival in Rome was not mentioned to young Marcus Titus. It had been agreed that it would be a surprise and that nothing was to disturb the boy's preparation for the competitions.

It had been five years since Marcus Aurelius had last seen his adoptive son. The boy was now sixteen years old. It was time to have the boy travel to the frontier to learn about life beyond Rome. Flavius had written that he recommended the travel as a way to broaden the knowledge of young Marcus beyond the walls and literature of Rome. Marcus Aurelius viewed it as his son's destiny.

The journey back to Rome was uneventful for Marcus and his legion. They had been replaced temporarily with a reserve legion and its commander. The rest and renewal was to be for four months. Marcus and his men looked forward to their return to Rome. Spirits were high as they arrived for the holidays.

Chapter 6. "The Amphitheater of Titus Statilius Taurus"

Marcus Titus had already gone to the Amphitheater with friends by the time his father arrived at the home of Flavius Titus. Flavius welcomed Marcus and Quintus as long lost friends. He excitedly told the two Roman soldiers about the boy's achievements, his preparation for today's games in the Amphitheater, and the physical changes in the boy since the Centurion last saw his son.

The three men then left the home of the teacher and walked to the Amphitheater.

The Amphitheater was filled with the citizens of Rome, legionnaires, and senators by the time that Marcus and his two friends arrived. Marcus, Quintus and Flavius took their reserved seats after exchanging greetings with acquaintenances in the Senate and from the city's elite.

After searching the arena for his son, he turned to Flavius and asked, "Where is the boy? Has he changed so much in five years?"

"He has Marcus. See that group of wrestling contestants?" Flavius pointed off to the right.

"Marcus looked to the right, "I do, but no one is recognizable to me."

Flavius smiled, "See the tallest among them? That is young Marcus."

Marcus laughed. "I cannot believe that that tall gangly boy is the baby boy that Quintus brought to Rome over sixteen years ago. What do you say Quintus?"

Quintus had a broad smile on his face. "It appears that we have brought forth a tall tree from a tiny seedling. The Gods smiled down upon us."

Chapter 7. "the ability to compete at arms.."

Flavius was correct as always in his assessment of young Marcus' skills at wrestling. Six matches resulted in six victories. His opponents, although all shorter than he was, were all more muscular and appeared to out weigh the boy by at least fifty pounds. Yet the speed and agility of young Marcus were too much for his opponents to overcome. He easily won all but his last match against a physically imposing red haired boy. That match went on for some time with each boy trying to find the weakness of the other. In the end, young Marcus took the red haired boy down with a swift movement that not only surprised his opponent but all those who were watching. It was an impressive win. Marcus was well pleased with Flavius.

Young Marcus stood beside his last opponent and as they both saluted an appreciative audience, Marcus recognized his father in the stadium. 'Flavius did not tell me.' He thought.

The boy ran to the edge of the arena as his father worked his way down to the field. As they met and embraced, the pride and the love of a father and son were apparent to all who saw.

They talked for a short time and then the boy told his father that he had to go back for the broad sword competition.

"Are you ready for this?" Marcus Aurelius asked his son.

"Ask Flavius. You paid him to teach me." The boy answered. As the boy started back to the center of the arena he called back to his father, "I will see you after the matches."

Marcus Titus rejoined the group of contestants that were now donning the armor designed to protect combatants from the bludgeoning of a broad sword on bone or skin.

Romans took great pride in their ability to use weapons of war. It was no surprise that the young boys who would soon fill the ranks of the Roman Legions also took great pride in their skill with weapons of war.

The broad sword competition was a favorite sport in the Amphitheater's holiday games. The edges and the end of the broad sword were blunted to protect the contestants from fatal or maiming blows to the body. Even so, there was always the chance for a broken bone as the result of the strength of a blow delivered by one of the more aggressive combatants. Having said this, there was also never a shortage of contestants ready to do battle in the broad sword competition.

The favored contestant for the day's competition was Lucius Neros. He attended one of the elite academies for young Roman citizens that concentrated on military skills and training with a secondary studies program in government. Lucius had been victorious in the broad sword competition since the age of sixteen. At nineteen years of age, he was about to join the legions. He was considered invincible in the arena.

The broad sword contests were exciting to watch. Many of the contests were fought at the same time and it was a single elimination. Most matches lasted only a few minutes and despite the protective measures taken to provide safety to the contestants, there still was a fair amount of blood and injury to those involved.

After an hour and a half, the finalists were identified. Lucius had demonstrated in contest after contest why he was the favored contestant for the day. A large red haired boy was also in the mix as well as the lanky boy who had won the wrestling tournament earlier in the day. The last finalist was not a Roman. He was a dark youth from the territories. He competed with a ferocity not often seen in what was considered to be friendly competitive contests.

The four drew arrows from a quiver to determine the semi final competition. The short arrows would compete with one another while the long arrows also competed. The two winners would compete in the final match of the day.

Marcus drew a short arrow as did the dark youth from the territories. Lucius would fight the red haired boy.

The final matches were held in the arena as the last events for the day.

The broad sword competition took place inside a thirty foot wide circle. The rules were simple. To win, you had to force your opponent outside the circle three times or force the sword from his hand.

Lucius and his opponent were first to enter the combat circle. Both young men were accomplished with the broad sword. They moved from side to side thrusting and parrying. Both showed equal skill and athleticism. Their swords crashed together with a thunderous clanging that brought the crowd in the stadium to their feet. Finally, after fifteen minutes of wielding their ever heavier blades, Lucius locked the hilt of his sword with that of his red haired opponent and with a quick twist of his blade, he sent his opponent's weapon hurdling out of reach. Lucius brought his blade up to his forehead in salute to a worthy opponent.

As they left the combat circle together, Marcus Titus and the dark youth from the territories entered from the opposite side. They both saluted the area where the Roman Senate was seated and then each other. The dark youth immediately sprang at Marcus with a slashing motion. Marcus side stepped and parried the blow away from his body. As his opponent spun around, Marcus thrust straight for his opponent's chest. The thrust was met with an upward swing that pushed Marcus' sword up and to the right. The dark youth followed with a thrust of his own toward Marcus' right side. Marcus brought his sword down so quickly and hard that it drove the dark youth's sword momentarily into the ground. Both were back in a defensive position before either could attack the other. Both boys fought hard as their swords rang out and sparks flashed as steel met steel. Both fought with determination and with heart. Lucius watched with admiration as the match continued for over twenty minutes with neither boy showing signs of withering in front of the other.

Then in a split second, Marcus glanced down and saw that his left foot had barely crossed the circle's boundary. Realizing in that second that his opponent had gained the first point, he began to lower his sword hand when his opponent seeing an opening swung down hard on the extended and exposed arm. A crackling sound was heard throughout the stadium as sword met bare skin and bone. Marcus's right arm went limp as his forearm shattered under the strength of the blow. He felt dizziness in his head and his stomach wretched at the pain. Marcus dropped to one knee as he looked up at the dark youth first in anger then with understanding.

The boy from the territories was wide-eyed with the realization of what had happened. He threw his sword to the ground and went to Marcus to help him balance and to keep him erect while others came to aid the wounded contestant. The boy apologized for what he had done. For Marcus, it was not necessary. He knew by looking into the other boy's face that he had not realized that Marcus had crossed the boundary.

The matches were called with Marcus' injury. His arm was set while the other combatants stood by and offered encouragement. Once the arm was set, Lucius asked Marcus why he had dropped his guard. Marcus explained that he had crossed the boundary.

"You mean that you called the point against yourself?" an amazed Lucius asked.

"Yes, I did. It was the rule of the game." Marcus answered.

"The rule is to win. You play the game until the official calls the point."

"I do not see it that way. Isn't it more important to do what is right than to do what it takes to win the game?" Marcus asked Lucius.

Lucius smiled, "I am not the one with the broken arm!"

They looked at each other hard for a moment, then both laughed, Marcus with some pain.

Chapter 8. "Friends"

The four months furlough went by quickly. Marcus Aurelius spent much of this time with his son. They learned much from one another. The father realized that his son was indeed a very special person. He realized that a decision made sixteen years earlier was not only right for him but was right for the world. It would have been a larger loss to the world had this boy not been spared. Marcus Aurelius was satisfied that he had made the right decision.

Young Marcus had a serious fracture of his lower right arm. He worked it daily to try and regain full use but it became obvious after two months that there would be some limited motion that he would have to accept. Marcus continued to work with his right arm but he also decided that what he could not accomplish with his right arm, he would excel at with his left. To the amazement of Flavius, young Marcus became as adept at using his left arm as he had been with his right. This could serve the boy well when he took on the responsibilities of manhood.

After their meeting in the Amphitheater, Marcus and Lucius became good friends. Lucius found in Marcus the intellect that he knew he lacked. He admired that intellect and he also admired the way Marcus worked at getting his use of his right arm back and his training with his left arm. It kept his friend from becoming a cripple for life. Marcus, for his part, enjoyed listening to the excitement in Lucius voice when he would talk about joining the Legion and going off to discover new lands to conquer for the glory of the Roman Empire. Lucius would say that Caesar, himself, would someday recognize him as a great Roman warrior and reward him for all that he would do for Rome.

Marcus would ask, "Which is mightier then, the mind or the sword?"

Lucius would answer, "I think the mind yields to the sword."

To which Marcus would add, "The sword is for the moment, the mind is for the ages."

Lucius would always finish these discussions with the same reminder, "Your mind is more expansive than mine but I am not the one who suffered a broken arm." Again the laughter.

Chapter 9. "The Journey"

In the summer of Marcus' nineteenth year, Flavius called Marcus to his garden for what would be the final discussion between teacher and student. They had often used the garden as a place of learning as well as reflection.

Marcus had watched his teacher age over the years that he had spent with him. Now Flavius was in the twilight of his years. Although his body had become frail, his mind was as sharp as it ever had been.

"Marcus, we have reached a point in time when our paths must, of necessity, go in separate ways. Your father, Marcus Aurelius, would like to have you join him on the frontier. I, on the other hand, wish to travel to Gaul. I am told that the women there are beautiful!" Flavius laughed at this touch of humor and Marcus politely joined in the laughter.

"Flavius, I thought that you might want to go with me to the frontier. We could spend some time in Greece along the way and visit Athens. You have often said that you would like to put to use your knowledge of the Greek language and once again cast your eyes on the remarkable architecture of that country."

Flavius gave the idea some thought and said: "Athens was once one of the most civilized cities in the world. I think that if I were to go back now, I would be disappointed."

"It cannot have changed that much." Marcus appealed.

"All things change, Marcus. Nothing remains the same. Places, people, institutions ...." Flavius waived his arms in the air as if encompassing the world in his comments. "My garden is beautiful because I give it constant attention but even as the sun goes down in the evening and rises the next morning, it shows change in just that short period of time. How much more change is there in a week, a month, a year?"

Turning to look at Marcus, Flavius went on: "Look at my pupil. How much you have changed. You were brought here a baby wrapped in a blanket. You will be leaving a man clothed with knowledge and compassion."

Flavius sat down on a short stone wall next to his reflecting pool. He picked up a small stone and dropped it into the pool of water. "Observe the circles that come from such a small stone. The circles of water multiply and widen as they move away from the small stone until eventually they will have touched the entire pool. Such is the nature of change." He lifted his eyes from the water and looked directly at Marcus. "You will see and be touched by such changes in your lifetime. You will be a part of those changes. It is your destiny."

Flavius then stood and beckoned his student to follow him into their home. "Marcus, always travel with an open mind. See what others do not. Understand that there is more to life than what is most apparent. While life can be beautiful as is my garden, it is wise to also be on your guard. Those with little knowledge and insight are envious and fearful of those who have the gifts which you possess. Always measure their strength against your own and act accordingly. If you do so, time will be on your side..." Flavius paused for a quick look back at Marcus and then finished what he was saying. "and you may live, as long as I have, to enjoy a trip to Gaul to see the beautiful ladies."

It was a sad parting when, eight days later, Marcus Titus said good bye to his teacher and longtime friend Flavius Titus to travel overland to the frontier. The only home and family that Marcus had ever known were in Rome. His friends, the city, its roads and markets, the people, they were all a part of him. He wondered as he left all of this behind, whether he would ever return and if he did, would it be much changed. Flavius seemed to think so. At nineteen years of age, it was hard to imagine.

Chapter 10. "Pharsalus"

Marcus Titus traveled to the frontier overland rather than by ship. His itinerary was planned in advance by Flavius and his father to be instructional and an opportunity to broaden his knowledge of the people and places under Rome's influence. The journey would take six to eight months and would encompass parts of Dalmatia, Macedonia, Epirus, Achaea, and Athens. From Athens, Marcus would sail to Lycia and then on to Judaea.

An old friend accompanied Marcus Titus on his journey, Quintus. This was the last assignment for the legionnaire before his scheduled retirement and he looked forward to traveling with the man that he had delivered to Rome as an infant.

The two Romans traveled the northern route, passing the uppermost reaches of the Adriatic Sea through Venetia, then down the rugged eastern shoreline of the sea and the Dalmatia coastline. Once they arrived in Greece, they turned east and continued to Pharsalus in northern Greece. Quintus arranged to visit with friends in the legion there and for Marcus to visit the battlefield where Julius Caesar defeated Pompey the Great and the legions loyal to the Roman Senate.

As Quintus, Calvinus, the centurion hosting the visiting Romans, and Marcus surveyed the battlefield, Marcus pointed to a rise at the right, "That is the point where Caesar's army defeated Pompey's legions."

Quintus explained to Calvinus that Marcus was a student of Roman military strategy among other things and was acquainted with the history of the battle of Pharsalus.

Marcus explained, "Pompey ordered his legions to hold their position and to let Caesar's army attack. He theorized that by doing this, Caesar's men would exhaust themselves and would be easily defeated. Pompey had almost twice the number of legionnaires that were in Caesar's legions.

Pompey also had his right wing secured by the river" Marcus pointed in the direction of the river. "He positioned his entire cavalry on his left wing along with all of his archers and slingers."

As the three men looked at the expanse before them, they could picture Pompey's vast army spread out in front of them.

Marcus continued, "Caesar spread his legions out where we stand. In addition to those he designated for a frontal assault, he created a third and forth line opposite Pompey's cavalry and archers. Seeing that Pompey awaited his charge, he ordered his legions to attack holding the third and forth line in reserve. His legions moved forward with the attack but halted half way to Pompey's lines for a respite, to regain the strength needed for the battle. These were men who knew what they required for battle. They then renewed the attack and upon reaching Pompey's lines, Pompey released his cavalry to flank Caesar's frontal assault. It was at this point that Caesar released his forth line. They rushed Pompey's cavalry with such force that those in Pompey's cavalry who were not killed turned their horses and retreated to the mountains. This left the archers and slingers unprotected and they were immediately cut down by Caesar's forth line. Pompey's left wing collapsed and as it did so, Caesar released his third line. The fresh legionnaires immediately forced Pompey's lines to break and the day was Caesar's."

Calvinus was impressed. "Young man that is a remarkable summary. You can add to your rendition that Pompey's loss was also the downfall of the Republic."

Marcus looked at the centurion. "A small pebble dropped in a pond will create ripples that will eventually touch the entire pond. Such is the impact that all things have in this world."

After four days of rest and exploration, Marcus and Quintus said good bye to Calvinus and continued on to Athens.

Chapter 11. "Athens"

Marcus had been looking forward to his arrival in Athens. He had an avid interest in Greece, its history, architecture, and forms of government. He was fluent in the Greek language and had read with interest the works of Socrates, Plato, and Aristotle.

Upon arriving in Athens, Marcus and Quintus immediately took note of the less than friendly reception that they received from the Athenians. They soon realized that even as Rome ruled the world, not all of the people under Roman rule were submissive to the Romans. Quite often there was visible tension between themselves and the Greeks with whom they dealt.

Marcus' knowledge of the language and history of Greece did however offer breakthroughs in their dealings with some of the populace.

While visiting the site of the Parthenon, Marcus and their guide had a lengthy discussion of the reforms that Pericles had instituted to strengthen Athenian democracy. Marcus expressed his admiration for Pericles' contributions to the culture of Athens including free theater for the people. Their guide, Atticus, was impressed. He invited Marcus and Quintus to his home for dinner. It was the first and only time that a Roman entered the home of Atticus. Atticus and his family would never forget the two Romans who talked late into the night about the battle of Plataies and the Athenian victory over the Persian army. Atticus found in Marcus a shared admiration for the military genius of Themistocles. Most Romans talked of Caesar's victory over Pompey. Here was a Roman who understood the pride of Athenians. He was a rare individual.

Marcus was also interested in the Athenian idea of democracy as a form of government. Long after Quintus had retired for the evening,

Atticus and Marcus talked about democracy and the personal freedoms that evolved from such a form of government.

As the first rays of morning light filtered into Atticus' home, Marcus observed, "It seems to me that the rule of law will suffer in a pure democracy."

"That would be true were it not for the fact that democratic principles are based upon the desires of the majority." Atticus responded.

"Then it becomes a question of the degree of knowledge and understanding of many versus the degree of knowledge and understanding of a few. And if that be true, then only an educated society can create a democracy that will last." Marcus looked at Atticus, "Do you agree?"

Atticus was a teacher by profession and a guide by avocation. He had also served Athens as an officer in its army. He gave serious thought to what Marcus postulated. There were times when leaders must dictate action and there are times when every man must be able to express his beliefs. Finally, he said, "I have to agree with you. Athens has always benefited from the knowledge of its sons. We can boast many of the world's greatest minds, Socrates, Plato." He waived his hand above his head. "Democracy has worked because we understand the responsibilities that accompany such form of governing. Education is an important factor in the decision making process and we have always placed education and knowledge on a very high pedestal."

Atticus invited the Romans to meet some of his fellow Athenians. They traveled with Atticus to the far reaches of the city. Marcus and Quintus learned much about the people of Athens and their feelings about their Roman rulers. Athenians longed for their "democracy" but they understood that the might of the Roman army would be too much for them to have any hope of a return to a democratic government anytime soon.

Marcus and Quintus spent a second night with Atticus' family before they said good bye to their guide. Marcus gave a silver chain that he had purchased in the market to the wife of Atticus and thanked her for her hospitality. He took Atticus' outstretched arm and bid him farewell. The Romans mounted their horses and turned toward the final leg of their journey and Judaea.

As they rode down to the harbor, Marcus thought about the reach and might of the Roman legions. A smile crossed his face as he remembered his friend, Lucius Neros. Lucius had left Rome three years ago to serve with the Roman legions in Judaea. Marcus wondered if their paths would cross again. 'If the gods will it.' He thought to himself.

Chapter 12. "The Anatolia Coast"

Marcus and Quintus joined the 80 oarsmen and 50 marines aboard the liburnia for their sea voyage to Lycia. The liburnia was a Roman Galley used by the Romans to control the seas and to insure that Rome's shipping and trading business was not threatened by pirates or other enemies of the state. It consisted of two rows of oars, and a mast and sail to provide power. It also had a closed deck that allowed it to carry men and supplies both above and below deck. Marcus had never traveled on a ship accept as a newborn. He enjoyed the experience.

One night, as the liburnia neared the shores of Lycia, Quintus joined Marcus on deck. "How goes our ship this evening?" Quintus asked.

"It goes well, Quintus." Marcus replied as he stared at the open sea, enjoying both the wind and the water's spray in the cool night air. "I am told that we should reach Lycia by late tomorrow if the winds and tide stay with us."

"Are you looking forward to visiting Rome's stepchild?" Quintus asked in reference to Lycia.

"Lycia has always interested me." He turned to Quintus. "Did you know that Flavius was a friend of Gaius Caesar?"

"The adopted son of Emperor Augustus?" Quintus asked.

"Yes. And after being wounded during the Artagira campaign, Gaius retreated to Lycia where he died. Had he not died, Gaius might be Emperor as we speak." Marcus looked at Quintus for a reaction. The weathered soldier took in this new information, shrugged his shoulders and said, "Life has its victims."

Marcus moved to another subject. "It is interesting that Lycia has really never been fully ruled by Rome. Flavius told me that they have a form of self-rule. I believed Flavius referred to it as a federation known as the Lycian League. Several city-states in Lycia have joined together to form this League. I hope to learn more about this federation during our stay in Lycia."

Quintus laughed, "Always the student."

"There is much we can learn about in this world of ours. We must always seek understanding of those things that determine our lives and our destiny." Marcus pointed to the sky as a falling star crossed high above the ship's mast. "What do you think that was?"

Quintus answered "A falling star."

"Why did it fall and where did it fall from? How far away was that falling star and why did it disappear?" Marcus prodded Quintus.

"I never gave it that much thought. Maybe the gods are throwing the stars so far away that they just disappear." Quintus smiled at his own clever answer.

"Maybe, but maybe there is something more going on up there." Marcus shook his head. "I may never have all the answers to all the riddles of life but there are some which, with a little effort and exploration, I may yet learn." He looked at Quintus and with a quick smile said, "When I do discover the answers, I will be sure to share them with you."

"My head already aches from what you have shared." Quintus laughed as he clapped young Marcus on the back. "But you are a good man in spite of your head full of useless questions and information!"

The wind was picking up and shifting away from the coastline. The ship's sail fluttered as the wind shifted direction. The helmsman swung the wheel and as the ship swerved hard to the starboard, Marcus and Quintus had to brace themselves in order to maintain their balance.

"It's going to be a different tact than had been planned on." Marcus observed.

Quintus looked at the rapidly receding shoreline. "I hope we don't get thrown off course. This is rugged country. We could lose several days going overland to Lycia."

That night the winds continued to pick up and change direction. By daybreak, the ship was too far north to make landfall at Lycia. The Captain opted for a nearer port. Those onboard were thankful to be off the sea and on firm land as a storm developed and pounded the Anatolia coastline. Ships were tossed about and several were swamped before the storm moved off the coast.

The storm damaged the liburnia as well as other ships in the small harbor. The captain informed Marcus that repairs would take several days. The delay coupled with the local mountain lure encouraged Marcus to alter their plans. Marcus decided that he and Quintus would travel overland to the city of Xanthos. He wanted to experience the Taurus Mountains and the Ak Daglar, one of the highest peaks in the entire mountain chain. He also wanted to learn more about the people that inhabited this rugged countryside. The two Romans bid farewell to those they had sailed with and rode toward the mountain path that would take them to the high peaks of Lycia and then on to Xanthos.

Marcus looked back over his shoulder as his horse carefully climbed the steep mountainside and entered the heavily forested foothills. Soon the thick forest would give way to the Ak Daglar's massive rock formations that created a great wall in front of them and then disappeared into the cloud cover high above them.

Marcus could still see the harbor and the town. He thought 'how fortunate were these people to be protected by the sea to the west and the high peaks to the north, east and south. It is no wonder that the city-states of Lycia have for centuries maintained their independence.'

He turned to Quintus, "I think it will be interesting to get to know the people of Lycia. I think that their thoughts on what fate has provided for them for the future will be quite different than what we may think."

Quintus had been concentrating on the climb. The trail had narrowed and ever the soldier, he was apprehensive about where this path would lead and what they may encounter. "I will be more interested in getting out of this forest and out into the open again where I can see what lies ahead."

Marcus laughed knowing what Quintus was alluding to. "Exactly! We are both interested in what lies ahead!"

Quintus looked at Marcus and shook his head. "I am speaking of our safe travel."

Marcus smiled, "As am I, Quintus."

The two Romans continued until night fall without reaching beyond the tree line. They set up camp in a small hollow on the trail that had been used by other travelers for the same purpose. The next morning they awoke to clear skies and warm weather. They continued on their way and by mid afternoon had reached the rock effacement of Ak Daglar. From there they proceeded on foot leading their horses along the narrow path.

"Quintus, look at that view." Marcus pointed to the vast expanse that spread out before them. Many mountain peaks could now be seen as well as the forested hillsides below them.

"The walls of heaven." Quintus answered.

"The walls of heaven." Marcus repeated. "Quintus you have described it perfectly. Very poetic for a soldier of Rome."

"I have my moments." Quintus laughed. "This is like a mammoth fortress."

"Yes. It is the reason why the Greeks, the Persians, the Egyptians, and even Rome never fully conquered this small country."

Another night on the mountain and on the third day they reached the summit.

"Quintus, I feel that I could talk to the Gods!" An excited Marcus exclaimed as he stretched both of his arms toward the sky and turned a full circle.

A small voice answered his exclamation, "Are you such a man that you have the ear of the Gods?"

Both men spun around to face the direction that the voice had come from. They were immediately confronted by a young woman wearing a cloth tunic and sandals.

The woman smiled and then looking to the skies said: "Ask them to allow us soft winds and fair skies for our journey over Ak Daglar to Lycia." She turned to face young Marcus.

"I didn't really mean that I could talk to the Gods." He half stammered.

For the first time in his life, he found words hard to come by as he stared into the crystal clear blue eyes of the young woman who now stood before him. He had never seen a young woman as beautiful as the person who now made light of his excited comments upon reaching the highest peak of Ak Daglar.

She looked directly into his eyes for a moment longer then turned to look at the vast horizon before them. "It is a wondrous sight to behold." Turning back to him, she asked, "Is this your first time on Ak Daglar?"

He hesitated and then answered "Yes." Nothing more came out as he again was struck by her beauty.

She stood about five feet six inches with a trim slender figure. Her golden brown hair had been woven into a loosely knit braid that reached half way down her back. Her skin was fair. Her lips were full and seemed to be continually in a sort of half smile. Her hands were smooth and delicate which indicated to Marcus that she was not a peasant living in the mountains.

Finally, Marcus regained some composure and asked, "Who are you and what are you doing up here alone?"

She looked at Marcus for a moment, then smiled and pointing a finger at him said, "Ask the Gods!"

With that she turned to Quintus and continued, "I travel back to Xanthos. Would you mind if we accompany you?

Quintus looked at the young woman, "We?"

"Yes. My Anora and I are on our way home. If you are traveling to Xanthos, we would be grateful to have the protection of Rome as we travel."

"You recognize what we are?"

"Yes. My father has had business with Rome and I myself have been to Rome. My name is Didyanna Atolia."

"Well," Quintus turned to Marcus, "what do you think Marcus? Should we provide escort to Xanthos?"

"Marcus again felt the rush of warmth flowing through his body as the young woman looked up at him. "Yes, of course. But who and where is your Anora?"

"She is down the path about 50 meters. She needed to rest. Anora is my chaperon. We have traveled quite far today. I was anxious to reach the top and came ahead. I did not expect to meet anyone else up here. Especially not someone who talks to the Gods!" Her eyes danced as the smile returned to her face. "Thank you for your willingness to have us accompany you to Xanthos. I know my Anora will appreciate the company."

Marcus and Quintus helped Didyanna bring Anora to the crest of the mountain. Didyanna explained that the two men were Romans on their way to Xanthos and had offered their protection for the remainder of their journey.

"Where were they when we were ascending this monster?" Anora flicked her head at Quintus. "You should have been there." Then looking at Marcus, she began, "He, I would be concerned about…." Her voice trailed off as she looked at the young man closer. "You are young but you have a knowing way about you."

Anora sensed rather than knew that Marcus was not like others his age. Anora also recognized that Marcus was not totally Roman. This was a unique young man. Finally after a few more studying glances at Marcus,

Anora said, "We have three days together." Pointing a crooked finger at Marcus, she went on, "I will know you by the time we reach Xanthos."

Marcus smiled at the older woman. "I will look forward to spending the time talking with you and with Didyanna." He did not look directly at Didyanna as he said this but saw that she immediately looked at him when her name was mentioned.

Quintus nodded to himself and mumbled, "Looking forward to getting to know the people of Lycia."

Chapter 13. "The Walls of Heaven"

It was decided that the four travelers would remain in camp just below the summit for the evening. This would provide Anora with some time to rest before the journey was continued.

Marcus constructed a shelter for the women while Quintus built a small cooking fire for the evening meal. Didyanna sat with Anora and talked about things of interest only to women. Occasionally, Didyanna would glance in the direction of Marcus but would say nothing. Anora took note of this and the fact that Marcus was equally interested in her charge. Quintus was too busy with his fire to notice anything.

As darkness closed in around them, the party had their dinner and sat by the light of the fire to enjoy the night and to talk.

Didyanna looked out into the darkness and said, "I always feel safe in our mountains. It is like having a wall around us."

"The walls of heaven." Marcus offered. "Quintus has to take credit for that observation. He came up with that view of your mountains this afternoon."

Marcus looked deep into Didyanna's eyes and went on. "I have to agree with him. These must be the walls of heaven for I have never seen such beauty in all my travels."

His meaning was not lost on Didyanna , who blushed ever so slightly, nor was it lost on Anora, who immediately asked, "Young Marcus, tell me about these travels of which you speak. I am interested in knowing what kind of judge you are... of beauty."

Anora folded her arms across her chest and stared across the fire at the young man.

Marcus lifted his eyes from Didyanna and swung his legs around so that he was sitting squarely facing Anora.

"Anora, beauty is in the eyes of the one who makes the observations. Physically, I have traveled from Rome to Athens by land and from Athens to the coast of Anatolia by sea. I have seen the Coliseum, the Parthenon, and the Aegean Sea in the moonlight. I have watched the moonlight sparkle on the waves and I have seen birds fly high into the skies and soar on the currents of air. I have seen the best athletes of Rome training to sculpt their bodies and I have read books. Books that have described far away places that are inhabited by strange and beautiful animals, flowers, and people. I have examined precious stones that catch the sun's light and capture it deep within its crystals then throw the light back out with many times its brightness and color.

Anora, all of these things have great beauty but tonight, inside these walls of heaven, there is a beauty that transcends all earthly images and is captured in the stars." He shifted slightly then stood, looking up at the stars. "Beauty has to be felt as much as it is seen. Here and now, for me, it has all come together and I feel it in the most inner parts of my soul."

This time he looked down directly at Didyanna. There was no one else there at that moment. He smiled at her. She smiled back and they both looked up at the star laden sky.

Anora was satisfied. Quintus thought to himself that their journey to the frontier had just gotten a lot longer.

Chapter 14. "Courtship"

The next morning, they packed their camp and began the descent that would lead them to Xanthos. The women had been leading a donkey which had carried their belongings. Today they rode on horses led by their Roman escorts. The donkey followed behind down the narrow path.

Marcus was unusually talkative as he led the horse carrying Didyanna. He told her about his father and about Flavius. He talked of Rome and his childhood. He gave her a verbal picture of their journey from Rome to the "walls of heaven" and all that he had seen along the way. She seemed to take in every word. By the time the small caravan stopped for a mid day meal, Didyanna had a pretty good idea of what Marcus was all about. It was also quite obvious to Anora and Quintus that Didyanna had more than a passing interest in this young man from Rome.

While the two women prepared the mid day meal, Quintus and Marcus saw to the horses and donkey. Out of hearing of the women, Quintus spoke to Marcus.

"Tell me Marcus, how many young women have you been with in Rome?"

Marcus frowned, "I don't understand what you mean."

"I didn't think so." Quintus said knowingly. "You are a smart young man but let me give your some words of advice about women." He paused to see if Marcus was listening. He was. "As interested as they may be in you, they would much rather be talking about themselves. I have had my share of experiences and I know that the women who have had the strongest feelings for me are those that I have taken the time to ask them about themselves."

Marcus thought about what Quintus was saying. He smiled at Quintus, "Guess I have been a little bit full of myself this morning."

"A little bit." Quintus confirmed. "The good news is that she is still interested."

Marcus glanced over the back side of his horse at the women. Didyanna was motioning for them to come for the mid day meal. He looked back at Quintus and said, "Never too old to learn. Thank you."

Marcus spent the rest of the day asking questions of Didyanna. He discovered that she loved to read and listen to music. She played the harp and had performed in the public theater in Lycia. Her father was a council member of the Lycian League and had been the League's emissary to Rome. He was also the administrator of the Xanthos school and a member of the Xanthos city council. Her mother was an accomplished artist and the daughter of a prominent merchant. Didyanna also had an older brother who was a career officer in the Lycian military. She was obviously very proud of her family.

They discussed literature and art at length and found that they both had an interest in Aristotle because of his varied scholarly interests. Marcus was amazed that a young woman from Lycia would have the sophistication and education that Didyanna obviously had. It was not what he would have expected.

Their second night together, they camped at the tree line. Marcus again prepared a shelter for the two women. The men opted to sleep under the star filled sky.

After dinner, Marcus asked Didyanna if she would like to go for a walk. She accepted.

The two young people walked through a small wooded area and then out into a clearing where trees again gave way to rock formations and slides. They found some stone placements that provided comfortable seating in the fresh night air and sat down to talk.

Didyanna spoke first to break the stillness. "How long do you plan to stay in Xanthos?"

"Long enough to learn about the people of Lycia. My teacher, Flavius, often mentioned your province to me. He was impressed with what little history he knew of your country. I think the fact that he was interested in Lycia made me curious as well."

"There are a lot of people in Lycia. It may take some time to learn about all of them." She moved her foot through the pebbles at her feet and looked over at Marcus.

His face lit up. "I think that that would be a good thing." He saw her lips part and blushed when he realized that she knew exactly what he meant.

She folded her arms and went on, "Why do you want to learn about us? Are we so different from Romans?"

"No! No." He stood up concerned that she misunderstood what his interest was. "I want to learn as much as I can about others so that I can better understand what makes people do the things that they do."

He stopped to see if she was listening. She was. He continued, "Rome acts to protect many different people within the Empire. It brings stability through its control. It brings culture, trade, and education to distant lands. Yet there are rebellions from within the Empire, even as we fight invaders to preserve the security of its people."

She was serious now. "Do you really believe all that? That Rome acts to protect us?"

She shook her head. "Lycia has a long history of successfully protecting itself."

Marcus saw that this could quickly go from a bad situation to a worse one. He raised his hands in surrender. "I'm convinced. You are the last person in this world that I would want to fight with." He lowered his arms.

"I cannot believe that I am sitting out here like this with someone that I have known for only a little more than a day." Her eyes betrayed her words as the fire he had seen a moment ago vanished and the softness returned.

Marcus was relieved. He knew that she believed and that she was not unhappy to be with him.

"My teacher, Flavius, told me once that the ones who take their destiny into their own hands and work hard at achieving their goals are the ones who will truly reap the rewards of this world. I have a feeling that that pretty much describes the people of Lycia."

She knew that he was trying to bring their time together back to what they both really wanted it to be. She sighed, "Flavius was an intelligent man."

He looked straight into her eyes and said, "Sometimes, I can be with people for only a moment and yet feel that I have known them all of my life." He looked away quickly and went on. "You are one of those people."

"I'm glad that I am Marcus." She stood, "Maybe we should be getting back to our camp."

Marcus nodded as he stood. "Yes, if we get an early start tomorrow, we can probably make Xanthos by nightfall."

As they walked back toward the camp, Didyanna asked, "Have there been others?"

"Others?"

"Yes." She looked over at him. "Have there been other girls that you have met, that you felt that you knew them for years?"

Nervously he answered, "Not that I can recall."

"If you felt like you knew them for years, I would think that you would recall them."

"I suppose that I would."

"Well if someone asks you if you felt like you had known me for years, will you remember that you did?" she laughed.

He reached for her hand and they stopped. She turned and looked into his face. They both knew what the other was feeling as they experienced a warm rush through their bodies from the touch of their hands.

Marcus took her other hand and said, "This moment is one that I will never forget. When I told you yesterday about the beauty of this place, about the walls of heaven… it was not the mountains, forests and sea. It was you."

He felt the slightest tightening of her hands around his. She leaned in to him and kissed his cheek then dropped one of his hands and walked back to the camp with him, holding onto his other hand.

Anora noticed the young people holding hands but decided there was nothing to be said. Quintus on the other hand, decided to get up from the fire and turn in for the night. As he passed the two he said, "Nice night."

They agreed.

Chapter 15. "Xanthos"

Once on the forest path, the horses could again be ridden. Anora sat astride her donkey while Didyanna rode with Marcus on his horse and Quintus rode beside them. There was a great deal of conversation mixed with laughter directed at Anora and her poor donkey. But Anora was very happy not to be walking. She also was very happy to be closer to the ground and traveling at a slower pace than she would have been had she been on horseback. The group arrived in Xanthos just before sunset.

Marcus was immediately impressed with the city. Its buildings were well constructed and maintained. The streets were stone not earthen. Though night was close at hand, there was still a great deal of activity. Surprisingly, a number of merchants still applied their trade. Overall, the city had the feel of prosperity and the people secure and well off.

A number of the people that they passed by recognized Didyanna and bid her hello.

Marcus looked over his shoulder and said with a smile, "I did not realize that I was in the company of such an important person."

"Best be on your best behavior." She retorted.

When they arrived at the Atolia household, word of their coming had already reached the councilor. He and his son came out of their home to meet the travelers and be introduced to the two Romans.

Marcus climbed down from his horse and then helped Didyanna down. He held her in his hands just a second longer than would have been expected. Her brother Cale took a step forward from behind their father but the councilor put out a restraining hand. Cale looked quickly at his father who shook his head slightly to indicate that the behavior would be tolerated, at least for the moment.

Didyanna did not notice the actions of her brother and father. She was enjoying the attention of Marcus but once down she turned and ran to her father.

"Father, I would like to have you meet these two Romans who have escorted us from the Ak Daglar." She led her father over to Marcus and Quintus as she spoke.

"This is Marcus Titus of Rome... And this is Quintus Tarasa, a Legionnaire in the service of Marcus' father."

Her father reached out to take the hand of Marcus. "Marcus, my name is Alex Atolia. Thank you for providing my daughter and her chaperon with an escort."

Alex Atolia then turned to Quintus and said, "Welcome to my home and to Xanthos. It is an honor to have a soldier of Rome visit our city. I would like to introduce you to my son."

Alex motioned for his son to step forward. "This is Cale, my son. As you can see by his uniform, he is in the service the Lycian army. We are very proud of him."

Alex looked from Quintus to Marcus for any sign of a reaction.

Marcus stepped forward to take Cale's hand. "It is a pleasure to meet you Cale. My teacher, Flavius, has great admiration for the Lycian army. He attributed the Roman victory over Mithridates to the assistance the Lycians provided during the Anatolia campaign."

Cale was taken back by this acknowledgement by a Roman of the importance of the Lycian army in the victory over Mithridates. "Thank you." was all that Cale could manage.

Alex Atolia put his arm around his daughter. "Anora, do you need help getting down from that donkey?" he asked.

Marcus immediately went over to help poor Anora down from her donkey. "I am sorry Anora." He held out his hand.

Anora took the young man's hand and slid carefully to the ground. Looking at the councilor she said, "There is more to this young one than you would expect." With that, she bustled around the group, across the stone walkway, and through the arch leading to the main house.

Alex laughed and turning to Marcus and Quintus asked, "Do you have arrangements for a place to stay this evening?"

"We do not." Marcus replied, "But I am sure that we can find something."

"I would be most honored if you would accept our hospitality and spend the night with us. It is getting late and we can spare you the search for tonight's accommodations."

Marcus looked at Quintus who nodded approval. Marcus answered for both of them, "We are a little worn out from our journey. I hope this is not an inconvenience?"

"Not at all. It is the least I can offer for the kindness shown to Didyanna and Anora."

Alex led everyone through the arch and up the stairs to the main entrance to his home.

Chapter 16. "Lycian Hospitality"

Alex Atolia suggested that the travelers take their time getting ready for a late evening meal. He asked his servants to prepare enough food to accommodate the household for the evening. Lamb with vegetables and herbs were prepared along with figs and other local produce. Cale brought out their best wine as was the custom when entertaining guests in Lycian homes.

Alex motioned for his guests to sit to his right while Didyanna and Cale sat to his left.

Marcus marveled at how beautiful Didyanna looked in the candlelight. She wore a white silk tunic that clung to every feature of her body. Its gold trim wrapped loosely around her neckline then ran along the edge of her frock down the left side of her body and cascaded over her left thigh where the tunic parted just above the knee.

Marcus almost missed the question asked by her father.

"Marcus, when I was visiting Rome on behalf of Lycia, I spent some time learning about the City and its educational facilities. My Roman host often mentioned an educator by the name of Flavius Titus as a recognized scholar in Rome and someone that I should arrange to meet. Unfortunately, that meeting could not be arranged in the short time that I stayed in Rome. I am curious, you are Marcus Titus and you mentioned when you arrived that your teacher was a person called Flavius. Might that be the Roman scholar that I was supposed to meet?"

Marcus nodded. "Flavius Titus is well known for his knowledge and the depth of his studies. I have seen many Roman citizens come to his home seeking his counsel. It would not surprise me that Flavius is the man that you were to meet. As for my name and his, my father was a pupil of Flavius before I was. My father sought to pay tribute to his teacher by giving me his teacher's surname."

Alex found this connection amusing. "Interesting. It is a small universe that we live in."

Marcus spoke, "Sir, may I ask a question of you?"

"Of course."

"Didyanna has told me that you are a representative with the Lycian League. I am interested in knowing more about this governing body and how it works. Could you explain its operation to me?"

"Are you interested in government, Marcus?"

"Yes sir. 'History is but a window to the future.' Or so Flavius always tells me. By understanding the past, I think that we can better deal with what lies ahead. We can build on the successes and avoid the mistakes."

"Well said. Anora was right."

"Anora, sir?"

"Yes, her advice to me: 'There is more to this young man.' Well, let me tell you about the League."

Alex and Marcus talked through the entire dinner and then late into the night about the history of the federation of city-states that had become known as the Lycian League. Alex explained that a representative body of 23 cities formed the council which they called the Lyciarch. Within the council it was recognized that certain city-states were much larger and therefore to truly be representative of the general population of Lycia, these larger city-states should have additional voting rights. It was agreed that 6 such city-states, Xanthos, Myra, Olympos, Patara, Pinara, and Tlos would all cast three votes while the remaining 17 would each be allotted one vote each. Meetings of the Lyciarch rotate from city-state to city-state so that each member state has a turn at hosting the governing council. It also provides representatives with an opportunity to meet and get to know the peoples of Lycia.

"The Lyciarch has a special agreement with the Roman Senate that allows us to govern and provide advice and direction to the Roman Governor of the Anatolia Province." Alex looked up and to his surprise, he and Marcus sat alone at the table. Didyanna had retreated to a divan in one corner of the room and had fallen asleep. Cale and Quintus had lost interest in the discussion of politics and had retired for the night.

"To my knowledge, Lycia is the only independent state within the Roman Empire." Marcus observed.

"I believe that you are correct Marcus. I will admit that under Roman protection Lycia has prospered. I believe that the arrangement with the Roman Senate has been a good thing for both parties."

"Do you think that Lycia will continue to enjoy the favor of Rome?"

"I have no reason to think that it will not. Why do you ask? Have you heard something that would make you believe that Rome will not continue to honor the Senate's agreement?" Ever the politician, Alex looked for double meanings even in the most innocent of comments.

"No. I have heard nothing. But I have always thought that the Senate serves at the will of the Emperor. Should the Emperor's chair be some day occupied by one not so kindly disposed to the Senate, the Senate and its agreements could amount to very little."

"Marcus, you are wise but youthful. Those thoughts might be thought treasonous in some circles. They best are left unspoken."

"As a Roman citizen, I have certain privileges. One such is the ability to speak about thoughts that cause me some concern."

Alex held up a hand. "Roman citizen, yes, but as you have said the chair of the Emperor may one day change and with that change you too might lose the very privilege of which you speak."

Marcus had often thought about this too. It had led to many lengthy discussions with Flavius. His teacher would always conclude their conversations on the subject with the admonition, "Never compete with the Legions of Rome." to which, Marcus would ask "But will the Legions stand with the Senate or with the Emperor?"

There was no answer.

Alex stretched and then stood up.

Marcus stood up with him and apologized. "I am sorry that I have kept you up so late discussing politics. I did lose track of the time."

"I love political discussions, Marcus. I enjoyed your questions and interest. Perhaps we can spend some time talking about Rome and the political climate there. It has been almost four years since I last visited that remarkable city."

"I will look forward to our talk."

Looking over at his daughter, Alex smiled. "I had better wake her so that she can retire to her room. That divan is not the most comfortable bed in the house."

Marcus sensed that it was time for him to retire to his room also. "Thank you again for your hospitality, sir."

"My pleasure, Marcus."

As the father crossed the room to wake his daughter, Marcus took one last long look at Didyanna and then left the main hall for his room.

Marcus woke early the following morning. As he looked from the veranda of his room at the garden below, he still had visions of Didyanna sleeping on the divan in her white silk tunic the night before. She was constantly on his mind.

As if he had wished her to appear, suddenly there she was in the garden looking up at him. He went down the half circle of stairs leading from his veranda to the garden where she waited for him.

"Good morning Marcus."

"Good morning Didyanna."

She was dressed only in an apricot colored, silk stola that again draped her figure in such a way as to capture her natural beauty. The arm openings were cut deeply and open to her waist. The neckline was low in the front and in the back. Her skin shone like the silk of her dress. The garment ended just above her knees displaying well shaped calves and braided sandals on her feet.

"It's a beautiful day. I love early mornings. Listen to the birds Marcus."

Marcus listened. "What manner of bird makes such a beautiful sound?"

"It is called a canary. We were given two of them by traders who found them on islands to the west of a country called Mauretania. My father is interested in determining if they will survive here in Lycia."

Marcus laughed.

"What are you laughing at?"

"I believe that the islands, of which you speak, are known to Romans as the Canis Islands. Flavius once pointed out a guard dog that had come from those islands and belonged to a Centurion. It protected his family while he was away on duty. The dog was quite large, quite capable of surviving anywhere, and apparently bred that way by the inhabitants of the Canis Islands." He laughed again but alone.

Looking at the still unsmiling Didyanna, he said, "Do you not see the humor. The Canis Islands were so named because of the big dog but those little green birds carry the islands name, canary!"

"It must be Roman humor. I just enjoy their music." She looked up again in the direction from which the birds were singing.

Marcus thought for a minute then said, "Being here with you, I believe I prefer the singing of a canary to the barking of a guard dog, too!"

This time he was rewarded with a smile.

They listened a moment longer to the melody being carried by the little green birds. Finally, Didyanna proposed that they go into the house and wake everyone so that they too could enjoy the day.

Cale helped Marcus and Quintus find lodging for their stay not far from the Atolia home. This gave Marcus the opportunity to spend time with Didyanna without imposing on her father's hospitality.

On the forth night of his stay in Xanthos, Marcus was invited to attend a celebration at Cale's post accompanied by Didyanna. They were entertained by a theatrical dance group with music and interpretive dancing.

As they walked back through the streets of the city following the performance, Didyanna asked, "How did you like the entertainment tonight?"

"I thought it was great. Lively, good music, great dancing. What did you think of it?"

"I particular liked the dancing." She answered as they reached the city park just before her home.

She laughed and took his hand first twirling away from him and then spinning back toward him so that his arm wrapped around her. She stopped with her body pressed against his. He could feel her warmth, smell the sweet fragrance of her perfume, and sense his own excitement. As they looked into each other's eyes, she reached up with her other hand and drew him closer to her. Their lips touched gently then kissed. For both of them, all time stood still. Then, they released each other both startled at what they had done. They turned and quietly walked the rest of the way to her home.

At the archway leading to her home, Marcus touched her arm, "Good night, Didyanna. I want you to know that this was the best night of my life."

Didyanna heard the deep sincerity in Marcus' voice and saw the seriousness of his face. She blushed as she realized the effect that she had had on him.

"It was a wonderful night for me too!"

They looked at each other for one last moment. Then both turned and parted holding onto the memory of a first kiss. It was a memory that would last a lifetime.

Chapter 17. "Message from Rome"

Quintus had spent much of his time in Xanthos visiting with friends at the Roman outpost. Several of the legionnaires who had served with him in Judea were now assigned to Lycia. It was a good posting for the men. They felt welcomed by the local people. They did not have the constant conflict in Lycia that they encountered in Judea.

The fifth morning of their stay, Marcus accompanied Quintus to the outpost. It was located just beyond the outskirts of the city on a mountainside with a commanding view. Quintus wanted his friends to meet the son of Marcus Aurelius. Several had served under the Centurion and the admiration for their commander ran high.

Marcus received a hearty welcome from Quintus' friends. Marcus' good looks, lean, sturdy frame, and standing at just over six foot in height assured him that other men would immediately be drawn to him as a leader. He also had the ability to draw other people into conversation and make them feel comfortable at being a part of whatever it was that was being discussed.

The legionnaires spent most of the morning sharing stories of the frontier with their new found friend. As the noon day approached, a messenger arrived and was escorted to Marcus.

The young messenger informed Marcus that his teacher and close friend for many years, Flavius Titus, had passed away. Marcus was asked to return to Rome.

The news of the death of his closest friend and surrogate father shook Marcus as he had never been shaken before. This was the first death of anyone close to him. Tears welled up uncontrollably in his eyes. He just sat in his chair staring at the floor. The legionnaires had all experienced exactly what this young man was experiencing. They had all lost close friends in battle. They knew it was time for them to leave quietly. One by one they touched Marcus shoulder and walked out of the room. Only, Quintus remained.

The two men sat in silence for a long time. Marcus was reliving a thousand memories. All the lessons, the studies, the training, the successes and the failures came flooding back. It was impossible for the young man to imagine that he would never again hear Flavius passing along some bit of understanding, some hint as to how to approach this thing that we call life.

Marcus remembered one statement in particular now: "Some day I will no longer be your teacher but I will always be there for you if you but think of me. You have the power to give to me an existence even after I am gone."

Marcus heard these words almost as if Flavius was standing in the room next to him. He looked up with a start, then, saw Quintus watching him. He had not realized that anyone else was in the room with him.

"Quintus, I must return to Rome as soon as possible."

Quintus walked over to Marcus. "I will make the arrangements." Quintus placed a hand on Marcus' shoulder. "Death is inevitable for all of us. As soldiers, we understand this better than most people do. Flavius had a good life. Remember the good things and thank the Gods for providing those times."

Marcus nodded.

Quintus walked away to make the arrangements for their passage to Rome.

As the Gods would have it, a merchant ship was preparing to leave for Rome from Myra on the morning tide. Quintus obtained passage for both he and Marcus.

Chapter 18. "The Parting"

Time to prepare for their voyage was short. It was agreed that Quintus would take care of their belongings and see to it that their horses would be ready for the trip to Myra. Marcus would go to the Atolia home to say goodbye. The two men agreed to meet at the stable within two hours. They would have to get to Myra by sunrise tomorrow.

Marcus half ran through the streets of Xanthos in order to have the opportunity to say good bye to the Atolia family and in particular to Didyanna. He knew that his time was short. He also knew that fate may make this parting a final one for him and his first love.

'His first love.' He thought to himself as he approached the archway leading to the Atolia home. He had known somewhere deep in the recesses of his mind that Didyanna was in truth his first love but now it surfaced when he was leaving her. As he knocked on the door, he wondered if she felt the same way about him. 'Was he her first love?'

He knocked again on the door. There was no answer. Marcus walked around the home to the garden. He could still picture Didyanna that first morning in her garden. The thought that he may never see her again tore at him almost as much as the death of Flavius.

He called out to the house. "Didyanna. Hello. Is anyone home?"

There was no answer. There would be no farewell. He turned away, walked again pass the house and through the archway. He turned and looked one last time at the Atolia home. It had been a happy place for him. He half nodded to himself and turned to go to the harbor.

As he walked through the open market near the harbor, he heard a familiar voice call his name. Cale had been in the market and had seen Marcus from a distance. The two men met in the center of the street.

"Cale, am I glad to see you. I stopped by your home to say goodbye to you and to your father." He hesitated a moment. "And to Didyanna. My good friend and teacher, Flavius, has passed away. Quintus and I leave for Myra within the hour. We sail for Rome tomorrow."

Cale could see the pain in Marcus' eyes. "I am sorry to hear about Flavius. I know that he was close to you by the way that you talk about him."

"Thank you Cale. Flavius was family." Marcus was lost in thought for only a moment then went on, "I was hoping to say good bye to Didyanna and your father before we sail."

Cale had come to appreciate Marcus after their first meeting. He knew that Marcus and Didyanna had special feeling for one another and he approved.

Cale looked at Marcus and smiled. "I do not know if I can help you find my father…." He paused, "but I might be able to help with Didyanna. She and Anora are somewhere here in the market. We were all shopping together but got separated."

Marcus looked about the market place. There were hundreds of shoppers spread over several city streets. "Where should I look for her?" He asked in an almost panicked voice.

Cale answered, "I last saw them over there." He pointed toward a fabric maker's tent. "I will help you look for her."

They both went in the direction of the fabric maker. As they approached the tent, Didyanna came out from under the flap with Anora by her side. Their hands were filled with baskets of material.

Didyanna looked up from her basket almost at the moment that Marcus first saw her coming out toward him. Their eyes locked and as they had experienced before, they were alone in the crowded market place.

Didyanna recognized a change in the way Marcus looked at her. Beneath his smile there was an expression of deep sadness. This changed her own feelings from one of joy at seeing him to a feeling of concern.

As they met, he embraced her then stepped slightly back, "I am leaving for Rome within the hour. Flavius has died."

"Oh, no!" She reached up with her left hand and softly touched his cheek. "I am so sorry, Marcus."

"Thank you."

"How did you hear of his death?"

"Friends in Rome sent a messenger. They knew that we had planned on visiting Xanthos."

"And… you leave today?"

"Yes. I have to go back. Flavius is… was…" Marcus again felt his throat tighten. "Quintus has made arrangements for us to sail with a merchant ship leaving from Myra tomorrow."

Cale and Anora had been standing by listening. Didyanna looked at both of them. She took Marcus' hand and said to her brother and her chaperon, "Please excuse us for a moment." She led Marcus to a small side street that was nearly empty.

She stopped and turned to face the man that she knew that she was meant to be with. She began, "I know that this is something that you have to do. It is the right thing to do. But, I am going to miss not being with you."

"I will miss you." Marcus was struggling with more conflicting emotions than he had ever experienced before in his life. He owed Flavius his life but he would have willingly given his life to Didyanna.

They embraced each other for one last time.

She looked at him, tears now falling from her eyes, and said simply, "Come back."

He bent down to her, gently kissed her once and said, "I will."

They walked back to Cale and Anora.

Looking at Cale, Marcus said, "Take care of her." Then Marcus turned and walked away.

Chapter 19. "The Funeral"

By the time Marcus returned to Rome, Flavius had been laid to rest.

Flavius had long ago made his plans for how his body and his estate were to be handled. He had a strong belief in the afterlife. He believed that each person had a soul that survived death and became a form in which a person moved on to the next world. Flavius believed that if a person led a good life in this world, he would be rewarded in the next. With this in mind, he borrowed a tradition from the Egyptians. He instructed that a gold coin be place in each of his hands and that he be buried with the coins so that he could use the coins, if necessary, to pay for his transportation into the next world. Although the Egyptians put a coin in the deceased's mouth, Flavius used his prerogative to leave his mouth free to communicate with those he met in the next world.

His estate was divided into two parts. One part was left to the School for Roman Citizenry. 'Civilization can not survive without a proper and adequate education.' Flavius stated in his will.

Never having had children of his own and with no close relatives, the other half of his estate was given, 'to my friend, my student and my teacher, Marcus Titus.' as stated in his will. Marcus was surprised at being referred to as 'my teacher' by Flavius but after some thought, he understood. Marcus smiled at the description.

Marcus had never given much thought to Flavius' financial position. After his death, Marcus was surprised to learn that Flavius was very well off. In life, he had lived comfortably but not extravagantly. Marcus knew that Flavius had come from a long line of aristocratic Romans. He knew that Flavius mingled easily with the upper class in Roman society. Even to the point of having had audiences with the Emperor. Marcus had attributed all of this to the wealth of knowledge that Flavius was well known for. But now, Marcus found that he had inherited lands in the northern part of Italia and along the coast of Illyricum on the Mare Hadriaticum. When the transfer of the entire estate was completed, Marcus was a very wealthy man at the young age of twenty-one.

Marcus Aurelius had joined Marcus Titus shortly after his son had arrived in Rome. He, too, had been summoned to Rome for his friend Flavius' funeral proceedings. The two men had visited the cemetery where Flavius had been laid to rest. They agreed to erect a monument on the site to the man who had provided their formal education.

They then returned to the home of Marcus Aurelius in Rome. The two sat together for a long time recalling their mentor and what he had imparted to them.

"What do you plan to do with your inheritance?" Marcus Aurelius asked his son.

"I shall plan to visit each. I understand that I not only have received the lands but also a responsibility for the peoples that inhabit them. I think that I may have enjoyed a lack of an inheritance more." Marcus Titus smiled at his father.

"Ah, Flavius still instructs, even from beyond."

"He used to tell me that the death and burial of a man only alters his earthly presence. That a man's soul is eternal if those he leaves thinks of him often." Marcus Titus paused then continued, "He has insured immortality, at least, for my life time."

"Quintus tells me that you met a beautiful young woman in Lycia. Will she be a part of your plans?"

"I would like her to be. If fate wills it, she will be."

"Fate is what man makes of it."

They spent four weeks together before Marcus Aurelius had to return to Judea. During that time Marcus Titus learned much about the turmoil in the East. He promised his father that he would join him on the frontier once he had performed the new tasks that he felt duty bound to perform in honor to Flavius.

"Life is short my son. Do not wait too long to do those things that are important to you. Flavius, for all his knowledge, never visited Gallia. He never saw his beautiful women."

After their short few weeks together, they said good bye, each following their own destiny.

Chapter 20. "Quintus"

Marcus Aurelius had furloughed Quintus several times over the last twenty years to assist his son and provide an additional safety net. Quintus had served the Centurion faithfully and unquestioningly. So it was that the Centurion called his trusted friend for one last time.

"Quintus, how goes it my friend?"

"It goes well, sir." Quintus always knew when Marcus Aurelius was about to ask a favor. It was never an order. It was always a request but an important one. He thought to himself as he was offered a seat by his commander, 'I am getting old and still Marcus has confidence in me.'

Marcus Aurelius looked out of the window at the city of Rome. "Quintus, young Marcus and I have been discussing the future. His, mine, …" he turned to face his fellow soldier, "and yours."

"My future?" Quintus asked a little in surprise.

"Yes, Quintus. Yours! You have been a loyal and true friend to both of us.

Marcus has, let me say, unique plans for his newly inherited estates. He plans to create what he refers to as a profit sharing arrangement with the people who work his lands. Over time, he is even considering granting property ownership rights to those who show that they are willing to work hard to acquire such rights."

The Centurion shook his head. "I have never heard of such a notion but young Marcus tells me that it is a system of economics that he and Flavius had several discussions about. He even speculates that this may have been part of what motivated Flavius to leave his properties to Marcus."

The Centurion paused for a moment to consider again the discussion he and his son had had about profit sharing. He went on. "As I was saying,

Marcus asked what I thought about a permanent furlough for you so that you could join Marcus in this experiment."

Marcus Aurelius watched Quintus for his reaction. Quintus shifted his position in the chair but never took his eyes off of his commander.

"Marcus believes that he needs someone that he can trust, someone with good judgment, and someone who has a sense of fairness, to help oversee his lands in Illyricum and northern Italia. He believes that you are that person."

Marcus Aurelius walked over to a chair next to his old friend and sat down. "What do you think of the idea? Young Marcus and I agreed that we would abide by your decision."

Quintus looked away from his commander for the first time since Marcus had begun the discussion. "What do you think that I should do? You have always directed me down the right path."

"Quintus, I have given much thought to this since my son and I spoke of it. My friend, neither of us is getting any younger. The challenges of the frontier never change. Life is dangerous for a legionnaire on the frontier. I would like to see my best friend in a safer surrounding. I would also like to have my son be able to receive good counsel in his new undertaking."

Quintus thought for a moment then said half jokingly, "I can still place a lance at twenty yards!"

"I did not mean it that way." Marcus wanted to be sure that he did not insult his friend.

"I know that you are not questioning my ability. I question whether I can provide the good counsel to young Marcus. His mind takes in much more than my simple one does."

"Always remember, Quintus, that two minds are often better than one. If nothing more than offering for consideration another idea, it has value."

"I do enjoy my time with young Marcus. He has a great appreciation for life. I have not experienced that feeling for a long time." He looked again at Marcus Aurelius. "I have enjoyed serving with you, too. You have saved my life on more than one occasion. I can never repay you for that."

"You repaid that debt many times. I am indebted to you not only for saving my life but also for all that you have done for my son."

Quintus thought to himself, 'This is a father's concern for his son." He nodded, "Then it is done. I will take my furlough and join young Marcus on his next quest. May the gods smile upon us."

Chapter 21. "A Man Among Men"

The northern provinces of Italia were highly civilized and very much a part of the Roman Empire. Many of their native sons served in the Roman Legions that had conquered the vast reaches of the Empire. The people were well traveled, well connected, and very loyal to their rulers and to each other.

Marcus was welcomed to his new holdings with open arms. He and Quintus arrived at the former estate of Flavius Titus almost six months after Flavius' passing. Still, to a person, the servants, slaves, and neighboring patricians paid homage to Flavius and sent their condolences to Marcus Titus as the heir and new patriarch of the Titus estate.

The estate consisted of over two thousand acres of farmland, forest, lakes, and stock. There were two Roman styled homes, each staffed and maintained by slaves whose families had worked as household servants for more than two generations. This was a latifundia in every sense of the word. The main house was surrounded by a vast vineyard that seemed to stretch beyond sight, connecting the lands of the larger of the two structures to the smaller of the two. Marcus discovered through conversations with other patrician families, that the Titus estate was a gift to a relative of Flavius Titus from Horatius after Rome's struggle to create the Republic.

Marcus soon learned that he owned over 300 slaves who worked in his homes and in his fields caring not only for his vineyard but also for his sheep and goats and tending to his olive trees. He had a stable of fine horses and even a few mules and one donkey.

Upon seeing the donkey, Quintus was reminded of his very first journey with Marcus as a newborn and the remarkable woman he had seen riding on a donkey in Judea. That night, he again recounted the story of that journey to Marcus describing in great detail the appearance and continence of the woman with the child. Marcus could see the woman in his own mind and wondered aloud, "What becomes of people whose paths one crosses?"

Quintus was reminded of another attractive woman whose path both he and Marcus had crossed. "Didyanna?" he asked.

Marcus smiled at the mention of her name.

Quintus saw the happy smile. Something that he had not seen since Marcus Aurelius had departed for Judea. "Have you written to her or heard from her?"

"One letter. I received one letter from her but have not written in return."

Quintus was surprised that his friend had not written back to this young woman. He had surmised that Marcus had deep feelings for the Lycian girl that they had met on the mountain top. "Do you no longer have feelings for the girl?"

Marcus walked to the Atrium's window and looked out at the stars in the sky. He remembered another night just like this one in a distant land. "I will always have feelings for Didyanna."

He turned to Quintus. "Unfortunately, we are worlds apart. I have much to do here and then we still have further holdings in Illyricum to visit and manage. It would not be fair for me to keep Didyanna from having a life of her own."

"Is that not her decision to make?" Quintus went to the window to exam the stars.

They both looked out at the vast sky above them.

Marcus spoke. "She might be looking at the same stars at this very moment in time. If she is then we are connected."

Quintus shook his head. "You are at once a romantic and an innocent. If I had the feelings that you seem to have for this young lady, I would not let that relationship die of neglect."

"You may well be correct Quintus. But I have a duty to Flavius that must first be met."

The following day, Marcus assembled all of his slaves. He knew that most of them understood the Latin language having lived their entire lives in Italia and on the Titus estate.

His slaves sensed that there was something very different about their new patriarch. There was something about him that stirred their empathy with him and made them instantly feel a connection to him.

Marcus greeted them in a familiar way. It was as though he had known them for their entire lives. He explained to them his relationship with Flavius. He told them of the many conversations that he had had with Flavius about them and about the goodwill that they had earned through their hard work. He then offered a gift of almost unfathomable proportions to each slave family on the estate. He would allow them to share in the profits of the estate and further allow them to become tenant farmers of the estate, eventually earning their freedom. He explained that this was something he desired and believed in and that he hoped that they would embrace the idea as well.

He paused to allow what he had said so simply to be fully understood by those who heard. Three hundred slaves sat in complete silence. Slowly tears of understanding appeared on the faces of several of the older slaves. Finally, perhaps the oldest of the slaves stood up. In broken Latin, he said, "You offer us life, Counsul. You offer us our self respect. We know that you are a citizen of Rome. As a patrician you have absolute power over us. Yet as a man, you have given us our manhood. You are a man among men. You, Consul, are blessed by the Gods." With that the old man bowed down from the waist and remained bowed down. All of the other slaves who had sat quietly listening now stood and they too bowed down from the waist."

Marcus did not know what more he could do. His obligation here had been fulfilled. Quintus brought his horse to him and they both mounted their horses. Marcus raised his right hand to the sky and looking down from his mount said, "May the Gods watch over you."

As they rode away from the meeting with his slaves, he heard the slaves responding, "May the Gods be with Counsul."

Chapter 22. "Always the soldier"

Always the student, Marcus explored the history of the region. He was amazed to find that the Titus estate had remained in tact despite a Carthaginian invasion from Spain and later the power struggle over the rule of the Roman Empire between Marius and Sulla.

Sulla eventually gained control of Rome and was known for his brutality and greed. Yet the Titus estate continued to function without interruption.

Julius Caesar had spent a night at the Titus estate on his triumphant return to Rome after crossing the Rubicon River in defiance of the Senate.

The estate had prospered under Augustus. Now, with Tiberius ruling the Empire, the Titus estate continued its long history of serenity and its people were happy to be a part of the Roman Empire. They had the protection of the military, the convenience of good roads, an abundance of food, water supplied by pipes running from nearby aqua ducts, and the comfort of brick homes with self contained heating systems.

The estate generated a substantial income for Marcus even after the payment of taxes to Rome. He was satisfied with his plans to share these profits with his workers and to allow them to work toward their own independence. His personal belief was that all men should have an equal opportunity to reach their own individual level of success.

After spending several weeks at the Titus estate putting proper procedures in place to assure his wishes would be carried out, he prepared for his journey to Illyricum. Unlike his properties in Italia, the Illyricum inheritance offered a much greater challenge.

The Senate in Rome had given estates in Illyricum to a number of patrician families in an attempt to Romanize the population. The Titus estate was in the northern most territory of Illyricum bordering on Pannonia. Although Illyricum was considered pacified after the Second Pannonian War, the Legions continued to be harassed by attacks from the north. The Pannonians were never completely subdued and unfortunately, the Titus estate remained under constant threat of danger.

Quintus approached Marcus. There was a concerned look on his face as he addressed Marcus. "Marcus, I think that I should be at your side in Illyricum. It is not Italia and I have the experience of combat that you do not have."

Marcus put a hand on the older man's shoulder. "Always the soldier, Quintus. You must understand that what we are attempting to do here is much more important than lands on a distant shore. I trust you to see to it that my dreams and those of Flavius are implemented here. That takes a strong man. A dedicated and loyal man. You are that man." He looked straight at Quintus as he spoke. "Not more than one hundred years ago, a similar experiment was attempted and was met with the death of its sponsors at the hands of a mob. I need a good man and a good soldier here."

Marcus convinced Quintus that his place was in Italia. On the day of Marcus' departure for Illyricum, Quintus gave his last advice to his young protégé. "The native peoples of Illyricum are hard fighters. Always keep them in front of you. If they attack you, strike back with everything that you have at your disposal. Never give them a second opportunity to come back at you. Let them know that you are every bit as hard as they are. Then they will at least respect you. That may count for something."

Marcus nodded that he understood. They each extended their right arms and grasped the arm of the other. With that exchange, Marcus mounted his horse and joined the fifteen other men that he had chosen for his travels to Illyricum.

Chapter 23. "Illyricum"

Marcus had selected fifteen young single men to accompany him to Illyricum. He was well aware of the danger that they faced as strangers in an unsettled land.

Five of the men were slaves. They would be responsible for the provisions, equipment and horses. The other ten men were furloughed to him by the Roman governor in northern Italia. Marcus paid a small tribute to the governor for his kindness.

The ten men were heavily armed, each wearing a helmet, leather breast plate, leg protectors and carrying a shield of wood and leather. Eight of the men rode horses from the Titus stables. The two remaining men rode in a chariot that carried several iron-headed javelins. All ten also wore a dagger and a sword. Mules were provided to the slaves and they too carried daggers at their sides. It was clear that if there were trouble during the journey, this band of men were prepared to deal with such problems. Marcus hoped that the appearance of his men would eliminate the need for use of the weaponry.

The Roman army had built excellent roads and bridges through the Pannonia and Illyricum provinces. The trip to the newest Titus estate was rapid and uneventful. Several times Marcus suspected that he and his men were being watched from a distance but he could never identify who it was that was watching them.

The land was rugged and mountainous to the east and sloped down to the Mare Hadriaticum in the west. On one such slope sat the Titus estate. It was in bad disrepair and had but a handful of slaves tending to it. There were a number of one room dried brick houses clustered together in the center of the one thousand acres of land that comprised the estate.

There was a large olive grove and close to one hundred hogs being farmed on the property.

Marcus and his men rode into what appeared to be the main complex of buildings. They dismounted and entered the largest of the structures in the small compound. Inside, they found slaves huddled together in the structures' atrium. When Marcus entered, he was surprised to see the fear on the faces of the men, women and children. He immediately tried to put them at ease, introducing himself as the new patriarch and asking who was in charge.

A young woman stepped forward. She had long black hair that hung loosely over her shoulders. Her eyes were a sea green color and her skin had an olive tint to it. Her body was hard and firm indicating that she was accustomed to a long day of work and labor. Her voice was unwavering when she spoke. "I am in charge here."

Marcus was not yet an expert in judging the ages of women but he guessed that this woman was not much older than he was. He was equally surprised that a woman identified herself as the leader of these people. He took one quick look at the others then turned back to the woman. "Do you have a name?"

"Yes. I am Cara."

Marcus looked directly at her. "Cara. Well Cara, I am Marcus Titus. My men and I have traveled from Italia to establish my claim to this estate. We are all tired from our journey. Is there a place for us to stay?"

Cara defiantly stared back at Marcus. She glanced slowly down at the young Roman then back up to his face. Despite the muscular frame, this tall Roman had a gentleness in his demeanor and in his eyes. After a brief silence, she slowly answered, "You were not expected. This is the largest building on the property. If your men do not mind using the alcoves, study and this atrium, this is the best we can offer." She paused realizing that this young man was her owner. She continued, "Unless you wish to move some of us out of our homes to make room for your men?" It was both a statement and a question.

Marcus smiled slightly. This was a very smart young lady. He said, "This will be fine. In the morning we will make a full appraisal of the estate. Since you have been in charge here, I would like to meet with you in the morning. Later, you can introduce me to the others." He motioned to the other slaves who were looking on with some concern.

"Very well. How would you like to have me address you?" she said again with a slightly defiant look.

"How have you addressed other owners?"

"The original owners were killed by Romans in the wars. We have had no owners in residence since being occupied."

"Consul." A voice from behind Cara spoke up. It was one of the slaves from Italia who had been listening. He had taken an interest in Cara and was becoming concerned that not only was she beginning to place herself in danger but that she was also endangering the slaves from Italia who had been promised the opportunity to earn their freedom.

Cara looked at the slave then back at Marcus. "Consul… Consul, if you need anything, I will be in the house just beyond the garden."

She turned and with a last look at the slave from Italia who had interceded, moved with the other slaves out of the atrium and back to their respective houses.

Marcus and his men settled in for the night.

The next morning, Marcus rose early. He dressed quickly and walked out into the garden. To his surprise, several of the household slaves were busy preparing breakfast under the direction of Cara. Marcus was pleased to see that Cara was as attractive in the morning sunshine as she had been in the firelight from the night before.

"You have gotten an early start this morning." He said as he approached her.

"It has been some time since we have had owners in residence. I hope that we have prepared a proper meal for you and your men. I have assumed that, at least for today, you would all be having the morning meal together."

Marcus nodded. "Yes, we will all be taking our meals together."

She turned back to her chores saying over her shoulder as she walked away, "Breakfast will be ready shortly."

She moved easily among the servants and the trays of food. Marcus summoned one of his slaves from Italia and told him to rouse the others. He then walked through the garden and out into the olive grove. It was already a warm day but in the grove there was a slight cooling breeze. Marcus thought about how far he had come in such a short time frame. A few years ago, he was a boy with very few real responsibilities. Now, he was a man, a man with many responsibilities. He had wealth, properties, slaves, responsibilities. He was not sure that all of this made him any happier.

He thought about Rome, Flavius, his father, Quintus, his travels, and last but not least, Didyanna. It was while he was thinking about her that a soft voice said, "Consul, your breakfast is ready."

Marcus suddenly realized that Cara had come to the olive grove while he was deep in thought. "Thank you Cara."

She had been watching him. "You were deep in thought Consul. I waited but you were far away somewhere and the food is ready."

He smiled at her. "It is alright. We have a lot to do today and I am hungry."

They walked back to the garden together.

Cara and Marcus spent the rest of the day together. She introduced all of the estate's slaves to their new owner. There were twenty-one adults, ten men and eleven women. There were also seven children, four boys and three girls ranging in age from a newborn to two seven year old children. All of the adults were married except for Cara.

Cara was the only slave that had received an education. She had had her schooling in Greece before being sold into bondage. At the age of fourteen she had been brought to Illyricum as a house servant. Her owners had fled the estate when the Pannonian War broke out never to return. The estate had been invaded by both Pannonian warriors and Roman legions. A number of slaves had been taken from the estate by the invaders. Now, only a small number remained. Each time that strangers came to the estate, those slaves that remained were afraid that they too would be taken.

Marcus took note of what Cara had told him. Later he assured his slaves that he and his men would provide them with a safe home and the security that they would need to again make the estate productive.

Over the next several months, Marcus and his men worked along side the slaves to bring back the estate to its former grandeur. They added rooms onto the main house, built from dried bricks, and brought in cement to build structures to house the horses and the men who had traveled with Marcus from Italia. Holding pens were built to accommodate additional hogs that had been purchased by Marcus as well as newly acquired chickens which Marcus had added to the estate's farming activity.

Marcus also detailed some of his men to begin building a wall around the homestead. It was constructed to provide protection to those living on the estate. Marcus had designed it so that there actually would be two walls, an outer wall and an inner wall. A protected walkway topped the inner wall which was two feet higher than the outer wall. This walkway allowed for a view over the outer wall and also a direct view of the twenty feet that separated the two walls. If unwanted guests breached the first wall, they would find that they were trapped between the walls and that only small numbers of intruders could approach the second inner wall at any one time.

The days were now hot with temperatures much warmer than usual in the day time and not giving much relief in the evenings.

Marcus was working on a new water site that he hoped would yield enough water to build a well for the northeastern section of his property. At midday he sent the three men who had been working with him back to the homestead for their midday meal and to get some rest. He had stayed at the site to finish the piping that they had installed.

Cara had walked out to where Marcus was working. The sun beat down on both of them and there was little shade in this section of the northeast slope. Cara hailed Marcus as she approached carrying a leather pouch filled with wine. "Consul, I have brought you some wine to satisfy your thirst. Even the youngest and strongest of us needs to have relief from this heat."

Marcus smiled as he took the offered pouch with both hands. "Would that be you or me that you are talking about?" He lifted the pouch to his mouth and drank the wine. "Thank you. It is hot."

He looked at her now noticing the beads of sweat on her forehead. He realized that she had walked out here in the midday sun to quench his thirst and that she too was suffering from the excessive heat.

Holding out the pouch to her, he said, "Here, share this wine with me. You have worked as hard as I have."

Cara slowly walked toward Marcus. She gently pushed the offered pouch off to his side saying, "Consul works along side his slaves and now offers to share his wine with them. You may be a Roman citizen but you are no Roman." She now was face to face with Marcus. The two had not taken their eyes from one another. She brought her mouth close to his then slowly ran her tongue along his upper lip and then back across his lower lip. Stepping slightly back from him she continued, "The nectar of the vine is indeed sweet to the taste."

She smiled at him in a way that he had not seen from her before. She lifted the pouch to her mouth and drank the cool red wine. Her cheeks were flush from the heat of the day, the taste of the wine, and the touch of his lips. When she finished with the pouch, she set the pouch down and, without speaking a single word, walked back down the sloping hillside. Marcus watched her until he could no longer see her.

That night, she came to him dressed only in a white silk tunic. The warmth of her skin, the touch of her hands, the firmness of her body, she was all that he had imagined since the night that he had first met her. No words were spoken. The quiet sounds of the night filled the air and for a moment, both found peace in a troubled world.

The next morning, Cara slipped away from Marcus before he or anyone in the household had stirred. When they later met each other they both knew that their relationship had changed forever. Within weeks it became apparent to everyone on the estate that they were no longer master and slave. At the end of the year, Marcus gave Cara her freedom along with the other twenty estate slaves and their children. All remained at the estate as paid servants.

Marcus also brought in additional hired servants to work the land and continue the construction of buildings in and around the homestead. The soldiers who had been furloughed to him by the governor in Italia were due to return to their post. Marcus gave a generous purse to each of the men as part of his thanks for their hard work and loyalty. The night before they were to leave Illyricum for Italia, Marcus held a celebration for the men. Patricians and freeborn people from neighboring estates were invited to enjoy the holiday as well.

It was an evening that would be long remembered for its abundance of wine, food and dance. Cara danced only for Marcus while others looked on with envy. Marcus was entranced and although he paid proper tribute and attention to his fellow Romans, Cara was the center of his attention. Years later, he would remember the holiday and see only Cara, dancing, twirling, laughing, smiling knowingly, and leading him away from the celebration.

Chapter 24. "The Confrontation"

Marcus had been hiring local freemen to work his property in Illyricum since arriving at the estate. Most of his workers had their own homes in the surrounding villages and would come to work his land and construction projects during the day and then return home just before dark. By the time his men from Italia returned to Italia, he had more than fifty servants to take their place.

Ever mindful of the danger that accompanied owning property on the border with Pannonia, Marcus had seen to it that some of his servants were trained in the use of weapons. He also had recruited several archers to serve as guards for the compound that he had created with the construction of his dual walled enclave.

It had been almost two months since the professional soldiers from Italia had returned home. Marcus had gone to a neighboring estate to discuss the purchase of some additional adjoining land to expand an olive grove.

Cara was working in the olive grove near the compound when two of the estate's servants came running to her. In between gasps for breath, they spit out the warning that Pannonian warriors had been sighted at the well on the northeastern corner of the estate.

Cara immediately summoned all those in the grove to hurry back to the compound. Once inside the compound's walls, Cara went up to the front tower and sounded the bell alarm that Marcus had constructed for just such a situation. All of the estate's servants and workers came running to the compound. The archers took up positions on the inner wall while other workers armed themselves with javelins and swords and then joined the archers along the walls. The drills that Marcus had rehearsed with his people had had their effect.

Now it was a time to wait. Cara thought back to the days when she and the other slaves would huddle together and wait for the invaders to take their belongings and occasionally one or more of the slaves away with them. Now, she stood with the others ready to defend themselves. She knew both fear and pride at that moment. Marcus had done this for her and for the others. He had given them their freedom and this was part of the price for that freedom. It was well worth whatever price they paid even if it meant giving up their lives.

Hours passed without any sign of the invaders. The defenders on the wall never left their assigned positions. Marcus told them that if an enemy ever approached the compound, the estate must look as strong as possible. To that end, every able person must appear on the walls of the compound. They would not leave until the threat had passed.

Toward dusk, Cara spotted Marcus and two of his men approaching from the south. She scanned the horizon for signs of the Pannonians but saw nothing. Marcus and his men were now turning into the olive grove and would be out of sight for a short time.

In the Grove, Marcus thought to himself, "It will be good to get home."

He felt more than actually saw a brief movement in the grove to his left. Instinctively he drew his sword from the sheath attached to his saddle. Marcus' swift drawing of his sword elicited the same reaction from the two men with him.

Marcus indicated with his sword the direction in which he had sensed the movement. The men watched the left side of the grove as they proceeded at a steady pace toward the far end of the grove. Another movement to his right set alarms off in Marcus' head. He had no idea of how many were in the grove but he knew that if they were moving with such stealth, they were not friendly visitors.

He was about to spur his horse to a gallop when more than thirty men, armed with spears and swords, appeared around them from the shadows.

Marcus commanded his men, "Hold."

Suddenly, a tall, dark, muscular stranger stepped in front of the others. Looking directly at Marcus, he spoke. "We have been waiting for you. You are the Patriarch of this estate?"

Marcus starred back at the stranger. "I am. You are standing in my grove."

The stranger laughed heartedly. "Yes and my men and I drank from your well, too."

"I hope you enjoyed the water."

Both men were taking the measure of the other. Both concluded the other was a worthy opponent.

The stranger asked, "Did you design the walls for the compound? They were not standing when last we passed this way."

Marcus had been taught that the longer an opponent talked, the more uncertain he was as to what he was going to do. He answered, "The last time that you passed by my estate did you notice whether anything that belonged to me went missing?"

This brought some murmurs from the others in the grove but the stranger raised his hand to silence them. He studied Marcus more closely. "Are you a Roman?"

"A Roman citizen, yes. And you, are you a Pannonian?"

"A Pannonian, no. Commander of Pannonians, yes."

Marcus smiled as he next spoke, "Does the commander of Pannonians need thirty men to block the path of three?"

"You are a brave one on a horse looking down at a man on foot."

This is what Marcus was hoping for. "Tell your men that you and I will determine who leaves this land and who stays and I will join you on the ground."

The stranger turned to his men and gave them a simple order. "If this Roman beats me, leave his land and never come back." He turned to Marcus, "If I beat you, I will destroy everything and everyone on this estate."

"Not with thirty men." Marcus challenged as he stepped down from his horse.

"Not thirty, thirteen hundred just beyond the horizon." The stranger responded as he took off his cloak disclosing a well honed fighting physique.

Marcus also took off his cloak exposing well muscled arms, hardened by the manual work that he had become accustomed to since leaving Rome. His old wound from the Amphitheater shone in the fading light of day.

Marcus kept his back almost against his horse. "I prefer to have all of your men in front of me."

The stranger showed his teeth as he ordered his men to move to his rear. They moved quickly behind their leader. It was obvious that they were both well trained and knew not to question his commands.

One of Marcus' men took the reigns of Marcus' horse.

Marcus and the stranger approached one another with swords pointing toward each other.

"Before I strike you down, tell me your name." the stranger half commanded. He swung a mighty blow at Marcus which Marcus easily parried away

Marcus followed with a thrust directly at the strangers head. The stranger ducked away just in time to avoid being impaled by the move.

Marcus recovered, "What you mean to ask is 'who is it that will send you back to Pannonia in a cart?"

The stranger wheeled around trying to take Marcus down at the knees. Marcus leapt to the left avoiding the sweeping blade of the stranger and then brought his own sword down with a slashing blow that sent the stranger's sword into the ground. The stranger stood straight looking directly at Marcus. Marcus indicated with his sword that the stranger should recover his sword.

The stranger bent down slowly, grasped the hilt of his sword and stood. He did not lift his sword to fight. Instead he looked long and hard at Marcus. "A long time ago, I fought another who believed in rules for warfare. Tell me your name."

This time, the stranger was not commanding but asking.

Marcus answered, "I am called Marcus."

The stranger nodded. "Marcus Titus?"

"Yes."

The stranger motioned to one of his men to come forward. One of Marcus's men began to spur his horse forward but Marcus instructed him to wait. If the stranger noticed this, he did not acknowledge it. Instead the stranger handed his sword to his fellow warrior and told the man to go back with the others to their encampment. The man hesitated eyeing Marcus and his two men. The stranger spoke, "I will be safe with this man of honor. Tell our men that this estate is not to be touched." Looking back at Marcus, he continued, "Tell them that nothing is to go missing."

Marcus threw his blade to one of his men who caught it by the hilt and placed it back in its sheath on Marcus' saddle.

The stranger walked over to Marcus. Both men were of equal height. The stranger looked from Marcus eyes to his right arm and the scar just above the elbow. He pointed at the scar and asked, "Does that still bother you?"

Marcus looked down at the scar then back at the tall, dark stranger. The realization struck him. "You? In the Amphitheater in Rome! That was you?"

The stranger nodded. "I have carried that fight with me for many years. First in shame, then in wonder. I have often wondered who would have won that day, had I not made that mistake."

"Is it that important, now?"

"No. It was a youth's mind that considered both. The fact that we both live is what is important to men."

Marcus smiled at this stranger's insightfulness. "We may not be able to enjoy that privilege much longer if we continue to challenge men to confrontations in the dark."

They both laughed as did Marcus' men.

Cara had sent two men from the compound to find out why Marcus had not yet come out of the olive grove. They saw the Pannonians leaving the grove and move away from the compound. Fearing the worst had happened, they ran back to the compound. They were reporting what they had seen to a near frantic Cara when the guards on the wall called to her, "Marcus comes."

The confrontation that night would be retold many times by the servants and guards at the Titus estate.

The stranger, whose name was Metros Scipia stayed late into the night with Marcus and Cara discussing the political situation in Illyricum. Marcus found it interesting that Rome was unable to quell the uprising along the border. But he also sensed that men such as Metros Scipia were not the kind of men who would go quietly into servitude.

At day break, Metros returned to his warriors promising Marcus that the Pannonians would never again attack or plunder the lands of Marcus Titus. That promise lasted the lifetimes of both Marcus and Metros.

Chapter 25. "A Return to Studies"

Marcus had a very keen insight when it came to people and to events. He knew that the promise made by Metros would be honored. From the day that the promise was given, Marcus never again concerned himself with the possibility of invaders from the north.

Marcus now longed to return to his studies. It had been more than eight years since he had spent much time on the arts, languages, and science. He decided that it was time for him to leave Illyricum and to travel to Greece. He had groomed a man named Normalus to supervise the farming on the estate and Cara was more than capable enough to oversee the entire estate and its operation.

When he announced his plans to leave Normalus expressed uncertainty about being able to measure up to the expectations of Marcus but Marcus assured him that he was more than able to do what needed to be done. In return for Normalus' loyalty and effort, Marcus gave a forty acre parcel to his trusted worker.

Cara was more difficult to leave. Marcus and Cara had been inseparable for five years. They thought alike. They had overseen the affairs of the estate together. And, they had enjoyed the intimacy that only a man and a woman can know. Cara begged Marcus not to leave. Marcus knew that he had to go. In the end, Cara resigned herself to his leaving but when the day of departure came, she refused to say good bye. Instead she quietly watched him from the front turret until he was far from view.

Marcus traveled through Dalmatia and down to Athenae. He purchased a home in Athenae, hired servants, and spent the next three years studying language, the arts, and the religious beliefs of the peoples of the eastern empire.

Chapter 26. "The After Life"

At the age of thirty, Marcus Titus received a message from his father that would dramatically alter his life. Marcus Aurelius sent word to his son that his health was failing. He wanted to see his son one more time before he departed this world.

Marcus Titus immediately closed his home in Athenae and booked passage on a merchant ship bound for Joppa.

Marcus arrived at Joppa. It was a bustling port city that offered a variety of goods to those who could pay the price. Marcus, being very well off, had no problem purchasing all that he needed for his trip to Jerusalem.

He reached his father's home in time to share his father's last few days with him.

Marcus Aurelus' only interest was in hearing about what had transpired in his son's life. It made him happy to know that he had been instrumental in allowing this young man to play a part on life's stage. As a father, he knew that destiny had touched his son at birth and that the stars had laid out a path for him that was far greater than anyone would have imagined thirty years ago.

Marcus Titus talked about his time in Lycia. He remembered Didyanna and talked of their relationship. Two very young people very much in love. He talked about Quintus and the lands that Flavius had left to him in the north of Italia. It was a beautiful estate with much history and even played a part in Caesar's return to the Republic. He described Cara, her dark beauty and her defiant spirit. He described his encounter with Metros Scipia and the promise that would protect his lands in Illyricum. Finally, he recounted how he had spent his time in Athenae studying the arts and religion.

The two men, father and son, discussed the last topic at great length. Marcus Aurelius was a religious man. He believed that he would be going on to another world filled with wealth and all the beautiful people that he had ever known. As for the Gods, he did not believe that he would ever actually see them but he did believe that they would provide for him in the next life. He had done well in this world and would be rewarded by the Gods in the next.

Towards the end, Marcus Aurelius expressed concern about what the Jews called the coming of a Savior. They believed in one God. They believed that their God was all powerful. Marcus Aurelius had concerns that if this was true then what would this God care about the things that a Roman Centurion had done with his life.

In the short time that they had had together, Marcus Titus learned much about his father's sense of what was right and what was not. He had seen the results of many of the good things that Marcus Aurelius had done for his servants and friends. He understood that his father valued honesty, fairness, love, hard work, and loyalty and that his father made it a part of his life to recognize and reward others for these traits. Marcus Titus assured his father that the good that he had done would be rewarded in the afterlife. These were the last thoughts shared by father and son. Marcus Aurelius passed on quietly leaving behind a son who mourned for the only father that he had known but with whom he had spent so little time.

Chapter 27 "A New Beginning"

Marcus Aurelius left not only a vast estate to his son but also a standing on the frontier of the Empire that was remarkable for a Roman. Jews and Romans alike had a high regard for the Centurion. That good will carried over to Marcus Titus.

As requested, Marcus Aurelius was buried just outside of Jerusalem in the land that he had come to love among the people who had been such a large part of his life. The outpouring of sympathy from people unknown to Marcus Titus moved him deeply. He was especially surprised with the number of people from the Jewish community that expressed their grief over the Centurion's death.

After the funeral proceedings, Marcus retired to his father's home. There, he spent several weeks taking care of his father's affairs and meeting with those who wanted to express their personal sympathy to the Centurion's son. Roman soldiers joined with Jewish craftsmen and noble patriarchs in paying their respect to Marcus Aurelius' son.

Among his father's servants was a man by the name of Joseph. Joseph had run his father's household for many years. Joseph had made certain that the Centurion received only the attention that he desired. He acted as an intermediary, screening all those who wished to have an audience with the Centurion when the Centurion had been in residence. He had had Marcus Aurelius' full confidence and now Joseph served the son with the same dedication.

Never far from his liege's side, Joseph took an immediate liking to young Marcus. He saw many of the father's worthy traits in the son. Joseph found that young Marcus had a sincere interest in the life of those around him. He often asked Joseph about the Jewish perspective on events that seemed to dominate the politics and culture of Jerusalem and all of Judea. He was especially interested in the relationship between Romans and Jews.

Joseph and Marcus spent many days together during the year following the death of Marcus Aurelius. They had many discussions about the Jewish faith, its culture, and the impact that the Roman Empire was having on what Joseph called 'Jewish Heritage.'

It was late one afternoon when Joseph returned from the market with the household servants. He and Marcus began what would be a life altering conversation about what Joseph had encountered while at the market place. Joseph had visited the temple in Jerusalem and had listened to a young man whom he knew to be a rabbi discussing religious thought with the Pharisees. Joseph was perplexed by what he had heard.

Upon seeing Joseph on his return, Marcus asked, "You look troubled Joseph. Did you have some difficulty at the Market?"

Joseph looked at Marcus then gazed at the room as he thought again about the young rabbi. He turned back to Marcus and said, "I witnessed a strange sight at the temple today. A young man sat among the Pharisees." He paused as he remembered the scene.

"Is it so unusual for a young man to sit with the Pharisees?" Marcus asked with a smile.

"It is when it is the young man who provides the lesson." Joseph shook his head.

"What kind of a lesson?" Marcus was curious. He had studied the Jewish faith enough for him to know that it was the Pharisees who spoke in the temple and it was for all others to listen.

Joseph went on, "The Pharisees were admonishing the young man for spending so much time with beggars and the unclean. They asked the young man why he wasted his time preaching to outcasts and sinners. They even accused him of counseling those outside the Jewish faith. The young man looked at each one of the Pharisees before he spoke. There was complete silence as he did this. Then he answered 'It is the sick that have need of the physician, not the healthy.'"

Marcus smiled, "He sounds like a wise man."

Joseph nodded in agreement.

Marcus asked, "Did you find out the name of this young man?"

"Yes. I have seen this young man before. Some call him rabbi. His name is Jesus. He is a Galilean!"

Marcus had already heard stories about this young man called Jesus. There were stories that he preached against Rome, even against Caesar. Marcus was interested in learning more about this Jesus.

Marcus asked Joseph, "Did you learn what it was exactly that this Jesus was preaching to the outcasts and sinners?"

Joseph nodded, "He spoke of redemption. He preached that there is but one God, the Father. That all people are the children of the Father, and that through the Father, sinners and all who believe in him, can be reborn pure of heart. That they will be forgiven for their past transgressions."

Marcus walked over to the window and stared out at the city before him. "All people are the children of this one God." Marcus thought long about this. It was a remarkable theology. "Through faith in this one God, the Father, his children are reborn, pure of heart. Forgiven by their Father. Given a chance for a new beginning." He thought about his last few conversations with his own father and wondered if his father, Marcus Aurelius, had met this man called Jesus.

Turning to Joseph, Marcus said, "If we are all the children of one God, then who is it among us that can say 'I am of higher rank than the others' before this God. This Jesus teaches quite a remarkable lesson! I would guess that the Pharisees would have considerable consternation at such teachings in the temple."

Marcus seemed to Joseph to have been transformed as he repeated what Joseph had told him. Joseph would later tell his wife that it was as if a great light had shown on Marcus. It was if a great door to a room full of treasure had just been opened and Marcus was seeing it for the first time.

Finally, Marcus looked at Joseph and said, "I would like to see this young rabbi for myself. Can you find out for me where I might find this man, this man, Jesus?"

"I will see to it." Joseph answered.

Later that afternoon, Joseph interrupted Marcus in his study. "A Roman soldier is asking to see you. He waits in the courtyard." Joseph saw that Marcus had been deep in thought. "Shall I tell him that you are occupied?"

Marcus looked up. "No, that will not be necessary Joseph. I was thinking about the lessons of the young rabbi. His words will be with me a lot longer than our visitor." Marcus smiled. "Tell the Roman that I will be with him momentarily."

Even the journey from childhood to manhood does not conceal the identity of a true friend. As soon as Marcus entered the courtyard he recognized the Roman soldier who stood before him. "Lucius Neros. I can not believe that you are here."

Lucius embraced his friend with both arms and with a wide grin. "It is I who find it hard to believe that you are here! You are a long way away from Rome my learned and cultured friend."

Lucius released Marcus and stepping back said, "I am most sorry about your father's death. He was a great citizen of Rome and a great soldier of Rome. You will find that the legions here and on the frontier had the highest respect for your father, Marcus."

Marcus looked at his friend. "Thank you Lucius. I have already been overwhelmed by the outpouring of sympathy. My father seems to have been admired by a great many people here in the east."

Marcus called to Joseph and asked him to bring some refreshments. He then invited Lucius to sit and talk. "Are you posted near Jerusalem?"

Lucius smiled. "I am in Jerusalem. I am in charge of the cohort assigned to the fortress of Antonio."

Marcus nodded, "That is an important position."

Lucius agreed. "It is important in that the fortress offers protection for Caiaphas, the high priest of the Temple and a close personal adviser to Herod Antipas, purported king of the Jews."

Joseph had entered the room and was laying out food and drink for the two Romans as they spoke.

Marcus continued, "I do not know much about the current politics of Jerusalem but would guess that the high priest is someone of importance."

Lucius laughed. "He is the 'politics' of Jerusalem. The governor rarely takes any action without first considering where Caiaphas may enter upon the issue." Lucius lifted the urn and poured some wine into a cup before continuing. "If Caiaphas has a request for the Governor, it receives the highest priority."

Lucius paused to see if Joseph had left the courtyard. Not seeing anyone else, Lucius went on with his conversation. "To be honest with you, Marcus, I do not understand why we play politics with these Jews. Rome could crush these people within six months and run this country in any manner that it wanted to."

Marcus asked, "Why would Rome do that?"

Lucius took a long drink from his cup. "There is much in-fighting among these people. They distrust one another. They have their own class system. Even among the Pharisees there is division. One group is identified with the House of Hillel while a second group identifies itself as being the House of Shammai. They cannot even agree on the form their beliefs should take." Lucius shook his head as if puzzled by all this.

Marcus laughed and said, "Lucius, this is a side of you that I never knew. You have become a religious scholar while serving on the frontier."

Lucius again shook his head. "It is a part of my duties. I must take all of this in and report to the governor." Lucius looked once more about the courtyard. Seeing no one, he looked back at Marcus and said, "Guard and spy."

Marcus thought to himself that perhaps Lucius might have some information on the young rabbi that Joseph had talked about. "My servant, Joseph, was in the temple today and heard a young rabbi speaking with the Pharisees. I wonder if you have heard of him. His name is Jesus."

Lucius immediately straightened his back. "Yes, I know of this man. I am told that he preaches sedition. He has a small but growing band of followers and he challenges the authority of Rome and the Sanhedrin."

"The Sanhedrin?"

"The Sanhedrin is what the Jews call their governing body. It is made up of the high priests and the elders of the Jewish faith. They govern and administer the local laws. Caiaphas is chief among them. They fear this Jesus and believe that he is attempting to undermine their authority. There have even been discussions between the high priest and the governor about arresting this Jesus and locking him away."

Marcus was surprised by both Lucius reaction to the name of Jesus and by what he learned from Lucius. It was obvious that this man called Jesus was a person of considerably more influence than Marcus had suspected.

"Where does this Jesus preach?" Marcus asked his friend.

"Wherever he can gather a crowd. In the streets, the temples, the synagogues, people's homes, everywhere. I have heard that he uses magic to impress those who listen to him."

"Magic!" Marcus repeated mockingly. "Surely you do not believe in magic?"

"His followers call his tricks, miracles."

"What sort of miracles?"

"Healing the sick, exorcisms, turning water to wine. He says that he receives this power from his God."

"Do you know anyone who has seen him do these things?"

"No. But I have heard that he has made the lame walk and the blind see." Lucius began to think that Marcus might suspect that he was accepting these stories so he quickly added, "With such power, I would like to see him avoid the sword of Rome." Lucius drew his sword and held it high to catch the glint of the afternoon sun. He went on, "This is real power. Words will be dashed in the dirt but the sword will always carry the day."

Marcus placed his hand on Lucius' shoulder. "Now that is the Lucius I remember."

The two friends returned to talking about old memories. Marcus was careful not to disclose his meeting with Metros Scipia, his other recent connection with their youth. Marcus sensed that such information might one day work to the disadvantage of either himself or Metros.

Lucius took leave of Marcus a few hours later but extended an invitation for Marcus to join him at Herod's Palace so that he could be properly introduced to the influential people of Jerusalem.

Chapter 28. "Journey Back"

Marcus awoke the next day having had little sleep. He called to Joseph, "Joseph, I have been remiss in not seeing to my father's horse. I have decided that I am going to take some time to see Judea and to travel to Bethlehem."

Joseph asked, "Why Bethlehem?"

Marcus smiled as he remembered Flavius Titus. "It's a journey back that I promised an old friend that I would do."

"Back?" Joseph asked confused by what Marcus had said.

Marcus ignored the question. "Joseph, who would you recommend that I have as a guide for such a trip? I need someone who knows the province well. Someone who will be able to give me a sense of what Judea is really about. Someone with a sense of history about this land and its people." He turned and looked at Joseph. "Do you know of such a guide?"

Joseph smiled as he gave the answer that both men knew would be forthcoming. "Humbly, I offer my services to you."

Joseph attended to the horses. Within the hour, the two men rode away from Jerusalem along the road that would take them south to Bethlehem. Most of those traveling to and from Bethlehem were on foot. Some took notice of the Roman and his servant riding on horseback while others looked away out of fear or their own sense of station in life.

Joseph saw that Marcus was taking note of the reaction they were receiving from passersby.

Marcus spoke, "Joseph, Bethlehem is not far, let's dismount and walk for a while."

After they dismounted and began walking, Marcus greeted those with whom he had eye contact as they walked by. This was an unheard of act by a Roman. Joseph could not even remember Marcus Aurelius performing such an act.

Joseph finally looked at Marcus and asked, "Why do you address total strangers with greetings when you do not know them?"

Marcus smiled, "I am hoping to get to know them Joseph. Now tell me what you know about Bethlehem and Judea."

Joseph steadied his horse and shortened his grip on the reins. "As you can see, Judea is a land of good soil and rolling hills. Farming is a way of life for many Judeans. Bethlehem... well in Hebrew, Bethlehem means 'house of bread'. For centuries, Bethlehem has been a major marketplace for farmers to sell their crops. It is also the birthplace of King David, the second king of Israel." Joseph paused, looked more closely at Marcus, and continued, "Bethlehem is also foretold to be the birth place of "Him" whose coming has been prophesized."

Marcus stopped and stood looking at Joseph. Joseph moved uneasily under the stare of his employer.

"Him, who's coming has been prophesized?" Marcus drew his horse in closer to shield his conversation from a merchant who was passing by. He went on, "This is the Messiah of your faith, the one who will lead the Jews to the promised land?"

Joseph responded, "There are those that believe that such a one has already appeared."

Marcus considered Joseph's words and said, "My friend, Lucius, tells me that there are several would be prophets that profess to be the Messiah..." Marcus paused and looking directly at Joseph, continued, "including the rabbi that you talked about seeing in the temple, Jesus."

Joseph's face colored slightly and he looked away. Marcus asked, "Joseph, do you think that this rabbi, Jesus, could be the Messiah?"

"Are you truly interested in my giving you an answer?" Joseph said as he half turned back to face Marcus.

"I am interested in what you have to say... and I am interested in this one called Jesus."

Joseph motioned to a small grove of trees just off the road to their right. "Can we sit awhile and talk?"

"A good idea." Marcus replied as he led his horse to the shade of the trees.

After they had found a knoll upon which to sit, Joseph spoke. "My people, the Jews, have long hoped for the promised one, the Messiah, to come to us and fulfill the prophecy of our deliverance. What your friend has told you is true. There are a number of men who claim to be the one whose coming was foretold. But, there is only one that I know of who fulfills the entire prophesy."

Marcus stirred, "The entire prophesy?"

Joseph nodded, "The prophets have said that Bethlehem shall be above all cities because it shall be the birthplace of 'Him' whose goings forth has been foretold."

"And this one they call Jesus, he was born in Bethlehem?" Marcus was truly interested. Joseph sensed that there was a real searching for truth and knowledge in the demeanor of his Roman employer.

"I have heard that he was. He was born in Bethlehem about the time that Herod the Great decreed that all male children of Bethlehem be killed so that the prophesy could not be fulfilled."

Marcus scuffed, "Yes. If the prophesy were to be fulfilled, it would mean an end to the rule of Herod the Great and his family. Many empires have survived because of the treachery of their rulers." Marcus then asked Joseph, "If Jesus was born in Bethlehem, during the reign of Herod the Great, how is it that he survived?"

Joseph was perplexed. "I do not know. I have never heard it discussed."

Marcus went on, "Why do they call Jesus the Nazarene if he was born in Bethlehem?"

Joseph was again perplexed. "I do not know the answer to that either."

Marcus had one last question before they mounted their horses and turned toward the city of Bethlehem. "How does one distinguish a Messiah from other prophets?"

Joseph was bothered by the questions he had been asked. They traveled the remaining portion of their five mile trip to Bethlehem in silence as each was deep in thought about the one called Jesus.

It was midday when they reached the outskirts of the city. It was not the attractive city that Marcus had hoped for. Its buildings were run down, streets dirty, and market crowded with Bedouins and peasants.

Marcus thought to himself, 'What life would I have had were it not for Marcus Aurelius?' He smiled, then, realizing that he would have had none at all as a result of the decree of Herod the Great.

His thoughts were interrupted by Joseph, "You smile! What is it that you see?"

Marcus looked up from his thoughts. "Life. I see life, Joseph. I see how the hand of fate touches each of us and some will be given a golden spoon while others are condemned to a squalorly existence."

"It is the hand of God that touches each of us. If not in this world then in the next." Joseph did not believe in fate.

"Joseph, do you believe that one can rise out of these humble beginnings and become a person of significance?"

"I believe anything is possible."

"I have always thought that if a man were willing to work hard and apply himself, there were few limits beyond one's own capabilities." Marcus hesitated and then finished his thought, "This I now know, the journey back is an education unto itself."

Chapter 29. "The Coming"

Marcus spent most of the day in Bethlehem watching the city's people go about their business. He and Joseph had agreed that they would return to Jerusalem after nightfall and then proceed on the seventy mile trip to Nazareth the following day.

Marcus purchased a jalaba while in the market place much to Joseph's surprise. "What do you intend to do with that?"

Marcus laughed, "First, I will wash it and then I will wear it!" Marcus tied the jalaba onto his saddle. "I want to be able to move among the people without instilling fear. Today, it was clear to me that as a Roman I intimidate those that I would like to get to know better."

It was Joseph's turn to laugh. "You think that by changing clothes you can hide the Roman in you?"

"We shall see."

After another restless night, Marcus arose early for his trip to Nazareth. To his surprise, Joseph was also awake and about his preparations for the journey north.

"Good morning Joseph. You are awake early today." Marcus greeted his servant.

"I wanted to be certain that all was in order for our travels."

Marcus sat down for the breakfast that Joseph had had the household servants prepare.

"Have you eaten Joseph?"

"Yes."

"Then join me while I finish my meal." Marcus continued to eat. "Is it possible that we will be able to see this prophet, Jesus, during our travels north?"

Joseph shifted on the divan he was sitting on to look at Marcus. "I have heard that He appears frequently in and around the Sea of Galilee."

Marcus asked, "How far is the Sea of Galilee from Nazareth?"

"A good day's ride."

"Joseph, I am very interested in seeing this prophet for myself."

"May I ask why you have such great interest in Jesus?" Joseph was very direct.

Marcus noted this and said, "Joseph, you ask a direct question. I have come to have great trust in you. I will share with you a story that was told to me by my teacher in Rome many years ago. I would appreciate having you keep what I am about to tell you in complete confidence. You will understand why I request this of you when I am finished with the story."

Joseph nodded and said, "Since the first day we met, I have felt a bond with you that I cannot explain. You are a good man and you have my complete loyalty. If you entrust me with what is yours, I will treat it as if were my own."

The two men understood their relationship without the need for further comment.

Marcus began his story. "About thirty years ago, an infant abandoned in the hills above Bethlehem was discovered by a Roman patrol. The child was taken to the commander of the watch. The origin of the child was unknown but at that time, Herod had decreed that all male Jewish children of Bethlehem be put to death. The commander made a decision to send that child back to Rome. He adopted the child as his own. The child was educated, trained, and lived in Rome through his formative years. His teacher and mentor kept nothing from the boy as to the boy's background and support from his adoptive father. The only piece of information that could not be provided to the boy was who were his real parents." Marcus paused.

Joseph looked at Marcus with compassion. "You are the abandoned child."

Marcus shook his head, "No, not abandoned. Marcus Aurelius was my father. He provided more for me than I could have asked for. Not only in terms of worldly belongings but in developing the person I have become.

Before he passed away, we had time to talk of things that only a father and son can share with one another. He wanted me to know that I have not only a Roman heritage but also the touch of this land upon my being. It is why he had such an affinity for Judea. He said that I gave him a home here.

Now, I want to be at home here as well. I want to be one with the land and its people. And I have this sense that this prophet is somehow tied to my connection with all of this. That is why I go to Nazareth and perhaps the Sea of Galilee. It is my destiny. It is my coming home."

Joseph hesitated before speaking, "I have heard that Jesus will be preaching near Bethsaida, three days from now. If you wish to know Him, it would serve you well to attend this gathering."

Marcus looked quickly at Joseph. He understood the significance of this information. Having discussed the local politics with Lucius, he was aware that any public preaching by this prophet was considered a seditious act.

"Joseph, thank you. I appreciate your trust in me. We will go to Bethsaida."

Chapter 30. "Loaves and Fishes"

Marcus and Joseph traveled east from Jerusalem until they reached the Jordan River. They then turned their horses north and followed a road that ran north along the banks of the Jordan River. It was a good three days ride to reach Bethsaida. On the morning of the third day, Marcus and Joseph crossed the Jordan River and rode north along the east bank of the Sea of Galilee.

Marcus marveled at the beauty and breadth of the Sea. "I never imagined a Sea so beautiful and as wide as this in this part of the country."

Joseph nodded. "Yes and the fishing is good! Do you see the fishermen and their boats along the horizon? They cast their nets and the harvest is almost always plentiful. My brother-in-law has a boat. He lives on the coast between Bethsaida and Capernaum. You may wish to return home along the west bank. We could spend the night with my sister and perhaps join my brother-in-law for a day at sea. Have you ever spent any time fishing?"

Marcus smiled. "No that is one part of my education that is lacking." He looked out at the blue water with the sun now reflecting off each small ripple in the water. "Do you think that your brother-in-law would be willing to take one with no experience out there to do a day's worth of fishing?"

Joseph threw his head back and laughed. "My brother-in-law, Jacob, has a good sense of humor. Taking a citizen of Rome out on his boat and showing him how to fish will give him many stories to tell in the years ahead." Joseph looked quickly at Marcus. "I do not mean to overstep my position. I mean no disrespect. Please take no offense in what I said."

Marcus reached over and put his hand on Joseph's shoulder. "I take no offense Joseph. Remember, only a part of me is Roman."

As they drew nearer to Bethsaida, they were joined by many other travelers. All went forth with a purpose which as they learned was to hear the prophet, Jesus.

Jesus was to appear on a small rise just south of the town but the crowd had grown so large that his disciples had suggested a larger hillside to the west of town. Moving the crowd to the other side of town was not an easy task. Many complained especially those who had arrived early hoping to receive the personal blessing of the Messiah. Some of those who had gathered had been in Bethsaida for more than a week. Most were poor, many showed signs of illness and many had not eaten for the past few days as they waited.

Marcus decided to stable the horses in town and walk out to the mount to hear and to see Jesus. He paid the stable keeper to feed and bed down their horses. He removed a jug of water from his mount and the jalaba from his saddle. After paying the stable keeper, he pulled the jalaba over his tunic and he and Joseph then walked west from the stable following the constant stream of people to the edge of town.

They reached the place where Jesus was to appear. It was one of the largest gatherings of people that Marcus had experienced outside of the Coliseum. Most were sitting on the ground in clusters talking. Some were excited about what was about to take place. Others complained bitterly that they had been waiting so long, had not eaten, and had been displaced by the move.

Joseph pointed to a man who was trying to quiet those who were complaining the loudest telling them that there was more to life than food for the stomach. It did not seem to have the desired effect on those to whom he was speaking. Joseph said, "That is one of Jesus' disciples. He is called Peter."

Marcus took note of the disciple. He was not what Marcus would have expected of a disciple. Marcus had imagined a more refined, scholarly, and religious bearing among the disciples. This man was short and stocky, well built, and obviously someone who was use to long hours of hard labor. His face was well tanned from toiling in the sun and his beard grew wild as did his hair giving him an unruly look.

Marcus asked Joseph, "Do you know this disciple, Peter? What does he do for a living?"

Joseph looked at Marcus a bit puzzled and said, "He was a fisherman until Jesus called him to follow. He actually was a friend of my brother-in-law, Jacob. They spent many hours together on the Sea of Galilee."

"Have you met him, Joseph?" Marcus asked.

"We have met but Jacob is the one who really knows Peter. My sister thinks that Peter is a wild man. Jacob and Peter spent many hours together, after the day's catch, sampling the fruit of the vine!" Joseph laughed. "She tells me that the best thing that has happened for her husband, Jacob, was Peter running off to follow the rabbi!"

They both laughed at that.

Suddenly, their conversation was overshadowed by a rising murmur from the masses of people around them. Marcus looked away from Joseph toward the direction of the sound and his eyes immediately locked together with those of a young man dressed in a well worn linen jalaba.

Marcus felt the deep gaze of this young rabbi penetrating his own mind and piercing his very soul. This man called Jesus continued toward Marcus while acknowledging and occasionally touching the throngs of people around him. His gentle smile seemed to calm those who could see him and his words gave blessings to those who heard.

When Jesus reached the place where Marcus and Joseph stood, he again turned to Marcus and looking straight into Marcus' eyes, simply said "Follow."

Jesus moved away and as he climbed the remaining distance to the top of the mount, Marcus and Joseph followed at a short distance away.

Peter, his brother Andrew, and two other brothers, John and James, had prepared a place for Jesus where he could be heard by all present.

Peter spoke first. "Master, many here are in need of food. They have stayed for days waiting to hear you speak to them but their need for nourishment preoccupies them."

John then said, "Master, many are sick or have young ones with them. It is they who are most needy of food."

Jesus raised his hand and looked at his disciples. He nodded and said, "As my father provides for you and me, so then must we provide for others. Go forth and ask all who are here to share what they have with their brothers and sisters. Bring to me what is offered that I may bless the generosity of those who are willing to share their food with others in such need."

The disciples went in among the crowd and after a time came back to the place where Jesus sat talking to a small boy who had come forward.

He finished talking with the boy and turned to his disciples. “What have you brought to me for my blessing?”

Peter replied, “Master, we have but five loaves of bread and two small fish. It is not enough to satisfy all that are hungry.”

Jesus looked at Peter and smiled as he stood up. “Have faith Peter, it is enough.”

Jesus then turned to all who were gathered. The thousands of people that were there, men, women, and children all became silent as Jesus looked down upon them. His voice deepened as he spoke. “Please sit down.” The multitude did as they were asked and sat down on the grassy slope that ran from the top of the hill to the edge of the town.

Jesus turned to his disciples and said, “Bring to me the food that my Father, who is in Heaven, has provided through those who seek his blessing.” Peter, Andrew, and John brought the five loaves of bread and two fish to Jesus. Jesus picked each one up in turn and holding each over his head said, “Our Father has taught us that it is more blessed to give to others in need than it is to keep to ourselves more than we need. Those of you who have offered up your loaves of bread and fish today will have our Fathers blessing on you and upon your family for all time to come. God knows each of you and bares witness to your generosity and good heart. Blessed be this food to our bodies and God’s blessing on your souls.”

Jesus then took the bread and broke it into small pieces. He handed the pieces to his disciple along with the fish which he had also cut into small pieces and asked that they serve the food to all who were in need. All those present witnessed this act of generosity and many shared what they had in the belief that God would bless those that had food enough, for the food that they shared with those who had so little. Baskets of bread and fish were passed among the thousands that came to hear and see Jesus that day and when all had eaten and were filled, the disciples were amazed that there were remaining twelve baskets still filled with pieces of bread and fish.

Jesus, seeing that all had been satisfied through the giving spirit, said to the crowd, “Let this be a lesson to you, treat one another always as you would have yourself be treated. Love one another as you would your family for all of us are the children of God, the Father. That which you do for the poorest among us, you also do for my Father. Now, go forth and do good work for the betterment of mankind.”

He then turned to his disciples and told them to disperse the crowd as he needed to be alone in prayer. Turning to Peter, he said, “Always have faith Peter. Now, take the others by sea to Capernaum and I will join you later."

Peter and the other disciples began dispersing the crowd.

Jesus then sat down on the ground for a moment deep in thought. Some in the crowd lingered for a last look at the one they called the Messiah. However, no one approached him believing that he was deep in prayer. When only a few remained, Jesus looked up and saw among those who had stayed, Marcus Titus. Jesus smiled, stood up and walked over to where Marcus and Joseph had been sitting.

Jesus looked directly at Marcus as Marcus stood to greet Jesus. Again their eyes met as they had in the crowd. Marcus spoke words that came not from his head but from his soul, "You asked that I follow."

Jesus smiled, "You have a destiny to fulfill."

Marcus seemed to understand what it was that Jesus was saying. "Yes. I believe that all men have a destiny to fulfill but I have this sense that my destiny is somehow a part of this land, and a part of what you are about."

Jesus turned away and saying to Marcus, "Walk with me for a while."

Moving away, Marcus looked back at Joseph. Joseph nodded and said, "Go with him, I will wait back at the stable for you to return."

As they walked away from the hillside and the town, Jesus asked, "Did you understand what happened here today?"

Marcus watched this rabbi as he spoke. "I think that the teacher was imparting a lesson not only to those who came to hear and to learn but to those who follow and must serve others."

Jesus smiled and asked, "Who are those that follow?"

The two men sat down on a knoll. Marcus responded, "They are known as your disciples. You are their teacher and for now they are your students. Someday, the students will become the teachers. I had a teacher who often told me that long after he was no longer of this world, the lessons that he taught me would live on because I would continue to bear witness to his teachings."

"Do you bear witness to those things that your teacher imparted to you?"

"I try to. He was a very wise and learned man."

"Are you always true to his teachings?"

"Not always but I asked him once if it would be wrong for me to disagree with him."

Jesus laughed and asked, "What did he say?"

"He said that the lessons of man are often flawed and that even he could be subject to error." Marcus smiled at the memory of his teacher Flavius. "He was quick to add that true though that may be, he could not recall the last time he was in error." Both men laughed at that.

Jesus then became more serious. "There is but one steadfast truth and that is the word of God. Those that strive to live by His teachings will have his blessings. They will find happiness and contentment and will abide with him for eternity."

Marcus shifted his position so that he was looking directly at Jesus. There was something about this man that was different from all others that he had known. He asked, "May I be very direct with you?"

Jesus nodded.

"I have studied many subjects among them the religious beliefs of different sects and have questioned many beliefs. The Romans for example have many Gods and it is even believed by some that Caesar is a God. In my travels through Judea, I have heard that you are the son of the God of the Jews. Many call you the Messiah. It is said that you perform miracles and that these miracles are proof that you are who others say that you are. Perhaps, I witnessed one of your miracles today when you fed five thousand with five loaves of bread and two fish. But how can a man know the face of God or for that matter the face of the son of God?"

Jesus picked up a small branch that lay on the ground near to where he was sitting. He drew a circle in the dirt and said, "This is the circle of life. All things in life are connected. There is a balance that is necessary for order and harmony. It is not an accident that this circle of life has been created. It is too great and too well pieced together to be a chance fabrication. God, my Father, crafted it so."

Raising the branch and point to the sky, Jesus went on, "You ask how one can know the face of God. My Father's face can be seen in the sky above, the soft gray clouds that float across a field of blue. He can be seen in the birds that glide above us and in the fish that swim in the sea. The rain that falls to the earth, the wheat that grows on the land, the trees that bloom in the spring, the fruits of summer, all this can be said to be the face of God, my Father. But to see him as you believe you have a need to see him, you can look into the eyes and upon the face of every man, every woman, and every child. He has made all in his own image. These are real images, not the imagined images of the Gods of other beliefs. The images of our faith you experience every day."

Jesus paused a moment. Marcus sat quietly trying to absorb all that was being said. Jesus turned to look toward the setting sun. It was beautiful sight as the sky turned from bright blue to an amber and finally to a deep purple hue. Jesus then went on, "This balance within the circle of life is very delicate. It is dependent upon obeying the commandments which my Father has given to his people. His commandments provide for a well ordered life, a balance within which each of us can be happy. One of his greatest commandments is that you 'Do for others what you would wish that they would do for you.' All other commandments flow from the one.

Today, I saw that when the loaves were passed you did not take even a single morsel for yourself but instead passed the basket on. Why did you not take what was being offered?"

Marcus had not realized that Jesus had seen this small act on his part. "I did not realize that you were watching. I have food enough and I surmised that there were others today who needed nourishment more than I did."

Jesus smiled, "It is sometimes better to give than it is to receive. In your heart, you had a good feeling about what you had done. A small thing but yet not so small when measured by a man and his small son who had not eaten for four days. Such a man and his son were seated not far from you. He noticed your act of generosity and prayed that you be blessed for your action."

Marcus' mind took note of all that Jesus said. "How do you know these things?"

"Through our Father in heaven, all that happens here on earth will be made known to those who have the faith to see with their minds and with their hearts.

I have been sent to remind my Father's people of his words and his commandments. I am one with the Holy Spirit. If there be truth in what I teach, all of it, then the truth is that I am he who I have said that I am. What I have told to you is all part of the fabric of my time on earth. You are as much a part of that fabric as I am. In time you will know the purpose that God intends for you

You ask how you will know the face of the son of God. In truth, you will know it in your mind and in your heart."

Marcus looked up at Jesus after having again looked down at the circle fading from view due to the darkness of the night. "I am not sure that I fully understand all that you have said. But I am curious, do you believe that your disciples understood the lesson that you preached today?"

Jesus answered with a question, "Tell me the lesson."

Marcus explained his understanding, "Peter and the others were concerned about the feeding of the people's bellies when the focus should have been on the feeding of their minds. The lesson was the commandment that you have just spoken of…that in the balance of life there is enough for all if all treat others as they would want to be treated themselves. The sharing of what morsels they had, with one another, proved to be more than enough to satisfy because they accepted what you taught them and believed. But there was more. Religion is also based upon faith. Yours is a faith in one all knowing God. Had Peter and the others truly had faith, they would not have been as concerned with the filling of the bellies of those present as they would have been for reaching their minds and hearts."

Jesus stood and seemed pleased with what Marcus had said. "You are correct about the lesson. The sharing today was a gift given to all those who came from the Holy Spirit. As the Spirit touched you so too it touched all."

Marcus also stood up. "I am a stranger to you and yet you have taken me in as a friend. Why?"

Jesus took Marcus by the arm and led him back toward Bethsaida. "When I first saw you, I knew you if not by name then by heart. You come from two worlds. My guess is that you have both the blood of this land and that of Rome flowing through your veins. But your eyes tell me that you are the one that I have been looking for. I have chosen twelve good and true men to be disciples and to carry forth the word of my Father. They still have much to learn but shortly they will be tested and the spirit will descend upon them and they will understand. I am charged now with finding the one who will record for the ages all that is said and done here. I believe you are the one that has been provided for that task."

Marcus stopped abruptly. "I do not want to mislead you. I am interested in your faith but I am not a Jew. My interest is scholarly." He thought for a moment and added, "Curiosity may also be a part of it as well."

Jesus was not put off by this reply. He expected it. "I know who you are for my Father foretold of your coming to me. You are learned and you have the ability to record what you witness in truth and with accuracy. The light of the holy spirit will shine down on you and in time you will do what is right."

Marcus shook his head. "I hardly know you. I am impressed by what I have seen but I still have many questions and more to learn before I would commit to such an undertaking."

Jesus looked at his new friend, "I have faith."

As they entered the town, night had fallen. In the darkness there was the distant sound of a coming storm. Jesus said, "Time is precious, use it well. I must go to my... students. There is more to be taught before they will be prepared to teach."

Marcus was about to say good bye when he realized that he had never introduced himself properly to this man who had asked him to record a personal history. "I know you as Jesus of Nazareth. I have been remiss in not introducing myself properly. I am Marcus Titus, adopted son of Marcus Aurelius, a Roman Centurion who lived most of his life here in Judea."

Jesus turned to Marcus and knowing his unspoken thoughts said, "You worry that your Roman background is a blockade to our friendship. It is more of a bridge. Marcus Titus, when next we meet I will know you. Though you are known to others as Marcus Titus, when I have gone to my Father, you will be known to all who seek redemption as Mark. The bridge will have been crossed."

With that they parted friends. Marcus made his way to the stable.

Chapter 31. "The Storm"

Joseph was waiting at the stable when Marcus returned.

"You were gone a long time. I was beginning to worry about you."

Marcus clapped Joseph lightly on the shoulder. "Your rabbi and I had much to talk about. He has great wisdom for one so young."

"He is known among the Jewish people as a great teacher. I have been told that he provides parables, stories, as a means to reach the minds of those who will listen. The message in these stories is not always clear but they do accomplish a purpose. Everyone listens." Joseph looked at their horses and continued, "Nightfall has come. My sister and her husband live an hour's ride outside of town, just off the road to Capernaum. Shall we spend the night here or ride on to stay with them?"

"Are they expecting us?" Marcus asked.

"I sent word to them that we would be there tonight or tomorrow."

"Well, then let's ride on. I am too full of thought to sleep anytime soon."

Joseph saddled their horses while Marcus bid the stable keeper good bye. They mounted their horses and road out of town along the coast toward Capernaum.

As they rode, they could see a great storm out to sea. Lightening flashed sending jagged streaks slamming into the water and it was apparent that the wind was whipping up the waves causing white caps to appear even at the distance from which Joseph and Marcus were watching.

"It will be well for us if that storm remains at sea." Joseph said to Marcus.

"I agree. I hope that if your brother-in-law decides to teach me fishing, it is on calmer seas than that." Marcus pointed to where the last bolt of lightening had struck.

"No ships sail when a storm such as that is brewing." Joseph assured Marcus.

As they rode up to the coastal house of Jacob and his wife, Miriam, Marcus caught a glimpse of what appeared to be a ship struggling on the stormy sea. He reined in his horse to watch the place where he thought that he had seen the ship. Joseph pulled up beside him. "What is it?"

Marcus continued to scan the sea. "I thought I saw the outline of a ship."

Both men looked out to sea. Another flash of lightening showed a ship struggling to stay afloat as the wind and rain drove harder at the sea.

Joseph leaped from his horse and shouted to Marcus above the wind, "I will get Jacob. They need help."

"I will stay here to mark the spot in case they should go down."

Joseph ran to his brother-in-law's home and returned quickly with his sister and her husband following.

"Are they still afloat?" Joseph asked.

"Yes, there!" Marcus pointed as another flash of lightening lit the sky.

Jacob saw the boat too. He shouted, "They are being tossed toward the reef and the shallows. If they hit that reef, their boat will be destroyed."

"What can we do?" Marcus began pulling off the jalaba in order to give himself more room to maneuver.

Jacob looked at the Roman clothes that had been covered by the jalaba then at the man. "A Roman, yet a man of action. I like that. We should go down to the shore and get my boat ready for the rescue."

As they began the climb down the cliff to the shore Marcus saw a lone figure walking toward the water. Upon reaching the water's edge, the man stepped off and as if being held above the sea, the man walked straight out to near where the ship was floundering.

Marcus, Jacob and Joseph reached the shore and stood there watching the man in amazement.

Then they saw one of the ship's crew jump from the ship into the sea and begin to approach the man in the water. Suddenly the crew member sank beneath the water but the man reached down and pulled the crew member up beside him. Almost at the same time as the man saved the crew member, the storm abated and the sea became calm. Both men then climbed into the boat.

Jacob motioned for help in getting his boat out into the water and he and Joseph and Marcus rowed out to the floundering ship to offer help.

As they approached, Marcus was startled by the recognition of the man whom he had seen walk out on the sea to rescue the ship's crew. The man was Jesus.

Jacob also recognized one of ship's crew. It was a fellow fisherman, Simon who lately had changed his name and wished to be called Peter. "Peter, how is your crew?" Jacob asked.

Peter looked up and upon seeing his old fishing friend, he raised his hands and said, "Saved by the Son of God."

Jacob offered the shelter of his home to the shaken disciples. They quickly accepted.

Later, Marcus marveled at the story told by Peter of what had happened. He and the other eleven disciples had done as Jesus had asked. After leaving the hillside outside of Bethsaida, they had gone to Peter's ship and set sail for Capernaum. An hour out to sea, a great storm had come up and the wind had been so fierce that they were forced to haul in their sail and ride the storm out. Peter was aware of the shoals and was afraid that his boat would be cast up on the shoals and destroyed.

Then they saw what looked like an apparition coming toward them on the water. All of them feared what it was and what was about to happen to them.

But then Jesus spoke telling those in the boat not to be afraid 'I am here for you.' Peter answered saying that 'If that be you, Jesus, call to me and I will join you.'

It was then that Jesus called out to Peter saying, 'Have faith in me that I will uphold you in more things than this storm." Peter jumped over the side of the ship and at first was able to walk above the water. But the storm tore at his clothing and his view of the man he thought to be Jesus blurred. He again feared for his wellbeing and in that moment of weakness, he sank beneath the water. His last cry was for Jesus to save him.

Jesus reached out, grabbed Peter by the arm and pulled him up to him. "How little is your faith in me, Peter. Did you have doubt that I would hold you up and save you from this storm?" Jesus then looked to the heavens and the storm ceased. Together they climbed into the boat where the other disciples marveled at what they had seen. They had all knelt down before Jesus saying, 'In truth, you are the Son of God.'

Fed by Miriam and now dried by Jacob's fire, the tired disciples soon were asleep. Marcus sat next to Jesus watching the embers of the fire. Finally, Marcus asked the question that had been stirring in his mind for the entire evening, "All here believe that you walked on the water. Is that possible?"

Jesus did not take his eyes from the fire. "What did you see?"

Marcus thought back to what had taken place in the dark of night. "There was little light for me to see. There was little light for you to see. Jacob has told me that even those most experienced with the shoals and shallows of the sea in this area could not have walked the distance from shore to their ship without sinking. I saw you do this."

Jesus then turned to Marcus and said, "Marcus, have faith in God's purpose for you and you will be upheld in all that life has to offer to you." Jesus turned back to the fire, "My Father's purpose tonight was to demonstrate the power of faith to my disciples so that they too would believe and have faith that their lives had purpose."

Marcus stared into the fire and said, "Am I to be a disciple?"

Jesus answered, "There are twelve who I have chosen to walk with me. They will follow closely unto death with me. Two shall be spared but their path too will be different than the one for which you have been chosen. You are my other disciple. You are the one who will insure that the work of the twelve and of myself will not perish from this earth.

Your education is what separates you from the others. In time, all will have understanding but none will have your learning.

Tomorrow, we will go our separate ways but soon we will be together again.

Believe in what you see Marcus. You have been given a great gift by my Father in Heaven."

Chapter 32 . "Follow"

The next morning, Jesus and his twelve disciples prepared to leave the house of Jacob. Jesus thanked Miriam and Jacob for their sharing of their home and food with him and with his disciples. He raised his hand and looking up said, "Bless this man and this woman for they have cared for thy son and for his disciples. Bestow on this home and family good fortune and make of it a respite for those who are tired and in need."

Jesus then looked at the man and his wife and continued, "Your goodness shall be rewarded a hundred fold. As you treat others, you will be treating me."

Jacob and Miriam knelt down before Jesus, kissed his robe, and nodded in understanding.

Jesus then turned to Joseph, "Serve your master well for in serving him you also serve me." Joseph bowed his head in acknowledgement.

Finally, Jesus turned to Marcus who had been taking in all that was said and done. "I will see you again in Jerusalem." He paused and then went on, "As Mark, my other disciple."

Peter looked from Jesus to Marcus and then back at Jesus. "Is he to become one of us?"

Jesus answered without looking away from Marcus. "Marcus, also to be called Mark, has a different discipleship from that which you and my other followers have been called for. Tho we may all parish, he will preserve all that is said and done that others may know the will and the glory of my Father in Heaven."

Jesus turned and left the house of Jacob and Miriam with his disciples following.

When they had gone, Marcus asked many questions of Jacob and Miriam.

"Jacob, is it possible to walk the shoals the distance that we saw Jesus walk last night without sinking into the sea?"

"I have never seen nor heard of such a thing! The depth of the shoals changes frequently and the location is constantly shifting. No one could know where it would be safe to gain a footing for that distance much less see such a footing in the dark of night. No, Jesus was held aloft by the Almighty, God. That is the only explanation for how he could walk across the sea and save Simon and the others."

Marcus accepted what Jacob had said. It was certainly an act of faith which took Jesus safely across the water. He also considered how quickly the storm had calmed once Jesus had made his way to the floundering ship. He remembered Peter sinking in the sea and Jesus reaching down and pulling him up. Not more than a few feet separated the two and yet Peter sank with his lack of faith and fear and Jesus had remained above the sea and was able to rescue his friend and follower.

Marcus turned to Miriam and asked, "What did you see last night?"

Miriam was a shy and quiet person who had said little since Marcus had arrived. She had served all her guests well and had spoken only when addressed directly by one of men staying in her home. She looked at Jacob and with his approving nod said, "I saw our Lord, Jesus, walk across the sea and save Simon, his bother Andrew and their friends from drowning because of the storm."

"You believe that he walked on the water?"

She replied, "I believe what I saw. Jesus is the son of God. All things are possible with him."

Marcus nodded and turned to Joseph, "My friend, tell me what you saw."

Joseph did not hesitate. "I too saw Jesus walk above the sea to rescue his disciples from the storm. Were it not for him, they might have been lost. I know it is difficult for you to accept our faith in the young rabbi as the Messiah but many have seen what faith in him and in our God can do. I have heard that he cures those who have been sick or afflicted with just the touch of his hand. His coming has been foretold for centuries. He has been recognized by our prophets as the one. Now, by my own eyes, I have seen proof that he is no ordinary man. He is the one that we have been waiting for."

Joseph received approving nods from both Jacob and Miriam.

Marcus shrugged his shoulders. "Faith is a powerful force. It has moved armies and changed the course of history. Do you believe that this man will change the course of history for the people of Israel?"

"So it has been foretold." Joseph replied with a hint of uncertainty in his voice.

Marcus realized that he was becoming too much the inquisitor with his questions. He was a guest in Jacob's and Miriam's home and should show some consideration for his hosts. He decided to move on to a more palatable look at their experiences. "The young rabbi and I talked late into the night. He told me that the first and greatest commandment of your God is to do for others what you would have others do for you. It is a great thought. I have been considering its application to all rules and orders and I must admit that I can not think of a single occasion when such a commandment would not apply for the general good. It is remarkable that such a simple precept can apply so broadly." He looked again at Joseph. "Do you know where Jesus received his education?"

Jacob spoke before Joseph could answer. "Simon has told me that he is a carpenter's son."

Joseph then added, "His education comes through his Father."

Marcus marveled at what he heard. Jesus evidenced knowledge and understanding far beyond that which he would have been able to receive in the home of a carpenter. Marcus knew at that moment that he would indeed seek out the young rabbi again and seek to learn more about this man called Jesus.

"Jacob, you know the disciple which Jesus calls Peter?"

Jacob laughed, "Simon and I have been friends for many years."

"Tell me about him."

Jacob warmed to this subject. "Simon was born in Bathsaida, the son of Jona. He grew up working on fishing boats out of Bathsaida and learning the trade. Eventually he saved enough money to buy his own boat. He moved to Capernaum, married and had a few children. But his real love was the sea. That is where I met him. We fished the same waters. He is a good man. He used to share wine with us and many is the time that he would spend his nights under his boat instead of going home." Jacob laughed. "He also had his share of quarrels with other fisherman but after breaking a few jaws and knocking out a few teeth, he would always buy drinks all around and all would be forgotten.

He even had his mother-in-law move in with him and his wife to provide companionship for his wife when he was gone fishing."

Marcus tried to imagine such a man as a disciple of Jesus. "Jacob, do you know how your friend became a disciple?"

"It is as amazing to me as it must be for you!" Jacob shook his head as in disbelief. "Simon's brother Andrew always was the religious one in the family. He would often go to hear a prophet known as the Baptist preach. Andrew would come back from one of the Baptist's preachings and tell us how he had confessed his sins and was forgiven by God because he was penitent. We would laugh.

Then, one day, Andrew was with the Baptist when Jesus came to the Jordan River. The Baptist upon seeing Jesus proclaimed 'Behold the Lamb of God.'

Andrew was very excited and came back to Simon and told him of what had happened. A few of us laughed but Simon was very serious and asked his brother to take him to meet this 'Lamb of God.'

Later Simon told me that when he met Jesus, Jesus looked straight at him and said, "You are Simon, the son of Jona. I shall call you Peter. Simon was surprised that Jesus knew him."

At this Marcus recalled his own meeting with Jesus and what had been said.

Jacob continued, "Simon spent some time with Jesus and then came back to his fishing with his brother Andrew. He would talk for hours about Jesus and what he had seen him do while he was with him." Jacob laughed again remembering one story told by Simon. "Simon said that while he was in Cana at a wedding with Jesus, Jesus took water jugs and filled them with wine. No one knew where the wine came from but Simon allowed how it certainly was preferable to the water that was in them!"

Miriam looked admonishingly at her husband.

Jacob took notice and proceeded, "Well, one day not long after Simon had traveled with Jesus, Simon and Andrew were tending to their catch of the day when Jesus appeared as if from nowhere. Simon and Andrew were obviously pleased to see him and were also pleased with all the fish that they had caught. I remember Simon saying to Jesus, 'If you would like to join us tomorrow, we will show you how to catch these fish." Jesus looked at Simon and Andrew and said 'Come follow me, and I will make you fishers of men.' Something moved Simon that day. Andrew did not surprise me but Simon did. He was a good fisherman and had many good catches. But he looked at Andrew, nodded and off they went, leaving behind their nets and boat, seldom to be seen in the trade since.

That same day, Jesus proceeded past me and some others who were there and approached two other fishermen, Zebedee's sons, John and his brother, James. He called to them to come and follow him. They, too, accepted the calling. They left their father Zebedee, who had a good fishing business, and became followers of Jesus."

Marcus had listened to all that Jacob had said. "Have you talked to Simon, Peter, since he decided to give up his trade and follow Jesus?"

"Yes. A couple of months ago, his mother-in-law came down with a fever and was not expected to live. I sent word to Simon, at the request of his wife, that he was needed. Simon returned home with Jesus to tend to his mother-in-law... And this is another amazing story. Simon's wife had not been very pleased that Simon had gone off with Jesus leaving her to run the household. But when Jesus and Simon came to tend to her mother, her whole attitude changed. I have been told that upon their arrival in Simon's home, Jesus placed his hand on her mother's head, said a prayer, then washed her arms, legs and feet, and within hours the fever was gone.

Since that time, Simon's wife has been as much a disciple of Jesus as has Simon.

Simon has told me of witnessing many similar healings performed by Jesus. People seek him out to be healed or to have family members healed. Simon said that once Jesus even healed the servant of a Roman Centurion when asked by the Roman to save his friend. Simon says that only the Son of God could cure so many with such serious ailments."

Joseph had been watching Marcus to determine what might be his reaction to all that he was told. Marcus sensed this and so he turned toward Joseph, smiled and said, "Jesus is like no other that I have ever met. I must admit that from the moment that I first saw the man, I felt something inside of me change. It was a good feeling. And when I spoke with him, it was like talking with an old friend. I will have to learn more about this man and his teachings. He is someone I would like to get to know well."

Marcus then turned to his host. "Jacob, I would also like to get to know a little bit about fishing. Joseph tells me that you are good enough to even teach a Roman how to cast a net successfully."

Jacob laughed, got up, and walked over to Marcus. Placing his heavy hand on Marcus' shoulder, he said, "Follow me young man and I will teach you the joy of hard work in one of God's most beautiful settings." He motioned to the sea below. "The Sea of Galilee."

Chapter 33. "The Sea of Galilee"

Marcus, Joseph and Jacob were joined by Elias, Jacob's fishing partner for their day's fishing. Marcus noted that unlike Joseph, these two men were much like the disciple Peter. Both were stocky, well muscled, short in stature but much at home on the sea. Elias had a long beard and mustache. His hair was unkempt which by now Marcus guessed was true of most fishermen. Grooming was not high on their list of important things to do.

Jacob had given Marcus a change of clothes commenting that a tunic does not lend itself well to the sea and to handling fish. Now as they dragged Jacob's boat to the water's edge, Marcus understood the wisdom of the choice.

The boat was heavy in the sand. All four men applied their weight to the effort to get the boat into the water. Finally the heft of the boat lifted as the water eased the load for the men.

Jacob held firmly to the bow as Elias climbed in and settled in the stern. Marcus and Joseph followed sitting down on the nets in the center of the boat. Jacob gave a shove at the bow and quickly jumped over the gunwale and into the bow of the boat.

The boat had two sets of oars tied down to oarlocks on both sides of the boat. At its center was a small mast which was used to hoist a sail when winds permitted. Fishing nets with cork floats on one end and deadweights on the other lay in the bottom of the boat. The boat had a length of about twenty-four feet and its width measured a little over eight and one half feet.

Marcus and Joseph were given the assignment of manning the oars, much to the amusement of Elias and Jacob. The fact the Marcus was a

Roman citizen and rowing their fishing ship was at the forefront of their minds. Jacob did take the rowing seriously and he spent a good amount of time explaining to his brother-in-law and his Roman guest the proper way to use the oars and how to time their strokes to get the most speed and glide from their efforts.

Once he settled into the rhythm of the stroke, Marcus relaxed and enjoyed the exercise and the fresh smell of the sea. Gulls circled overhead in a sky of blue. The storm clouds of the night before were all but forgotten and the sun sparkled on the ripples in the water. Marcus thought of his conversations with the young rabbi and of the circle of life drawn on the ground. 'Everything connected in a perfect harmony.' It certainly seemed so at this moment.

Jacob set the sail about an hour out to sea as the breeze picked up. Once the sail was tied down, it filled with wind and ship moved on effortlessly through the small waves that now spread across the sea. Again, Marcus marveled at the beauty of the sea, the sky, and the vastness of what lie ahead of them. Jacob saw the look on Marcus' face. "Nothing like it." He said to Marcus. "This is why we love what we do so much. We are masters of our own fate out here. To know our God, you have to feel the waves beneath your feet. You have to smell the clean fresh air and feel it blow across your face and through your hair. You have to be able to look out over the bow and know that in all of this, as far as the eye can see, it is just you, the sea, and your Maker." He had been looking out to sea as he talked but now he turned to Marcus. "When we strike a catch," he curled a fist and drew his arm to his chest, "and you start hauling in your nets as fast as you can so as to not lose any of the fish, you will feel the excitement, the thrill of the craft, and the satisfaction of a good days work."

Marcus acknowledged what Jacob had said. He asked, "When will we be casting the nets?"

Jacob looked at some motion on the sea. "A timely question. Look over there. What do you see?"

Marcus looked out and saw the flickering on the water. "Something appears to be stirring up the water."

"Small bait fish." Jacob replied. "They are running from the bigger fish. Now, we go after the bigger ones and our nets will keep them from running from us."

The sail was dropped and this time Jacob and Elias rowed as hard and as expertly as anything that Marcus had ever seen. The boat cut through the water in front of the bait fish and then swung hard to the port side.

The men were all up, Jacob and Marcus casting their net to the starboard side and Joseph and Elias to the port side. They all held on to the nets as they felt the sudden impact of the school of larger fish. "Haul!" Someone shouted and they all began pulling in the nets as fast as was possible. The catch was good. After about an hour, the boat was filled with fish and Jacob announce it was time to sail for home.

"Well, what do you think?" Jacob asked Marcus.

"Nothing like this!" Marcus exclaimed. "As my old teacher would have said, 'Exhilarating!'"

They all laughed.

Elias had brought a small flute with him and as he pulled it out of his carrying pouch, Jacob explained that it was a sort of tradition with him and Elias to have music after a good day of fishing. They played and sang their seafaring songs and laughed at their two novice crew members during the trip back to their harbor. It had been a good day for Marcus filled with many memories. After a meal of fish, bread, figs and wine, all of which Miriam had overseen, he bid all a good night, went to bed and slept well into the next morning.

Chapter 34. "The Best Man"

Marcus woke to the sound of the sea and a gentle breeze blowing in through an open window. As he climbed out of bed, he realized that he had used muscles that had not been exercised in quite some time. He had aches where he had not had them before. He thought to himself, 'No wonder these fisherman are built like rock walls. I haven't felt this soar since those first few weeks in Illyricum.'

At the thought of Illyricum, a vision of Cara, dressed in her white silk tunic took form in his mind. He wondered how she was faring after all this time. 'I have traveled far in my lifetime. I have been very fortunate in meeting some wonderful people along the way. The question now is, will I continue to be so fortunate.' His thoughts then went to Didyanna, Flavius, his father, Marcus Aurelius, and then Jesus, the Nazarene. "Could he be the Messiah, the Son of the God of the Jews?"

Joseph half heard Marcus talking to himself and entered the room in which Marcus had spent the night. "You said something?" He looked at Marcus who was now dressed and adjusting the sword which he wore at his side.

Marcus looked up and smiled, "I think the workout that your brother-in-law gave me yesterday has taken its toll on me! Between the turn at the oars and hauling in those nets, I am having trouble moving!"

Joseph laughed and shook his head in agreement. "I too am having difficulty. It took me several minutes before I could stand up straight! Every movement is an effort."

"We are out of condition, Joseph. We need to apply not only our minds but also our backs or we are going to be old men before our time."

Joseph had not seen this lighter side of Marcus before. He sensed that he and Marcus were bonding in a way that friends often relate to one another. No longer the Master and the Servant but still he told himself to remember that he was in the employ of this Roman who he had become very fond of over the last few weeks.

They walked out into the main room of the house to a table set with fruits, breads, and wine. Miriam gestured to the chairs around the table, "Please eat before you go. I cannot have my brother and his Master leave us on an empty stomach."

Marcus looked from Miriam to Joseph and shook his head, "Not Master, friend and guest." He smiled at both of them, "I am hungry and you have set a wonderful table for us. Thank you."

After the morning meal, Marcus and Joseph thanked Miriam and Jacob for their hospitality and Jacob for the lesson in fishing. Marcus invited both to come to Jerusalem and be his guest at his home. They were astonished by this invitation to the point that neither could speak. Finally, Jacob said, "You pay us the highest honor but we could not so impose."

Marcus placed a hand on Jacob's shoulder and looked directly into his eyes, "It would never be an imposition. You and your good wife will always be welcome in my home. I insist that you plan to visit."

As Marcus and Joseph rode off along the west bank of the Sea of Galilee, Jacob said to his wife, "That man is one of the best Romans I have ever encountered."

His wife answered, "That man is one of the best men that you have ever encountered."

Chapter 35. "Caiaphas, the High Priest"

A week after their return to Jerusalem, Marcus received and invitation from Lucius to join him for a midday meal at the Fortress of Antonia to be followed by a meeting in the Temple with Caiaphas, the high priest of the Jews. Lucius knew from his first meeting in Jerusalem that his friend, Marcus, was interested in learning more about the Jewish faith. Although Lucius thought this a complete waste of time, he felt that it was something worthwhile that he could do for his friend.

As commander of the guard at the fort and provider of Roman security for the Temple, Lucius had some standing with Caiaphas and the Sanhedrin. The Sanhedrin were the chief priests and scribes of the Temple and with the elders of the faith, formed a governing council for the Jews. They made the law with the consent of Rome, and together, Rome and the Sanhedrin proscribed the proper order for Judea.

Marcus joined Lucius on the appointed day at the gates of the Fortress of Antonio.

As they climbed the long high steps leading to the entrance of the fort, Marcus observed, "A well designed and constructed fortress."

"It is impregnable! It is a fortress within a fortress. When we reach the ramparts, you will see that the shear height and massiveness of these walls would defy any intruder. We are protected on all sides. Even though we enjoin the walls of the Temple, we are higher and in fact have a clear view of the ground within the Temple from our turrets. This is a Roman masterpiece."

Lucius immediately led Marcus to the southeastern turret to view the city and the Temple grounds.

Marcus, ever the student, commented, "The walls are formidable, yet the distance to the top of these walls is more than halved by the top of the Temple's wall which adjoins the eastern wall. Is that not a possible exposure for the fortress?"

Lucius looked down at the top of the Temple's wall. It ran the entire length of the fortress's eastern wall and in fact was but a scaling ladder's length to the top of the fortress wall. He looked quickly at Marcus, "It is good that you are a Roman, or I would have to kill you for that observation." He smiled but behind the smile Marcus detected in Lucius a new concern for his impregnable fortress.

Lucius became serious for a moment, "Thank you Marcus. I am not aware that anyone has ever made note of the proximity of the two walls before now. It is something that we will have to address. I trust that your observation will remain a point of consideration between you and me?"

Marcus answered honestly, "It is merely a question. I have no reason to raise the matter with anyone but my friend, Lucius."

Lucius relaxed. "A fresh objective look at our defenses is a helpful thing. Today's ally may be tomorrow's enemy. Again, my thanks, my friend."

Lucius escorted Marcus throughout the fortress eventually coming to the hall where meals were served to the Roman garrison. There Marcus was introduced to the officers of the Garrison many of whom knew Marcus' father.

Following the midday meal, they walked to a well guarded, great iron door that led to the western entrance to the Temple of Jerusalem. The entrance to the Temple was also well guarded by soldiers of Herod Antipas, the son of Herod the Great.

Lucius was obviously known to the soldiers on both sides of the wall and he and Marcus proceeded to the Temple grounds without interruption.

Marcus marveled at the shear size of the Temple. He had learned from Joseph that the Temple had been a gift to the people of Jerusalem from Herod the Great, then King of Judea. It had been constructed from plans upon which Solomon's Temple had been built but Herod had sought to build it larger and more grand than Solomon's had been. There was no question in Marcus' mind that on the Frontier, this was indeed the structure of structures.

Inside the Temple, Lucius led Marcus down a long corridor to the inner chamber of Caiaphas. There were several guards along the corridor and at the door to the inner chamber but again they gave Lucius and Marcus only respectful nods as they entered the chamber.

Marcus was impressed with the inner chamber. It was heavily adorned with sculptures and tapestries. The furnishings were rich and plentiful. A lone figure sat at a desk reading a manuscript when they walked in.

"Caiaphas, I have brought an old friend from my days in Rome to meet you."

The man addressed by Lucius rose and turned to greet his new arrivals. Marcus was surprised at the appearance of this high priest. He was a tall slender man with a shallow complexion and a long pointed beard. He had no mustache as was the usual custom of the day and his hair had been fashioned into several long braids that flowed from his head to almost shoulder length. He wore a heavy robe with a belt of gold and on his feet he wore gold sandals.

Caiaphas walked over to Marcus and extended his hand. "A citizen of Tiberius' Rome and a personal friend of Lucius is always welcome to my chambers."

"You are very gracious. I thank you for the opportunity to meet you and to visit this great Temple." Marcus replied keeping eye contact with the high priest. Caiaphas noted this and was not altogether pleased that the Roman did not seem intimidated by his presence.

"I am told that you are the son of Marcus Aurelius, a well respected Roman here in Judea."

"Yes, I am his son."

"You have large shoes to fill then Marcus Titus! Your father was one of those rare people who moved easily between Romans and the rest of the world without causing any disruptions. Are you of equal talent?"

Marcus understood the challenge being given to him by Caiaphas and he responded without hesitation, "My father was indeed a very special person. I have come to know that he is missed by many. I am sure that in part he is missed for the very reasons that you now suggest. My talents, such as they may be, have yet to be seen."

"Then, let us hope that when they are seen, they match those of your departed father."

Caiaphas turned away from Marcus to address Lucius. "I have received word that the man, the Nazarene who professes to be the son of our God, continues to be a problem. He has been in the North of late, near the Sea of Galilee. I am told that in the land of Gennesaret, many of our poor who were sick and lame went to him and that by merely touching his garments, they became well again. This is trickery but the masses are beginning to believe in these lies. He preaches sedition Lucius. He talks of a kingdom in which he will rule over all of us. He leads people to believe that he is the fulfillment of the prophecy of the book of Micah… that he is the Messiah who will lead Israel back to greatness and shall rule over all the land. This cannot be tolerated. It is not only blaspheme to our Jewish faith it is a threat to Rome."

Marcus could see that his friend was visibly shaken by what Caiaphas had said. Marcus looked at Caiaphas and said, "Pardon me if you will. I am a student of many religions though I know very little about your faith. I have not heard of this Micah and his prophecy. Would you indulge me with a little education so that I can understand what it is this man is claiming to be?"

Caiaphas was accustomed to Roman ignorance. He smiled at the opportunity to educate this outsider to the true faith. "As a matter of fact, I was reading the prophecy of Micah when you entered my chamber."

Caiaphas walked over to the manuscript that he had been studying and began to read selected portions of the script, "Now gather thy troops against those who have laid siege to Israel, for one shall come from Bethlehem who shall be ruler of Israel, and he shall lead Israel to overthrow those who have laid siege to her, and He shall reign over all until the end of time." Caiaphas looked up at Lucius and went on, "You see my friend, this Jesus claims to be the fulfillment of the prophecy of Micah. He makes claim to the throne of Israel which is a direct affront to Herod Antipas. He claims to be the one destined to rule to the ends of the earth. This is a direct challenge to Caesar. We must put an end to him before the entire country rebels against Rome and against Herod."

Marcus sought to calm Lucius by asking a question of Caiaphas. "Although I have been in this land only a little while, I have seen no evidence of a threat to Rome's authority. Where are the armed camps that would threaten the power of Rome?"

Caiaphas gave Marcus a hard look. He wondered if this was ignorance, naivety, or cunning on the part of this Roman citizen. "This man, Jesus, stirs the masses with his speeches and his trickery. There are always those who seek to overthrow existing authority either out of greed or out of a lust for power.

Lucius knows this for he has dealt with these bands of thugs outside the gates of Jerusalem. It is only through the presence of the Roman legions and Herod's army that we keep the peace."

Caiaphas now resumed his manipulation of Lucius. "Lucius, we both know that Caesar wants there to be peace on the frontier and in this province. After years of war and turmoil which finally came to an end with the arrival of Varus, the Roman governor of Syria, and his two legions, a tenuous peace now exists. Samaria, Idumera and Judea are united as one. For twenty-four years we have enjoyed peace and prosperity under Herod Antipas thanks to the support of Rome. We are counting on that support to continue."

Lucius responded, "Caiaphas, you know that Rome supports Herod Antipas as I support you. What you have said is true. Years of peace and prosperity have been good for Rome and for Judea. As a province of the Roman Empire, you shall be protected by Rome against any who would seek to take away the authority given to you by Caesar.

If this man called Jesus is such a threat, we will take proper action to remove that threat."

Caiaphas smiled, "Rome is blessed to have one such as you defending her frontiers. Thank you Lucius. I am greatly relieved of my concerns."

Caiaphas then turned to Marcus, "Any friend of Lucius is always welcome in our temple. I trust that our discussion will be kept in confidence. It has importance both for the nation of Israel and for the Roman Empire." He smiled and finished, "Please come again."

Caiaphas then escorted his guests to the outer corridor. "Heed my words Lucius. This man, Jesus, is trouble. King Herod, himself, has inquired as to what the Roman Governor intends to do about him."

Lucius answered, "If the Governor has concerns, I am sure that he will consult with King Herod. Thank you for your time Caiaphas. Marcus has always been a student of history. I thought that it would be worthwhile for him to see your great temple and to meet you."

Caiaphas acknowledged both with a nod. "May Rome and Israel always share a history together."

The two Romans bowed their heads and then returned to the fortress.

Once back in Lucius' quarters, Marcus asked, "What do you think about Caiaphas' pronouncements?"

Lucius removed his sword and sheath from his side and threw them on his bed. "Caiaphas sees threats everywhere. Today it is this man, Jesus. Tomorrow it will be someone else. For months he was obsessed with a preacher who was baptizing people in the Jordan River. He told Herod that the man was a threat to his kingdom."

Lucius shook his head as he sat heavily in a chair. Marcus took another chair as Lucius continued. "I saw this preacher. A barbarian. He was a big man with a thundering voice but a man nevertheless. He was not a threat as Caiaphas and Herod's wife constantly prophesied. The Jews finally took him into custody and beheaded the man."

"For what reason?" Marcus was astounded.

Lucius half smiled, "That is the most incredible thing of all. Herod had him beheaded as a gift to his adopted daughter, Salome."

"A gift?"

"Yes, a gift. I am told that Herod lusts after Salome as he did her mother." Lucius paused to watch the impact of what he was saying to Marcus. He went on, "Ah, but you do not know the whole story. Our good Jewish King divorced his first wife to marry the wife of his half brother, the mother of Salome. As righteous as these Jews seem, Caiaphas did not have a problem blessing this second marriage nor does he have a problem supporting Herod Antipas' reign over the Jews."

"Why does a high priest support such a ruler?"

"Politics. Power. Influence. Herod and Caiaphas understand that one without the other would not have any of those things. It is a treaty born out of necessity."

"And does Rome support this as well?"

"For now my friend, for now."

"What will you do about the man called Jesus?"

"Wait and watch." Lucius finally came to the subject that he wanted to discuss with Marcus. "We have people who report to us on preachers such as Jesus. We need to be observant for there are many in this land that would prefer not to have Rome's authority here. They await the Messiah that Caiaphas read to us about today." He again studied Marcus for any sign of understanding.

Marcus knew Lucius well from their former life together in Rome. He suspected where this conversation was leading. He said, "Lucius, I have spent some time traveling the country since my arrival. Not long ago, my house servant, Joseph, and I were in Bethsaida and saw this Jesus. He was preaching not sedition but doing for others as you would have them do for you. If there is a threat there, I do not see it."

"Actually, Marcus, I was there as well."

"You were there?"

"Yes."

"I did not see you." Marcus said with some surprise. "But there were many there."

"Yes there were many."

"Why did you not call out to me Lucius? I would have welcomed a chance to talk with you about that event."

"Had I been alone, I would have called to you. But I was acting as a guard for another who was there and could not leave my charge nor call attention to her."

Marcus was again surprised that not only was Lucius in Bethsaida but with a woman. "I know better than to ask about your charge. But tell me your thoughts about Jesus."

"He is a powerful speaker. He moves people to do extraordinary things. For that reason if for no other we are ordered to watch him and listen for signs of sedition."

Lucius considered his time in Bethsaida before answering. "No. I did not hear anything in Bethsaida that would have given me cause for concern. But let me ask you a question my learned friend. How do you explain the feeding of five thousand with just a few loaves of bread and a couple of fish?"

Marcus understood the question for he had struggled with it as well. "I, too, have been thinking about that and about all that happened that day. You may recall that Jesus told everyone there that they should treat one another as they themselves would want to be treated."

Lucius nodded in agreement, "Yes, I remember that. Something about the first and greatest commandment from his god!"

"That's correct. He also told his disciples that as they had been provided for so too should they provide for others."

Lucius shook his head. "I still do not understand."

Marcus stood and began walking around the room. "I believe that the rabbi, Jesus, was teaching a lesson, first to his disciples and then to the masses. I have asked others and have been told that there are people all over Judea who offer their homes and their food to Jesus and his disciples. They provide the necessities through their labors so that Jesus and his disciples can preach the word of their God and minister to his followers.

I think that the message at Bethsaida was that if you will do this for him and his disciples it would be well to do it for all who are in need. He directed his disciples to bring forth that which people were willing to share. Five loaves and two fish were brought forth. He blessed those who had shown their generosity and then broke the bread and cut the fish into smaller pieces. Giving the small morsels to his disciples he said, 'Love one another as you would your own family for all of us are the children of

God. All of us are a part of His family. That which you do for the poorest among us, you also do for my Father.'"

Marcus stopped in the center of the room and looked at Lucius. "I believe that at that moment something moved all those present to act with compassion and share what they had with those who were not as well off. In sharing what they had there was more than enough to satisfy all.

How often have you witnessed such generosity of spirit, Lucius? I can tell you that I have never seen such even in the wealthiest of circles. I counted twelve baskets of bread and pieces of fish remaining after all had eaten.

Those that believe that this man Jesus is the son of God have told me that a Holy Spirit descended on the crowd at Bethsaida and filled them with the power of the Lord."

Lucius struggled to comprehend what Marcus was saying. He had witnessed all that was said and he could not deny the truth of what was seen. He shifted uneasily on his bed and said, 'Do you believe that this Jesus is the son of a god?'

"I believe what I see, what I hear, and what I feel. I have seen this man move thousands to do things that I would have believed impossible. I have heard his lessons and so far those lessons are truthful. I have had a very strange feeling about this man since the first time I heard about him. He is not like other men that I have known or read about."

Lucius looked at Marcus as he spoke and noticed that his friend seemed to be talking to him but his mind appeared to be on other things. "Is there more than what you and I saw at Bethsaida?"

Marcus went on. "Later, much later that same day, my servant Joseph and I were proceeding on horseback along the Sea of Galilee when a storm arose in the night. We could see the lightening flashing in the sky and the waves rising up and crashing on the sea. A lone ship was in distress on the horizon. We went for help and as we approached the shore, we all witnessed a man walking out into the storm toward the ship."

Lucius interrupted, "Walking where?"

Marcus raised his eyebrows, "Walking on top of the sea, out to where the ship was floundering!"

"You saw this?"

"I saw it as did the others who were with me. One man in the ship jumped into the sea and stood for a moment before sinking into the water. The man who had walked to the ship reached down and pulled him from the sea. As soon as both men were in the ship, the storm gave way to a clear star lit night. The man was this Jesus."

"Marcus, if anyone else had told me such a story I would not have believed it. But does this make him a god?"

"Lucius, it makes him different from all of us. His disciples were in that ship. His faith that his god would uphold him in all that he did allowed him to walk across the sea in a ragging storm. I found out later that he called out to those in the boat and one professing faith jumped into the water with him. That man told me that he believed that Jesus would uphold him and keep him safe but when he saw new lightening and heard the thunder so close he cried out to be saved and sank below the surface. He said that it was then, in the dark of night and beneath the dark sea that he felt Jesus grip his arm and pull him out of the swirling waters. Jesus then said to this disciple, 'How little faith you have in me even after I told you to come to me. Did you think that I would let you drown?'

It was a lesson. Planned or accidental, I think that Jesus was again teaching his disciples that as with the food at Bethsaida so too if they but have faith in their god and abide in his teachings, they will be upheld in all ways by their god."

Lucius walked over to Marcus and sat down next to him. "My friend, I do not know what to make of all that you have said. I shall have to think more about it. But this I do know, if this man from Nazareth or Bethlehem preaches sermons that defy the teachings of the scribes and Pharisees, he will need to be able to do more than walking on water to protect himself."

Marcus agreed. "Having met the high priest, I think that you are correct Lucius."

Later, the two friends parted each knowing that this would not be the last time that they would talk about the rabbi named Jesus.

Chapter 36. "The Lame Shall Walk"

Within the week, Joseph brought word to Marcus that Jesus was coming to Jerusalem.

Marcus felt something stir within him at this news. He immediately determined that he would go to Jesus in order to learn more about this man.

Marcus rode out of the city alone and turned west on the road to Emmaus. He had been told that Jesus and his disciples were coming to Jerusalem from that direction.

The road climbed steeply through the mountains and occasionally Marcus would pass by men and woman on their way to Jerusalem. He would ask those who appeared to him to be Jewish if they had seen the rabbi, Jesus. No one had any news to share.

As he reached the peak of one of the mountains in the region, he saw a group of people not far below him. His heart jumped when he recognized the rabbi sitting in the midst of the assembled group of people. He made his way down the road and arrived in time to witness yet another remarkable event.

A woman was kneeling before the rabbi with a small boy lying by her side. She reached out to him and said, "Lord, my son lays here a cripple. We have been abandoned by his father and by our family. I can go on no longer. I pray to you to intercede with your Father in Heaven and give us peace."

Jesus knelt down beside the woman and cupped her hands in his. He wiped the tears from her cheeks as he looked into her eyes. "You have great faith in me woman. How do you think that I can help you?"

She looked back at him and said, "You are the son of God. He is in you and you are in Him. Through you all is possible."

Jesus smiled, "Your faith is great. Blessed be your son for his mother sees what others do not."

Then Jesus directed his disciples to hold down the boy. Andrew and James took hold of the boy's shoulders while Peter and John held fast to his arms. Marcus dismounted from his horse and walked closer to see what was being done.

Jesus place a hand on the boy's forehead and said, "What is your name?"

"Jacob." The frightened boy replied.

Jesus then said, "Jacob, your mother has great faith in me. Do you know who I am?"

Jacob answered, "You are our Lord, Jesus of Nazareth, and the son of God."

Jesus smiled, "Do you want to be able to walk again?"

"Yes!" the boy said as the fear left his eyes replaced by a new hope.

"I am going to do some things that may hurt you for a short while. You may cry out but know that what I do, I do for you and for your blessed mother."

Jesus then reached down and grabbed a hold of the boy's crooked right leg. He grasped the leg just above the knee with his right hand and with his left hand he took hold of the boy's ankle. Then Jesus pulled on the ankle over and over again with all of his strength. He began working the leg forward so that its twisted bones crackled and heaved. At last he had stretched the right leg out until it was straight. As he did this, the boy screamed in pain.

The disciples looked at Jesus questioningly but held onto the boy so that he did not move.

Jesus then took the boy's other mangled left leg and again working with all of his strength, Jesus repeated the procedure. Beads of perspiration formed on the young rabbi's forehead. He continued his work until he managed to straighten that leg too.

As he completed his work, a bead of perspiration dropped from Jesus forehead onto the boy's left leg. At that moment the boy's screaming stopped and he opened his eyes for the first time since Jesus undertook his care.

Jesus looked up at the boy's mother who had stood by silently watching even as her son cried out. Jesus nodded to her as he stood up. She looked down at her son and at his straightened legs. Their twisted, mangled form was no longer a part of her son's body. She fell down to her knees, weeping and thanking Jesus, and kissing his robe. Jesus took her up into his arms as she thanked him over and over saying 'Thank you Lord!'. He said to all present, "No greater faith have I seen than this mother has shown this day."

Looking back at the woman he said, "Woman, bathe your sons legs in oil every day for a week. You are to move his legs straight up and then down several times a day. After a week, you will then begin helping him bend his legs at the knees. Do this several times a week, also. Keep your faith and he will walk with you as my Father wishes. Bless you."

Jesus kissed the woman on her forehead and then as he turned to Marcus said, "Marcus, how is your faith?"

Marcus did not know what to say. He did not think that Jesus had even notice that he was there.

"I have much to learn." Marcus replied.

"Follow me and I will teach you." Jesus put his arm around Marcus' shoulder and looking at his disciples said, "Our friend who was with us on the Sea of Galilee has returned. He will be with us for a while so that he may learn the ways of my Father. Treat him as one of us for so shall he be."

Most of the disciples acknowledged what Jesus said with a nod. Although Marcus sensed that not all were as pleased at his presence as was Jesus.

"The boy?" Marcus did not ask more.

Jesus looked quickly at Marcus, then answered, "He will be fine. He is in my Father's care now." Nothing more was said.

Chapter 37. "The Disciples"

Marcus took note that not only was Jesus accompanied by his disciples but that there were woman and children in his entourage this day. They helped lift the lame boy into a cart with wooden wheels that his mother used to move the boy. The boy was quiet, looking first at his straightened legs and then at Jesus then back at his legs. Finally, the boy collapsed into a deep sleep leaving behind the ordeal that he had faithfully suffered that he might walk. Marcus thought that he saw a smile on the boy's face as he slept.

Evening was approaching and the group decided to spend the night in the foothills before proceeding to Jerusalem.

The women began setting up cloth shelters and laying out blankets for the group while the disciples set about building a fire for cooking the evening meal. Everyone seemed to know what their role was and all that needed to be done was completed in short order.

While they were preparing the meal, Jesus introduced each of the disciples to Marcus.

"Marcus, this is Bartholomew. Bartholomew was called from Cana where he lived with his mother Tolomai. He is one of my steadfast followers. Always open with me in thought and in word. I have complete trust in him and know that he will carry the word of my Father to the vast frontiers of our faith when it is his time to do so."

Bartholomew responded saying, "That I can only be worthy of your trust in me." He then extended a hand to Marcus.

"Marcus, this is Thomas. Thomas is not unlike you. He believes in my teachings and is first among my disciples in understanding the parables but the Holy Spirit has not yet entered his soul. To be one with our Father, it is necessary that not only the mind and the body be committed but so too must the soul."

Thomas smiled. "Your wisdom exceeds anything that I have witnessed of the Priests and Pharisees. This much I know. God looks down on you and grants you the wisdom of the ages. Prophet or Son of God, I believe in you above all men. You are my Savior and my Lord."

After greeting Thomas, Marcus commented to Jesus, "Thomas looks much like you do."

Jesus smiled and replied, "Yes, we have sometimes been mistaken for one another. He too comes from Nazareth."

Jesus then led Marcus to Mathew. "This is my disciple, Mathew. Before Mathew came to us, he was a tax collector for Herod Antipas in Capernaum. We met there and talked about the work that he did and the work that I do. Mathew was kind enough to invite me and my disciples to his home for dinner and to spend the night. We talked late into the night about many things. I found in Mathew greater compassion than even he recognized in himself. The next day, he asked if he could join with me in my work. I could see that this was right for him and so he did become a disciple. He gave all of his worldly wealth to those in need. By this single act of faith, Mathew gained greater wealth in my Father's Kingdom than he will ever imagine."

Mathew laughed and said, "The Pharisees are none too happy about a tax collector being called to the ministry. But God's forgiveness for my past transgressions helps me to serve others and to lead them to righteousness and the rewards of a better life. I can never thank my Lord enough for showing me my true calling." He took Jesus' hand and kissed it.

Next, Jesus introduced Marcus to James. "This is my disciple James. He is often teased by the others because of his shortness in height. But James has inside of himself something much larger than all of the others. James has a true sense of what is right and what is wrong in this world. We became close when I decided to make my home at Capernaum. He is the son of my mother's sister and the brother of one of my other disciples, Jude. He is a student of scripture and much respected by all in spite of his physical limits."

Marcus took note of James' appearance. A short man with long hair, unshaven face, thin frame, wearing a single tunic and barefoot.

As Marcus and Jesus moved on to the next disciple he commented to Jesus, "Does James have some affliction on his legs? I noticed that his knees appear to be heavily blistered."

Jesus looked at Marcus. "Prayer. James spends a great deal of time in prayerful deliberation. My Father is well pleased with his devotion and has given him a gift. He will be respected by all who know him and will be wise in the ways of faith beyond his time."

Jesus stopped by a disciple who was busy preparing fish for the meal. "Marcus, this is Jude. In addition to being little James' brother, he is the second son of my mother's sister. He is also an outstanding preparer of food. I think that we might starve were it not for Jude's extraordinary ability to make a meal taste better than it should."

After meeting Jude, Marcus asked, "Do the others call him little Jude as they do his brother? They are both about the same height and build."

Jesus laughed and said, "No. You see with James there are two but we have only one Jude and with Jude's zeal for all that he does, we may be well off that there is but one."

Two men walked over to where Jesus, Jude, and Marcus were standing. Both were tall and had similar appearances though one was considerably larger in girth than the other. They were laughing as they approached.

The heavier one extended his hand to Marcus and said, "You are the Roman that we met by the Galilee! We were all so exhausted that we never had time for formal introductions." Placing his hands on his ample stomach and again laughing, he went on. "I am James the greater! You can see why my skinny brother, John, and the others enjoy addressing me with this honorable name."

Marcus laughed along with James. "I had an old friend by the name of Quintus. He used to go out of his way to find men who had some size to them. He believed that they worked harder and thus consumed more than others who were not so well turned out!"

Jesus too laughed at this. "I do not know about the work but there can be no doubt that James the greater consumes more than the rest of us!"

At this, the thinner of the two introduced himself. "I am John, James' brother. When we were children in Capernaum, my older brother did do the work of three. My father, Zebedee, had a fishing business and often hired men in the village to work his ships. At the age of twelve, James could do the work of three men because of his size." He paused looking admiringly at his older brother. James was basking in the praise being received from John. John went on. "Of course that was before he added one hundred and fifty pounds most of which found its way to his middle!"

James took a good natured swing at his brother as they all laughed.

Jesus then said, "We all have a good time with James the greater but in truth he has a very special place with us."

"You are my Lord, the healer, my teacher, and my salvation. If I can be half of what you are I will be blessed." James the greater turned to his serious side so quickly that he startled Marcus. Marcus saw the devotion and zeal that this disciple had for Jesus and his admiration for his master. It was quite a transformation.

Jesus took hold of both of James the greater's arms and smiled at him.

John looked at Marcus. "Our mother, Salome, always favored James. I used to say that he received twice the love because he was twice my size!"

At this, an older woman who had been preparing food, came to them. "I heard that John and it is not true!"

John laughed and taking the woman in his arms and hugging her, he said to Marcus, "And here is proof, my mother Salome. While my poor father slaves at his boats on the Sea of Galilee, my mother is here cooking for her oversized son!"

Salome bowed her head in greeting to Marcus and then gave John a light poke in his rib cage. "What kind of a mother would I be to let my sons roam far and wide, doing the good work of our Lord, without a proper meal."

Jesus came to Salome and put a loving arm around her also. "Salome not only prepares our food but often provides it through her generosity and that of her husband, Zebedee. My Father will have a special place for her at his table when her time has come."

The man that Marcus knew as Peter interrupted the good natured conversation of the group by announcing that the meal was served.

Looking at Marcus and then down to the sword at his side, he said, "I do not think that you will need that at our table."

Marcus looked down at his sword and then back to Peter. "I apologize if it offends you, I will be happy to leave it with my horse." He removed the sword from his belt and took it to where his horse had been tied. Peter shook his head at Jesus. "Why do you let this man be one with us, Lord? I do not understand. He is different from the rest of us. He is not worthy..."

Jesus held up his hand to silence Peter. "Do you not have faith in me Peter?"

Peter immediately regretted expressing his concern about Marcus. "Lord, you know that I have the strongest faith in you."

Jesus responded, "Strongest yes but so often in doubt about what I say. In the eyes of my Father all men have worth. He created all giving each the opportunity to be that which my Father intended for them to be. Peter, though you faith falters at times, my Father knows that you are the rock upon which our faith will be built. Marcus has yet to find his true calling but he knows that and he is searching. When he finally finds that which he is looking for, his faith will be the faith of the ages. He is the one who will insure that what we all do will be passed on from generation to generation."

Jesus looked at Peter to determine if he accepted what Jesus had told him.

Peter knowing this said, "Lord, I accept what you will."

Jesus knew that he had more work to do with Peter but he also knew that that was true for all mankind. It was Jesus purpose for being. He had to pray to his Father for divine guidance that he may yet teach all those that would hear the way to the kingdom of God.

Marcus rejoined the group. After being served a plate of food by Salome, Jesus led Marcus to yet another disciple who had already begun the meal. Sitting down beside the disciple, Jesus said, "Marcus, I want you to meet my first disciple. This is Andrew, brother of Peter."

Marcus was immediately interested in this disciple both because he was Peter's brother and because he was the first to follow Jesus.

"How is it that you are first among the disciples?" Marcus asked.

"May I Lord?" Andrew asked of Jesus.

"Of course, Andrew."

Andrew set his plate of food upon a rock and looked directly at Marcus. "I was a follower of a great prophet who was called by many, John the Baptist. John had been given the word of God and preached by the Jordan River.

As a fisherman, I had lived life hard both in work and in my leisurely hours. John showed me a different side of life. In truth, I thought that he was the Messiah that we all longed for.

John told me that if I repented my sins and accepted his baptism by holy water, God would restore my soul. Upon John's baptism of me in the Jordan, I did feel a new life within me and knew that my destiny was to follow my Lord.

I told this to John and then asked if he was the one God destined to be the Messiah. John could be fearsome at times and he took great exception to what I had asked. But as quickly as his temper flared at me, he became calm all of a sudden. Looking at those who gathered to join me in baptism, he pointed to one who stood apart from the others and said, 'Behold the Lamb of God.'

I looked at he to whom John pointed." Andrew looked to Jesus and bowed his head. "The man was Jesus, my Lord and the salvation of our world. John told me to go and seek what I searched for with the Lamb of God. But one night at my Lord's side and it was made known to me through the Holy Spirit that Jesus is the Son of God."

As he finished he and all near Andrew stood up for a woman who had been listening near by and now came to them.

As Marcus noticed her approach, he too stood up, knowing in his inner most reaches that this was truly a woman among women. Jesus went to her and introduced her to Marcus. "This is my mother, Mary."

Marcus could not take his eyes off of this gentle woman. Deep in his mind he recalled a description that seemed to be a portrait in words of the woman he now beheld. 'Her composure was like no other woman that I have ever seen. There was an inner beauty that shone around her. A beauty that was not of this world.'

Marcus bowed his head to Mary and taking her extended hand said, "It is my great pleasure to meet the mother of one as kind and caring as your son."

Mary looked long at Marcus without saying a word. It was as if all were suspended in time. Finally she smiled and asked, "Are you from Bethlehem, Marcus?"

The question not only startled Marcus but all who heard what was asked. "Yes. Yes I am." He answered honestly. "But how did you know?" Marcus could not believe that Mary could know his true birthplace.

"Mothers often know a great many things, if not by their instruction then by their hearts."

Mary gently squeezed Marcus hand. "You have come to my son to complete the circle. I know you as you know me. You are much welcomed among us." She let go of his hand.

Marcus had many questions that he wanted to ask. 'What did she mean by completing the circle? How did she know him? What did she mean that I know her?' It was then that he remembered that it was his old friend Quintus who had provided the description. He had told Marcus many times of their journey from Bethlehem to Rome. He had made special note of the woman he had seen riding on a donkey, carrying a baby.

Quintus had said that there was a look in her eyes like none other that he had ever seen before or since.

He came back to the present to see Mary still looking into his eyes. It was then that he understood. She smiled and spreading her arms said, "Please eat, all of you. Your food will be getting cold."

Turning back to Marcus, she said, "Come and visit with me at my home in Nazareth. I would enjoy talking with you."

"It would be my great pleasure." Marcus felt a tremendously warm feeling flowing through his body. He felt happiness for the first time in many years. He attributed this feeling to Jesus and his mother, Mary. They seemed to be opening a door to his inner most being. He sensed the light on the other side of that doorway.

Chapter 38. "Mary, mother of God"

Andrew listened to the conversation between Marcus and Mary, the mother of God. He sensed the renewal of life that Marcus felt for he had had the same experience less than two years earlier.

Later that evening, Andrew joined Marcus by a small fire that burned late into the night.

You have been given a very special gift, Marcus."

As Marcus looked at Andrew, he saw the burning passion with which this disciple was filled for Jesus. He asked, "Andrew tell me why you follow Jesus as the son of God."

Andrew was more than prepared to give witness to his Lord. "The Jewish faith has long believed that there would come a time when a Messiah would come to lead the people of Israel to take their proper place within the world.

One of our prophets, Isaiah, spoke of a virgin who would bear a son, Immanuel, God with us. Mary, the mother of Jesus, was a virgin when she conceived her son.

That he is God on earth, I have no doubt. You must be impressed with his knowledge and his ability to heal others?"

Marcus nodded in agreement as Andrew continued.

"Marcus, I will tell you two stories about Jesus as young boy. These stories I have heard from the holy Mother and from others as well.

Jesus was playing with some other boys his age. Several of the boys had slings with them so they began picking up stones and hurling them with their slings at many things including a bird that had been nesting in a nearby tree. One such stone struck the bird and knocked it down to the ground. Most of the boys cheered at showing such skill. But Jesus ran to the bird that lay motionless on the ground. He picked it up and saw that it had been killed by the stone.

The others scoffed at the loss of life but not Jesus. Tears appeared in his eyes as he carried the bird home to his mother. Mary confirmed what Jesus had surmised. The bird was gone.

Then as Mary watched her young son, he held the bird up in his hands and cried out, 'Father as you would heal me so heal the least of your creations.'

Mary then saw a ray of light shine down on her son and the bird in his hands. The bird moved lightly in her son's hands.

Jesus then showed Mary the bird as its eyes again opened to the world. Jesus bent down and breathed the breath of life into this small creature. Opening his hands the bird spread its wings and took to the sky.

Jesus then said to his mother, 'My Father loves all that he has created, even such small creatures as that bird.'

Not long after the rebirth of that bird, Jesus was playing in his backyard when his mother called to him to come to dinner. Mary has told us that Jesus did not come when she called to him so she went outside to find out why he had not come into the house for the evening meal. She found him kneeling beside their well, fashioning birds out of water and clay. She said to him, 'Jesus what are you doing?' He responded to her saying 'I am about my Father's work.' She did not understand at first and again called him to come into the house for the evening meal. Jesus stood and clapped his hands together. What appeared to be birds of clay and water immediately flew off into the sky as living creatures. Mary, the mother of the Son of God, understood."

Marcus sat quietly contemplating what he had heard. Andrew decided to go on.

"At the age of twelve, Mary and her husband, Joseph, traveled to Jerusalem for the feast of the Passover. There were great crowds of people in Jerusalem celebrating along with them. Sometime during the celebration with family and friends, Jesus wandered off without telling anyone where he would be. As the Passover feast was coming to an end, Mary discovered that her son was nowhere to be found.

For three days they searched for him. Finally, they went to the Temple to seek help. There they found Jesus, sitting with learned men, doctors, scribes and even priests.

Mary has told me that she was astonished by what she witnessed. Her son at twelve years of age, the son of a humble carpenter, was asking questions of those around him and responding to their questions as well. The answers that he gave amazed all who were with him. He had an understanding far beyond his years and education.

When he was finished he came to his parents. Mary scolded him for leaving without telling them where he was going. She said to him, 'Your father and I have been worried to death that something had happened to you.' Jesus answered his mother saying, 'Why do you worry about me mother, did you not know that I would be doing my Father's business.' Mary told me that it would be years later before she understood what Jesus had meant by this. But she remembered his words and in time she understood that this was the beginning of his ministry here on earth."

Marcus could picture the scene in the temple - the vaulted ceilings, long corridors, tall columns, and a small group of intellectuals sitting with a small boy. He, too, wondered how a boy of twelve could feel comfortable in such surroundings. Where would a carpenter's son, if he were a carpenter's son learn enough to ask questions much less answer the inquiries of a group of learned scholars? The answer that he kept coming back to was that Jesus had the knowledge that only the son of God could have been given. These were powerful considerations for a man like Marcus who also had had an exceptional education. He thought of Flavius and wondered how his old teacher would respond to what he had seen and heard here in Judea. 'Flavius would have enjoyed the challenge!'

Chapter 39. "And then there were Thirteen."

Marcus accompanied Jesus and his disciples to Jerusalem. On the way to the city, they were joined by three disciples who had come out of Jerusalem to meet them. Jesus introduced the three men to Marcus.

"Marcus, I would like to have you meet, Judas Iscariot, Philip of Bethsaida, and Simon, our Zealot."

Marcus shook hands with all three men.

Jesus then gave a more complete introduction as they walked on together to Jerusalem.

"Judas Iscariot is our keeper of the purse. Money donated to us for our preaching is held in trust by Judas and he in turn provides us with our basic needs. Judas is very good with money and with numbers. In fact that is why these three went ahead of us to Jerusalem."

Judas Iscariot immediately interjected, "I have procured food and lodging for us with a friend who has a small inn near the south gate to the city." He looked to Jesus for approval.

Jesus nodded at Judas. "You have done as I expected. Thank you."

Then turning to Philip, Jesus said, "This is my disciple and my good friend from Galilee. Philip has been with me almost as long as Peter and Andrew. He spends more time with me than I ever expected of him. He has a wife and several beautiful young daughters back in Bethsaida."

Philip spoke up. "My life's desire has been to serve our Messiah. I have found what I have searched for in my Lord, my Savior. My prayers have always been thus and were well known to my good wife and my daughters.

That I stay by your side surprises no one. Man's path to salvation is through the Son of God, our Messiah."

Marcus asked, "How does your family manage with you gone for such long periods of time?"

Philip responded, "My wife's family is able to care for her. My daughters will soon be married and will have their own lives to lead. Unlike the others, I understand the sacrifice that must be made in this world in order to be received in the next, in the glory of the Kingdom of God. I am willing to make that sacrifice in order to see my Holy Father."

Jesus put his hand on Philip's shoulder. "I am happy with all that you do. Philip, your family will be blessed for the sacrifice that they are making on behalf of my Father in Heaven. The Holy Spirit will be with your seed for all time."

Jesus then directed his attention to the third man. "Simon is a zealous student of Jewish law. He advises me on what is expected under the law of those of the Jewish faith. We often have in depth discussions of what is meant by the law and how it should be applied."

Simon smiled. He thought about the many challenges that Jesus had raised to the law as Simon knew it before he met Jesus. "I have learned a great deal at the feet of my Master. He has brought reason and purpose to laws which until my calling I accepted blindly."

Jesus went on, "Simon will one day take his understanding of God's laws to places where it is not known and will build on our faith by his good works and steadfast compliance with our Father's commandments."

"How many disciples do you have?" Marcus was curious to learn how many people Jesus was enlisting as leaders for his faith.

"Twelve have been called by my Father through me. You have now met the twelve."

"Will you call others?"

"Yes. But for different reasons will they be called. As you know, Marcus, I have indicated that you have a calling to be with us. The Twelve have witnessed much of ministry here on earth. They will take from what I have done here and will be the seeds of a new tree that will have many branches. Most of them will sacrifice as will I to insure that my Father's work is done. Their rewards will not be here in this world but in the next where they will be glorified for their service to God, the Father.

Many more will come after us. Disciples who will spread the word of the Father to all the nations of the world. Those who hear will be saved.

Those that act upon what they hear and repent of their past transgressions will find that God's Kingdom will be open to them here on earth.

Yes, Marcus, there will be others but you will be my next disciple. You alone have been given a seat at my table to remember and record all that you hear and witness of God's work here through my ministry. Your education has prepared you for this. Your position will insure that you survive to complete the work that God, the Father, has planned for you to do. You will sacrifice but you will endure. As with the scribes that brought forth the testament of our forefathers, you will give birth to a new testament that fulfills the prophesies of the past and provides direction for the future.

As I look to Peter to be the rock upon which to build a foundation, I look to you to provide the walls within which the lessons will be given. You will do this in remembrance of me."

Marcus saw a sadness in the expression on his new found friend's face. He listened carefully to all that Jesus said and had a sense that this rabbi, this teacher, this Messiah, knew that he and his followers were traveling down a road that would lead to their destruction. Rome would not tolerate any discordant note to their balance of control over their empire. From what he had observed in the Temple, the Pharisees and priests also would not welcome any reform movement within their province of control. Jesus, himself had said that Marcus would do what he was destined to do in remembrance of him. Jesus was prepared to die and was asking Marcus to record His acts so that he would not be forgotten.

Marcus thought to himself, 'The circle of life again brings me around to my beginnings. There can be no doubt that Flavius would put pen to paper to record such marvels as I have seen and heard. That is what Flavius would have done were he now here!'

Suddenly, the direction that Marcus had been searching for became clear to him. His pathway had always been pointed in this direction, of that he was certain. Marcus determined that he would accept the calling that Jesus had given and become the Thirteenth Disciple.

Chapter 40. "Jesus in the Temple"

Marcus returned home after accompanying Jesus and his entourage to the gates of the city. He and Joseph talked about all that he had seen and about those that he had met. He did not disclose his calling but Joseph could readily see that Marcus had changed after spending this time with Jesus.

Not many days after his return, his friend Lucius arrived at his home for another visit. The two men had their evening meal together in the dinning room of Marcus' home and then adjourned to an adjoining balcony that had a view of the city.

Lucius took another sip of his wine before broaching a new subject for the day. "Marcus, I know that you have been seen with the rabbi, Jesus, again."

Marcus looked at his friend as if insulted and said, "Lucius, do you spend all of your time keeping track of my comings and goings?"

"No, but we do spend a great deal of time keeping track of the man you know as Jesus. Yesterday he and his followers were at the Temple taking an evening meal within the view of the Pharisees and priests.

Jewish law requires men to wash before they eat. It was seen that this law was not followed by Jesus and his people."

Marcus observed that Rome had no such law.

"Yes, but we are not in Rome and Rome has given recognition to Herod Antipas and his priests. They have the right to rule under Jewish law if it does not conflict with the laws of Rome."

Marcus questioned, "And what became then of this violation of Jewish law?"

"Jesus was asked why he and his followers, guests in the Temple, would so transgress Jewish law and custom. Why he and the others did not honor their mothers and fathers traditions? Jesus was admonished by a priest who recited to him a law that 'He that curses his mother and his father, should die rather than live with such a sin."

Marcus laughed. "That is quite a leap to judgment from not washing before a meal to cursing one's mother and father."

Lucius cautioned, "You and I may think so but the Pharisees take this quite seriously."

Marcus could imagine where this was leading to but asked the question anyway. "What was Jesus response to the priest?"

"He stood up and called out to all within the Temple's walls to come and hear this discourse. He then called the priest and Pharisees hypocrites. He said that they honor his Father with their lips but not with their hearts. He accused them of teaching laws and traditions of man not God. He warned that those that followed the priests of the Temple were as blind as were the Pharisees and that if the blind lead the blind, they all shall perish."

Marcus again laughed to keep the conversation with Lucius cordial. "I cannot take issue with what happens when blind men follow blind men. Can you?"

Lucius went on. "He was not finished with his condemnation of the Pharisees. He said that every plant that his Father did not plant shall be uprooted. That their laws were like foreign plants because they were made by man not God. It was their laws which defiled God not eating the evening meal with unwashed hands."

Again, Marcus sought to calm his friend. "Lucius, how many times have you eaten your food with unwashed hands? Certainly, this was so when you were confronted in battle. It was so when I traveled from Rome to Jerusalem."

Lucius agreed. "For you and me what you say is so. But not for the Pharisees. They see in what this rabbi said the seeds of revolt. Revolt against their teachings. Revolt against their traditions. Revolt against their laws. They want Jesus arrested."

Marcus now became serious. "Surely you do not plan on arresting this man for not washing his hands and for saying that such a law has nothing to do with the worship of their God?"

"No. This time he will not be arrested though even Caiaphas has requested that it be done. In point of fact, Jesus and his followers departed from the city immediately after the confrontation. It is my hope that they do not return."

Marcus felt relieved but also disconcerted that Jesus was no longer close at hand. He wanted to spend more time with Him and his disciples so that he could begin to answer his calling.

Lucius changed the subject of their conversation. "Have you kept up with your practice with that sword you wear?"

Marcus looked down at his sword. He thought of Peter wanting him to remove it and now of Lucius wanting him to use it. "In truth, I have not."

Lucius smiled. "You may want to brush up on your practice. In these times of revolt, your ability with that sword may be more practicable than your search for learning."

Marcus considered their long term relationship and decided to give Lucius an opportunity to see Jesus as he, Marcus, saw him.

"Lucius, you know me to be both a scholar and a fighter. I am always searching out the truth of those things that are new and strange to me and I do so without fear."

Lucius spoke. "Is that why you seek out this young rabbi, Jesus?"

"Yes it is Lucius. Let me tell you what I have seen and heard. I want to hear your opinion once you have heard what I have to tell you."

Marcus retold the stories of Jesus as a young boy healing a bird and turning clay into living creatures. Then he described in detail what Jesus had done to the lame boy, Jacob, on the hillside. Lucius asked if Marcus had seen the lame boy walk. Marcus admitted that he had not but that the boy's legs were now straight rather than mangled beneath him and that that was remarkable in and of itself. Marcus recounted again Jesus walking on water in the dark of night and other stories told to him by the disciples as they all had sat around a camp fire late at night.

Lucius finally said, "Marcus, bring this lame boy to me and show me that he walks. Then and only then will I believe that this man is the Son of God."

Chapter 41. "Nazareth"

Marcus drew out his sword after Lucius departed from his home. He looked down the length of the blade and remembered the hours of lessons that Flavius and Quintus had given to him. He passed the sword from his right hand to his left hand with a quick flick of his wrist and then back again to his right hand. He felt comfortable with the weight of the sword in either hand. This had been born out of necessity as a result of his competition in the Coliseum. As he swung the blade up and around as he had done as a youth, Joseph entered the room.

Joseph immediately stepped back in complete surprise at seeing Marcus wielding his sword.

Marcus caught a glimpse of Joseph out of the corner of his eye and began to laugh. "This is the other side of me, Joseph. The side you have not known."

Joseph relaxed. "Your father often talked about your appearance in the Roman Coliseum. He was proud of your skill at arms."

Marcus held out his arm to reveal a large scar that was his legacy from his day in the arena. "Did he tell you how that day in the Coliseum ended?"

"Yes he did. With honor. He said that you were the victor even in defeat."

"My friend Lucius would most likely argue the point. He likes to tell me that the mind yields to the sword and that I, not he, was the one who was injured that day because I played the game as the rules required."

Joseph humbly replied, "It is not my place to offer a judgment but I can tell you how your father saw the outcome. He said that he was proud of you because you not only had the ability to use your strength but demonstrated good judgment in its application."

Marcus returned his sword to its scabbard. "Thank you Joseph. I hope that I never disappoint my father's memory in that regard. By Lucius' estimation, the time may come when I will have to exercise both strength and judgment in that regard again."

Marcus knew what he must do after his visit with Lucius. He planned to leave for Nazareth the next morning.

Nazareth was almost seventy miles north of Jerusalem. Located in a hilly region of Israel, it was protected on all sides by sloping hillsides and woodlots. It was home to Jews and Muslims who had managed to live side by side for hundreds of years. Marcus had obtained as much information as he could about the town and its people. He also was given a description of the route to take to travel to Nazareth by Joseph. Joseph offered to accompany Marcus but Marcus declined the offer knowing that it was now his time to travel his journey alone.

Marcus rode for four and one half days along the roadway leading north. Finally, he sighted the town he was seeking. His first stop would be at the Roman post that had been established there almost a century earlier. The Romans had built a small fortress just outside of the main part of the town. It had three walls of varying height ranging from four feet at the outer wall to almost ten feet at the innermost wall. It was a construction idea that Marcus was very familiar with. It was designed to slow any attack on the fortress and to entrap any intruders.

As Marcus entered the fortress, a Roman sentry approached him to ask the nature of his business.

"I am a citizen of Rome and only just arrived in Nazareth. I wish to announce my presence to your commander and to inquire of a particular person that I am looking for."

Marcus wore the familiar seal of Rome and by his clothing and his mount, the sentry accepted what Marcus had said. The sentry pointed the way to his commander's location.

Marcus nodded to a second sentry stationed at the door to the commander's office as he dismounted. "Is the commander available?"

The sentry responded, "Please wait here, and I will ask if he is able to see you. Who may I say requests an audience?"

"Please advise the commander that Marcus Titus, late of Rome, and now in residence in Jerusalem, wishes an audience."

Seconds later the commander of the garrison appeared with the sentry. He walked over to Marcus and extended his arm in Roman fashion to greet his guest. "Octavius Syracusa, Centurion of Nazareth, welcome Marcus Titus."

The centurion was of medium height with dark, closely trimmed hair, brown eyes, and well muscled body.

Marcus bowed his head quickly and said, "It is a pleasure to meet you Centurion. I am the son of the late Marcus Aurelius. He too served Rome in the Legions."

The centurion straightened up at the mention of Marcus Aurelius' name. "This then is a double honor to have you with us! Your father was well known and respected within the Legions of Rome. In fact, I had the pleasure of serving under him for a short time before assuming my post here in Nazareth."

Marcus looked away momentarily then back at the centurion. "Unfortunately, my time with my father was limited. He sent me to Rome to study when I was a child and growing up, I only saw him on furloughs and when he was in his final decline."

"I am sorry." The centurion responded with true emotion. "Tell me, Marcus, do you have a place to stay in Nazareth?"

"No. I do not. Perhaps you could recommend an inn?"

The centurion smiled. "In the morning. For tonight, you will stay with us. It will be a great honor for us to entertain the son of Marcus Aurelius."

Marcus accepted the kind offer of lodging. It would be worthwhile to become acquainted with those posted to this fortress even if only for a night. He decided to wait a while before asking for the information that he hoped would lead him to Mary, the mother of Jesus.

The Romans talked late into the night. Marcus telling them stories about growing up in Rome and the others talking about life in the legions and about their experiences with the inhabitants of Nazareth.

The next morning, Marcus was up and out early. He understood the order of garrison life and was not surprised to see the soldiers of this post busy going about their duties at an early hour.

Marcus proceeded to the stable to saddle his horse. Inside the stable, he found Octavius also saddling a horse.

"Good morning Centurion."

"Good morning Marcus. How did you sleep?"

"Very well. I think that between the trip here and the wine that we consumed after dinner, there was never any doubt that I would rest easy."

"I want you to know that we enjoyed hearing about Rome. I was intrigued with your studies. Will you go back to Rome soon to continue your pursuit of knowledge?"

Marcus saw the opening that he had waited for. "I do not know when I will return. Actually, one of the reasons that I came to Nazareth had to do with my pursuit of knowledge."

The centurion seemed surprised. "You came here in the pursuit of knowledge?"

"Yes. I am interested in knowing more about the religious beliefs of the inhabitants of this land."

The centurion shook his head. "It is very confusing. Jews believe in only one God. The Phoenicians believe in a different God. Some have no beliefs! Some even believe that their God is about to come down to earth to lead some type of rebellion. That is why we have been posted here. At the first sign of rebellion, our charge is to quash any revolt quickly and thoroughly."

Marcus nodded in understanding. "Have you seen any signs of rebellion?"

The centurion laughed. "These people know better than to challenge Rome. No there are no signs of rebellion here. We do have some interesting preachers though."

"Oh?"

Marcus seemed interested so the centurion went on. "Yes. There was a young carpenter who gave up his father's carpentry business to preach about forgiveness if you confess your sins to him. I do not know who forgives these people but he has some people listening to him."

Marcus asked, "What is the name of this carpenter?"

"He is called Jesus."

"Does he live in Nazareth?"

"He used to but he moved to Capernaum and only visits his mother periodically."

"His mother lives in Nazareth?"

The centurion nodded yes as they both finished saddling their horses. "Yes. She lives here.

I have business in town and will be riding passed her home. Are you interested in seeing it?"

Marcus was anxious to say yes but needed to explain to the centurion, why he had such an interest. "I would like to see the home of this man, Jesus. I am trying to understand how the Jews can have only one god when we accept the fact that there are many."

The centurion mounted his horse and Marcus followed by mounting up onto his own horse.

"Marcus, their beliefs are beyond any rational explanation. But you can ask them and see for yourself. Let's go and I will get you started on your research."

As they rode together out of the fortress and into the town, Marcus again experienced a good feeling, almost a happiness, at the thought of seeing Mary once again.

The centurion led Marcus to the outlet from the street on which Mary's home was located. "Marcus, if you ride to the end of this street you will see a small cut stone house built into the hill side. That will be the home of Mary, the preacher's mother."

Marcus thanked the centurion. "Octavius, I wish to express my sincere thanks for your hospitality last night and for guiding me to this place today. If you ever travel to Jerusalem, you are always welcome at my home."

The two men clasped each others arm and then went their separate ways.

Chapter 42. "Mary"

As Marcus dismounted and tied his horse to a small tree in front of the cut stone house, the front door opened and Mary appeared in the entryway.

Marcus walked toward the house. "Good morning Mary."

Mary's smile radiated warmth and welcome. "Good morning Marcus. I am happy that you decided to accept my invitation and come to Nazareth. Please come inside."

The inside of her home was well furnished. It was very evident that either her son or her husband had provided very fine crafted furnishings for their home.

Mary offered a chair to Marcus and proceeded to bring a cup of cool water to the Roman.

"What brings you to me?" Mary asked as she sat down on a chair across from Marcus.

"I came to talk with you to learn more about your son. I also would like to ask if you know of his whereabouts." Marcus instinctively knew that Mary would know what was in his heart so there was no need for guise when talking with her.

"My son and his disciples have left the country for a little while. I believe that they are along the cost of the great sea in a town called Tyre."

"Do you know why they left the country?"

"Yes I do. Peter was concerned for my son's safety. Something happened while they were in Jerusalem. Peter felt that they should all go up along the coast for a while."

"Did your son also fear for his safety?"

"My son has a mission in life. He has told me that when his time has come to go to meet his Father, neither I nor anyone else should morn for him. That, his time here on earth is within the province of his Father. He says that he will be happy when the day arrives that he can rejoin his Father who is in Heaven.

I think that he decided to go with Peter and the others to Tyre more out of concern for their safety than for his own."

Marcus understood what Jesus had told Mary. Often, he had thought about all those that he had responsibility for and he too knew that his wellbeing was never as much of an issue as was theirs.

Marcus continued with his desire to learn more about Jesus and Mary. "I have been told that your husband was a fine carpenter. Your home is very nicely furnished. Is this his handiwork?"

Mary looked around the room and a gentle smile appeared on her face. "Yes. Much of what you see was crafted by my Joseph. He was a good carpenter and a good man. He and my son made this table together." She ran her hand along the side of a table that was in front of them. "Jesus has the same skill that my Joseph had. I am afraid that it is one talent of his that will not see much use now."

Marcus looked into Mary's eyes trying to discern how she was feeling at that moment. "Are there not times when he takes some time away from his preaching to return to his carpentry?"

Mary for the first time showed an expression of concern. "My son, Jesus, tells me that he must be about his Father's business for his time is short and there is still much for him to do."

"But, isn't his father's business that of carpentry?"

Mary looked deep into Marcus' eyes. "You ask a question that deep in your heart you know the answer to."

Marcus did not look away. Deep in his heart he did know the answer to his question. Mary simply confirmed by her response that which he knew. "Yes. He is the son of God."

A glow seemed to surround Mary as she then spoke. "Marcus, Jesus told me that you would come. That is why I was waiting for you. He has told me that you are the one who will write one of the greatest stories ever written. He has said that although his time is short, you will complete what he has started by preserving his words and actions for the ages.

Do you believe in him and do you believe that you are who my son believes that you are?"

Marcus still did not look away. "I do."

"That is good. Jesus bid me to tell you of things that I have seen so that you might remember them in the history that you shall write about this time."

Marcus settled back in his chair. "I am most interested in hearing anything that you wish to share with me."

Again, Marcus saw a glow that seemed to surround Mary as she smiled and nodded. She began, "At first, even knowing what I knew, it was hard for me to accept that my boy was conceived by the Holy Spirit and would grow in knowledge and understanding of things that were not of this world but of a greater world, the kingdom of God."

She looked at Marcus in wonderment. "Did you know that my son was born under a magnificent star? It was a sign from Heaven of his birth. My husband was amazed at that light." She paused caught up in her thoughts. "Shepherds saw the star and came to see my son as he lay in a manger. He had many visitors that night. Three men of wealth came from far away lands with gifts for my son. They said that they had been following the light from the star for many days. When I asked them why they came, they told me to pay honor to the one who was prophesized to one day be the king of the Jews." Mary smiled at this.

She bowed her head and then went on. "When he was twelve years old, Joseph and I found him teaching priests and scholars in the great Temple of Jerusalem about things that neither Joseph nor I ever taught him nor did we fully understand. When we asked him why he would do such a thing he said to us, 'Did you not believe that I would be doing my Father's business?'

That night Joseph said to me, 'Mary, I have accepted all that has gone before because of my love for you. But truly I now believe that our son is the son of God. There is no other way that I can explain the knowledge which he has about life and about God for I have not nor could I ever teach him of the things that I heard him say today.' I too felt this for I knew that though my good husband had taught my son much about his craft, the things that I heard him say in the Temple that day and the way in which he was able to talk with and answer the questions of those around him, was not of this world but truly God given."

Marcus had heard the stories of Jesus birth and of his day in the Temple before. But now he had confirmation from Jesus' mother who had witnessed all of this first hand. He had to admit that it was truly a God given gift to have the knowledge evidenced by Jesus in all that he said and did.

Mary continued with her memories of her beloved son. "In my husband's last years, he and Jesus spent much time together. They worked hard and had a great deal of time to talk while they worked. Joseph loved Jesus as a son. When Jesus was in his early twenties, Joseph told me that they had talked about death and that he took comfort in what Jesus had said. In the last moments of his life, my Joseph said to me, 'My blessed Mary, you have been my love and my life here on earth. I will look forward to the day when we will be together again in the kingdom of God.' He then smiled at Jesus, who was with me by his bedside, squeezed my hand, and was gone."

A tear slowly made its way down her cheek. She excused herself for a moment and left the room. When she returned, she said, "I am sorry. I miss my Joseph. I should be happy that we will one day be together again for all eternity."

Marcus asked, "Your son, Jesus, I have heard that he prophesies that there will be eternal life for those that believe. Is this so?"

Mary sat down opposite Marcus again. "Yes. Much of his teaching is about the kingdom of heaven. After my Joseph passed on, my son began his ministry in earnest. He would preach in synagogues throughout Galilee. People would come to him to hear his message and to be healed of their sicknesses. Eventually, the synagogues were not large enough to hold all those who wished to see him and hear his message."

She paused to focus again on her guest. "Can I get for you some more water?"

Marcus thanked her but said that he was fine. "Please go on." He said.

"On one occasion, when my sister Elizabeth and I were with him, a huge crowd had gathered to hear him. People came from Galilee, from Decapolis, from Judea, from Jerusalem, from Syria, and from beyond the Jordan. Gentiles, Muslims, and Jews all had gathered to hear my son speak." Mary looked at Marcus to determine if the magnitude of what she was telling him was realized by him. It was.

"He talked about the kingdom of God that day saying, 'Blessed are the poor in spirit, for theirs is the kingdom of heaven; Blessed are they that mourn; for they shall be comforted; Blessed are the meek' for they shall inherit the earth; Blessed are they that hunger and thirst after righteousness; for they shall be filled; Blessed are the merciful, for they shall obtain mercy; Blessed are the pure of heart; for they shall see God; Blessed are the peacemakers; for they shall be called the children of God;

Blessed are they which are persecuted for righteousness sake; for theirs is the kingdom of heaven.'

Every man, woman and child who were there that day heard his words. And when he finished his sermon and walked down the mountain, all there went down on their knees and called out Messiah, Lord, Savior, and Son of God.

A ray of light came down from the sky as he moved away and shone on him. In that moment, we all knew that God was pleased with his son." Mary sighed. "In my heart, I always knew. That day, everyone knew because God let the holy spirit descend down upon them and through His son, gave them understanding and hope."

Marcus marveled at what he had heard. He asked, "How do you remember his sermon so well?"

She smiled at him and said, "A mother remembers all things about her child, great and small."

Again remembering that day, she said, "As we walked among those who were gathered there, a young man with leprosy knelt down before us and said to my son, 'I am a leper and suffer much. Lord, I believe in you and know that if you so will that I be cleansed of this curse, it will be so.' My son bent down and placed his hand on the head of the leper and said, 'I so will that your faith in me and in my Father will provide for your cleansing.' We walked on and as I looked back, the young man removed his wrappings from his face and hands and all signs of leprosy were gone."

Marcus responded, "I would have liked to have been with your son to hear his words and bear witness to his healings."

Mary said, "There was one such as you who was there. A centurion. He came to my son and said, 'Lord, my servant lies at my home sick with palsy and very much in pain.' To this my son looked upon the centurion and seeing good in the man said, 'I will go with you to your home to see your servant.' The centurion answered saying, 'Lord, I am not worthy that you should come to my home. But you have but to say the words and I know that my servant shall be healed.' My son looked again upon the centurion and then to all of those around him. Looking back at the centurion he said, 'Truly, I say to you, that I have not found so great a faith in all of Israel as you have shown me this day. Go home to your servant and by your faith your servant shall be healed.' The centurion bowed to my son saying, 'I do not need to go home to know that my servant is healed. Because you have said it, it is so.'

She looked into Marcus' eyes. "You see Marcus, by your own words, I have heard you call him rabbi but he ministers to all. Jews, Romans, Gentiles, in his eyes all are one."

Marcus thought about the sermon on the mountain. He thought about the centurion and wondered, 'Did his father have such faith?' He thought about all men being treated as one, equals in the eyes of God. He thought, 'Why should it not be this way?'

Mary watched Marcus and knew that he was considering all that she had told him. She said, "I think that you have heard enough from me for today. Let me fix some food for us and you can tell me something about yourself."

There was something that Marcus wanted to tell Mary and so while she prepared the mid-day meal, he preceded with his story.

"Mary. Many years ago, in fact, the year that I was born, a soldier serving with my father, carried me across the plains and mountains of Israel on our way to Rome. That soldier's name was Quintus.

Quintus often told me about our journey out of Bethlehem and how he came upon a man and a woman carrying a baby and riding upon a donkey. He described the woman as having a beauty unlike any other woman he had ever seen. He said it was a beauty that radiated from within. It is that same beauty that you have. I am wondering if you might be that woman."

Mary remembered the Roman soldier with the woman and child. He had smiled at Joseph and Mary. At first, they had been concerned that their child might be in danger. King Herod had ordered all male children born in Bethlehem to be put to death. It was for that reason that Mary and Joseph were traveling with their new born son out of Israel to Egypt. When they saw the soldier smile, they had felt safe once again.

"Quintus." She repeated. "I often wondered who the Roman soldier was that smiled at us as we traveled on our way to Egypt. Quintus. We were so alike and yet so different, the three of us and you three! And yet our paths crossed, then as they have now. God works in strange and wonderful ways. Marcus, I believe that you are meant to be by my son's side. May God bless you and protect you," Mary paused then added, "and my son."

When they had finished eating, Marcus thanked Mary and said that he must continue on and find her son, Jesus. Mary provided him with directions to Tyre and wished him well.

Chapter 43. "The Coasts of Tyre and Sidon"

Marcus took the road west to Accor and there he spent the night. The next morning he traveled the road north along the coast and by mid-afternoon he had reached the Phoenician city of Tyre.

It only took a short while for him to learn that Jesus had given a sermon while in Tyre and that though there were few Jews in the city, a great multitude had gone to hear him speak. He also learned that Jesus and his followers had then left the city and were traveling on to Sidon.

Marcus continued his journey following in the footsteps of Mary's son. He thought about Mary and her belief that God meant for him to be at her son's side. If so then for what reason? Jesus had said that he should record all that took place so that future generations would know what happened here. He wondered though if there were more reasons for him to be by Jesus' side. Certainly he could write about what he experienced. Then Lucius appeared in his mind admonishing him to be ready to use his sword should words fail.

Marcus reached the village of Sarapta by nightfall. As he rode into the village there was a celebration underway. He was invited to join in.

"What are we celebrating?" He asked.

"The miracle of our Lord!" Came the answer.

"What miracle?"

A woman came out of the midst of the crowd with a young girl holding her hand. "This miracle!" The woman shouted and again everyone cheered. "My daughter was possessed by the devil! She cried uncontrollably and cursed all around her. I begged my Lord to have mercy on us even though we are Cananites.

At first he told us to leave him thinking that I was not sincere when I called him my Lord. But I followed after him and again begged him for mercy. I fell to my knees and prayed that he would take pity on me and my daughter. When I opened my eyes, he was standing before me. He looked at me and knew I was sincere for he heard my silent prayer.

It was then that he reached down and took hold of my daughter's head. She immediately fell silent, her ravings gone. Jesus said, 'Woman, great is thy faith, what you have prayed for shall be so.' And with that he released my daughter's head and walked on leaving me with my dear child.

Look at her kind sir. She has returned to me whole."

At that, all assembled cheered again and repeated, "The miracle of our Lord!"

Marcus asked one of the revelers if Jesus had gone. The answer was yes.

Marcus decided that if he stayed the night, he might again miss Jesus at Sidon. He stopped at an inn and purchased some bread, some cheese and some wine to take with him as he pushed on through the night.

Just outside of the town of Sidon, Marcus came upon the disciples and Jesus encamped on a mountain side. As he rode into the campsite at the dawn of the morning, James the Greater stirred and looked up. Seeing a man on horseback, he immediately stood up. He recognized Marcus saying, "Marcus, you keep strange hours for a civilized man."

Marcus laughed quietly as he climbed down from his horse. "I never thought of it that way but of course you are right."

They shook hands and moved over to the warmth of a dwindling fire of embers and flame. As they seated themselves, Jesus appeared. "Marcus! What brings you to our encampment at this hour of the day?"

Marcus immediately stood back up. "A warning. Caiaphas the high priest of the Temple in Jerusalem has asked that you be arrested for sedition."

Peter had now also joined the group. "I told you Lord. They fear the things that you say and do."

Jesus looked from one man to another. He then knelt down by the fire and softly said as he poked a stick into the embers, "My life in this body has a time to light the way and a time to die much like the fire here before us that only hours ago burned brightly but is now but dying embers." He then stood up and looking again at each man said, "My time to leave you is drawing close but I will always be with you in spirit and when you have need of me, I will be there."

Peter protested, "They will have to deal with me before they lay hands on you."

James likewise said, "And I, my Lord. Only say the word and we will raise an army of ten thousand, a hundred thousand if needed and place you on the throne of Israel."

Jesus' face saddened. "Have you not heard all that I have said. It is my Father's will that shall be done here on earth. If it be my time to join my Father who is in heaven, no man shall be able to stand in the way."

With this Marcus spoke up. "My Lord, what you say is true. I believe that when our time to leave has arrived, it is preordained. Yet, I also believe that as a man I make certain choices that can either hasten the day of departure or delay it for its true time and place."

Peter was struck by the fact that Marcus referred to his master as 'My Lord.' He listened to Marcus and then asked of Jesus, "Surely you must agree with Marcus. Is that not why we came to this land?"

Jesus answered Peter, "We came to this land to spread the good news of the kingdom of God and the forgiveness of sins. But I see now that we must return to Galilee if my Father's work is to be completed. Come, we must make ready for our trip home." Jesus moved to where he had been sleeping in order to pack his few worldly belongings.

"Marcus, will you be coming with us?" Jesus smiled.

"My Lord, I will be your constant companion."

Jesus laughed, "Ah yes, my mother has been talking to you."

Chapter 44. "The Return Home"

Jesus and Marcus talked about many things during the journey back to the Sea of Galilee.

"Marcus, you are a learned man. I know that your mind has been well trained. Let me tell you a story and have you tell me after what is its meaning."

Marcus nodded in agreement. Peter and several others watched and listened.

Jesus proceeded with his story. "A sower went forth to sow his seeds. Along the way some seeds fell to the ground and birds came and ate those that had fallen. Some of his seeds fell in stony places where there was not much ground. These seeds sprung up quickly because they had no soil depths to push down in. But when the sun was up, they had no root and withered away.

Some of the seeds fell among thorns. The thorns sprung up before the seeds and choked the growth from the seeds. But some seeds were sown in good ground, took root, and brought forth fruit, some a hundred fold.

Now tell me Marcus, what is the lesson of the story of the sower of seeds?"

Marcus thought for a moment and then answered. "The seeds are like grains of knowledge. My old teacher, Flavius, use to say to me that he could instruct a hundred students with the same lesson and he would be happy if ten learned what was intended. Something inside of you has to be able to accept what is being taught and has to put the lesson in a proper perspective."

Jesus smiled, "Can you apply that to my teachings?"

Again Marcus thought for a moment before answering. "I have not heard all of your teachings but those lessons that I have heard not only made sense to my mind, they struck a cord deep in my heart.

You said when you were at Bethsaida that one of God's greatest commandment was to do for your neighbor that which you would want for your neighbor to do for you. I gave that much thought and applied that lesson to many different situations that came to my mind. I reached the conclusion that if all men followed that commandment, we might truly have a peaceful world and a world that is a much better place in which to live. It is a lofty lesson yet so simply said."

The disciples were impressed with how Marcus responded. They had struggled with the meaning of this parable until Jesus had explained the lesson to them. Jesus had said that he used parables as keys to open the doors of the kingdom of heaven to those who would have the eyes to see, the ears to hear, and the hearts to understand. Marcus was now one of them.

Jesus nodded his approval and said, "Let me share with you yet another parable and ask you for your interpretation. When the sower had come to his field, he sowed his seeds in good ground. When he was finished he retired for the night. During the night his enemy came and sowed thorns in his field. When the seeds later sprung up from the ground, the good seeds brought forth fruit, but the bad seeds brought forth thorns. The sower's servants questioned whether the seeds sown were from a bad basket to which the sower replied that the bad seed had been sown by his enemy but the good seeds were sown by his own hand. They then asked what to do and the sower said to them, gather up the thorns and tie them in a bundle that they may be burned. Then gather up the fruit of the good seed that we may bring them into my barn."

Jesus looked at Marcus for his response.

"You are the sower. Those who speak against you are the enemy. In this world, there will be those that hear you and believe in you. They will be like the good seed. Those that listen only to they that speak against you will be like the bad seed.

You have taught about repentance, forgiveness, and the kingdom of God. Those that see what you show them, hear your words and receive both as truth will be brought into the house of God, as the good fruit was brought into the sower's barn."

Peter turned to Andrew and said in amazement, "I have truly underestimated this man."

Jesus smiled at Marcus, "My belief in you is well founded, Marcus. It is time that you follow your true destiny. Watch, listen, and remember what transpires in the coming days. My time on earth is in your hands."

All those that heard, misunderstood Jesus' meaning. Even Marcus thought that Jesus was referring to his security rather than something greater for which Marcus was destined.

When they reached the shores of the Sea of Galilee, they were again greeted by a vast crowd of people. Many suffered from physical illnesses and disabilities. All sought the blessing of the man of God, the messiah.

Jesus went up onto a hillside to pray for them. All knelt down with him and for three days and nights he fasted in prayer. On the third day he stood and turned to his disciples. "For three days these people have fasted and prayed with me. They have asked for mercy from me and from my Father who is in Heaven." He raised his voice so that all could hear.

"Your faith in the power of God, my Father, who is in Heaven, shall be rewarded if not in this world then in the next. It is my Father's wish that all here be fed that he may bestow his blessing on you."

Jude spoke softly to Jesus. "How shall we feed them Lord? We have but seven loaves and a few fish."

Jesus looked at Jude then asked for the loaves of bread. He took the bread and broke it into small pieces saying, "It is right that we should share what little we have with those who have less than we do. For as much as I do this for you, if you shall do it for others, yours will be the kingdom of Heaven."

A great light came down from the sky and shown on Jesus. He lifted his bread up over his head and then taking one bite passed the bread to the others around him.

Marcus watched while his own heart seemed to be touched by the demonstration of sharing. Jesus had gone three days without food or water. Now he had but one bite of bread and had passed his food to others. As Marcus looked out over the crowd, he saw others doing as Jesus had done, offering what little they had to others who had less. He guessed that there were at least four thousand people present including men, women, and children. As at Bethsaida, when all had eaten there were several baskets of food remaining. Marcus knew and accepted what Jesus had spoken of, 'the Holy Spirit had descended upon the people, and had brought peace and understanding to their hearts.'

His thoughts were interrupted by the voice of a young boy who had approached him. The boy walked with the help of a stick but nevertheless stood tall and straight before him. The boy said, "Kind sir. I remember you from Jerusalem. I am Jacob. Your Master made me to walk. I have come to thank him. Would you help me to get to him?"

Marcus was stunned. It was the boy from the hillside outside of Jerusalem. Marcus looked down at the boys legs. The legs were still as thin as rails but the boy could now use them and he was walking.

Marcus offered his horse to lead the boy to Jesus but the boy shook his head.

"I would like to walk up to my Lord." The boy said proudly.

"And so you shall." Marcus replied.

As they walked slowly up the hillside, people saw them coming and moved out of their way. Some commented that the boy was lame and now made to walk because of Jesus. Others moved because a Roman was stepping forward.

As they reached the spot where Jesus was sitting, Jesus saw the boy and stood to greet him. "Jacob, your mother's faith and your own have served you well."

The boy handed his walking stick to Marcus and with some effort walked the last few feet to Jesus without any support. "Thank you Lord." The boy could say no more as tears rolled down his cheeks and he wrapped his arms around Jesus. Jesus embraced the boy as the boy's mother came up to stand beside Marcus.

Looking on, the woman said to Marcus, "Jacob wanted to do that on his own two good legs. Praise be to God and to his son here with us!"

Marcus looked at the boy's mother and saw the relief in her eyes from the years of pain. Relief that Jesus had given to her and to her son because she believed and had faith in him.

Marcus next looked at the boy, weeping tears of joy for being released from the bondage that he had labored under since birth. No longer was he bound to a wagon. He could walk. He could go wherever he desired now. He had been given a gift by the son of God. He had received a new life with new experiences and new opportunities. All things were possible through Jesus. The people who gathered here to see their Messiah understood this, believed this, were saved by this. Jesus had returned home.

Chapter 45. "A Prophesy of Death"

Jesus spent many days by the shore of the Sea of Galilee. Occasionally, he would climb up into the surrounding mountains for prayer and meditation. Always when he returned from a day of prayer, there would be people waiting for him to ask questions, to offer repentance and beg forgiveness, or to be cured of an illness.

Marcus witnessed a man who brought his son to Jesus claiming that his son was possessed by the devil. He told Jesus that his son would sometimes throw himself into a fire, or into the sea though he could not swim. He said that he had sought help from Jesus' disciples not wanting to burden Jesus with his son's suffering. But the disciples were unable to give his son peace. The man said, "Only my Lord, the son of the most high, can rid my son of his affliction."

Jesus looked at the man and his son then at his disciples. He shook his head at the disciples saying, "How long must I be with you before you have faith." Placing his hand on the head of the man's son, he continued, "That which brings heart ache to the father shall be removed from the son from this time and forever more. The love of the Father toward his son makes it so."

Jesus removed his hand from the boy's head. The boy looked up smiling and asked, "What has happened to me?"

Jesus replied, "The devil had your soul but my Father in Heaven has dispersed the devil so that your father on earth may have the joy of his son in his own house. Your father's love for his children has made it so."

The disciples then asked Jesus why they were not able to cast out the boy's demons as had Jesus. They asked that had not Jesus often told them that they would have the same power over evil and illness in this world that their Lord had through the glory of God.

Jesus answered saying that they were unable to do so because they still had doubts about what was possible through a belief in God the Father and through his son. "You have seen and yet you still have questions. If you truly believed in me as the one that I say I am, my Father would give you the power to move mountains."

Jesus saw that they still did not understand, so he said, "The son of man shall be betrayed into the hands of his enemies. They will kill me and on the third day I shall be raised again. Then you will believe all that you have seen and heard."

Marcus moved forward and said, "Lord let me protect you."

Peter and James the Greater also stepped forward saying, "I too will not let this happen."

Jesus shook his head. "You do not understand. My course has been planned long before this time. I must die so that others will live. But my Father will raise me up that I may show you and everyone that there is a kingdom that will welcome all those who have faith and who truly believe in those things that I have taught while I have been with you."

Still not understanding, Thomas asked, "Lord, who is the greatest in the kingdom of heaven""

Jesus answered, "You ask this because you question why I must die that others may be saved."

Jesus then called to a small child who came immediately to him and sat down in his lap. As the child smiled up at Jesus, Jesus spoke to his disciples saying, "Unless you are converted and become as a child such as this, with unquestioning faith, you will not enter the kingdom of heaven." He paused and then looked directly at Thomas. "Thomas, you must humble yourself so that you have the faith of a child, a child such as this. A child who comes unquestioning to Him who is the Father, the Son, and the Holy Spirit. He who does this is the greatest in the kingdom of heaven."

Jesus again addressed all of his disciples. "If you receive one such little child in my name then you receive me as well."

Andrew asked, "What is the meaning of this, Lord? Did we not do so in trying to cure the man's son?"

Jesus responded to Andrew by asking a question. "Was it in my name that you attempted to cure the boy or was it by the power that you perceived was your own that you tried to cure the boy?"

Andrew bowed his head in understanding.

Jesus again spoke to all of his disciples. "You should never despise any of God's children. In heaven the angels of children behold the face of my Father. My Father has sent me here to save those children who are lost.

If a man has one hundred sheep and one of them goes astray, he will leave the ninety-nine and go to look for the lone one that is lost. And when the man finds the sheep that has gone astray, he celebrates more at the coming home of that sheep than he does the ninety-nine that did not go astray.

Our duty, yours and mine, is to find those that are lost. My Father in heaven does not wish to lose even one of his children. It is his will and not ours that saves those that are lost."

Philip then asked, "If it be your Father's will and not ours that saves those that are lost and heals those who are ill, what then is our responsibility? What then is our purpose?"

Jesus answered Philip, "Because you have chosen to follow me and believe in me, whatsoever you shall bind on earth shall be bound in heaven. If two or more of you shall agree on anything that others ask for in the name of my Father, it shall be done. If two or three of you are gathered in my name, there I will be in your midst. Father, Son, and Holy Spirit, one within the trinity of God."

Marcus watched and listened as Jesus taught his disciples the meaning of his faith. As Marcus watched he saw that the words which Jesus used to convey his teachings seemed to bore into each of the disciples. They absorbed every lesson offered and seemed visibly shaken by the power of the implications of what Jesus was giving to them. He was giving them the same authority which they recognized had been given to him by God, his Father. Some of the disciples visibly shook while others paled. John became ill and had to leave for a short time to relieve his illness.

When Jesus had finished his discourse with the disciples, he moved to where Marcus had been sitting. "Marcus, tomorrow it is time for me to leave Galilee and travel to Judea. My time is getting shorter and I have much yet to do."

Marcus responded, "Why do you believe that your time is getting shorter? I have offered my assistance. If it comes to that, I could provide you with safe passage to one of my holdings far from here."

Jesus understood the compassion of Marcus as evidenced by his offer. "My friend, your heart means well, but understand this. There is no place on earth that I could not go to if it were the will of my Father. But it is my Father's will that I do his work here until the hour of my calling back to him. When it is my time to go, you will be there. I know this. That is why I must ask you not to interfere with what is ordained to be. You are to write the story for others to tell. Above all else, you must survive!"

Jesus looked hard at Marcus as he spoke. The emphasis on Marcus' survival struck Marcus to the core. For the first time in his life he felt fear for what lie ahead of him. But almost as quickly, that fear was replaced by a stronger emotion of rising up to combat anything or anyone who would be a threat.

Marcus looked back at Jesus and said, "I will write your story and I will see to it that it is told across the world. Together, we will continue to do the work of your Father, the one living God."

Jesus smiled. "It is good that you believe Marcus. Hold onto your faith for the entirety of your life. There will be times when your faith will be challenged but my Father will give you the strength that you need if you believe and if you ask for his guidance."

Marcus took Jesus' arm and said, "Your lessons have shown great wisdom. If all men lived by what it is that you teach, this world would be a far better place. For one man to have such understanding and knowledge, it truly has to be through divine inspiration. The son of God cannot perish. I will not let it happen. And, if I do not let it happen then it is God's will that I am able to do so."

Jesus bowed his head and said softly, "Just remember, above all else you must survive to do the work which I have asked of you, the work that my Father has chosen for you to do. You must write down all that has happened, all that has been said, and all that you have witnessed. If you do not, my time here on earth may well have been for nothing."

Marcus reassured Jesus that he would do as Jesus had asked. Marcus also decided that it was important for him to talk with his friend Lucius when they returned to Judea.

Chapter 46. "The law of Moses"

Jesus and his followers departed from Galilee and traveled along the west bank of the Jordan River until they arrived at Jericho. As they entered the city, they saw that great crowds had gathered to see him. People were proclaiming him to be the Messiah, the Savior.

The Pharisees had also come to see Jesus. It was their mission to challenge him and his teachings. They wanted to give Rome the proof needed to have Jesus arrested and put in prison. Some, including Caiaphas, even wanted him dead.

Jesus stopped and sat down on a short wall just outside of the city. As the crowd began to come and sit down around him, one of the Pharisees asked, "Teacher, you have taught many lessons that puzzle me. I would like to know if it is lawful for a man to divorce his wife for any reason."

Jesus knew that this was a question designed to create a trap for him. He answered, "Have you not read the Old Testament? It states that in the beginning, He made them male and female. For this reason, shall a man leave his mother and father so that he may cleave to his wife. That together as man and wife, they shall become as one. That they shall no longer live separately but shall be forever entwined.

What therefore God has joined together, let no man put asunder."

The Pharisee then asked his second question hoping to catch Jesus forsaking the law. "Under the law of Moses, why did God give a command that there should be a writing of divorce so that a man could divorce his wife?"

Jesus sternly responded, "Moses allowed divorce because of the hardness of your hearts toward your wives. But in the beginning it was not the law handed down from my Father.

God, our Father, commanded that 'Thou shall not commit adultery.' I say to you that whosoever shall divorce his wife, except for fornication, and shall marry another, commits adultery."

The Pharisee then objected, "Your teachings violate the law of Moses."

Jesus answered back, "Adultery violates the law of God."

Another man within the crowd then spoke. "Good Master, what good thing shall I do that I may be certain that I will be granted eternal life?"

Jesus looked at the man who was dressed in good garments and wore silver on his wrists and around his neck. He said, "There is but one Good Master and that is God. To gain eternal life, keep his commandments."

The man asked, "Which shall I keep?"

Jesus said to him, "These, thou shall do no murder, thou shall not commit adultery, thou shall not steal, thou shall not bear false witness, thou shall honor thy mother and father, and thou shall love thy neighbor as thyself."

The man then said, "All that you have said, I have done since my birth. Do I lack anything else?"

Jesus looked at the man for a long time before answering. "If you want to be perfect in the eyes of God, go and sell all of your possessions. Give the money that you receive to the poor and you will have treasure in heaven far exceeding that which you have here on earth. Do this and then come and follow me."

All that heard this were astounded. The man shook his head saying, "I have many possessions. I can not part with them to follow you. I have labored long and hard to have some wealth in this world. I am truly sorry."

The man stood up and slowly walked away with his head hanging down.

Marcus thought of his own wealth and wondered if Jesus were to ask him to make this kind of sacrifice, could he?

Jesus sensing what everyone was thinking said to all around him, "Rich men shall hardly enter into the kingdom of heaven because of their wealth alone. It would be easier for a camel to go through the eye of a needle than for a rich man to enter into the kingdom of God."

Jude then asked, "How then can any of us be saved?'

Jesus answered saying, "With men this is impossible but with God, all things are possible."

Peter then said, "We have forsaken all, and followed you, shall we not be saved?"

Jesus answered Peter, "All who sacrifice in my name, believe in me, and keep our faith, shall inherit everlasting life in the kingdom of God. Obey the commandments, be kind to others, help those who are less fortunate, and forgive those who sin against you, and you shall receive the glory of God."

Jesus then walked among the crowd spreading the word of God to all who listened. He admonished them to repent their sins and seek forgiveness from the God who made them. "As he has given me life so too has he given you life. As the father forgives his son his transgressions, so too will our Father in heaven forgive us our transgressions if we truly repent. Pray to Him who gave you life on earth that He will grant you eternal life in heaven."

After the crowds had dispersed, Marcus spoke to Jesus. "Lord, why have you not asked that I sell my possessions and give my wealth to the poor?"

Jesus smiled, "My friend, you have already given much. Wealth is not measured by possessions alone. When the time comes, you will give your life to me. Man has no greater possession than that to give."

Marcus then said, "I know that tomorrow you plan to travel to Bethphage. I must return to Jerusalem to attend to some things that need to be done."

Jesus nodded saying, "Yes, you should return to Jerusalem. You have been away for some time now.

I will be coming to Jerusalem before a fortnight has passed."

Marcus then said, "I will welcome you with open arms. I hope that you will do me the honor of staying in my home while you are in Jerusalem."

Jesus looked about to see if anyone was listening. Seeing no one he turned back to Marcus. "My time is near. I fear that I will be betrayed by one who is close to me. You must not be involved when this happens. I have told you that you have a destiny, a purpose. You must survive. You must fulfill your purpose in life. Through your hand, you will bear witness to the word of God, as I have given it.

I will look forward to your welcome but I fear that our time together will be short."

All Marcus could say was that he hoped that Jesus was wrong about the betrayal and about his time for dying being near.

Chapter 47. "The Teachings at Bethphage"

The next day, Marcus traveled to Bethpage with Jesus and his disciples. He then continued on to Jerusalem knowing that he needed to talk with Lucius as soon as possible.

Jesus was again beset by large crowds at Bethphage. He and his disciples came to a spot known as the mount of Olives and decided that this was the place to rest. A Samaritan came to Jesus and asked to be forgiven his sins. "Oh son of God, I am not worthy of your forgiveness but as I know you to be who you are, know me that I truly repent and beg salvation."

Jesus looked with favor on the Samaritan and said, "Go in peace for my peace I give you. Your sins are forgiven."

Peter then asked, "How is it that a Samaritan should be given such grace?"

Jesus answered, "In the eyes of God, all of his children, who repent their sins, deserve a place at his table."

Jesus paused to let his statement to Peter resonate with all those who were listening. He then went on, "Peter, there was a Jewish merchant traveling along a road to the marketplace when he was set upon by robbers. He was beaten, they stole his money, and they left him beside the road wounded and unable to move. A priest came along and seeing the man beside the road, passed by on the opposite side. A Levite also came along the same road and seeing the wounded man, he too passed by on the opposite side. Then a Samaritan came along and seeing the Jewish man lying wounded next to the road, he crossed over to the man, tended to his wounds, and then took him to an inn and paid for him to be cared for.

My Father has said that we should love our neighbors. That we should do for them what we would hope that they would do for us if we were in a like situation. Our neighbors are those in need. As this good Samaritan showed his love for the wounded man lying beside the road, so too does God love his children. They may be Jew, Samaritan or even Gentile. If they have a need, He is there for them if they but ask for his help."

Hearing this, a Gentile stepped forward asking, "Lord, please forgive my sins for I have squandered my family's wealth on riotous living and gambling. It has left me with nothing."

Jesus lifted the man's bowed head up with his hand. "You still have a soul. That is your most valued possession. It was given to you by God. Your past sins are forgiven but if you do not set your course on the right path, your future sins will suffer you to eternal damnation. Now, go forth and do good deeds. Earn your family's forgiveness and sin no more."

After the man had gone, John asked Jesus, "Will his family forgive him?"

Jesus looked out at the Olive grove as if peering into the future before answering. "A man had two sons. His older son was a hard worker who tended his fathers flocks long after others had gone home for the day. The man had due respect for his older son and provided for him what he had earned. The man's younger son was beloved by the man but was not given to hard work. The younger son preferred instead to spend his time playing and enjoying the more pleasurable pursuits of life. One day the younger son asked his father for his inheritance, that he might set off to see the world around him. The father gave him his due and the young son left his father and his home.

While the older brother stayed on and continued to work hard with his father, the young son squandered away all of his wealth and was reduced to living in squalor and debt.

Finally, with no place else to turn and with his life almost at its end, the young son decided to return home and ask his father's forgiveness.

When his father saw his poor son yet a long way off, he ordered a feast to be prepared. When his son arrived home and asked for forgiveness, the father gave it to him, happy in his heart that his son who was lost had now been found."

John then asked, "And what of the older brother who did not leave but stayed with the father and continued to labor beside him?"

"A father has room in his heart for all of his children knowing that each one is different. His love of his children knows no bounds. He loves each of them as they are his. Thankful is he for his children that stay the course and forgiving is he for those children who are lost and then they are found."

Chapter 48. "Brothers at Arms"

Marcus sent word to Lucius that he would like to meet somewhere where they could talk in private. They agreed on an inn in the northeastern corner of the city beyond the Hippodrome. Marcus arrived before Lucius and was talking with the innkeeper when Lucius arrived.

They ordered drinks and took a table in the far corner of the inn where few would notice them and they could talk in private.

"So, what is the big secret that has us hid away in this miserable excuse for an inn?" Lucius laughed as he took a healthy drink from his cup.

"Jesus." Marcus answered knowing the reaction he would get from his friend.

Lucius immediately put down his cup and looked directly at Marcus. "Your infatuation with this man is going to get you into serious trouble." Lucius looked around the room to see if anyone was paying attention to them. He noticed two men on the far side of the room look away as he turned to face them. He was not certain if they were looking at him with more interest because of his legionnaire's uniform or because it was an unlikely twosome that he and Marcus made for this remote inn. In any event the two men soon left the room leaving Marcus and he alone for their conversation.

"Marcus, you already know that Caiaphas wants this man in prisoner or even dead. He claims that Jesus has proclaimed himself the King of the Jews. Herod laughed at this at first thinking it absurd. But now, even Herod is concerned about the following that this man has. I have been informed that thousands turn out to hear this man speak wherever he travels. I have even heard from my post in Nazareth that you visited with his mother."

"Lucius, I told you that I was interested in finding out more about this man."

"And did you Marcus? Did you find out more about Jesus?"

"Yes, I did. He is remarkable. He heals the sick. He teaches that man should love his neighbor. That in the eyes of God, all men are equal, because God made man."

Lucius interrupted Marcus. "You and I have been through this before. I told you then that if you brought to me the lame boy who could walk, then I might believe these stories that I hear. But until the boy walks, I…"

Now, it was Marcus who interrupted Lucius. "He does walk."

"Who?"

"The lame boy named Jacob. I have seen him."

"Are you sure you saw the same boy?"

"Yes, I am sure. In fact I spoke with both him and his mother. They came to a place where Jesus was speaking to thank him for enabling Jacob to walk."

"I can not believe it."

"Believe it, Lucius. I can bear witness to it."

"What else have you seen, Marcus?"

For the next hour, Marcus told Lucius all that he had seen and done over the last several weeks. Lucius sat still and said nothing. Finally, when Marcus had told him everything including what Marcus now perceived his purpose in life to be, Lucius spoke in a low tone saying, "I concur with the last advice that this prophet gave to you, you must survive. If Jesus comes to Jerusalem and incites a crowd, I fear that Rome will have no choice but to have him arrested."

"Why?"

"Politics, religious reasons, it does not matter. Herod will ask the governor to have him arrested and the governor will comply. You look on this man as half god half man. Pilate will only see the man. Herod will see a person vying for his title of king of the Jews. Caiaphas will see him as a false prophet who is disrupting the true beliefs of the Jews.

Your Jesus has too many powerful enemies. For that matter, Caesar will not tolerate such turmoil in the territories. You know this better than I. You have studied our history."

Marcus realized that all of what Lucius was saying was true. "Jesus is not a threat. The kingdom that he talks about is in the after life not here and now. He does not speak of rioting and violence. He talks about love and peace."

Lucius shook his head. "It is not so much what he says as it is the reaction that he evokes from those that hear him. The Zealots among the Jews have been looking for a person to rally around to lead them in their attacks upon the Empire. Jesus could very well be the one that emboldens them. He should not come to Jerusalem."

"He will come."

"He seems to respect you Marcus. Can you not convince him to leave Judea and take his message to others in distant lands. Why not go to Egypt?"

"As he sees my purpose in this world so too does he see his own. He told me that he will be betrayed by one of his own. He knows that he faces death here."

"Then why does he come?"

"One night, I asked him that question. His answer was that he will die and then be raised up from the dead so that others seeing this will know that there is life after death and that the kingdom of God will be for all eternity unlike the finality of this world."

Lucius leaned back in his chair. "I hope that your prophet is right. I would like to believe that when I leave this world I will find something better in the next. But that is the unknown. For now, I want to do all that I can to survive in this world. If I am not mistaken, you have been given that same advice by this same person."

Marcus nodded in agreement. What Lucius said was all true. Marcus did not like the thought that his new friend and teacher would soon be leaving him. His heart ached at the thought. He could feel the void already as the meaning of all that would transpire touched his soul.

"I will do what I have to do."

Lucius got up, paid for their drinks, and said to Marcus, "You have always been wise. Do not allow your emotions to cloud your judgment."

As they walked out of the inn into the small alley that ran out to the main street, they were suddenly confronted by a dozen men wielding swords. The leader of the band was one of the men Lucius had seen in the inn.

Lucius drew his sword and ordered, "Step back, I am a Roman Centurion."

The leader answered back, "And I am the one who will cut you from end to end. Death to all Romans."

The men charged forward as Marcus instinctively drew his sword. In the small alleyway, only four or five of the attackers could engage Lucius and Marcus at one time. They were no match for the brothers at arms from the Amphitheater in Rome.

The first of the attackers to fall was their leader. He brought his sword down hard at Lucius head but Lucius parried the chopping motion and with a chopping motion of his own, Lucius severed the arm of the would be destroyer of Romans.

Marcus skillfully disarmed three other attackers and using one as a shield dispatched a fourth with a thrust straight into the attacker's mid section. Lucius was back at the others and was soon joined by Marcus as the two slashed and cut their way through their attackers with a fury that neither had experienced before.

The battle was over within a few minutes. Ten men lay dead or dying in the alleyway while two others had escaped but not without injury. The innkeeper had heard the fighting and had sent for help. As Marcus and Lucius leaned against a wall to recover their strength, several Roman soldiers came running into the alley. Recognizing their commander, they immediately took custody of the Zealots that were still alive.

"Are you hurt Commander?" One of the soldiers asked.

Lucius nodded, "No, I am alright thanks to my educated friend." Lucius looked over at Marcus who had now stood away from the wall that he had been leaning against. "There is always a place for you in the legions of Rome." Lucius added.

Marcus looked down at his bloody sword. As he put it back in its sheath he said, "Love thy neighbor. I certainly did not honor that commandment today."

Lucius laughed and pointing with his sword toward the place where their attackers lay sprawled out on the ground said, "Your neighbors did not give you a chance to do that. Come with me. We will go back to the fortress and get washed."

Marcus looked at both himself and at Lucius. They both were covered in blood though none of it was their own. Washing this off his body seemed like a good idea.

The soldiers marveled at what the two Romans had done. Ten Zealots had been beaten in that small alleyway by a centurion and a private Roman citizen. The story of the attack and ensuing battle would be told over and over again that night and in the days ahead. It gave the legionnaires one more reason to believe in the superiority of the Roman Empire.

The story also made its way to Caiaphas and the Pharisees. It gave them a reason to continue to fear the power of Rome and Rome's presence within their kingdom. Caiaphas knew that Lucius was a force to be aware of but now this Roman citizen apparently was another that he would have to contend with.

Marcus and Lucius returned to the Fortress of Antonia to take advantage of the hot baths and get some clean clothes. The clothes that they had been wearing when the attack occurred had to be discarded as they were beyond repair.

Lucius gave Marcus a uniform of the Roman legions saying, "We should make that permanent." He gestured at the well fitting uniform.

Marcus looked at his garments. "Well, at least they are clean."

Both men laughed.

"What does your Savior say you should do when you are attacked as we were today?"

Marcus thought to himself, 'A good question.' He looked up at Lucius and said, "I do not know what he would say. I have never heard him advocate violence in any form."

Lucius walked over to a cabinet and took out two glasses and a bottle of wine. Uncorking the bottle, he poured a drink for Marcus and himself. "This is a weakness in your new found religion. We live in a violent world. Today, your training by Flavius Titus saved both your own life and probably mine. I could not have survived an attack by twelve Zealots without you.

Rome understands that it is might that rules and maintains order. It is not the higher calling to books and education that makes Rome strong. It is the sword and shield."

Marcus shook his head. "Lucius, this is an argument that you and I have been having for years. I agree that the sword rules and can be used to maintain order but to what purpose if not for the laws established by man based on his history, experience, and knowledge. And what of the advancement of civilization? This is the result of man's pursuit of learning and has nothing to do with the power of the sword."

Lucius raised his hand. "Ah, but if the sword did not maintain order and if the Empire did not reach out into the frontiers and bring this civilization to the uncivilized world, how then would such learning and development survive?"

Marcus had to admit that some of what Lucius was proffering made sense. "You have become a philosopher since leaving Rome! Perhaps there is a good argument that both the sword and learning go hand in hand."

Lucius clapped his friend on the back. "Well, perhaps there is still hope for you."

Later, when Marcus returned to his home, he thought about his conversation with Lucius. He would have to ask Jesus what was expected by God when an enemy attacks without warning and without cause."

Chapter 49. "Moneychangers in the Temple"

As Jesus had promised, he returned to Jerusalem to fulfill the prophesy that the King of the Jews would enter Jerusalem riding on an ass.

All of Jerusalem was aware that Jesus was coming and great crowds gathered along the road leading to the gates of the city. People lay their robes and blankets on the road as a demonstration of their respect for the son of God. Others cut palms from nearby trees and lay them before him as well. A great cry went up from the multitudes shouting Hosanna to the son of God, Hosanna in the highest.

Lucius and Marcus watched from the great wall that surrounded the city. It was a sight that no man would ever forget. Thousands of people were falling down on their knees as Jesus and his disciples passed by. All were shouting his name and praising him as the son of God, the Messiah, the Savior.

As Jesus entered the city, a band of men began chanting, 'Praise Jesus, King of the Jews." The chant was picked up by others as Jesus proceeded down the streets and through the inner walls of the city toward the Temple.

Upon reaching the Temple, Jesus and his disciples entered into the Temple's courtyard. To Jesus' dismay, the courtyard had been turned into a marketplace, where merchants were selling all manner of produce, trinkets, and wares. It was part of an arrangement with the Sadducees that the merchants would share their profits with the priests and Pharisees.

Jesus became irate upon seeing what had become of the Temple built to honor God. Filled with a great rage, he began overthrowing tables and ordering the merchants and those buying from them to get out of his house. He shouted at all there. "It has been written that My house shall be called a house of prayer. You have made it a den of thieves. Let no one remain who has visited such sacrilege on My house!"

Those that had proclaimed Jesus as King heard his words and rushed in to remove the merchants and their wares. Chaos ensued and the courtyard erupted into fighting between the merchants and those that had come into the courtyard with Jesus. There were too many of Jesus followers now inside the courtyard. The merchants escaped taking with them as much of their possessions as they could and still be safe from the crowds now forcing them out.

Jesus and James the Greater climbed the stairs leading to the Temple and walked inside. Jesus went before the alter and lay down before it on the floor. With his arms outstretched, he prayed to his Father that the children of God would see and understand. James stood in the doorway to protect his Master.

When Jesus was finished with his prayer, he sat in front of the alter and heard the prayers of the blind, the lame, the sick, and the possessed. He healed all who worshiped him as their Savior and as the Son of God.

The priests of the Temple watched as Jesus ministered to the sick and heard those that came to him call him the Son of God. One priest stepped forward and asked, "Do you not hear what they call you? They are referring to you as the Son of God in God's Temple."

Jesus was still angered by what he had found in the Temple's courtyard. He answered the Priest saying, "Have you never read that out of the mouth of babes comes true praise? I say to you that they see what you, who are sinful, will never see. The kingdom of heaven is reserved for the pure of heart."

The priest retreated with the other priests present. Jesus remained the rest of that day in the Temple listening to the prayers of those who truly believed. At the end of the day, Jesus asked that his disciples remain in the city so that the needs of those who had not been seen by him would be met.

Marcus had arrived with Lucius and a detachment of Roman soldiers while the merchants were fleeing with their belongings. The soldiers had restored order in the Temple's courtyard. Marcus had joined James the Greater at the Temple's doorway. When Jesus had ministered to the last of those who sought him out, he had come out to the doorway and greeted Marcus saying, "You will be with me from now until the end." He then gave his instructions to his disciples and together Marcus and he left the disciples and went to Bethany.

Chapter 50. "Bethany"

Jesus and Marcus accompanied by Matthias, a constant follower of Jesus, entered the village of Bethany. They were greeted by a man named Simon who bowed down before Jesus and begged that Jesus and his two companions enjoy the hospitality of Simon's home. Marcus later learned that Simon had been a leper and had been cured by Jesus upon Simon's declaration of faith.

Simon and his wife prepared a great feast for their three guest serving lamb, figs, and other assorted fruits and vegetables. After the evening meal, neighbors gathered to hear the words of Jesus.

Jesus sat down under the night sky in front of Simon's home and all gathered around him. Looking up at the stars, he said to them, "Try as you might, you can never count the number of stars that shine in the night sky. So too, are the number of blessings that my Father will give you in heaven if you obey his commandments here on earth."

One of the neighbors asked, "What can we do to honor you, Lord?"

Jesus smiled and said, "When I am hungry, you feed me. When I have no place to lay my head, you provide a bed for me. When I have no clothes, you provide me with clothing. When I thirst, you give me drink.

I say to you, that as you do for me do likewise for the stranger. If he be sick, tend to him. If he thirsts, give him drink. If he hungers, give him food. If he is naked, cloth him. For as much as you do this for a stranger, you do it for me.

Do these things as I have commanded you and you shall be received into eternal life."

Then a woman came to Jesus with an alabaster box. Inside the box there were very precious ointments. The woman took the ointments from the box and applied it gently to Jesus' head.

Matthias, seeing this, objected saying, "Why do you allow this waste of good ointment when it might be sold and the profits from the sale given to the poor that they may eat and be clothed?"

Jesus answered, "You will have the poor for all time but my time with you is short."

Then looking at the woman who had tears in her eyes, Jesus said, "This woman knows in her heart that what I say is true. She prepares me for my burial for she knows that I will be taken away soon. Her faith in me by this act shall be like a memorial to her.

I say to you that my time is coming but I will be raised up and shall join my Father in heaven. The angels shall rejoice and in their rejoicing shall receive all of you who repent and accept the truth of what I have told you."

The hour was late when all retired accept for Jesus and Marcus. They sat quietly for awhile gazing up at the star filled sky. Presently, Jesus asked, "What is on your mind Marcus?"

"Recently, a friend of mine and I were attacked by Zealots without cause or warning."

"What did you do?" Jesus asked without showing any emotion or surprise at what Marcus had just said.

"I drew my sword and killed or wounded those that attacked me."

"And having done this, how do you feel now?" Again, Jesus asked the question without emotion.

"I am bothered by what I have done. It happened so quickly that I did not think. I just reacted. Had I not fought, my friend and I would probably be dead."

Jesus looked into Marcus' eyes then looked away. After some time, Jesus said, "If a man shall strike you on the cheek with his hand, you should offer him the other cheek. My Father has handed down a commandment that thou shall not kill. I say to you that if you kill without just cause you shall not see the kingdom of heaven. You must decide if my Father will see your actions as just or unjust.

This much I will tell you. My Father made the light to shine on all things, both good and evil. He sends the rains down on both the just and the unjust. So before you take away that which he has given, you should have exhausted all other possibilities."

"Lord, you have said to me that above all else I must survive. Do I survive by the sword if I have no other choice?"

"You will always have a choice. Pray to the Father for guidance and wisdom. He will guide your actions."

"And what of the laws of man? Are they to be obeyed?"

"Where the laws of man do not conflict with my Father's commandments, they are in harmony. But a man cannot serve two masters. You will not be able to serve God and Rome.

The greatest of all commandments given by my Father is that thou shall love the Lord thy God with all thy heart, with all thy soul, and with all thy mind. The second greatest commandment is not unlike the first, thou shall love thy neighbor as thyself. These two commandments must be the foundation upon which all other laws rest. If the laws of man conflict with either of these two commandments, they are not just and proper.

Marcus, God knows what you will need. You have but to accept this in your heart and in your mind and God will provide you with direction and purpose."

Marcus listened to what Jesus was saying to him and a sense of relief came to him. He had had a sort of sickness in his soul after the attack in the alleyway. He had felt conflicted by his actions having been exposed to the teachings of Jesus. Now, he reasoned that he had had no alternative to the path he had taken. He instinctively knew that this would not be so from this day forward.

Jesus saw that Marcus relaxed now. The Holy Spirit had descended upon him and given him peace.

Jesus and Marcus both inwardly sensed that time was precious for both of them. There were many things which Jesus wanted Marcus to hear and understand. And so, Jesus and Marcus sat beneath a star laden sky while Jesus gave to Marcus the knowledge and insight that he would need for the days, weeks, months, and years ahead.

"Marcus, I know that you are man of law. It is in your nature. To be able to discern which laws of man are compliant with the laws of God, understand these which I now give to you.

Do not use the Lord God's name in vain; do not lust after another's wife nor commit adultery; do not commit murder; do not take from others that which is not yours; and do not bear false witness against others.

You also should understand that as I give to you the prohibitions so too do I give to you those commandments which glorify God.

If a man has need of a coat, offer him your cloak.

If a man hates you, show him love that he may learn from you.

Forgive those that curse you, or despitefully use you.

Remember that what you do for the least of those which God has created, you do for Him. So, do not horde your treasure on earth but use it for good works. God will see these good works and give you a greater reward in his kingdom of heaven.

I have seen many, including the Pharisees and the Sadducees do good deeds in the Temple to win the praises of man and then go about their private lives violating the laws and the commandments, and thinking only of themselves. God sees these as they are and their only reward will be that which they receive in this world.

Those that do good deeds in secret, not for the praise of man but for the praise of God, will receive their just reward in the kingdom of heaven.

Likewise, when you pray, do not pray with vain repetitions. Your Father in heaven knows what are your needs before you ask him. Pray from your heart and from your soul. Ask for his guidance and care. He shall hear and shall answer you."

Marcus watched a star fall from the sky as he sat listening to what Jesus was saying. Looking back down at Jesus, he asked, "How do I begin to pray to the Lord our God? I am a mortal and have never been taught by any others than mortal men."

Jesus answered by asking Marcus, "Do you believe me to be mortal?"

Marcus had known for a long time that this was a question that Jesus would one day ask of him. He had given the question much thought. He had relived all that he had seen Jesus do and all that he had heard Jesus say in the time that he had known him. Now, the question was before him. He responded to Jesus without hesitation. "I accept you as my Lord, the son of the one God, who reigns not in this world but in the next. I believe you to be immortal, to be one who will last through all eternity."

Jesus smiled and placing a hand upon Marcus' shoulder said, "Then hear me well Marcus and remember for this is how you will begin your prayers to my Father:

'Our Father, which art in Heaven, hallowed be thy name.

Thy kingdom come. Thy will be done in earth, as it is in heaven.

Give us this day our daily bread.

And forgive us our debts, as we forgive our debtors.

Lead us not into temptation, but deliver us from evil, for thine is the kingdom, and the power, and the glory for ever.

Amen.'

As I have taught this to you and to all of my disciples, so too, you must teach it to all those who seek to pray to my Father. It is only through me that He will hear your words for I am He and He is in me.

Do you understand what I am telling you?"

Marcus did understand and answered, "Yes."

Jesus then stood up to stretch his body after a long day. He spoke as though he were talking to the heavens but his word were for Marcus to hear.

"Often I have taught others through parables with the hope that by example they would understand the complex lessons that I would never be able to teach them if I were to convey the lesson to them directly.

With you, I have known since our first meeting that you knew and understood from the beginning.

But when you write all of this down for others to read and to learn, you too must recite my parables. To that end, ask and receive from my disciples the parables that I have given to them. Some they may not yet understand but they will remember the story if not the meaning." Jesus smiled gently and went on. "In time, the Holy Spirit will descend upon them giving light to the darkness. They will then go forth with the word and shall preach to all that will hear, what they have witnessed and learned."

Marcus wondered aloud if he was to go forth and preach as well. This was something that had not occurred to him before this moment. "Am I to go forth and preach your teachings as well?"

Jesus' face saddened and he rubbed his temples with his hands as he said, "Almost all of my original twelve disciples shall suffer as shall I at the hands of others. Those that will preach, will teach lessons that non-believers will take issue with to the point of persecution and death.

This is not what my Father has in mind for you Marcus. You are to create a testament for all those who accept the word of my Father. It is that testament that shall offer mankind hope and the keys to eternal happiness. Your reach will be the greatest of all my disciples. It will endure for generations.

That is why, Marcus… that is why you must survive."

The sun was just beginning to come up in the eastern sky. The outline of the mountains could be made out in the distance as the stars were quickly fading from sight.

Jesus turned to walk back inside his host's home. "We must thank Simon for his hospitality."

Marcus asked one last time, "Must you return to Jerusalem?"

Jesus looked at Marcus and both knew the answer to Marcus' question.

Chapter 51. "Preparation for the Celebration of Passover"

Jesus, Matthias, and Marcus were joined by Mary and Martha, sisters of Lazarus, who also lived in Bethany for the journey back into Jerusalem.

It was obvious to Marcus that these two women were very close to Jesus by the very nature of their ease of conversation with him. He would later be told, by one of the disciples, that Mary had always thought that one day she and Jesus would become husband and wife. Marcus never learned if this was discussed between the two of them but he did come to understand that it was something that all of the disciples were aware of.

Just outside of the gate to the city, they met the other disciples who were seated beneath a fig tree, heavy with leaves to block the midday sun, but with no fruit.

Jesus then said, "This tree bares no fruit though it is rich with leaves. Yet its purpose is to provide fruit for those who are hungry. From this day forward and for ever this tree shall not bear any fruit." The tree withered before their eyes.

The disciples were amazed. Jesus, seeing the amazement in their eyes, said, "I tell you that if you have a faith and believe in me, you will not only be able to do as you have seen me do, but whatever you ask for in prayer, believing in me, you shall receive."

Then, Peter asked, "Where shall we go Lord? The Pharisees have threatened to imprison us if we enter the gates to the city."

Jesus said to Peter, "My time has come to go into Jerusalem and to do the work of my Father. I must go to his Temple for the Passover Feast."

Jude then spoke for all saying, "If you are to go there then we shall all go there. Your fate will be our fate as well."

Jesus and his disciples then proceeded to the Temple. A crowd began to follow Jesus knowing that the authorities had issued an order of restraint against him. They wanted to witness what would happen to Jesus when he entered the Temple.

The crowd continued to grow as Jesus and his followers entered the temple. Once within the Temples gates, Jesus went to the steps of the Temple and there began to teach another lesson to those around him.

"I am often asked why I spend time trying to save sinners, those who are sick, and those who are poorest among us. As the shepherd tends to his flock and tries to heal the sick and save the poorest among his sheep, I am the shepherd of my flock and should do no less. If one of my flock goes astray, I must find him and show him the way back."

Caiaphas, upon learning that Jesus had entered the Temple and was teaching on the outside steps, went with the other priests and elders to confront Jesus. Caiaphas was enraged at the audacity that this man should come and teach within his temple. He demanded of Jesus, "By what authority do you come into this temple to teach?"

Jesus turned to Caiaphas and said, "I will answer you after I ask you one question. The baptism of John…was it from heaven or from man?"

Caiaphas knew that if answered from heaven, Jesus would ask why then he did not believe what John had told them and if he answered from man, the people might rise up against him for they believed in John as a prophet.

Caiaphas finally said, "I cannot tell."

Jesus then responded, "Then neither can I tell you by what authority I come to this temple to teach."

Jesus then said to Caiaphas and his priests and elders, "Hear this parable that you might profit from it.

There was a certain landowner who planted a large vineyard with a long hedgerow all around it. He built a tower and a winepress in the middle of it and hired husbandmen to tend it while he traveled to a far country.

When the time came to harvest the fruit of the vine, the landowner sent his servants to vineyard so that he could receive the fruits of his vines.

But the husbandmen who he had hired beat one servant, killed another, and stoned the third.

He sent other servants who met the same fate as the first.

Finally, he sent his son saying surely they will revere my son and not do harm to him. But the husbandman saw the son and said let us kill him and seize all of the fruits of the vine for ourselves.

And so, they killed the son also.

Now, tell me what will the landowner do to the husbandman when he comes?"

One of the elders answered, "The landowner will destroy the wicked men and will hire out his vineyard to those who will render him the fruit of the vines in their season."

Jesus nodded in agreement then said, "The Scriptures say it and I tell you that if you reject the stone upon which the temple is built, the kingdom of God shall be taken away from you and given to a nation bringing forth his fruits."

The disciples feared that Caiaphas would have them all seized for what Jesus had said. But Caiaphas was also afraid. He was afraid of how the crowd would react inside the temple if he ordered a prophet seized within its walls.

Caiaphas spoke briefly with one of his priests and then went back inside the temple. The priest remained and said to Jesus, "Master, we know that you always speak the truth and that you teach the way of God. Tell us, is it lawful under God's commandments, to give tribute unto Caesar?"

Jesus saw the wickedness in the priest's heart and said, "You seek to trap me you hypocrite. Show me the tribute money."

The priest held up a coin.

Jesus asked, "Whose image is on the coin?"

The priest answered, "Caesar's."

Jesus answered the priest saying, "Then render unto Caesar the things which are Caesar's, and unto God the things that are God's."

Marcus marveled at how adept Jesus was at responding to the obvious attempts by the priests to entrap him into defying Rome. This was not a man preaching sedition. This was God's son preaching redemption. He wondered how many in the crowd understood this.

Jesus' message, to all who truly heard, was that God is the cornerstone upon which the temple, the Jewish faith, is built. If they rejected the son of God, they rejected God, the Father, also. The cornerstone would give way and the temple would fall. They would lose their covenant with God. Then another nation might rise out of the ashes and accept the word of the son of God. If so, that nation would bring forth the fruits of his teachings and create a new order in the world.

As he thought through all that Jesus had said, Marcus realized that the real threat to the existing order was not the man but his ideas. If God saw all men as one, if he created all people in his image and sent them forth as his children, then how could man justify one man having dominion over another? He realized that this was the threat that Caiaphas must fear most. It would eventually be a threat that Rome also would have to address.

Marcus suddenly feared for the well being of his friend, Jesus of Nazareth.

As Jesus and his disciples were leaving the temple, one of his disciples, Judas Iscariot, came to him and advised that he had made arrangements for their evening meal and a place to stay.

Marcus thought that it might be safer if Jesus and his disciples stayed with him in his home while they were in Jerusalem.

"Let me offer you the comforts and the safety of my home while you are in Jerusalem."

Judas immediately objected. "Master, I have arranged for the Passover meal to be served in keeping with our faith. There will be no need for concern for our wellbeing during the feast of Passover. It is a holy time respected by Jews and Romans alike."

Marcus did not feel comfortable with the tone in Judas' voice nor his insistence upon being the one in charge of the group's wellbeing.

"I mean no disrespect to the Jewish faith, but as you, yourself, have just pointed out, some that call themselves believers believe more in what is best for them than what is best for the general welfare." Marcus looked to Jesus expecting agreement.

Jesus said, "Thank you Marcus for your offer. Judas has been the one who has provided for our wellbeing, our food and lodging for almost three years now. There is reason enough for us to allow his work in this regard."

Andrew then turned and looking at the temple buildings said, "These buildings and walls are magnificent."

All those present turned to admire the buildings within the walls of the temple courtyard.

Jude observed, "It is said that Herod the Great built this temple using the same plans that Solomon used in building his temple."

Jesus became angry with his disciples and raising his voice said to them, "Do not be impressed by what Herod has built and the Pharisees maintain. The day is not far off when there shall not be left standing one stone upon another. All of this will be thrown down and ground into dust."

He then turned and walked away. The disciples realizing that Jesus was upset with them followed at a safe distance.

Marcus walked beside Jesus in silence for a time. Jesus finally spoke to him. "Marcus, the others wisely walk behind us. Do you know why I became upset with them?"

Marcus offered his assessment, "They admired the physical representation of your faith rather than the spiritual?"

Jesus looked over at his companion. "You are all that I could hope for." He turned back to the road ahead leading to the mount of Olives. "I have labored for three years to bring the word of God to my disciples and to the His people. I do not know if I have succeeded. Sometimes, I believe that they have heard and understand. I believe that the Holy Spirit has entered the darkness of their souls and provided them with light. But then, as just now, they become distracted by the things of this world and lose sight of the next."

Marcus said, "They are human. The son of God does not have the failings that mortal men have."

Jesus sat down on a fallen tree trunk and nodded in agreement with what Marcus had observed. "Thank you. Patience is what I need to remember. My only concern is that my time is short and they still have much to learn."

Marcus picked up on this last comment. "You seem worried about the quickness of your days. Why not let me provide you with some degree of safety so that you may have the time you need to teach your disciples all that you wish for them to know."

Jesus laughed softly to himself. "We may both be old men before that day would arrive. My disciples were chosen because they are all good men. Devoted and loyal followers. Most seeking to know the truth. To find their way to the Lord, our God. They will be sorely challenged in the days ahead. They will learn and grow not by just what I impart to them but by the life lessons that my Father has planned for them.

You, too, will learn from life lessons as you go forth. But you already have the knowledge that I teach. Your basic instincts are God given as are the instincts of all men. The difference is that in a chosen few, the realization of those instincts, those gifts, is apparent and known. In others, it is something that must be discovered. The discovery is part of the life lessons that I refer to."

Peter and James the Greater finally felt that it was time to join their Master. They walked over to where Jesus was seated. Peter asked, "Master, you have said that the time will come when the temple shall be destroyed, and those that persecute us shall pay the price. When will this happen?"

James added, "Will there be a sign that it is time to rise up and throw off our oppressors? Who will lead us?"

Jesus answered them. "Be careful not to be deceived. It is written that a Savior shall come and he shall be called Christ. That he will lead you, the chosen people of God, to throw off your oppressors and establish a new kingdom.

I tell you that many shall come in my name. There shall be wars. Nations will rise up against nations. There shall be famines, earthquakes, pestilences and floods in many different lands.

Many will revile those who preach for my name's sake. Those who chose to follow in my footsteps will be set upon and many shall die. But I tell you that if you follow in my footsteps to the end, you shall be saved.

The gospel of my Father's kingdom shall be preached and its text shall be written so that the entire world will have the opportunity to know the Lord thy God. And though I die and the world as we know it shall pass away, yet my words shall not pass away. You will be my surrogates. You will be given the power here on earth to open the doors to the kingdom of heaven."

Jesus then spoke of many parables so that his disciples would understand what was coming and what would be expected of them. He foretold his betrayal and crucifixion after the feast of the Passover. He promised them that he would be raised up again after his death. They asked him how they would know that he had arisen. He told them that he would go before them into Galilee and there they would see the truth.

Marcus, again, asked Jesus to spend the Passover under his protection. Again, Jesus declined the invitation saying, "My disciples have arranged the Passover meal with a good man in the city. I must honor our good host for the work that he and his family have done in the preparation of our Passover meal."

Marcus had a bad feeling about the coming night. He took Peter aside to talk with him. "I am concerned about our Lord's safety here in Jerusalem. He has made enemies of the high priest. I have seen how Caiaphas treats his enemies."

Peter asked, "Would the high priest violate the Sabbath?"

Marcus nodded, "To rid himself of a threat to his authority, it is possible that even the high priest of your faith would send his followers to do harm to Jesus."

Marcus took Peter by the shoulders and looking directly at him, said, "I know that you and the others are men of peace. You have accepted the master's teachings and are willing to turn the other cheek to those who would strike you. But now, you must be vigilant. If threatened you must remove yourself from the threat or you must remove the threat. If you do not do this, you may all die."

Peter looked from Marcus to the other disciples gathered around Jesus. He knew that most of the others were not given to fighting even if they were so inclined. "In my day, I might have offered a fist instead of a cheek. But, I have come too far with my Lord to do that now. If it is my fate to perish beside my Lord, I will gladly do so."

Marcus stood away from Peter. He admired Peter's devotion to Jesus. Jesus had told Marcus that Peter was like a rock when it came to his steadfast adherence to the teachings of God. For the first time, Marcus understood exactly what Jesus had meant when he had said this to him.

Marcus also looked at the other disciples. Turning back to Peter he said, "I promised his mother that I would stay by his side. This I will do."

Chapter 52. "Passover"

That night, Jesus went to the house of his Passover meal host with his thirteen disciples. He said to Marcus, "You are welcome to celebrate the feast of Passover with us."

Marcus had already determined that he would keep a watchful eye for any signs of trouble. "This is your feast. It is a time for you to spend with your chosen twelve. John has told me that you will be celebrating the liberation of the Jews from Egyptian bondage. With such a celebration it may be best if I rest awhile here at the gate."

Jesus smiled. "What will happen, will happen. It will not matter if you are here or inside."

Marcus was surprised that Jesus knew what his real intention was. "I prefer to see it coming than to be surprised."

Jesus placed an arm around Marcus. "The Scriptures will be fulfilled. There is nothing that you can do to change that. You and I have our different callings. The next few days will be hard for both of us. Remember, all that happens is as my Father wills it. As the Father wills it so too does the son. It is our will that you survive. It is our will that you prepare the gospel of my time with you. That is your purpose."

Jesus turned and left Marcus at the gate. He and his twelve disciples went into the home of their host to celebrate the feast of Passover.

A short time later, a woman by the name of Miriam came out of the house carrying a small plate of food and a cup filled with wine. "Sir, I have brought out for you some food from our Seder."

Placing the plate and cup of wine down on the low wall that surrounded the house, she went on, "There is unleavened bread, roasted lamb, herbs and wine."

She removed a towel that she had carried over her arm and offered it to him. As he took it from her she said, "One end of the towel is wet, the other end is dry. Our custom for the Seder is to wash our hands before we eat."

This was a new experience for Marcus. He knew that Passover was one of three major holidays for the Jews. He wanted to learn more. "May I ask your name?"

The woman blushed as she answered. "Miriam."

"Miriam, I do not know the custom of this celebration. Would you explain it to me?"

Miriam looked at Marcus. She thought that for a Roman he did not seem to be like others that she had seen. He had a kinder face and she thought, 'He is a friend of the Master.'

She decided to give to him that which he wanted to know.

"Passover celebrates the birth of the Jewish nation. Before that time, we were held as slaves in Egypt. The Pharaoh was our Master. Moses rose up from among us to receive the word of God. He carried God's commandment to Pharaoh telling Pharaoh to let our people go. But, the Pharaoh would not listen and so God brought ten plagues on the Egyptians. The last of the plagues was death to the first born of every house.

Moses told his people to sacrifice a young lamb to God and place the lamb's blood on their doorways that the plague would pass their households by. Our people were spared but not the Egyptians. They suffered great loss as did the Pharaoh. It was then that we were allowed to leave Egypt. Due to the haste of our people to leave behind the bondage that they had suffered under, they ate unleavened bread and herbs that they found along the way.

Tonight, we celebrate the Exodus by eating the young sacrificial lamb, the unleavened bread, and the herbs just as did our forefathers in their time of deliverance."

She realized that Marcus never took his eyes from her as she told him the history of her people. He was truly interested.

"Thank you Miriam. I have long been a student of the history of nations. Your history and tradition is well worth knowing."

She offered a quick smile, nodded and went back inside the house.

Marcus had finished his meal and was watching two older men walking down the street toward a nearby house when John came out to join him. John was usually very animated and generally a happy person. But, this night he did not show any signs of his usual personality.

"What is wrong John?" Marcus was immediately concerned.

"Our Lord. He has said that one of us who shared the Seder meal with him tonight will betray him."

Marcus straightened up. His senses immediately sharpened and his hand brushed by the sword at his side. "Did he say who it was that would betray him?"

John seemed beside himself. "No. Only that it would be one of us."

"Did he say anything else?" Marcus was searching for clues as to who the betrayer might be.

"Only that the one who would betray him would better not to have been born than to suffer the wrath that would befall him."

"Anything else?"

John looked at Marcus as if seeing him now for the first time. "My Lord said that he shall go as has been written in the Scriptures. He then directed us to henceforth remember him. He took the unleavened bread and broke it into twelve pieces giving a piece to each one of us. He held his piece up and said, 'Take and eat this. This is my body.'

Then he took up his cup, gave thanks to the Lord, and after first drinking from the cup, he passed it to each one of us saying, 'This is my blood of the new testament, which is shed for many for the remission of sins, drink this in remembrance of me.'" John shuddered at the thought of what he had witnessed.

Tears began to run down John's cheeks as he went on. "My Lord then said that after tonight he would not taste the fruit of the vine again until he would drink it in the kingdom of his Father."

At that moment, the door to the house opened and Jesus stepped out into the night air followed by the rest of his disciples.

As he came to John and Marcus, he said to them, "Let us walk back to the Mount of Olives. I have need of prayer.

When they arrived at the Mount of Olives, Jesus again spoke. "This night, you shall abandon me for it has been written that when the shepherd shall be smitten, the sheep of his flock shall be scattered."

Peter immediately stood and said, "Though others may abandon you, I will never leave you Lord."

Jesus turned to face Peter. "Peter, before the cock crows at daybreak, you shall deny me three times."

Peter objected saying, "I will never deny you even if it means my death."

The other disciples likewise stood and proclaimed their loyalty unto death to their Lord.

Chapter 53. "Gethsemane"

Jesus and his disciples then went into the garden of Gethsemane at the foot of the Mount of Olives. There, Jesus asked his disciples to wait while he, Peter, John and James went further into the orchard to offer up prayers to God.

Marcus noticed that Jesus seemed more distracted than he had ever seen him. There was an edge in his voice and in his words now. Jesus, turned to Marcus and said, "Are you to stay with us awhile longer."

Marcus had always been a person who understood the language of the body as well as of the mind. He answered, "This night, I will be at your side."

Jesus bowed his head in acknowledgement and seemed slightly more at ease knowing that Marcus would be there.

Once they were away from the others, Jesus said to Peter, John and James, "My soul is very troubled this night, even to the point of feeling that my death is near. Please, stay here and keep watch while I pray."

John answered, "We will be here. Comfort yourself knowing that we will keep the watch."

Jesus touched John lightly with his hand and then walked a short distance from them. He knelt down and stretched out on the soft undergrowth in the garden. It was if he hugged the earth and almost wished that he could become a part of it at that very moment. After a few minutes, Jesus raised his head and looking through the branches of an olive tree at the sky above said, "Father, if it is possible, let this cup pass from me that I not have to taste death." In the silence of the night, he bowed his head for a moment and then looking again toward the heavens, he said, "Not as I will but as thou will."

After meditating on his fate, Jesus returned to find that all three of his disciples had fallen asleep. He roused Peter and said to him, "Could you not even keep watch over me for one hour? You must pray that you not enter into temptation when I am no longer with you, for the spirit is indeed willing but the flesh is weak."

Peter was not fully awake. Jesus returned to his place of prayer.

Marcus observed Jesus' movements from a distance but could not hear his words. Most of the others were sleeping or near sleep when Judas Iscariot approached him. "Marcus, the hour is late. I am going to tell the innkeeper that we may yet come for the night. I shall return."

Marcus nodded. He had learned from the others that Judas was the one that handled all of the financial affairs of the disciples and arranged for food and lodging as they went about their travels. After Judas had disappeared down the street leading away from Gethsemane, he turned back toward Jesus. It looked as if the three who had gone with him were themselves asleep and that Jesus was kneeling in prayer.

Marcus thought to himself, 'The hour is late and all but the Master sleep. How strange that this man who moves so many should be watched over by so few. By only me.'

Jesus rose and looking skyward said, "Oh my Father, if this cup may not pass away from me, except that I drink from it, let thy will be done."

Walking back to where Peter, John and James were sleeping, he woke them and said, "You have had your sleep. You are rested. But, behold the hour has come. The son of man has been betrayed into the hands of sinners. Rise, let us go back to the others. He who has betrayed me will soon be here."

The three immediately jumped to their feet. In each of them there was fear at what Jesus had said. They looked back at the gate but only saw Marcus.

James said, "Look Lord, Marcus stands watch."

As they reached the other disciples, they all heard the sound of many footsteps approaching. Marcus stepped inside the garden to stand beside Jesus.

Judas rushed ahead of men bearing swords and lances. He ran through the gate and up to the man that he had followed for almost three years. The man who he had seen do wondrous things. The man who made the blind to see, the lame to walk, and the sick to heal.

Judas kissed Jesus on the cheek and said, "Help Master."

Jesus looked at Judas with great sadness. "Oh you of little faith, what have you done?"

The guards from the Temple surrounded Jesus and the disciples. One of the guards advanced on Jesus waiving his sword and pointing it at Jesus. At that moment, Marcus threw off his cloak and stepped between Jesus and the advancing guard. With the quickness of a leopard, Marcus drew out his sword and in the same motion struck the Temple guard on the left side of his head, cutting off his ear. The movement had been so quick and so unexpected that for a moment all froze where they were standing. The Temple guard collapsed to the ground felled by the blow to his head.

Marcus quickly picked up the fallen guard's sword and holding out both swords, one in each hand, he was prepared for what was to come.

"And behold, one of them which were with Jesus stretched out his hand, and drew his sword, and struck a servant of the high priest's, and smote off his ear. Then said Jesus unto him, Put up again thy sword into his place: for all they that take up the sword shall perish with the sword." Matthew 26:51-52.

Jesus stepped out from behind Marcus. As all present watched and listened, Jesus looked directly at Marcus and said, "Put up your swords. All those that take up the sword shall perish with the sword. That is not what I have intended for you.

Do you not know that if I prayed to my Father for help, he would send twelve legions of angels to protect me? But then how would the Scriptures be fulfilled? Thank you Marcus. There is nothing more for you to do here. Now, stand back."

Jesus then turned to those who had come for him and said, "You come to seize me with swords and lances as though I was a thief. Only yesterday I taught you in the temple as would a Rabbi and there you did not seize me. What has changed between then and now?'

There was no answer from those that were there to arrest him and take him back to Caiaphas. A detachment of Roman guards appeared at the gate.

Jesus looked at all of them. Sensing that his time had come and that there was a need to avoid further confrontation between these sinners and his disciples, he said, "The Scriptures must be fulfilled. You have no quarrel with these, my followers. Do with me as you will but let my disciples go."

The Temple guards immediately took hold of Jesus and began to lead him away. As they did so, all of the disciples except for Marcus and Peter fled from the garden. Some of the Temple guards who were now caring for their wounded comrade began looking toward Marcus. One said, "What about the one with the sword?"

There was hesitancy at the gate by the other guards. One of those who held Jesus said, "He looks to be a Roman."

Jesus interrupted, "You have come for me not him."

The Roman detachment at the gate stepped inside. Their commander gave an order to the Temple guards. "You were ordered by Caiaphas to arrest the man called Jesus." Looking at the wounded guard and surmising what had happened, the commander continued, "If I find that you have exceeded your authority or worse have attacked a citizen of Rome, you will pay with your lives rather than a mere ear. Now, do as Caiaphas instructed you to do."

The threat was clear. The Temple guards moved off with Jesus.

The commander then approached Marcus. "I have seen you at the fortress with Lucius." Looking back at the last of the Temple guards to leave the garden, the commander smiled and went on, "I guess they have not heard of the Roman citizen that dispatched ten zealots with but one sword. Caiaphas' men were fortunate that they were not all killed by you."

Marcus heard the commander but thought of what Jesus had just said to him. 'Those that take the sword shall perish with the sword.' He said to the commander, "You said that they are taking Jesus to Caiaphas. For what purpose?"

"To answer charges brought against him by the priests and elders of the Temple. We were alerted by one of the priests that the guards had been dispatched to arrest this Jesus. Apparently, one of this man's followers received thirty pieces of silver to deliver the prophet to Caiaphas at a place and time when there would be few to protect him. Our centurion, your friend Lucius, thought that you might be with him and sent us to insure that Rome's interests in the matter would be protected." Again the commander smiled, concluding, "Or maybe it was to protect the interests of the Temple guards." The others in his detachment laughed at this as well.

Marcus turned to Peter who had been standing back a few feet. "I am going to the fortress with these soldiers to find out what is happening."

Peter nodded but said nothing. As Marcus left with the Roman detachment, Peter followed at a distance.

Chapter 54. "Rush to Judgment"

Marcus and the detachment of Roman legionnaires went immediately to the fortress. Lucius was waiting at the gate when they arrived.

Marcus saw his friend and said to him as he passed through the gate, "Up late Centurion?"

"No later than the citizens of Rome! How many of the Temple guards are in need of a doctor?"

Marcus just shook his head in answer but the commander of the detachment answered for him. "He took off the ear of one then took his sword. Armed with both swords, your friend was ready to take on the twenty or thirty Temple guards by himself."

Lucius smiled. "That's the disciple I love."

Marcus looked back and saw a Roman soldier at the gate detaining Peter. He turned to Lucius for assistance. "Lucius. The man at the gate is called Peter. He is the chief disciple of Jesus. Can you provide him access to the Temple?"

Lucius looked at Peter and called to the soldier detaining him. "Is he armed?"

The soldier performed a quick search and answered, "No Centurion. No weapons."

Lucius then said, "Let him come forward."

Peter approached cautiously.

Lucius said to him, "I can get you into the Temple's courtyard but make no attempt to enter the Temple. If you are recognized, they may kill you." Lucius instructed his men to take Peter to the gate that led directly from the fortress to the Temple and see that he was passed through.

Marcus then asked, "Is there any way that I can gain access to the Temple?"

Lucius shook his head and answered no. "It would be a fool's errand for you to go to the Temple. Surely, the Temple guards would recognize you as the one who tried to prevent the arrest."

Lucius waived his men forward with Peter in the direction of the Temple access gate. He then took Marcus to his own quarters. "I want you to stay here. I will go to the Temple and will be back with the information you seek as soon as I am able. Get some rest. I will have my servants see to any needs that you may have."

Marcus had to agree with Lucius regarding his position now. He would indeed be recognized and most likely killed if he entered the Temple. He took Lucius' arm and said, "Thank you for your help, both at Gethsemane and here."

Lucius smiled at his friend. "We are brothers at arms." With that, Lucius left Marcus and went with his second in command to the Temple.

Within the walls of the Temple, there were several small campfires with Temple guards gathered around each. It was a strange sight to Lucius. He did not recall ever seeing this many guardsmen in the courtyard in the early morning hours.

Lucius saw Peter sitting with some guards and some elders by one of the fires. As he passed, he heard a female servant of the high priests ask Peter, 'Are you not one of the followers of Jesus of Nazareth?' Peter answered, "I know him not nor do I understand what you are asking."

As Lucius went up the steps leading to the Temple, Peter stepped away from the fire and walked over to a place in the corner of the steps which was nearer to the Temple.

The woman servant followed him and as two Temple guards walked by her she said to them, "This is one of the disciples of Jesus of Nazareth."

The guards looked at Peter and laughed. "We have this courtyard completely sealed off. It would not be possible for one of that rabble to get within these walls." They walked over to Peter with the servant woman. "She contends that you are a follower of Nazarene. What say you to that?"

Peter again felt the fear that he had experienced in the garden at Gethsemane. "I do not even know the man."

Another guard had now joined the group to listen to what was being said. He observed, "I do not recognize you. You are not an elder."

Peter explained that he was a vendor who had been forced to leave the Temple by the crowds. He had come back to claim his goods that were left behind. He had not yet met with the priests to process his claim.

"What is your name vendor?" They asked.

"I am Simon."

"By your dress and by your speech, I would judge you to be a Galilean. Surely you are one of the Nazarene's followers."

Peter began to swear and curse to prove that he was not a follower for no follower of Jesus would ever act that way. For a third time, he denied being a follower of Jesus. As he did so he heard the crowing of a cock with the dawning of a new day.

Peter then went to the gate of the Temple wall and walked out of the courtyard. Once outside the wall, he leaned against it and began to cry. He remembered the words of his Master, "Before the cock crows, you will deny me three times."

Caiaphas had called together the chief priests, the elders, and the scribes. Witnesses were called to accuse Jesus of blasphemy and seditious acts. One said that he threatened the very destruction of the Temple within which he was now being brought to trial. But, their testimony so conflicted one with another that the council was reluctant to act.

Jesus had remained silent, staring at the floor, during all of the testimony brought against him by his false accusers. Caiaphas became enraged at the inaction and finally stood up and said to Jesus, "Have you nothing to say? Do you not have any defense to offer?"

Jesus remained silent.

Caiaphas stepped down from the podium where he had been presiding and walked over to where Jesus stood. "I asked you if you have a defense against the accusations that have been made against you."

Jesus again remained silent.

In frustration, Caiaphas demanded of Jesus, "Are you the Christ, the Son of the Blessed One, our God?"

Jesus looked up at Caiaphas and said, "You have said it. I am. You shall see the son of man sitting on the right hand of power and coming in the clouds of heaven"

Caiaphas reached out and ripped the clothing off of Jesus shoulders. He turned to the elders who had sat in disbelief at what they had seen. "We have no need of further proof. By his own words, in God's Temple, he has blasphemed. What is your verdict?"

They all condemned Jesus to death, some spitting on him and others striking him with their hands as they passed by him.

Caiaphas then ordered that Jesus be bound and tied and taken to the Roman Governor, Pontius Pilate so that the death penalty could be carried out as was the custom.

Lucius witnessed all of this. Although a hardened soldier, he felt sympathy for this man they called Jesus. Nothing that had been said justified the sentence of death that the Jews had pronounced for this man.

Lucius returned to his quarters and to Marcus. Marcus had been waiting impatiently for his friend's return.

"What is happening?"

"Nothing good my friend. The council has found Jesus guilty of blasphemy and sentenced him to death."

It was not that Marcus was surprised by what he heard because he had known that the risk was real. It was hearing the actual pronouncement, 'guilty and sentenced to death' that struck him to his very core. He half gasped, "This can not be."

Lucius sat down on his bed. "I saw the entire proceeding. There was no real evidence against the man. They had a steady stream of false accusations, most of which contradicted one another."

Marcus looked at Lucius. "How then was he convicted?"

Lucius stood up saying, "Caiaphas asked Jesus if he was the son of God. And, Jesus said that he was. There was a rush to judgment."

"What will they do?"

Lucius walked to the doorway of his quarters. "Only Rome can carry out a sentence of death. Caiaphas has sent Jesus to the Governor with the Council's recommendation of the death penalty."

Marcus then crossed the room to the doorway. "We must go to the Governor and plead his case."

Lucius placed a hand on Marcus' chest. "We will go but you must say nothing. I will plead his case. Only I, as a witness to the Council's deliberation, have standing to hold forth before the Governor."

Lucius looked directly into Marcus' eyes. "You must agree to this or you may not accompany me to the Governor."

Marcus understood and agreed.

Chapter 55. "Pilate"

When they arrived at the Governor's Palace, Pilate immediately received Lucius and Marcus.

"Welcome Lucius." Pilate said as he looked over at Marcus. "This must be your friend that I have heard so much about." Pilate held out his hand.

As Marcus took the Governor's extend arm, Lucius introduced Marcus.

"This is my boyhood friend from my days in the Amphitheater in Rome. He is the son of our former centurion, Marcus Aurelius."

Pilate nodded his approval. "Your father was a long time friend. It pleases me to have his son here in Jerusalem. You are always welcome at the Governor's Palace."

Marcus thanked Pilate.

Lucius then spoke. "Governor, we are here concerning a prisoner who has been sent to you by Caiaphas and the Sanhedrin."

Pilate turned and walked over to his desk. "Yes. The prophet called Jesus of Nazareth. I have heard much about this man." He turned to face his guests. "They say he can turn water to wine. He would be a valuable guest." He then turned and walked to the window to look out at the grounds below. "I am told he holds himself out as a prophet, a Messiah for the Jews. In fact some, I have heard that some even call him the King of the Jews."

Lucius looked from Marcus to Pilate, "Governor, if I may speak?"

Pilate looked at Lucius. "Please do Centurion."

Lucius took a deep breath. "I witnessed the proceedings in the early morning of this day. Witness after witness came forward with accusations that gave evidence of nothing. In many instances what was said by one witness contradicted what had been said by others. I saw no evidence of any Roman or Jewish law that had been broken by this man. He is a prophet and teaches only lessons that these Jews themselves should accept."

Pilate raised his hand. "Caiaphas has said that this man professed to be the Son of their God. Is that true."

Lucius acknowledged this. "Yes, he did say it was so. But I know of no Roman law that makes this a crime punishable by death."

Pilate considered this for a moment. He then turned to Marcus. "Your father provided good counsel when he was alive. He told me of you once saying that you were first and foremost a student and a scholar. Is religion one of your avenues of study?"

Marcus paused and then responded, "I have studied several religions."

Pilate then asked, "Do you believe it possible that this man is the son of a God?"

Marcus studied Pilate to determine if this was asked for a reason other than a truthful response. He determined that it was a direct question that deserved a direct response. "In Rome there are many that believe that Caesar is descended from the Gods. I have found that in Judea and even here in Jerusalem, there are many that believe that Jesus is descended from God."

Pilate looked from Marcus to Lucius. He hesitated a moment in thought, smiled, and said, "Come with me. Let us examine this King of the Jews."

As Pilate led them down the hall to the Great Room of the Palace, he said to Marcus, "I too have heard that Caesar is descended from the Gods." He then laughed aloud.

Outside the Governor's palace a crowd was gathering having heard that Jesus had been arrested. Several of the disciples mixed in with the crowd but stayed well clear of any Temple guards or Roman soldiers that were also among those who had gathered.

Pilate was greeted by Caiaphas and several high priests and scribes as he entered the Great Room. Caiaphas was not pleased to see Marcus with Pilate and asked for a word with the Governor.

"Governor, do you know that the man with you interfered with the arrest of the prisoner that I have brought before you?"

Pilate answered truthfully. "I did not know this. Tell me Caiaphas, do you know that this man is the son of former centurion, Marcus Aurelius, commander of the 10th Legion and an advisor of the Governor?"

Caiaphas looked at Marcus and Lucius who were both looking directly at him. He answered Pilate. "I did not know this. The resemblance is not apparent."

Caiaphas stood up less conspiratorial now and said, "My nephew was one of those who apprehended the prisoner early this morning. Marcus Aurelius' son cut off his ear with a sword."

Pilate looked surprised. "How is your nephew?"

Caiaphas almost hissed. "He will survive but will never be as he was."

Pilate turned and walked up a flight of steps leading to his seat. Caiaphas followed in silence. Lucius and Marcus were shown to one side by one of Pilate's guards. The room was filled to capacity with legionnaires, priests, elders, scribes and local officials.

Once seated, Pilate ordered, "Bring in the prisoner."

Jesus was brought before Pilate bound with his hands behind his back. Marcus bridled at the sight of Jesus. It was obvious that he had been beaten. His clothes were ripped and his body covered with bruises.

Marcus started to push forward but Lucius held him back. "Easy my friend."

Pilate looked at Jesus for several minutes before saying anything. In all that time, Jesus simply looked down at the floor.

Finally Pilate said to Jesus, "Tell me, are you the King of the Jews?"

Jesus slowly looked up and answered Pilate, saying, "You have said that I am."

Pilate turned to Caiaphas and asked, "What do you say, High Priest? Is this your King?"

Caiaphas in anger shouted, "He says that he is King of the Jews. This same day he professed to be the Son of our God. He has said that he wishes to create a new kingdom here on earth and to throw off Roman rule. He has threatened to tear the great Temple of Jerusalem down so that not one stone will stand upon another."

Caiaphas then called upon his priests to come forward with their charges which they did.

Throughout the proceeding, Pilate was amazed as he watched Jesus listen to all that he was being accused of and yet he said nothing in his own defense.

When all of Jesus' accusers had finished bringing forth their charges, Pilate stood and walked down the steps. He approached Jesus accompanied by two of his guards. He stopped before Jesus and said, "You have heard many charges brought against you by these many priests and scribes. Yet, you have said nothing in your defense. I offer you, now, the opportunity to answer all that has been said against you."

Jesus did not reply. He stared down at the floor.

Pilate looked back at Caiaphas then said to all present.

'Your Chief Priest has brought this man to me under sentence of death by your Council. I must have some time to deliberate on what has been presented to me. I ask that you all leave me and adjourn to the courtyard. I will be with you shortly."

Pilate had Jesus taken to a holding room.

When all had gone, Pilate's wife came to him and said, "I have had many bad dreams this night while I was sleeping. This man Jesus, he is an innocent man. I beg you to have nothing to do with passing judgment on this just man."

Pilate promised his wife that he would do what was just and proper. He told her to leave him to his deliberations.

The courtyard of the Governor's Palace was now filled with people from all parts of Jerusalem. They had come to see what would happen to the prophet. While they waited for Pilate's decision the priests and elders mixed with the crowd and encouraged them to reject Jesus saying that he sinned against God and man.

After much consideration of the options he had available to him, Pilate finally had Jesus brought before the crowd.

He said to all present, "It is the feast of the Passover. I will release one prisoner from prison and commute his sentence in honor of your holy day."

Several zealots who had mixed in with the crowd began shouting, "Release Barabbas."

Marcus and Lucius were watching from another window in the Governor's Palace. Marcus turned to Lucius and asked, "Who is this Barabbas?"

"A zealot. A stabber who murders the innocent in the name of his religion. He has been sentenced to death also."

Meanwhile, Pilate again said to the crowd, "If it is your will that I release the King of the Jews, I will do this."

The priests and the scribes mixing with the crowd picked up the cry of the zealots and again shouted, "Release Barabbas."

Looking at Jesus and then at the crowd, Pilate asked the multitudes, "What will you have me do to this man whom you called the King of the Jews?"

Again the priests and scribes stirred the crowd to answer, "Crucify him."

Pilate could not understand why the crowd responded this way. He held his hands up and quieted them. Then he said, "I can find no fault with this man"

Again the cry went up to crucify Jesus.

Pilate had one of his servants bring him a bowl filled with water. He again raised his hands and dipped them in the water saying, "I am innocent of the blood of this just man."

Then someone in the crowd shouted, "If not Pilate, then let his blood be on us and our children." Again the crowd shouted, "Release Barabbas."

He ordered his soldiers to release Barabbas as he had promised the people and to carry out the sentence of death of Jesus.

Chapter 56. "Golgotha, the place of the skull"

Marcus walked away from the window with many conflicting thoughts. He said to Lucius, "How could those people ask for the pardon of a criminal instead of the one who has offered them peace and salvation? I have seen how he cares for them and yet when he needed them most, they turned on him."

Lucius tried to comfort his friend. "That is what sets us apart from the rest of the world. We, Romans, are loyal to Rome and to Caesar. I am sorry that these Jews have made the choice that they have. The Governor was ready to pardon Jesus if they had but asked that it be so."

Marcus, in response to Lucius, overlooked the fact that Rome itself had had its share of in-fighting for the throne. He was concerned with what was happening here and now. He turned to his friend and asked, "Can not Pilate pardon Jesus of his own accord?"

Lucius answered. "He has the authority to do as he will. But he also has his orders from Rome. Those orders are that he maintains peace on the frontier and that he work with King Herod Antipas to that end. Caiaphas is the chief priest of King Herod. You have seen him. You know that he is a politician as well as a priest. He wields great power among the Jews.

Looking away from his friend Lucius went on, "No, the Governor will not pardon Jesus now that the rabble as well as the priests have called for his death."

Marcus slumped down in a chair. With his head bowed, he said, "Then it is a sad day for the Jews and a sad day for Rome."

Jesus was taken by the soldiers of Pilate to a common hall. One soldier step forward saying, "Here is what I think of the King of the Jews." He raised a wooden staff and struck Jesus across the head.

Jesus fell to his knees.

Another soldier took a whip to him, shredding the back of what remained of his clothing. Then a group of soldiers approached Jesus with a scarlet robe and threw it over his shoulders. They bowed and offered mocked praise of him as the King of the Jews. Then they forced him into a chair, placing crown of thorns on his head. One brought forth a reed and stuck it in Jesus' right hand.

As Jesus sat there, the soldiers spit on him and mocked him saying, "Hail, King of the Jews."

At that moment, their commander entered the common hall and ordered them to stop the mockery. "That will be enough. Bring the prisoner out. His cross is waiting."

The soldiers cheered. One pulled the scarlet robe off his shoulders and threw the blood stained garment behind the chair. Two others lifted Jesus out of the chair and threw him forward. Jesus stumbled, still weak from the whipping. The soldiers kicked him and prodded him with wooden staffs to force him to his feet.

Outside, they had prepared a heavy wooden cross for him to carry to the place of his crucifixion. They forced him to pick the cross up and put it over his back. Again they prodded him with wooden staffs and led him through the streets to Calvary and Golgotha, the mount of skulls.

Those that had demanded that he be crucified had waited in the courtyard of the governor's palace to follow him to Calvary. They wanted to watch their verdict carried out. Every so often, the crowd would shout for the soldiers to bring to them, Jesus.

As Marcus and Lucius were talking, a great cheer went up from the courtyard. Both Lucius and Marcus returned to the window.

Below, they saw soldiers moving the crowd aside, forming a corridor through which Jesus was now being led.

Marcus gasped at the sight of his friend and the man that he now believed was holy, the son of God. "What have they done to him?"

Lucius knew what was to come. He had seen many crucifixions and although he accepted them as punishment for criminals, he was not comfortable with the method. "Marcus, I think it would be better for you if you not witness this man's death."

Marcus turned away from the window. He could not bear watching Jesus struggle with the cross that had been placed on his back. He was sick at the sight of Jesus blood stained head and body. His emotions were mixed with anger. He had a desire to take to his sword to save the man to whose mother he had made a promise.

Jesus had commanded him to stand down but surely Jesus did not foresee all this. Finally, he said to Lucius, "I must be there for him."

Lucius was not sure what Marcus meant. "To fight?"

"I would if I could. But Jesus commanded me to do otherwise. He teaches that those who take up the sword shall perish by the sword. He has commissioned me to be his historian so that the work that he has done while he has lived will not be buried with him when he dies. It was his last request of me."

Marcus reached down and removed his sword from his belt. Handing it to Lucius, he said, "It would be best if you kept this. The temptation for me to make use of it this day, may be more than I can manage."

Lucius took the sword. "These are bad times and this is not Rome."

"I know but I have agreed to follow the path that he has shown me." Marcus again looked out the window. Jesus was no longer in sight having passed through the gate and now going along the road to Calvary.

Marcus turned back to Lucius. "I must go."

Lucius placed Marcus' sword in his belt opposite his own sword. "I will go with you. You may have need of both me and your sword."

The two men went out of the palace and onto the streets of Jerusalem.

To their surprise, the crowds had swelled to untold numbers to watch the procession as the soldiers led Jesus to the place where his crucifixion was to occur. Lucius ordered people out of the way as he and Marcus rushed onward.

They heard a shout go up ahead of them and pushing through the remainder of the crowd in front of them, they saw that Jesus had fallen under the weight of the cross. Soldiers grabbed a large man in the crowd and forced him to pick up the cross and follow as they again prodded Jesus with their staffs to move onward.

In the next section of the road, Jesus again fell to the ground. A woman removed her scarf from her head, poured water on it, and wiped his face. Jesus looked at her with thanks. Again, the soldiers dragged him to his feet and pushed him onward.

Marcus looked at the woman as he passed by her. He recognized her as one of those who had been with Jesus in Galilee. Her tear filled eyes caught his and for a moment they held but then he moved on.

Marcus and Lucius were now at the back of the soldiers holding back the onlookers. No longer were these people calling for Jesus to be crucified. Many were shouting for him to save himself. They were calling for him to bring the wrath of God down on those who were his captors. Fearing an uprising from the masses that were gathering, the commander of the detailed soldiers ordered that their weapons be drawn. This had the desired effect and the crowds became less restive.

The man who had carried Jesus cross now faltered under its weight. The soldiers ordered Jesus to again take up his cross. As he struggled to lift it, a boy broke through the ring of soldiers and helped place it up on his back. Jesus looked at the boy and said "Jacob."

The boy looked at Jesus saying, "My Lord. My Savior."

A soldier grabbed the boy and yanked him back outside the perimeter of soldiers. Though handled roughly and shoved by a much larger man, the boy stayed on his feet.

It was then that Marcus recognized the boy. He took Lucius by the arm and led him to where the boy was now standing. The boy saw the Roman soldier coming toward him and then saw that the soldier was being led by the friend of Jesus.

Marcus said to the boy, "Do you remember me?"

"Yes." The boy nodded. "You were on the hillside when the Master healed me."

Marcus turned to Lucius. "You once said that if I brought the boy who was lame to you and showed you that he could walk, then you would accept that Jesus was the Son of God."

Lucius looked at the boy as Marcus introduced them. "Lucius this is Jacob, the boy that Jesus made to walk."

A great cry went up from the mount where Jesus had now been taken. Marcus, Lucius and Jacob all moved quickly to get to Golgotha.

As they came out of the city to the mount, Marcus saw two men hanging on crosses with their arms outstretched and tied with ropes. Their limp bodies had little life left in them.

Beneath the two, Jesus was being nailed to his cross. The sound of the hammer driving the nails into flesh and bone made Marcus weak. Jacob fell down and cried.

Soldiers were holding Jesus down as they crucified him. People watching were screaming out in agony drowning out any screams that may have come from the victim himself.

Then with great effort, the man and the cross were hoisted up and placed between the other two who had suffered his fate. A sign had been placed above Jesus' head that read, ' King of the Jews.'

Some still mocked him. A few priests who were there to witness the carrying out of the verdict called up to Jesus, saying, "You who sought to destroy the Temple, if you are the son of God, save yourself. Come down from the cross." They turned to each other and mockingly observed, "He who sought to save others can not even save himself."

The long watch then began. Many in the crowd had seen enough and departed from Golgotha. The soldiers relaxed now and put their weapons away. They gambled for the clothes that those crucified were wearing.

The sky began to darken and still more of those who watched went away. Lucius sensing that Marcus wished to move closer said to Marcus, "I think that it is safe for us to move closer, if that is your desire."

Marcus nodded. As they walked toward the soldiers, the commander looked up. Recognizing Lucius as the Centurion at the fortress, he stood.

Lucius said to the soldiers, "My friend would like a closer look at those that have been crucified."

One of the soldiers stood up and said, "He can accompany me. It is time to give them drink." He took a sponge, stuck it on a reed, and dipped it in vinegar. He went to the first of the three hanging on a cross and wiped his mouth. The thief cursed but there was little life left in him. Then he went to Jesus. As he wiped the sponge filled with vinegar across Jesus' parched lips, Jesus opened his eyes. He said nothing but Marcus thought that his eyes had caught Marcus and seemed to be less strained.

When the third man on the cross was given vinegar, he snapped his head to the side rejecting it. Then seeing Jesus, the man called to Jesus, "Lord, if you cannot save us, please remember me when you come to your kingdom." Then he looked down at the soldier and in a voice struggling for air, said, "We have been justly punished for the bad deeds that we have done. But, he has done nothing wrong."

Jesus hearing this looked at the man who was crucified with him and said, "Your faith has willed it, when our hour has come you shall be with me in heaven."

Now, though it was still mid-afternoon, the sky was as black as a starless night. The only light that shown was from the campfires which the soldiers had built. Marcus and Lucius sat with the relief guard that had been sent from the fortress. Though many had left, those who were true to Jesus were scattered throughout the hillside. Woman were wailing and men including several of the disciples wept though they remained a far distance from the place of the skull.

From a distance, a man approached the soldiers posted at the foot of Golgotha with three women. Marcus had his eyes fixed on the cross and did not see their approach.

The man said to the guards, "This is the mother of Jesus, her sister and a friend. They would like to go to her son."

The guards looked at Mary and understood in their hearts that she rightfully should go to him. Without a word, they stepped aside and let the small group go to the cross.

Marcus now saw them as they drew near. He recognized the disciple John, Mary the mother of Jesus, Mary's sister who was also called Mary wife of Cleophas, and the woman who he had seen wipe the face of Jesus as he bore his cross to this place.

They knelt down before the cross and as they prayed, Jesus opened his eyes and looked down at them. He spoke to his mother. "Mother, look up at thy son." She looked up at him with tears filling her eyes. He went on, "Know that I love you deeply. Soon, I will be joining my Father who is in heaven."

Then looking at John, Jesus said to him, "Look to my mother and care for her as you would your own."

Again looking into his mother's eyes, he smiled and closed his eyes to rest. John took Mary, the mother of Jesus, in his arms and the group moved away.

In the eighth hour, the two criminals crucified with Jesus died. Jesus had not moved nor opened his eyes for some time. Believing that he too had perished, one of the soldiers took a lance and pierced Jesus' side to determine if he was gone. Jesus' head went up in agony and he cried out.

Lightening struck out violently across the sky. A great wind blew across the earth and the ground quaked. Rocks tumbled as the ground beneath Golgotha shook and in the distance the earth parted and the Temple's wall split in half.

The soldiers were now on their feet, not knowing what to do. They had never seen such a tempest. Their fires went out and the only light came from the constant flashing of lightening in the darkened skies.

Marcus went to the foot of the cross bearing Jesus. Lucius followed. No one stopped the Centurion and his friend.

Jesus looked up at the heavens and cried out, "My God, my God, why have you forsaken me?" He hesitated for a moment staring blankly at the sky then he looked down at those below. His eyes rested for a moment on Marcus. Marcus saw the pain, the fear, a momentary loss of understanding. Then as if all pain and fear were taken from him, Jesus' face relaxed, his body gave up its rigidity, and he accepted his fate.

Jesus slowly raised his head to the heavens and with one last gasp for air, he sighed, "Thy will be done." His head slowly went down to his chest and he was gone.

Chapter 57. "Resurrection"

Marcus offered Mary, John and the others who were with them his home for as long as they needed a place to stay. Marcus' servant, Joseph, had kept watch with the others during the long day's vigil. Marcus asked that Joseph escort Mary and the others back to Marcus' home.

"Joseph, provide for their needs. I must return with Lucius to the fortress to determine what next will be done." Looking back at the three who hung motionless on their crosses, Marcus went on, "He cannot remain their like that."

Lucius, who had said very little over the course of the final hours of the vigil, looked at the crosses with Marcus. He thought of all that Marcus had told him about this man, Jesus, He thought about the lame boy, Jacob, who now walked. The skies suddenly cleared. Lucius looked about him at the destruction caused by the wind, the quakes, and the lightening. He felt a tremor run through his body and it was as though something, a great burden, was lifted from his soul.

All who were with him were shocked by what the Centurion then said. "Truly, this was the Son of God."

The soldiers felt that same tremor, that same lifting of a great burden. Each accepted what none had dared to say, this man Jesus, was in truth the Son of God.

Though she grieved for the loss of her son, Mary knew in her heart, at that moment, that her son's greatest gift, the one that he had so often talked about, had been given. The Holy Spirit was with them and their sins had been taken away.

Marcus and Lucius returned to the governor's palace. Pilate received them in his private chambers.

Pilate said, "It is done."

He appeared very discontented as he went on. "You were there?"

Lucius answered, "We were there."

"I washed my hands of this. You both saw that. His blood was not on my hands. It was those envious priests who call themselves servants of God." Pilate shook his head. "They are no servants of God. They are the murders of the Son of God."

Marcus was again surprised to hear another Roman accept this fact.

Pilate ran to the window. "Look out there. I am told that at the moment he died, all of this occurred. Who else but God could do this? The Temple's wall, it is split in half." He turned back to Lucius and Marcus. "That storm! Never have I seen such a tempest. The sun was taken from the sky." Pilate collapsed into a chair. "Just as we took the Son of God from this earth."

Pilate was drained. He had reached the point of collapse. Marcus thought it was time for him to speak.

"Governor, what is to become of the body of Jesus?"

Pilate looked up. He said, "A friend of mine, a wealthy friend, Joseph of Arimathea, came a short while ago and asked permission to remove the body from the cross and place it in a tomb. I agreed and gave him my written order."

Marcus and Lucius looked at each other. Then Lucius said to Pilate, "We will go back to Calvary to see that it is done." With that, they left Pilate knowing that he would forever blame himself for what he had done.

Joseph of Arimathea went with a friend, Nicodemus, to Golgotha and presented Pilate's orders to the Captain of the guard. They then took Jesus' body down from the cross with the help of some soldiers.

Respectfully they wrapped the body in fine white linens covering it with spices of myrrh and aloes. This was the Jewish custom for burial. Then they carried the body of Jesus, followed by his mother Mary, John and the others, to a burial place where a new sepulcher had been hewn in the stone and never before been used. They laid Jesus' body inside. Then, all knelt down to pray. When they had finished their prayers, one by one they touched his body and departed until only his mother remained.

She took his hand, saying, "My son, rest in peace. I know that you are in heaven with your Father. My love goes there with you." She wiped tears from her eyes, took one last look at her son, and departed.

Marcus and Lucius arrived at Golgotha just after Jesus had been carried away. The soldiers who were there showed them the way to the sepulcher. By the time they arrived, a great stone had been rolled in front of the opening to the tomb by Joseph of Arimathea, Nicodemus, John and Joseph, Marcus' servant.

John told them that the Jewish custom was to observe the Sabbath day which followed and that then they would return to take care of the final preparation of the body on the first day of the week. Lucius posted a guard to watch over the tomb to insure that it would not be disturbed. Marcus then left with Mary, John and the others to go to his home.

On the first day of the week, Mary Magdalene, the woman who had wiped Jesus' face, Mary, the sister of Jesus' mother, and Salome went to the tomb to prepare the body. As they approached, the earth again rumbled and an earthquake shook the ground causing the stone in front of the sepulcher to roll back from the entrance.

The posted guards had seen much in the last three days. They feared for their lives thinking that God in his anger made the earth to quake where his son had been laid. They hid themselves from sight and did not interfere with the three women as they approached the tomb.

The three walked into the sepulcher. Shocked, they saw that Jesus' body was gone. Then from the side of the sepulcher, there appeared a young man wearing a long white garment. The woman huddled together in fear.

The young man in white said to them, "Be not afraid. You are here to find Jesus of Nazareth who was crucified. As you can see, he is risen as he said he would. Go and tell his disciples that he is risen from the dead and that he goeth before them to Galilee. There they shall see him."

The woman ran from the sepulcher. On the road back to Marcus' home they met Peter and Marcus, who themselves were on the way to the sepulcher. Mary Magdalene cried out, "They have taken Jesus out of the sepulcher and we do not know where they have taken him to."

Peter began running to the sepulcher. Marcus, being younger and stronger, also ran to the sepulcher arriving at the empty tomb first. He stopped at the entrance to the sepulcher and looked inside. He saw the white linen clothes but the tomb was empty. Peter caught up to Marcus and went inside the tomb. There he saw the linen clothes and in another place the napkin that had covered Jesus' head. Marcus entered behind Peter and seeing that which Peter saw, he believed. Jesus had told him that three days after his death, he would rise and enter into his Father's kingdom. Marcus said to himself, "So might it be."

"Peter therefore went forth, and that 'other disciple' and came to the sepulcher. So they ran both together: and the other disciple did outrun Peter, and came first to the sepulcher.

Then went in also 'the other disciple', which came first to the sepulcher, and he saw, and believed." John 20:3, 4 and 8.

They left the sepulcher to return to Marcus' home. Peter turned to look back. Suddenly, he knew what he must now do. "Marcus, I thank you for your hospitality. I must now leave you to call my brothers together. My Lord would want me to bring his apostlet disciples together."

Marcus knew that Peter would be guided hence forth by the Holy Spirit for this too Jesus had told to him. Peter would be the rock upon which the new religion would be born. They shook hands and parted.

That night of the first day of the week, the disciples gathered in the upper room of another's home. They gathered behind shuddered windows and locked doors for fear of what the Jews might do to them. All were there except for Judas Iscariot, the one who had betrayed Jesus.

They ate the evening meal in silence until a knock came at the outer door. All were afraid that now their time had come but for Peter. He went to the door. "Who knocks?" He called out.

"Mary Magdalene. Please open the door and let me come in."

Peter opened the door, letting her in. He quickly looked out beyond her and seeing no one, he closed the door quickly and locked it.

"You bring news?" He asked.

The woman seemed half out of her mind as she cast a wild look about at the other disciples. Rather than answer only to Peter, she answered to all of them. "I have seen him."

John stood up to sooth her. He said gently, "Who have you seen Mary?"

"The Master. He spoke to me"

Jude was now standing as well. "You have both seen and talked with our Lord?"

Thomas added, "How is it possible?"

Mary went on. "I was weeping and He said to me, 'Woman, why do you weep? Whom are you seeking?' Without looking up I said, 'I seek Jesus of Nazareth. If you know where he is tell me and I will go to him and take him away.' Then I heard his voice for he knew me by name and called to me saying Mary. It was then that I looked up and saw him.

I started to run to him but he raised his hand and bid me to stay back. He said to me, 'Do not touch me Mary. I am not yet ascended to my Father.'

Then he told me to go to you and tell you this good news. He has risen. He said that soon he would go to his Father and your father; his God and your God. But, that before he ascends into heaven, he will come to you and appear before you."

The disciples looked at one another and did not know whether the woman was telling truth or imagining all that she had said.

Peter offered Mary Magdalene a chair and some drink which she accepted.

Bartholomew asked, "Peter, what are we to do now?"

Peter answered, "We wait. In God's time we will receive the truth."

Some slept while others talked of things that they had seen the Master do. There had been many miracles. There had been many more lessons from his teachings. They wondered aloud if they would be able to recall all that he had taught them.

In the light of the oil lamps they saw an image appear in their midst saying 'Peace be with you.' And suddenly, Peter said, "My Lord."

Jesus held out his hands to show them where the spikes had been placed. He then showed them his side where the lance had pierced his skin.

All there fell down on their knees crying out, "Master, Lord, Savior."

Jesus again said to them, "Peace be with you."

They became quiet and listened as he spoke to them. "As my Father sent me, now I send you to do our father's work. He walked among them and as he did so he passed the holy spirit to each of them saying, "Receive the Holy Ghost."

Andrew looked up at Jesus and said, "Command me Lord."

Jesus nodded his head and said to all, "Whosoever sins you forgive so too shall your Father forgive. And, whosoever sins you retain, so too shall your Father retain.

To those who truly repent and ask for the remission of their sins, you should show mercy. Those upon whom you show mercy shall dwell in the house of the Lord forever."

Philip asked, "To what nation do we minister?"

Jesus responded, "You are to go forth and teach all nations. Baptize them in the name of the Father, and of the Son, and of the Holy Ghost. Teach them to observe all things that I have taught to you. And, fear not that you will forget, for I am always with you, even unto the end of the world."

Jesus went then to Peter saying as he left them, "Peter take care of my flock. What two or more of you bind here on earth, the same shall be bound in heaven."

The disciples rejoiced in the knowledge of the resurrection of their Lord and Savior. They went forth as commanded, teaching not only in Jerusalem but in all Judea. Later, they would travel to lands far from Galilee where most of the disciples had been born, raised, and had spent all of their adult life. Many were amazed that these disciples, coming from humble beginnings and being unlearned, were able to speak in foreign languages and show great knowledge of things that the ignorant should know little of.

Chapter 58. "A Warning to Depart"

In the weeks and months that followed, Peter and John took God's message directly to the Temple in Jerusalem. There, they would repeat the teachings of Jesus and many would gather to hear their words.

One day, when entering the Temple, a lame man lying by the gate, begged alms from them. Peter and John looked together at the man and felt sympathy for him. Peter knelt down and said to him, "I have no silver or gold to give to you. But such as I do have I will give to you."

Reaching down and straightening the man's legs, Peter spoke to him, "In the name of Jesus Christ of Nazareth, rise up and walk."

John reached under one of the man's arms and Peter reached under the other. Both lifted the man to his feet. As they did so, the man felt strength returning to his legs and slowly he began to walk.

The man shakily walked behind Peter and John into the Temple. All within the Temple recognized the man as the cripple who daily would lie outside the gate begging. When told by the beggar that the disciples of Jesus had given him the ability to walk, the people in the temple were amazed.

Peter saw that the people now looked at him and at John as though they should be revered. He said to them, "Why do you marvel at this? Why do you look so earnestly at us with reverence because we made this man to walk? Do you believe that we did this by our own holiness?

Do you not know that what we are able to do, we do by the grace of the Holy One that you murdered. You delivered he who was truly holy to be crucified when Pilate gave you a choice between the Son of God and a common criminal.

He is the one who allows us to heal the sick for he has been raised up by God from the dead. This we have witnessed. What we do we do in his name."

Peter pointed to the man who had for years lay by the gate begging. "This man was healed by the power of God and by this man's own faith.

You have greatly sinned by violating one of the commandments of God. As the Son of God was crucified by the Romans so too were you as guilty as they for you rendered the judgment. Yet God is a forgiving God. Therefore, if you truly repent of your sins and ask for God's forgiveness in the name of his son, Jesus Christ, you may yet be saved. When it comes time for you to come face to face with the Lord, he will forgive you your sins if you truly repent. Jesus gave his life so that this lesson could be given to the people of Israel. He gave his life for the remission of our sins."

Many of those who heard Peter accepted Jesus Christ as their Savior. There were those though that had doubts. They went to the Captain of the Temple Guard and to the high priest and told them of what Peter and John had said and done.

Peter and John were arrested and placed in prison. Finding no crime for which to levy punishment, the Sadducees set them free but ordered them to no longer preach in Israel and to leave the country. They were threatened with imprisonment if they did not do as ordered.

Peter and John went immediately to the other disciples and told them all what had happened at the Temple. They told the others that they had been warned that all of Jesus disciples would suffer if their blasphemy continued.

Philip asked Peter, "What shall we do? If any of us are found doing as you have done, will we not also be put in prison?"

Peter considered these questions but had no answer as to what course the disciples should follow. Finally, he said, "Let us pray for guidance. Our Lord will show us the way."

Chapter 59. "Moving On"

Marcus had returned to his home after he had left Peter at the sepulcher. Joseph and the household staff were waiting when he arrived.

Joseph welcomed Marcus home. He informed Marcus that Mary, the mother of Jesus, and her two sisters, Mary and Salome were resting comfortably but that they had shed many tears after arriving at his home. John had brought them to Marcus' home but had then departed to join the other disciples.

"This has to be one of the most difficult moments in a mother's life. A mother has lived too long when she survives her child." Marcus thanked the rest of his staff for the care given to his house guests.

Joseph motioned to Marcus that there was something else. He took Marcus aside and said in a low tone of voice, "Your Roman friend was here earlier. He asked me to tell you that he has an urgent matter that he must discuss with you."

"Did he say what it was about?"

"No. He simply said that it was urgent and that I should convey his message to you as soon as I was able to."

Marcus thought about this. So much had happened in such a short time that he knew anything was possible.

"Joseph, it is late. Have the staff retire. I am going out into the garden for awhile. I have some things that I need to sort out in my mind."

"I will get some food and drink for you before we retire." Joseph dismissed the staff as Marcus nodded and walked from the room to his garden in the back of his house.

As he walked about his garden, he had a sense of loss much as he had had when Flavius had died and when his own father, Marcus Aurelius had passed on. Jesus had become almost a part of his inner being in the short time that he had known him. He wondered how one man could have so profound an impact. Then, he knew the answer almost as he thought of the question. Jesus was the Son of God.

Jesus was also Mary's son. He thought about how lonely she must be now. He thought about how hard the days ahead would be for her. Jesus had been her shinning star. Now, he was gone, never to be held by her again. He remembered Quintus' description of the countenance of the beautiful mother as she held her child close to her heart. Does anyone ever come to terms with the loss of a loved one?

Joseph interrupted his thoughts as he brought out some fruit and a cup of wine. "I am sorry to intrude but I thought that you needed some refreshment."

"Thank you Joseph. Actually, I could use some refreshment. This has been a very bad day."

Joseph set the tray down on a marble bench in the center of the garden. "If you need anything more, just call. I will be resting in the anteroom."

"Thank you, Joseph. In the morning, I will go to see Lucius. I am interested in what it is that he has to tell me. I trust that you will take care of whatever needs our house guests may have."

"It is my honor to serve the Holy Mother."

Marcus had never thought about that, the Holy Mother. Yes, it was true. Mary, the mother of Jesus, was the Holy Mother. God would take care of her and give her peace.

The next morning, as Marcus was preparing to go to the fortress to visit Lucius, Lucius appeared at his door.

"Lucius, I was just preparing to go to the fortress to meet with you. I am surprised to see you here." Marcus shook his friends hand as Lucius entered the house.

Lucius drew out the sword that Marcus had given him. "Marcus, I ask you to take back this sword."

Marcus looked at the sword then at Lucius. "I can not."

"I know that Jesus spoke against it but I fear that your safety is at risk. Even if you have this sword that you use so well, you will still be in great danger!" Lucius was very serious. He took Marcus' hand and placed the sword in it.

Lucius continued. "Caiaphas and the other priests are determined to rid Judea of all those who followed Jesus. Already, they are petitioning Pilate to arrest and jail those who speak on behalf of Jesus.

They have given a list of the disciples of Jesus to Pilate and have indicated that King Herod seeks to have those who threaten his kingdom removed. You are listed among the disciples."

Marcus looked at Lucius. He did not question what was being said. He asked, "How did you learn of all this?"

"Pilate summoned me for consultation. He told me that you were among those listed."

"What will he do?"

"Nothing for now. He will wait to see how Herod and Caiaphas deal with what he believes is a Jewish problem."

"Then, for the time being, I am safe."

"Safe from Rome but not from Israel. It is but a matter of time before Herod orders his own soldiers to act. They will act directly when given cause and by stealth where no cause exists. That is why you must take your sword and use it when needed."

Marcus shifted the sword in his hand. Its grip was familiar to him. The sword had been a gift from his old mentor and friend, Quintus. It seemed like ages ago now. The sword was perfectly weighted for him. He moved it in a circular motion and then walked to a table and laid it down. Turning to Lucius, he said, "My days of the sword are over. I made a solemn oath to my God that I would no longer travel down that road, even if it means my death."

Lucius knew that his friend had been moved greatly as a result of his association with Jesus. Lucius had experienced this also at the crucifixion. He accepted the fact that Jesus was the Son of God. But, he also believed that in the world in which he lived, more than good deeds were required to survive.

Lucius walked to the table and lifted up the sword. He held it up in front of him as he addressed Marcus. "My friend, we have been through a lot together. I tell you that if you do not take this sword and use it on your enemies, they will use their swords against you."

"I am sorry Lucius. I know that you say this to protect me but I believe that God has something greater for me to do. He will provide whatever protection I need."

"Marcus, if you do not want to think of yourself, what about those under your roof. What if Herod's men come here and decide to destroy everything and everyone here. Then will you take up the sword?"

Marcus had not thought about that happening. Joseph, his staff, and what if his guests were here when this happened. He would be forced to do that which he had given a promise not to do. No, he would not go back on his word to his God. He would have to find another path to follow.

"Lucius, trust me when I tell you that I will be safe. I will also find a way to guard against harm coming to others."

Lucius shook his head. He placed the sword back on the table. "Go back to Rome. There you will be honored as you should be. Live out your life there in peace. Here, on the frontier, you and the other disciples have nothing to look forward to except hardship and death."

Marcus smiled at his friend. "Lucius, you are forever the pessimist. But tell me, what will happen to you. A centurion, Primus Pilus here in Jerusalem and a believer in Jesus as our Savior. What will you do if you are ordered to support whatever it is that Herod and Caiaphas decide to do?"

Lucius walked to the door to leave. He turned to Marcus. "I will pray to our God that that day will never come. Be careful my friend. May God be with you."

Marcus walked over to Lucius, took his arm, and said, "And you be careful. I would not want to see you perish by the sword."

Lucius left the house. Looking back at Marcus, standing in the doorway, he laughed, "Nor would I."

Chapter 60. "The Journey Begins"

Mary and her two sisters joined Marcus for the morning meal. As Joseph and the household servants served them, Mary said to Marcus, "You have much on your mind this morning. My son and I often shared those times with one another."

Marcus understood why Jesus would have shared his innermost thoughts with his mother. She had a divine aurora about her. Her eyes gave one to know that she had an insight into one's deepest feelings. She was now concentrating solely on him.

"Holy Mother, do not trouble yourself with my concerns. At a time such as this, you should tend to your own needs."

Mary smiled and said, "I am."

Marcus understood that he should tell Mary of his concerns. Perhaps, she and her sisters would understand what he knew he would have to do.

"This morning, a friend of mine, a Roman Centurion, warned me that the High Priest, Caiaphas, has asked that I and the other disciples be arrested and be put to death, as was your son."

Mary's two sisters, Salome and Mary, gasped upon hearing what Marcus was saying. The Holy Mother rose up from her seat and walked over to Marcus. Placing a gentle hand on his shoulder, she said, "My son and I spoke of the times to come after he was gone."

Marcus was surprised at this. "Spoke of the time after he was gone?"

Mary released her hand from his shoulder and walked to a window. She gazed out into the garden. 'It was so peaceful there.' She thought for a moment on this and then the violence of the outside world. 'If only men could see the world through a mother's eyes.'

She turned back to Marcus.

"My son told me that many of his disciples who followed in his footsteps would suffer his fate."

Again her sisters gasped.

"My son said that you must do what he has asked of you. You are to provide written testament to the truth of who he is."

Marcus thought to himself, 'Who he is? Who he is not who he was.' He looked at her and again he saw that divine glow that seemed to flow from her very being."

She knew his thoughts. "Yes Marcus Titus, who he is. He is not gone from us but is with us now, even as we speak. His holy spirit will be with you always. His hands will guide you as you do his work. As with the original twelve, he has given you his authority to do what he willed."

Marcus got up from his chair and walked to Mary. He knelt before her kissing her hand. "Thank you Holy Mother. I will do all that he asked of me."

In the days that followed, Marcus made arrangements to sell all of his holdings in Judea. He instructed Joseph that the proceeds from his holdings be used to provide for Mary, and for the wives and families of Peter and the other disciples.

John had been asked by Jesus to care for his mother. Marcus gave a part of his wealth to John so that this could be easily done. John along with Barthollomew also called Nathanael, accompanied the Holy Mother, Mary, back to Nazareth. Before they departed, each of the disciples, including Marcus, visited with her and paid homage to her son.

Marcus then made arrangements to provide financial support for the disciples to do what each knew they must do having been inspired by Jesus and filled with the Holy Spirit. He spent some time with each of them discussing their plans and asking questions about their time with the Lord and Master.

The apostles, in turn, were given to know the calling for Marcus. They willingly imparted to him all that they had seen and all that they had heard. As they talked with Marcus, they were amazed at their own understanding. It was as if some divine light had shined down upon them and they were filled with the knowledge that had eluded them until this moment. Suddenly, the parables and teachings of Jesus became clear to them. Their purpose was likewise clear to them. They knew that they would preach his message even unto their own death. They no longer lived in fear. The time that they spent with Marcus was part of the divine plan.

During this time, Lucius sent word to Marcus that Judas Iscariot was found dead after hanging himself. He also advised Marcus that he had confirmed that Judas had betrayed Jesus to Caiaphas for the sum of thirty pieces of silver. Marcus thought of how little life is worth to some that they would destroy it for thirty pieces of silver. How wrong it was for one man to take the life of another, of a creation of God. He wondered how it was that a good man turned to the dark side of life. Surely, a child is born in goodness. Sometime between birth and adulthood, something takes place turning the good in some people to evil. Is it by choice? He did not know but he now believed that those who accepted Jesus and lived by his teachings would always make the right decisions in life.

When Peter learned of the death of Judas, he called together the original eleven to appoint a replacement for Judas. They gathered together outside the town of Anathoth. For three days, the disciples discussed those who would qualify to carry forward with their apostolic responsibilities. They agreed among themselves that the person who would replace Judas would have to be someone who witnessed the life, death, and resurrection of Christ. Two people were considered, Joseph called Barsabas and Matthias. Both were known to be good men and both had been followers of Jesus from the very early days of his ministry. The disciples prayed for guidance. Their prayers were answered when they all agreed by unanimous consent that Matthias would be the one to carry on in place of Judas.

Matthias gladly became a part of the apostolic disciples accepting the responsibilities placed upon him as a disciple of the Son of God.

Peter, as the anointed head of the Jews who accepted Christ as the Son of God, told the other eleven that they must now be about their responsibilities. They must take their new faith in God and in Jesus Christ, his son, to the ends of the earth.

The twelve began their own ministries. Those who heard the word of the Lord and accepted Christ were called Christian Jews. They believed in Jesus but continued to obey the laws of the Jewish religion. This was something the priests in the Temple could not abide. They began to persecute the Christian Jews and deny them in the Temple. In response, Peter and the other disciples established Christian communities that no longer followed Jewish law but rather they followed the teachings of Christ.

Peter met with Marcus on the day of Marcus' departure from Jerusalem.

"Peter, what will you do now? You know that with each day you are at greater risk."

"My flock is here in Jerusalem and in Judea. For the time being, I will stay and spread the word of my Master and Lord."

"You know that there are those who speak against you?"

"Yes, I know this. But, I thank you Marcus for your concern.

I must tell you now that when you first came to us, I did not think kindly of you. You were not a Galilean and not a Jew. You were so different from the rest of us that I could not see how you could ever be one of us.

I also think that your education intimidated all of us. Most of us have no formal education. You were a man of letters. You were a citizen of Rome, our rulers. A fisherman, a man of the sea, has his own pride. You threatened that self esteem just by your presence.

Jesus knew you. We should have seen that and trusted in our Lord.

I know now that your calling was from the Father. The Holy Ghost will be with you always. When you commit to writing what the Holy Spirit imparts to you, send me the written word. I will see that it is circulated to all."

Marcus had listened quietly to all that Peter said. He had known that Peter had trouble accepting him as a disciple for some time. He was glad that Peter now recognized that what had separated them since their first meeting was not real but only imagined.

"Peter, what is in the past is behind us. We go forward as brothers. Your future and mine will be linked no matter how many miles and how many years separate us."

The two men embraced and then said good bye.

Marcus' last visitor before he departed from Jerusalem surprised him. An elder Pharisee appeared at his gate and asked for an audience.

Marcus went out to greet the man. "Welcome. What may I do for you?"

The Pharisee looked long at Marcus before answering. "I have heard that you were a friend of the Rabbi, Jesus."

Marcus no longer denied Jesus to anyone. "That is true. I have accepted Jesus as my Savior and God."

The elderly man nodded. "Strange that you a Roman and I, a Pharisee, hold the same beliefs."

Marcus invited the Pharisee into his home and gave the man a cup of wine.

The Pharisee took a drink from the cup and then looked around the room. "I have been here before. This was the home of Marcus Aurelius."

Again, Marcus was surprised. "You knew my father?"

"Yes. I admired your father. He moved as easily among the Jews as he did among the Romans. He was a great man.

My name is Nicodemus. I am both an elder of the Temple and a ruler of the Jews. I knew the Rabbi for a long time. We would meet at night so that no one would know that I sought out the Rabbi.

We would talk of many things. His intellect was beyond his years and beyond his training. He was a carpenter's son, an apprentice of the trade."

Marcus remembered that he too had thought these very things when he first heard Jesus preaching.

Nicodemus continued, "He once told me that in order for a man to enter the kingdom of God, he must be born again. I did not understand how this could be possible. Could an old man enter the womb?

The Rabbi explained that this rebirth that he spoke of was not by the flesh but by water and of the spirit. If a man accepts the son of God, repents his sins, and is baptized, he may be forgiven. Such a man may see the kingdom of God.

He said to me that whosoever believed in him will not perish but have everlasting life."

The elderly man looked into the face of Marcus and asked, "Do you believe this?"

Marcus did not hesitate to reply, "I do."

Nicodemus looked away saying, "I do too. That is why I have come to you as his friend." Nicodemus looked back at Marcus. "I come to you because I know that you are his other disciple. You drew your sword as his protector in the garden of Gethsemane. You were the disciple that followed him to the Temple after his arrest. You have witnessed his miracles as have I. And, you have been given authority to write his history so that the world will not forget."

Nicodemus then asked Marcus, "Is not all that I have said true?"

Marcus looked the man squarely in the eye and answered, "Yes."

Nicodemus bowed his head. He knelt down in front of Marcus and asked, "As the other disciple, will you baptize me in the name of my Lord, Jesus Christ?"

Marcus saw that Nicodemus was visibly shaking. He felt sorry for this Pharisee. He understood the gravity of this act and what it must have taken for Nicodemus to come to him. Without any reluctance, Marcus walked to a pitcher of water that had been placed on a table. He brought the pitcher of water over to where Nicodemus was still kneeling, head bowed.

Marcus raised the pitcher above his head saying, "Bless this water to our use and bless us to thy service." He poured some water on the head of Nicodemus and then poured water over each of his hands. Placing his hands on Nicodemus' head, Marcus asked, "Nicodemus, do you seek forgiveness of your sins and acknowledge Jesus Christ as the son of God and your redeemer?"

The elderly Pharisee continued to shake as he answered, "I do."

Marcus stepped back and said, "Then rise up Nicodemus. Your sins are forgiven. Go with peace of mind and sin no more."

The Pharisee stood up no longer shaking. He felt as if a great weight had been lifted from his shoulders. He knew that through this disciple of Jesus, he had been forgiven. His years were short but he rejoiced in the thought of seeing the kingdom of God.

Nicodemus looked one last time at Marcus, then bowed and left Marcus' home without saying another word.

Marcus watched the elderly man walk through the gate. A beam of sunlight came through the clouds and brightened the doorway where Marcus stood. He did not know how the words and acts that he had just performed came to happen. He only knew that it was right and that God had allowed him to pass God's forgiveness on to this old man. Remembering what Jesus had said, Marcus believed that the son of God was now acting through him. He knew that it would be so for all of Jesus' disciples.

Chapter 61. "To Know the Way"

Joseph saddled Marcus' horse while the other servants secured Marcus' baggage on a mule. It was a sad time for all of them. They knew that they might never again see the man that they had come to respect and now honor as one of the disciples of their Lord.

Marcus took one last walk through of his father's house. From his bedroom, he looked out at the well kept garden. It was a sad occasion. He wondered how often his father had walked through that garden to think about life. He wondered if his father had thought about him while out there. Were the circumstances reversed, he would have. Marcus drew the curtains shut, closing out a part of his life forever.

He walked out to the courtyard where his staff was waiting. He personally embraced each one of his servants, thanking them for their service to both his father and to him. When he reached Joseph, he said, "You have been my most trusted servant and friend. If you ever decide to come to Rome, you will always be welcome as my guest in my home."

Joseph knew that this invitation was heart felt by Marcus. He marveled at the fact that servant and master could have such a relationship. But, then too, he knew that Marcus had accepted Jesus as his Lord and Savior. He knew that this citizen of Rome was the thirteenth of those chosen to follow. Marcus was a man to be honored.

Joseph also knew that Marcus had been given authority by Jesus to set down for history all that had happened and all of the lessons of Jesus' ministry. It seemed a daunting task. Somehow, Joseph knew that Marcus would succeed at it.

Joseph answered Marcus, "God willing, I will see you again. If not in this lifetime then in the next."

Marcus climbed up onto his horse. "Peace be with you, Joseph."

"And with you."

Marcus took hold of the pack mule's rope and led the animal through the gate. Once out of the city, he turned onto the road to Emmaus. From there he would go to Joppa and then on to Caesarea.

At Caesarea, he would take passage on a ship to the island of Crete. From Crete he would sail to the island of Malta and then to Syracusae in Sicilia. The final itinerary would take him from Syracusae through Messanae straits and on to Rome.

Upon arriving in the town of Emmaus, Marcus was surprised to learn that Andrew was preaching in the local synagogue. He made his way to the synagogue and arrived just as Andrew was finishing his sermon.

As Andrew walked out of the synagogue, he immediately saw Marcus standing by the roadside.

"Hail Marcus." Andrew was filled with joy to see Marcus.

"Hail Andrew. This is a great surprise for me to find you here in Emmaus."

The two men embraced as others looked on. Someone said, "It is another disciple of the Son of God."

Another said, "It is the Roman disciple, Marcus."

Both Marcus and Andrew heard the comments. Andrew gave his usual hearty laugh. "The Roman disciple? As a man from Galilee, I never thought that I would hear such a thing! I often wonder if the Baptist had any idea of the far reaching impact his announcement of the coming would have on this world."

Marcus had spent time with Andrew. He knew that Andrew was originally a follower of one called John the Baptist. The Baptist had pointed Jesus out to Andrew as the one who had come to give light to the world. Andrew had told Marcus that he immediately knew in his heart that Jesus was the Messiah.

Marcus said, "I am on my way back to Rome…"

Andrew finished Marcus' statement for him, "To write the gospel, the truth about our dear Lord."

"Yes. I have been called to do this."

"We all know that, Marcus. You are numbered thirteen among us. Many more disciples now follow. It is our destiny that we each go our separate ways spreading the truth about Jesus Christ, the son of God. We must provide the opportunity for others to find the Lord. We must use the authority given to us by the Master to appoint others to carry on after we are gone. This is our mission."

"Where will you go, Andrew?"

"Wherever God wills. I am his instrument now. John and I are traveling through Judea preaching the given word to those Jews who have not yet accepted Jesus as their savior. Soon, I plan to travel to Syria and on to Galatia to bring the word of God to the Gentiles."

Marcus thought about Andrew's journey ahead. This was a man that spent his entire life in and around Judea. A fisherman by trade and now a disciple of the Lord. "Do you know the way?"

Andrew smiled, "God will guide me."

Marcus nodded. "May peace go with you."

Andrew reached into a pouch that he had tied to his waistband. He pulled out a hand carved cross and held it up before Marcus.

Marcus looked at its very recognizable shape. "What is this?"

Andrew took Marcus's hand and placed the cross in it. "This is our sign. Peter, my brother, has authorized it as the symbol of our Christian beliefs. It reminds us that our Lord suffered and was crucified so that our sins may be forgiven. This we should never forget."

As Marcus thanked Andrew for the sacred gift, he thought, 'I will never forget!'

Marcus climbed back up on his saddle. He said to Andrew, "Be well Andrew. Your path is a difficult and hard one."

Marcus always enjoyed being with Andrew. Andrew was big, happy fellow. He was an ardent believer in Jesus Christ. Marcus sensed that this was a blessing but one which would lead to much sacrifice and suffering for his friend. He could say no more to Andrew. But he did say a silent prayer that Andrew be rewarded in heaven for his faithful service here on earth.

Marcus rode away leaving behind one of the original twelve.

Marcus spent two days in Joppa. He had been told by Quintus that this was a jewel on the Great Sea and a place where a man might find peace. His first evening there, he had to agree that Joppa offered beautiful sunsets that seemed to fill the entire sky with a bright red glow that was reflected off the clear blue waters that washed up against the shore.

Marcus rode his horse casually through the tidal water as it washed up onto the sand that stretched out for miles along the coast. In the distance he could make out the outlines of ships entering and leaving the harbor.

He rode south for a while. He tried to put the terrible sights that he had witnessed out of his mind. He had been told by Andrew that Jesus had risen. He hoped beyond all hope that this was true. If so, he tried to form a picture in his mind of a risen Christ rather than a crucified Christ.

He pulled on the reigns to bring his horse to a halt. He climbed down from his saddle, letting go of the reins so that his horse had some well earned freedom. He walked to a place above the break water and sat down to watch the last vestiges of daylight sink into the sea.

The sun was but a sliver of a giant ball of fire on the horizon. Again he thought of a risen Christ. An image of Jesus came to him as he let his mind travel in its own direction. He saw the image clearly now. Jesus eyes were looking down at him. His arms were raised high and he appeared to be pointing toward the heavens. As he smiled, he seemed to be lifted up, higher and higher. The sun finally sank out of sight and with it went Marcus' vision of his Savior.

Marcus' horse gently nudged Marcus with his nose. The horse sensed that with the coming of night, it was time to be off to the inn and stable.

Marcus climbed back up on his horse and turned back to Joppa and the comfort of the inn he had found on the coast just outside the city limits.

Once he had taken care of stabling his horse with his mule, he went into the inn for the evening meal. As he sat at a table waiting to be served, he reached into a pocket and pulled out the cross that Andrew had given him.

'What had Andrew said? Peter had decided that this was to be the symbol of Christ. A symbol to all that one was a Christian, one who believed in Jesus as the son of God.'

His thoughts were interrupted by a barmaid who had come to take his order. Upon seeing the wooden cross in his hands, she gasped, "Oh! Why do you carry such a thing?"

Marcus looked up at the girl. Seeing the shock on her face, he realized what this symbol might mean to those who had not seen or heard of the Messiah. What it might mean to those that did not have the same perspective that Peter had.

Marcus spoke as gently as he could to the young barmaid. "Have you heard of the young Rabbi called Jesus?"

"The prophet from Nazareth?" She answered.

Marcus was surprised by her answer. "Yes, prophet as some call him, Son of God as others would have it."

She looked at Marcus as if she were trying to form a judgment of him. At that moment the innkeeper joined them, saying, "Is there a problem sir?"

Marcus set the tiny wooden cross on the table. "No, there is no problem. I am afraid that I caused some concern with this young girl because of this cross." Marcus pointed at the symbol in plain view on the table.

The innkeeper looked at the cross then back to Marcus. "It is a strange relic for someone to carry with them. I have heard from other travelers that the Romans have recently crucified a prophet on one of those over in Jerusalem."

Marcus bowed his head. The image of Jesus, suffering on the cross, was again in his mind's view. As a tear rolled down his cheek and he felt as if his inside were about to break apart, he said, "That is true. I was there."

The innkeeper put his arms around the young barmaid and hugged her close to him. "This is my daughter, Rachel. She saw the prophet once when he came to Joppa. She had a friend who was tormented by the devil. A young girl her own age who would have uncontrollable seizures and would throw herself to the ground. The man that you say that they crucified in Jerusalem was the one who freed my daughter's friend from her demons."

Marcus looked up with reddened eyes and saw that both the young barmaid and the innkeeper had tears in their eyes as well. Marcus picked up the cross and holding it said, "Peter, one of Jesus Christ's disciples has said that this is to be a symbol of Jesus sacrifice for all of us. He has said that this will remind us of that sacrifice and of all the good that the Son of God taught us and did for us while he was here among us."

The innkeeper's daughter looked at the tiny wooden cross and then touched her heart.

Marcus was so moved by the gesture that he took the girl's hand and placed the little wooden cross in it. He said to her, "You have a good heart and a blessed soul. Take this cross and remember the good thing that the Son of God did for your friend. Think also that he has done a good thing for you as well. You have recognized in him what others failed to recognize. You have been truly blessed."

The girl looked at Marcus. "Why did he have to die?"

Marcus smiled at her. Again the answer he gave came from within. "He is risen. He goes to another place to be with his Father who is in heaven. I have seen the risen Christ. Those that believe in him shall also see him in his time. Cry no more, young one. Be happy with the thought that the Son of God is not dead but lives and will come again to accept you into his house and into his kingdom."

The girl understood. The Holy Spirit had indeed filled her soul. She tightened her hold on the cross and said to her father, "May I go and tell Ester?"

The innkeeper nodded his approval and his daughter immediately left the room. Turning back to Marcus, he said, "So, you too are a disciple of our Lord?"

Marcus immediately took note of two things that the innkeeper had just said. First, that he, Marcus, was not the only disciple that the innkeeper had spoken to. And, second, that he referred to Jesus as 'our Lord' which meant that here too was another follower, another Christian.

Marcus answered the innkeeper. "Yes, I am a disciple. Have you spoken to another disciple recently?"

"I have. He was here yesterday. His name was Matthew. He is going north to Caesarea."

"Was he alone?"

"Yes, as far as I know. He stayed one night with us. He told me of the crucifixion. He said he has a mission, a promise that he must keep to our Lord."

Marcus sat back in his chair remembering the former tax collector turned disciple. He was the man that Jesus directed to give up all his worldly belongings if he wished to follow the Master. So deep was Matthew's belief in Jesus as the Messiah, the promised one, that Matthew had willingly given away all of his wealth.

Jesus had told Marcus that he received the loudest protests from the Pharisees for having a tax collect preaching the word of God. The Pharisees had labeled Matthew a sinner. Jesus had responded to this criticism by saying, 'They that are whole have no need of physicians, but those who are sick do have a need. I came not to call the righteous, but the sinners to repentance.' Jesus had wondered if the Pharisees ever understood the message of God. God was forgiving of those who repent their sins.

The innkeeper excused his delay in taking Marcus' order for the evening meal. Marcus had the innkeeper bring to him what it would be that the innkeeper would recommend.

After he finished his meal, he went to his room on the upper floor. In bed, he thought about the risen Lord until he fell asleep.

During the night, a storm arose and by early morning the waves were crashing along the shore and rain beat hard against the window of the room where Marcus slept. He awoke to the steady drumming of the rain on the roof.

Marcus got out of bed and went to look out the window. The storm reminded him of another storm on the Sea of Galilee. It seemed like many years ago now. So much had happened since the night that he saw Jesus walk on top of the water to the floundering boat.

There were no boats floundering at sea this day. No doubt the fisherman had decided that this was not a day for fishing. He had hoped to get an early start so that he might overtake Matthew on the road to Caesarea. Looking out at the weather, he knew that that would not be possible for as long as the storm lasted.

'There is something beautiful about a storm at sea.' He thought to himself. He watched the rain coming down in great torrents. The waves were at least as high as he was tall and maybe even higher as they lashed the shoreline. The sky was dark with just a hint of morning light somewhere far above the storm.

Marcus pulled a wooden chair from the corner of the room over to the window. He sat down to take in nature's fury. There were flashes of lightening, here and there, above the sea. The low rumble of thunder could be heard some distance away. It took him back again to the hilltop at Golgotha. It was a barren hillside now but the shadow of those three crosses still hung over its stark landscape. Marcus wondered if the spot would remain that way always. 'Many civilizations have come and gone through the centuries. Where one had once stood, now another has been built over it. Would this happen to Jerusalem and to the spot where Jesus had been crucified? Jesus, himself, had prophesied the destruction of Jerusalem.' He had no doubt that this would come to pass.

'My kingdom is not of this world.' How many times had he heard Jesus say that to his disciples and to others? 'If he has risen will he remain with us or will he go to his kingdom. He had said that his was the kingdom of Heaven. I wonder if I will see him in this world. Hopefully, I will be worthy to see him if not here then in the next life.'

Looking again out the window at the shoreline, he remembered yesterday. He had been deep in thought and had imagined Jesus as risen and standing before him. The image was still clear in his mind. The arms raised, the hands pointing to the heavens, the comforting smile and then the ascension. 'Was it my imagination or something more?'

He suddenly had the thought that perhaps this was the Son of God's way to show him the way. Jesus had given him what he needed most and had not realized it. Hope did not end with the cross. It began there with the risen Lord showing the way to everlasting life.

Marcus knew that his writings must convey this message clearly. He must point the way as shown to him by the Son of God. The image is not one of the crucified Son of God but one of a risen Son of God inspiring mankind's salvation.

Chapter 62. "Return to Rome"

Marcus never did have an opportunity to find Matthew before he sailed from Caesarea on the long voyage back to Rome.

Marcus enjoyed the many days at sea. During the day, he would help the ship's crew with their work. At night, he would talk with them about their experiences at sea. On the way from Crete to Malta, the seamen discovered that Marcus had known the man called Jesus who some had seen and one had heard preach while in Galilee. They were very interested in hearing about this prophet, this man of God.

Marcus began holding nightly sessions with the men. At first, he told them of the things that he had seen Jesus do. Marcus took note that the seamen particularly enjoyed the story of Jesus chasing the moneychangers from the Temple of Jerusalem. Eventually, Marcus began sharing the parables and teachings of Jesus. There were many questions but by the time the ship reached Rome, many of the seamen were converted to Christianity.

Marcus knew that it was not his stories and lessons that had caused the acceptance of Jesus as their Savior and Lord. It was something greater. He concluded that the Holy Spirit had entered the souls of these men of the sea.

He thought about this, about the ever present danger they faced out away from land. Yet they loved the sea and all that God had created above and below it. He knew from his many nights spent talking with them that they had a reverence for what nature had provided. He too felt it when late at night he would stand alone on the deck of the ship and look up at the vastness of the night sky and the millions of stars that filled the heavens. Somehow it all made sense knowing that there was one great and all powerful force behind it. That force was God.

The ship docked at Ostia, a coastal town on the Roman peninsula. It was but a short ride to Rome from Ostia.

As Marcus entered the outskirts of one of the greatest of all cities in the world, he marveled at its beauty. The architecture, the landscape, even the roads all bespoke of wealth and power. It was a remarkable contrast to the cities and villages of the frontier. Marcus had a renewed sense of why Rome commanded the world. As his horse's hooves quickened on the hard road surface, he tried to image how Rome and Christianity might go forward side by side.

Marcus Aurelius' home in Rome had changed very little since the date of his passing. Marcus Titus had inherited the home in Rome and its belongings along with the home in Judea from his father. While Marcus had been in Judea, a few trusted servants kept up the Roman residence and took care of its needs. With the return of Marcus, the servants now hastened to restock the pantries and open up those rooms that had been closed for years due to the lack of use.

The chief steward of the house was a man by the name of Alexander. He wondered how much young Marcus would have changed. He had heard conflicting reports. As legionnaires had been furloughed to Rome, stories of the Roman citizen who together with one Centurion had dispatched twenty to thirty religious zealots in an alleyway had come back to Alexander. It was told that Marcus Titus son of Marcus Aurelius was that Roman citizen.

Others who had been on the frontier talked about a prophet who drew thousands of followers everywhere that he spoke. One such follower was a Roman citizen called Marcus. Alexander had been led to believe that this Marcus who followed the prophet also was Marcus Titus.

As he prepared the household for the arrival of its owner, Alexander thought about the young boy who had been tutored by Flavius Titus. Young Marcus had shown that he was both a scholar and an athlete. He had learned much from Flavius Titus. Alexander reasoned that both reports about Marcus Titus could be correct. He looked forward to Marcus' return. He would learn for himself which Marcus was the real Marcus, soldier or saint.

Marcus dismounted at the front entrance to his home. As he looked at the outside structure, he saw that little had changed. Columns supported the portico over the front door. The white stone façade was weathered to a rich cream color. Two large doors swung open to the inside to reveal white marble floors and walls, all of which were highly polished and gave off much light from the high windows on either side of the doorway.

As Marcus entered the house, he was greeted by Alexander and a servant by the name of Cassandra.

"Welcome home, Marcus." Alexander greeted Marcus with a warm smile and a slight bow.

Marcus remembered Alexander from his boyhood days as one of his father's favorite servants. Even during those years when his father had been serving on the frontier, Alexander would visit young Marcus and Flavius at Flavius' home. Marcus learned later that Alexander was bringing both financial stipends as well as news of his father to Flavius. This was evidence of the trust that Marcus Aurelius had of this servant. Young Marcus had continued with that trust by retaining Alexander as chief steward to manage his affairs in Rome after his father's death.

"Alexander, it is good to see you after all these years." Looking around the room, Marcus continued, "It is good to be home." His eyes came to Cassandra.

"Marcus, this is Cassandra. She has been here for two years and provides some of the best meals in all of Rome."

Marcus smiled, "Cassandra, it is a pleasure for me to meet you. After many weeks at sea, a well prepared meal will be a wonderful homecoming for me."

Cassandra was a short young woman of about twenty-four or twenty-five years of age. She had dark brown eyes, long dark black hair, radiant smile, and apparently did not sample her own cooking too often. She was as thin as a reed. Marcus later learned that Cassandra was a source of constant energy and hard work. He attributed her lack of any weight to the fact that she was constantly in motion.

She smiled at Marcus. "It is good to have you home. I have heard so much about you that I feel that I already know you. Let me go and prepare a meal that I hope will meet all of your expectations." She bowed slightly and left the two men alone.

Marcus turned to Alexander. "Where did you find her?"

As they walked from the entry way into the great room of the house, Alexander answered, "Actually, she found me."

"Found you?" Marcus asked with a frown.

"Yes. She appeared at the door a little over two years asking for you."

"Me?" Marcus stopped in surprise.

"Yes. She told me that she had come from Lycia where a friend had asked that she inquire after your wellbeing."

Marcus was stunned by this news. "Lycia." Thoughts of Didyanna came rushing back to him from somewhere buried in his mind long ago.

Alexander saw the immediate change in Marcus' composure. "Would you like to have me summon Cassandra to come back?"

Marcus knew that he would have many questions for his newest servant. "No. I will talk with her after the evening meal. Lycia was a long time ago. I will be very interested in hearing all that Cassandra will be able to tell me. I suspect that it will take some time. For now, I need to have my things unpacked, my horse and mule seen to, and I need to freshen up."

"I will see to your animals and have a bath drawn for you. Do you remember your way around the house?"

Marcus looked around the great room. Yes, he remembered his father's house well. "Yes Alexander, I remember my way. I always loved visiting here when my father was in residence." As Marcus started in the direction of bedrooms, he turned to Alexander and said, "Thank you for seeing to my animals. I would like to have you and Cassandra join with me for dinner this evening."

Alexander smiled, "We will look forward to that."

Chapter 63. "The past may be prolog to the future."

Cassandra had prepared a virtual feast for Marcus. Sliced cabbage and lettuce with a cherry sauce and grated cheese would serve as the first course. Then a wine and honey mixed drink served with a platter of snails, shellfish and sliced porpoise. The main course featured roast pork cooked with vegetables and red wine. She had also made a pudding for dessert.

In accordance with their patron's request, three places were set at the table. When Marcus walked into the dinning room he was immediately impressed with the table setting and the variety of food provided.

"I haven't seen a meal so well prepared and displayed as this is in many years."

Cassandra gave one of her most brilliant smiles as Alexander pulled out a chair for her to sit in.

With a nod from Marcus, all three took their places at the table.

"Cassandra, how did you find such delicacies on such short notice?"

"Sir, we were informed of your coming two days ago. Alexander and I went to the market yesterday to stock the pantry for your homecoming."

Alexander nodded, "Rome is a city that runs on information and rumors. You are a celebrity of sorts. A sailor from Syracusae saw you and announced that you were on your way to this city."

"How is it that he or anyone here in Rome for that matter would have an interest?"

Cassandra was quick to answer Marcus' question. "All of Rome has heard of the Roman citizen who with the help of but a single Centurion dispatched thirty to forty barbarians on the frontier. I know of many here who would like to meet you."

Alexander followed Cassandra, saying, "There is also the report of a citizen of Rome being a follower of a Jewish prophet on the frontier. Some say that it is the same citizen who dispatched the Zealots."

Marcus smiled with amusement. "It seems that communications in Rome have reached a degree of accuracy and speed which should be the envy of the entire Empire."

"Are you saying that what we have heard is true?" Alexander asked.

"To a degree, what you have heard is correct." Looking at Cassandra, Marcus laughed, "Thirty to forty barbarians is a bit exaggerated."

Turning to Alexander, Marcus went on, "Do you remember my boyhood friend, Lucius?"

"The boy from the Amphitheater?"

"Yes, the very same. He is the Centurion who was with me when we were attacked by ten religious Zealots outside of an inn in Jerusalem."

Alexander laughed and turned to Cassandra. "Marcus and Lucius were the final contenders in the games at the Amphitheater. Both represented their teachers in combat with broad swords and lances. My guess is that a dozen Zealots would be at a huge disadvantage when tested against the skills of these two Romans."

Cassandra gazed admiringly at Marcus. "Still, a dozen men against two, it is something that the Romans that I have heard speak of with pride."

Marcus shifted uneasily in his chair. "I have found in my travels that there are other things in life which require greater skill and which are to be treasured more."

Cassandra looked puzzled. "What kind of things?"

"Things like faith, like hope, like forgiveness of and charity to others." Marcus lifted is cup of wine and honey. "We are fortunate to be here in this great city of Rome and to have the opportunity to live a life that is plentiful. I have seen many, many others who are not so fortunate."

Marcus set his cup down without taking a drink. "In Judea there was one called Jesus of Nazareth. Some called him a prophet." Looking at Alexander, Marcus said, "I would not identify him as a Jewish prophet. Most of the high priests of the Jewish faith did not accept him or what he preached as being in accordance with Jewish law and teachings."

Alexander asked, "Patron, I have heard that this man, Jesus, preaches revolt and rebellion against the Empire?"

"What you have heard is not so. His teachings were about love of our fellow human beings. And, he was not a man, Alexander. He was the son of God."

"I do not understand." Alexander spoke with some hesitancy.

Marcus understood. "As you know, I have been a student of history and religion for many years now. One of the reasons that I went to the frontier was to learn first hand about Judaism and Islam.

Upon my arrival in Jerusalem, I was told about a rabbi who preached a new form of Judaism. I sought out this rabbi only to discover the one called Jesus.

I saw him feed five thousand followers starting with only five loaves of bread and two small fish. I saw him walk on top of a raging sea to rescue men who were his followers, his disciples. I saw him take a boy who had been crippled since birth and make him rise up and walk. These things I saw for myself. There are many more things that I have heard that this Jesus of Nazareth did to help the sick and the disabled.

Alexander, you have heard that I am a follower. I am that and more. I am a believer.

I listened to this man, who was raised as a carpenter, talk of things that even the priests of the temples were amazed at. His knowledge far surpassed many who listened and who had been highly educated.

He spoke of another kingdom. A kingdom where there was but one God. A God who was the creator of all that we know. A God who looks upon each of us as his child. Jesus said that he was sent to us by God, who was his father, to let us know that those who accepted this truth and believed in him, would find eternal life when it was time to depart from this world.

Jesus preached that there were certain principles that God expected each of us to live by. Among those principles were two commandments that transcended all else: to love God with all your heart, and to treat your neighbor as you would want your neighbor to treat you.

I have spent a long time now thinking about Jesus and what he gave to me. I am a follower, I am a believer, and I am his disciple."

Both servants were amazed at what they had just heard. They could find no words to respond to what Marcus had told them. Neither had ever heard such things before and neither had ever expected to hear such things from a Roman citizen.

They both recognized the same realization as they sat there. Marcus had talked of only one God, not the many that Romans generally worshipped.

Marcus had witnessed miracles and magic with no other explanation. Marcus had expressed the belief that the man, Jesus, was the son of a God. Did that mean that this Jewish man on the frontier was holding himself out to be the equal of Caesar? If Marcus believed this, how could he be loyal to Rome and to this son of God at the same time? Both were suddenly frightened, not only for their patron but for themselves as well.

Alexander was the first to speak. "Patron, why do you tell us these things? You can not know us so well that it is safe for you to share such thoughts with us."

Marcus calmly looked at his two servants. "Alexander, it is my calling to say these things not just to those who I know well but to all who will listen. I went to the frontier in search of not just further knowledge but in search of my purpose in life. I believe that the God that I have now accepted as my one true God, showed me my purpose through his son, Jesus Christ.

Things happen in life that are beyond mere chance. Alexander, you remember Quintus. He is the one who brought me here to Rome at the request of my father.

He often told me the story of our journey and how he at one point came upon the most beautiful mother and child that he had ever seen. The memory of them was forever etched in his mind.

I met that mother and child when I was in Judea. The child was Jesus and his mother Mary was the woman that Quintus so well remembered.

I cannot believe that our paths crossed at so young an age and then again as adults without some purpose. There is a reason why this happened.

Jesus and I talked of this while I traveled with him. He told me that it was God's will that I write the gospel, the absolute truth about his life and its meaning so that God's word is not lost to future generations. He said that my training in the languages and my education uniquely prepared me for this purpose. That God had selected me to be the one who would write this history.

I walked with the Lord and I saw Jesus crucified on a wooden cross by Roman soldiers. While he suffered, the skies darkened. Lightening flashed across the skies as if thrown by some great force against the earth. The ground broke apart. Total darkness covered the earth for hours when otherwise it would have been light.

I saw his earthly life slip from him. I watched helplessly as our Savior was taken from us.

Jesus told all of us, his disciples, on the night before he was taken, that he would arise from death as his Father had promised so that we would know that what he had taught us about his Father's kingdom in heaven was true.

He did this three days after his burial. I went to his tomb and saw with my own eyes that it was empty.

Later, as I rode alone along the shore of the Great Sea, I saw him and I knew, at that moment, that truly he was the son of God, our risen Lord.

He said that by his resurrection he would provide a light to the world and proof that there is eternal hope for life everlasting in God's kingdom. A kingdom not of this world but in a world to come. It is that hope that gives me faith that what he has committed us to on earth is what is rightful if we are to see what has been set apart for us in Heaven.

For these reasons, I must do as I believe I was born to do. I must spread the good news that Jesus offered to all of us by word and by my writings."

Alexander listened to young Marcus without saying a word. He could see the commitment and almost a fervor that his patron had to this new faith that he had found on the frontier. When Marcus had finished, Alexander spoke. "I am considerably older than you are my patron. I have witnessed the benevolent rule of Caesar Augustus, the poor treatment of Jews and their banishment from Rome by Tiberius, and now the cruelty of Tiberius' appointed protector of Rome, Sejanus, commander of the Praetorian Guard.

If you speak publicly as you have just now spoken to us, you will be arrested, tortured and killed before you write a single word.

I humbly implore you to use your time wisely. I do not know of such things as Gods in heaven and here on earth. But, if it is true, that you have been chosen by one God who reigns supreme to write the history of his son in this world that should be accomplished before you risk your life with any public utterances."

Marcus considered the advice he was being given. "Alexander, there is wisdom that comes with age. I will take your advice under consideration. It does make some sense."

Looking then at the table, Marcus said, "Neither of us have been wise enough to appreciate the hard work and effort that Cassandra has put into giving us this great feast. Let's enjoy our evening meal."

Marcus picked up his eating utensils and sampled the cabbage and lettuce salad with cherry sauce and cheese. "Cassandra, this is delicious!"

After they had eaten dinner and Marcus had received all of the latest news and gossip from his dinner companions, Marcus leaned back in his chair and looked directly at Cassandra.

"Cassandra, I am guessing that you know the daughter of Alex Atolia."

Cassandra smiled knowingly. Marcus could see that he was correct by the way Cassandra looked at him.

"Yes, I know Didyanna very well. We have been friends for a very long time."

"Alexander indicated that you came here two years ago. Have you heard from Didyanna since your arrival in Rome?"

Cassandra could see that Marcus was still very interested in her friend. She was glad that she was here upon his return from Judea. "Yes, we exchange letters. Her father represents the Lycian League here in Rome. He and his son visit the city about every two months. Cale carries our letters for us."

Marcus thought that he noticed a reddening of Cassandra's cheeks when she mentioned Didyanna's brother's name. "How is Didyanna?"

"Beautiful!" Cassandra exclaimed. "As you may remember, she has all of the best features of the Lycian women. Long golden brown hair, slender body, fair skin, and crystal clear blue eyes like the water from a mountain spring! She has many young officers in the army and some not so young pursuing her." She was now enjoying her conversation with her patron. "Her brother thinks that it is time for her to select a husband and begin a family."

Marcus remembered the beautiful girl that he had met very well. He made an attempt at casual interest but both Cassandra and Alexander could see that Marcus had more than passing interest. "Has she come to a point where she is considering someone?"

Cassandra again smiled. Though this young man was her patron he could just as easily have been one of her friends. "Didyanna is very careful about such things. She does not speak of it even to her close friends. But, I think that there could be someone."

Marcus sat up in his chair while still looking at Cassandra. "If she keeps such things to herself, what makes you think that there may be someone, someone that she may care about?"

"I have seen her in the twilight of the evening when stars first appear in the sky. She walks alone in her garden smiling at the stars above and sometimes hums music as she goes along. This is something I recognize. I am a woman too. It is a sign that love is in the air."

Marcus was distracted by all of this. Leaving Xanthos seemed like a lifetime ago. He was no longer the youthful young man that had spent a wonderful few days in a place he remembered as peaceful with a young girl that he remembered as perfect. He had experienced several lifetimes since then. He knew that he had aged. He still saw Didyanna as she was when they first met. That young girl and he were no longer the match that they had been. It was painfully obvious from Cassandra's description of Didyanna that she had not changed. He knew that he had.

Marcus suddenly was aware that nothing had been said for an uncomfortably long period of time. He left his memories behind and said, "From my memory of my brief time with the Atolia family, Didyanna deserves to find happiness."

Marcus rose from the table. "I want to thank you both for joining me tonight and for making me feel at home. I have enjoyed our conversation and have a lot to think about."

As he walked away, he turned and said "Tomorrow I will need to make some decisions. I have more to do than I had realized but it is good to be home. Good night."

Chapter 64. "A Step Back in Time"

Marcus woke up early the next morning. After dressing, he took an apple from the kitchen and left his home. He wanted to walk the paths that he used to walk as a young boy. His first stop was the home that belonged to Flavius Titus, his old teacher. Flavius had left the building with all of its books, maps, charts, and his writings to the city to be used as a school for young people interested in furthering their education. He had endowed the school so that no child who sought to learn would be denied.

As Marcus paused in front of the school, he smiled at all the activity. The garden just inside the gate was filled with boys and girls laughing and talking about the things that they were learning. Marcus thought to himself, 'Flavius would be well pleased with this.'

He walked on for several streets to the market place where he and Flavius always did their shopping. He was pleased to see that little had changed there in the last twenty years. Most of the vendors were new but the goods and merchandise were the same.

As he passed through the market, an older woman called out. "Marcus? Is that you Marcus Titus?"

Marcus looked in the direction of a small vegetable stand. It's wooden frame and cloth walls were a familiar sight. So too was Octavia, the proprietress who had sold her family's produce there for as long as Marcus could remember. Her stand was always a favorite with Flavius. He would mull over a certain group of vegetables for what seemed like hours, negotiating a price with Octavia. Then both would agree on what was a fair transaction. Finally, Octavia would wrap the vegetables in paper as Flavius would turn to Marcus and say, "It is important to eat well. That's what makes us what we are."

Marcus smiled at the old woman as he approached her vegetable stand. "Yes Octavia, I have returned to Rome."

"The Gods be praised. I thought that I would be dead before I would ever see you again."

The old woman embraced the young man as tears welled up in her eyes. She stepped back, wiping her tears away with the hem of her dress. "Where have you been young Marcus? Let me look at you."

As Marcus answered, the old woman took a closer look at him. "I have been to the frontier, to Judea."

"You have aged since last I saw you, Marcus. You are still as handsome as I remember you but you are no longer a boy."

Marcus grinned. "And you are as pretty as ever. It is no wonder that Flavius was excited by you!"

Octavia blushed. "Watch what you say. Flavius gave no thought to me. I am but a street vendor."

Marcus shook his head in disagreement. "You forget that I handled his estate. I know that you do not have to sell your produce at the market in order to earn a living. Flavius saw to that when he left us."

Octavia again felt tears forming in her eyes. "He was a good man."

Marcus agreed. "He was a great man. And, he did like you. Why else would he spend hours negotiating with you for a cabbage?"

They both laughed.

Octavia turned serious. "What did you find in Judea, Marcus?"

"I found my purpose in life. That is why I have come home. I have a story to write. A story of faith, of hope, and of love."

Octavia did not take her eyes from his. "This faith that you will write about, is it a religious faith?"

Marcus answered, "Yes, it is. A man by the name of Jesus provided me with guidance."

Octavia took Marcus by the hand and led him to a place by her stand where there were two chairs. She motioned for him to sit. "Your eyes. That is what is different about you Marcus. Please sit here for a minute."

The old woman went to a vendor across the way from her stand. She spoke briefly with him and then returned. "Athros, a Greek who sells figs here in the market, is going to join us. He has been to Judea and often talks about a prophet that he heard speak there."

Marcus was surprised to hear this. He did not think about the possibility that anyone in Rome would know of Jesus.

A short man with a heavy beard came almost at a run to meet Marcus. Marcus stood up as he approached.

"You have seen Jesus?" The short man asked as he stopped in front of Marcus.

"Yes, I have seen Jesus." Marcus answered.

The short man raised both hands to the sky and shouted, "Praise God!"

Several shoppers looked over at the short man then at Marcus and Octavia.

The short man paid no attention to the interest of the others. "I have seen and heard Jesus!" He said as he pounded his chest with his hands. "He is my Savior! I have seen him heal the sick. With my own eyes, I saw him heal a blind man so that he received back his lost eye sight. I listened to him. He confirmed that he is the son of the one God who rules over all of us. I believe him." The short man shook his head vigorously agreeing with his own words.

Marcus smiled at the short vendor. "You are right to believe him. I believe him too."

Octavia raised her hand to her heart. "Athros talks about this prophet, Jesus, constantly. I did not know if he was making these things up as a result of too much wine on his buying trips or too much time in the sun. But you, Marcus, you too believe that this man is the son of a God?"

Others near by had been listening. They drew nearer to hear what was being said.

Marcus saw the expectancy in Athros' eyes. Marcus put a hand on Athros shoulder and said in a clear voice so that all could hear, "Jesus Christ is the son of God."

Turning to face the dozen or so people who were now around him, he said, "Jesus was sent by the one true God to teach us the path that we must follow to obtain salvation and everlasting life. There is no other way than by living as Jesus has taught that we should live."

A stranger asked, "What way is that?"

Marcus turned to the stranger and answered, "You must treat others as you would want them to treat you."

Another person asked, "How do you know that this man was the son of a God?"

Marcus answered, "Not the son of a God, Jesus was the son of the God. There is but one God and his kingdom is not of this world but is in Heaven.

I know that Jesus Christ is the son of the one God because I saw him crucified and then later rise up and go to be with his Father, who is in Heaven."

Athros shuddered. "He was crucified? This cannot be. Why would God allow his son to be crucified?"

Marcus looked at Athros and saw the shock on his face at the news that Jesus had been crucified. "Jesus, on the night before he was arrested predicted that he would be arrested and crucified. He said that this would happen to fulfill a prophecy that the son of man would be killed so that the son of God could rise up from the dead and save our souls. If we believe in him and that he has risen and gone to his Father's kingdom then we can accept the fact that there is life after death because he has shown us that this is true. For us to join him we have but to follow what he has taught us."

The section of the marketplace where Marcus was speaking was now crowded with over one hundred people. All of those people were coming together to hear Marcus. Vendors had left their stands unattended. Shoppers had stopped to listen and even a few Roman legionnaires, who had happened by, drew near to hear what Marcus was saying.

Marcus went on to describe Jesus' teachings and to speak of the parable of the prodigal son and the forgiving father. He likened the parable to the one God that he spoke of.. He was a forgiving God who would forgive those who had sinned but who repented of their sins and sought forgiveness. Much as the father had welcome his prodigal son home, so too would God welcome home those who had sinned but who were now truly repentant.

Athros then asked, "If Jesus has been crucified and has left us, who will lead us on?"

Marcus answered, "There will be others who come with the authority of God. Jesus has selected his disciples to go out into the world and to preach his word. He has said that what they bind on earth shall also be bound in Heaven.

Jesus has said that God's kingdom shall have no end. So too his word shall have no end."

With those parting words, Marcus knew that his first and foremost duty was to write the gospel of Jesus so that in truth Jesus' words would have no end.

He bid good-bye to Octavia and Athros. As he walked through the crowd, the people stepped aside in silence. They sensed that there was something very special about this man. He had a calling. Somewhere, deep down inside of each of those who heard him speak, there was a sense that this was a man with a holy passion. It touched them and would remain with them. He offered hope and a path to eternal life. He believed it and he led them to believe it also.

Marcus returned to his home determined to spend the time needed to create a history of the life of Jesus, his teachings, and his promise for future generations. For the next few weeks, he spent all of his time on his writings. He knew he must complete his promised task.

Chapter 65. "Roman Repression"

Word of the man in the marketplace spread quickly. As with all rumors, the story grew as it spread. When it reached the commander of the Praetorian Guard it evidenced sedition and revolt against the rule of Rome.

Sejanus had heard of the radical cleric in Judea named Jesus. He had fomented revolution in the frontier province and had reportedly been put to death for his attacks on the legitimate government in Judea. Now it seemed that one of his disciples had come to Rome and was attacking the government in Rome. Sejanus demanded that his guards find out who this rebel was and arrest him.

Less than a month from the time that he had visited the marketplace, Marcus was interrupted from his writings by Alexander.

"Patron, you have a visitor. A woman from the marketplace by the name of Octavia."

Marcus immediately rose up from his chair. "Have her come in, Alexander."

Alexander went out and escorted the older woman into Marcus' library room.

"Octavia, what a pleasant surprise. I hope all is well with you."

Octavia looked nervously at Alexander. Alexander knew instantly that she preferred to say what she needed to say to Marcus without him being present. He bowed to the old woman and said, "Excuse me. I will be outside if either of you need anything."

After he had gone, Octavia quickly told Marcus why she had come. "Early this morning, the Praetorian Guards came to the marketplace. They went directly to Athros' stand and questioned him about his recent statements about the Jewish revolutionary in Judea, Jesus of Nazareth.

Athros declared for all to hear that Jesus was not a revolutionary but the son of the one, all powerful God. He said that the one God reigned supreme and that he would lead the way for all to have a better life." As she said this she faltered and had to grasp the back of a chair to remain standing.

Marcus rushed to her side. "Then what happened?"

"They beat him. They punched and kicked him and called him vile names. They destroyed his stand and threw his produce into the street.

Then one of the soldiers picked him up and held a sword to his neck. The soldier said that he would ask only once for the name of the rebel who spoke treason in the market three weeks ago.

Athros looked only for a moment at me then turned to the soldier and said 'Jesus is my Savior.'"

Octavia collapsed in Marcus' arms. He lifted her up and took her to a couch. He gave her water to drink.

After a sip, she went on, "They killed Athros. They killed him in front of all of us." She began to cry. Through her tears, she said, "They are looking for you, Marcus. You must leave Rome. They will find you and when they do, they will kill you."

Marcus heard her words but he was thinking of the short merchant with the heavy beard. The little man who had heard the Master and had believed in him. He said a brief prayer for Athros' soul.

He called to Alexander who appeared quickly from the outer room. He explained what Octavia had reported and the need to move quickly.

"It is possible that someone may have followed Octavia to my home. If they knew about Athros, they may well have know that Octavia knew me also.

I am going to take Octavia away from here. We will find a ship to take us back to Judea. Tell the staff that I will sail within the week. Say no more.

In six months time, sell my home and divide the profits among the staff. Give an equal share anonymously to the family of Athros, the merchant. God willing, our paths will cross again but if not, I deeply appreciate the service that you have given to my father and to me." Marcus embraced Alexander for the last time before leaving the library with Octavia. He collected a few personal items and enough money for the trip ahead and put them into a carrying sack. He and Octavia then disappeared through a passage in the wall that led to a nearby alleyway.

Marcus guided Octavia through sections of the city that she had never seen before. He was happy with the knowledge that not much had changed here either and that his boyhood escapes worked even now that he was a man.

Once outside the city of Rome, Marcus turned northwest. Octavia looked at him at one point and said, "This is not the way to the sea."

Marcus smiled at her. "No, it is not. We are going to Ancona on the east coast. I did not want to give our travel plans to anyone. We are in great danger and the fewer people that know what I have in mind, the better off we both will be."

Octavia looked at Marcus as they walked along the side of the road. "I am an old woman, Marcus. I have lived a good life. Now, I only slow your escape. Leave me to my fate and do what you can to save yourself."

Marcus smiled back at her. "I would never do that Octavia. You most likely saved my life by risking yours to warn me. I will do no less. Beside that, what if I should die and meet Flavius in the next life. What would I say to him if he knew that I left you to take care of yourself?"

They both laughed but they both also understood the dangerous choices that they were making.

It took them nine days to make the trip northeast to Ancona. Marcus purchased new clothes for them and a pair of mules to ride. At Ancona, they sold the mules and booked passage on a merchant ship sailing to Salone on the Illyricum coast. His hope was to get them both to his holdings in Illyricum in order to provide a safe haven for Octavia.

The winds were with the ship as they sailed east across the Adriaticus arriving a day earlier than expected. They spent the night in Salone to allow time for Octavia to rest and then continued to his estate in Illyricum.

Chapter 66. "A Second Homecoming"

She saw the two figures in the distance coming directly toward the gates of her home. As they drew closer, it appeared that it was a young man and his elderly mother. The man was walking, tall and straight. The woman rode on a donkey, her head held high though her shoulders sagged with age. She thought to herself, they must be lost.

Cara asked one of her workers to go down to the gate and welcome the travelers. "Have them come up to the main house."

She took one more look at the two people about to enter her enclave. For a brief instant, she thought to herself that there was something familiar about the way the young man carried himself. But, she dismissed the thought as quickly as it had come to her.

Marcus was impressed by what he saw as he walked up the stone road that wound its way through the cultivated hillside. A lot of work had been done to expand the farm lots that he and his men had cleared and planted years ago. He wondered if Normalus was still overseeing the farm work. He had been a loyal worker and Marcus had put him charge of the farming when he had left Illyricum.

Marcus also thought about Cara, the woman who he had entrusted his property to. She had faithfully forwarded profits from the estate to Alexander in Rome. Alexander had in turn sent them on to Marcus in Judea. From the increases that were evidenced by what had been given and now as he looked over his lands, he knew that his trust in Cara had been well placed.

Marcus and Octavia were greeted at the entry gate by a servant who was unknown to Marcus. "Good day sir, madam. The mistress of the house sends greetings and has asked that I escort you to the main house."

Marcus thanked the servant and as he followed the man toward the main house, he noticed that there were several armed men standing guard along the walls of the enclave. He wondered if they were there for Romans or for Pannonians.

As he walked up the steps of the main house, Cara came out of the front entrance. Both stopped in their footsteps at the recognition of one another.

"Marcus!" Was all that Cara could say.

"Cara, you have not changed. You look the same as you did that first day when we met."

Both went to each other and embraced. Octavia and the servant shifted awkwardly at the exchange.

Marcus stepped back. "Cara, I have brought this kind woman with me from Rome. This is Octavia. She is a long time friend of my father and of my teacher."

Cara took her eyes off of Marcus to look at Octavia. "Welcome Octavia. It will be a pleasure to have you here with us."

Cara then turned to the servant. "Ransus, please go and find Metros. He will want to welcome Marcus."

She looked back at Marcus.

Marcus had a surprised look on his face. He asked, "Is Metros Scipia here?"

Cara looked down at the floor. Then, with resolve, she looked directly into Marcus' eyes and said, "Yes, Metros is my husband."

Marcus was again surprised but this time he managed not to show his feelings. After a slight pause, he quickly said, "I am happy for both of you. May you both be blessed."

His choice of words confused Cara but before she could speak, Metros walked into the hallway. "Marcus Titus!" He shouted. "Praise the Gods. Welcome back to Illyricum."

The two men shook hands and clapped each other on the shoulder.

"Metros, you look bigger and stronger than I even remember you. It is good to see you."

Metros smiled a big toothy smile at Marcus. He always had liked this Roman. "You look very fit yourself Marcus." Looking Marcus over, he suddenly frowned. "No sword?"

Marcus smiled, "That is a long story. But, let me introduce a friend that I have brought with me from Rome. This is Octavia."

Metros bowed slightly to the older woman. "Welcome Octavia. Any friend of Marcus is my friend as well." Again he flashed his toothy grin.

Octavia had first been somewhat alarmed at Metros appearance but once he smiled that broad smile, she was put at ease. "Thank you." She said.

Marcus took Metros by the arm over to where Cara was standing. Taking Cara's hand he said, "I am so happy for you both. Cara has told me that you are married. That is a very good thing. You must tell me how all this came to pass."

They walked into the main room of the house. Cara sent another servant out to get refreshments while they sat down to talk.

Over the next few hours, Metros and Cara told Marcus how they had to first deal with the Romans and then with the Pannonians to keep the estate together. They had organized the local patricians to band together and had finally worked out a negotiated truce that had been kept for three years now. During that time, they had expanded the farming with the help of Normalus. They had also begun breeding horses which they sold to both the Romans and the Pannonians. This too helped keep the truce in effect. Their horses were among the finest bred and were highly prized by those who purchased them.

Over time, each of them had come to appreciate one another and the hard work that each was doing. Their appreciation blossomed into love. A little over a year ago, they were married.

Marcus was truly happy for them.

Marcus then began his story about what he had experienced since leaving Illyricum. He spent most of his time, describing all that had happened in Judea and the impact that Jesus had had on his life. He related his calling with such emotion and passion that all in the room were swept up in his fervor.

"I must do what God has willed for me to do here on earth." He said as he bowed his head almost in exhaustion.

Cara felt great sympathy for the man she had once loved. She now loved him in a much different way. She was moved by the story of Jesus. She was in awe of the resurrection and what it offered to her and to everyone. Her intuition confirmed to her that Marcus was the person to write the history of his new found faith and of his witness to the son of God.

Metros never believed in either a place that exists after death or in the existence of Gods who were greater than men. But he knew, first hand, the courage and integrity of Marcus. As he listened to Marcus, he was struck by the fact that Marcus was so moved by what he had seen. He also saw the truth in some of the teachings of Jesus that Marcus had shared with them. Marcus had seen a boy crippled from birth rise up and walk because of this man, Jesus. This was a powerful image for Metros. If Marcus gave testimony to having seen this with his own eyes, he could not doubt that this Jesus was more than a mortal man. For the first time in his life, Metros considered the possibilities that opened up for him and all others in this world.

Metros asked, "Will you stay here with us Marcus?"

Marcus shook his head. "No, it would be too dangerous. You have established a truce that works well for all in this valley. My presence could destroy that peace."

Metros objected, "This is your home Marcus. All of us would willingly defend you to the death."

Marcus raised his hand. "I am not about death any longer. I am about life. Jesus has arisen to show us a better way to live. I must be true to the example that he has set for all of us."

"Where will you go?" Cara asked. The concern she had clearly showed in her eyes.

"I will go where God leads me. But, I do have a favor to ask."

Metros responded by saying, "Anything."

Marcus looked over at Octavia who had sat very still during the entire evening's conversation. "Octavia saved my life in Rome. Of this, I have no doubt. I would like to leave her here in Illyricum, under your protection Metros. I do not believe that Rome will come here to look for her so I do not believe that she will endanger anyone here.

If they look for anyone, it will be me. For that reason, I will be leaving early tomorrow morning. All that I will need is one of your prized horses and a certain sum of money for my continued journeys.

I have given this much thought. In return for having you do as I have requested, I am going to turn over this estate, that you both have worked so hard to develop, to you. It will be my wedding present to you."

Metros and Cara both objected to the gift and said that Octavia would be treated as family for as long as she wished to stay in Illyricum.

Marcus said that what he willed would be done. He did not have need of so much wealth and with his calling, having such wealth would be a burden.

Early the next morning, he bid farewell to his friends and rode off leaving his written transfer of his Illyricum property in Cara's hands.

Metros and Cara climbed the stairs to the top of the enclave's protective wall. They watched Marcus disappear down the road. Marcus never looked back.

Chapter 67. "Home is where the heart is."

Marcus knew from the moment that he had arrived in Rome, what his ultimate destination would be. As he rode south along the Adriaticus Sea toward Macedonia, he thought about his decision. Although Rome had some influence over the place that he was going to, it had managed to remain mostly independent. It was made up of separate city-states that had joined together in a Federation for their common protection. It had its own army, a representative assembly, and a culture that thrived on its separate identity from Rome. It also helped that its land was protected by dense forests and that its steep mountains protected the rich river valley areas. It would be very difficult for Rome to effectively move its armies across the rugged mountains and through the tangled forests. They would have to engage an army that was thoroughly familiar with the terrain and that had fortified the mountainsides. Marcus believed that it was a safe place for him to go and spend time writing about the life of Jesus. Lycia was also the home of Didyanna.

For the most part, Marcus' journey was uneventful. He traveled to the city of Heraclea, then west to Pella, and then south again to Cassandrea. From there he boarded a ship bound for Ephesus, a coastal town on the Aegeum Sea.

Again traveling west, he crossed Asia entering into Lycia from the north. The road was rugged as it climbed steeply into the mountains. It gave Marcus a sense of security. He knew that these were the kind of roads that Rome would have to navigate in order to destroy the Lycian League. With a homeland army defending the passes, it would be impossible to take control of the country from the land. Only the coastal plains around Patara and Myra could be threatened.

Five days after entering Lycia, Marcus arrived at Xanthos. His horse was pretty well worn from the travel and so was he. He decided to find an inn and stable where both he and his horse could get some much needed rest and food. He would contact Didyanna after he had an opportunity to recover.

Finding accommodations was an easy task. Xanthos thrived on merchant trade and there were many suitable inns both on the outskirts of the city as well as in the city itself. Marcus selected an inn just outside the city. He did not want his arrival to be known until he was fully ready to explain his sudden return after so many years.

That night, Marcus sat up late into the evening wondering how he would be received by the Atolia family. 'Would Didyanna be happy to see him again? How would her father look upon the return of someone who had all but vanished from his daughter's life years ago? Someone who had not even written to his daughter for all of this time? Would Didyanna think that he had taken for granted her caring for him?'

Marcus had thought that he had his plans all worked out. But now that he had arrived in Xanthos, his plan did not seem so clear to him. More than once during the night, he thought about abandoning his plan all together and leaving Xanthos without a trace that he had ever been there. Finally, he fell into a deep sleep and did not wake until mid-morning the next day.

Marcus had saved his best clothing for the time when he would again meet Didyanna. As he dressed, he examined himself in a mirror. He wondered how different he would look to Didyanna. He hoped that his clothing would hide the years and the toll that those years may have taken upon him. Finally satisfied that there was no more that he could do to improve his appearance, he went to the stable, saddled his horse and rode into the city toward the Atolia home.

Marcus remembered the way. Not much had changed in Xanthos during the years that he had been away. Actually, now that he was back, it did not seem all that long ago. Fond memories flooded back into his mind and occupied him until he reached the Atolis home.

He dismounted and tied his horse to a tether post just outside the gate that wound its way around the graceful home inside the courtyard. He walked through the gate and directly to the main doorway. He pulled on a golden chord that hung down along the right side of the doorway. A bell resonated above and moments later Didyanna's brother, Cale, appeared in the doorway.

Cale immediately recognized Marcus. "Marcus Titus, welcome back." Cale extended his arm in greeting.

Marcus took Cale's offered arm, saying, "Hello Cale. Thank you for making an awkward moment less painful."

Cale looked puzzled. "Awkward moment? Marcus, you are always welcome in the Atolia household."

As they went into the inner entryway, Didyanna appeared in the hallway. She stood there, tall and straight, as beautiful as Marcus had remembered her. Everything around him seemed to disappear. He was in a world where it was just he and Didyanna. Neither said a word to the other. As if they were both propelled by some invisible force, they rushed to one another, embracing and then separating just enough to look into one another's eyes.

"Oh Marcus!"

"Didyanna."

They drew close together as their lips met and they became lost in the warmth and emotion of each other.

Cale smiled and quietly left the two lovers alone in the hall way.

Cale returned to the main room of the house. He looked at his father and mother and then to Cassandra. "Marcus has arrived."

There was a sigh of relief from all of them.

Alex Atolia motioned for his son to sit down. "It is good that he is here. When we did not hear from him, I was concerned that he may have been taken prisoner by the Romans before he was able to leave Italia."

Alex's wife, Cecilia, asked, "Do you think that Romans will seek him here?"

Alex shook his head. "No. I think that the active interest in Marcus is only in Rome. Tiberius rules the Empire, Sejanus only rules Rome. From what I have heard, Tiberius is not happy with Sejanus and will soon have him removed. Amidst all this political intrigue, I doubt that much effort will be made to capture Marcus."

Marcus and Didyanna entered the main room. They were noticeably flushed with a healthy glow as they were greeted by the family and Cassandra.

Marcus was surprised to see Cassandra in the Atolia household. "Cassandra, this is a pleasant surprise."

Cassandra smiled. "You left Rome rather hastily. I decided that I too would be better off coming home to Lycia." Looking at Didyanna and then back at Marcus, Cassandra said with a mischievous expression, "I thought that I might see you again."

Marcus nodded, appreciating the wisdom of Cassandra. "Lycian women are blessed with a wisdom that exceeds all conventions! It appears that my surprise visit to Lycia was only a surprise to me!"

Everyone in the room laughed.

Later, as Marcus and Didyanna sat alone in the garden, Didyanna put her hands to his face and looking into his deep brown eyes softly whispered, "Welcome home my love."

Chapter 68. "Life after Death"

Marcus and Didyanna spent the next month learning the inner most thoughts and feelings of each other. She told him of her abiding deep love for him. She had agonized over his leaving and had worried constantly about his safety. She had asked her brother Cale, and her father to seek any information that they might obtain of him on their trips to Rome. They had reported that he had inherited several estates previously owned by his teacher and that for a while it was believed that he resided in the northern provinces of Italia.

She looked at him sadly and went on. "Then they told me that they had learned that your father had died and that you were living in his frontier residence in Jerusalem." She shuddered as she went on. "There was a report that you and a Roman centurion were attacked by rebels in Jerusalem. I died a thousand deaths after that piece of information."

She paused then went on, "I knew that the Gods would bring you back. It could not be otherwise."

Marcus put his arm around Didyanna. "You are right in all that you have said but for one thing."

Didyanna pulled away from him to look at his face. "One thing?"

Marcus was deadly serious now and it disturbed her to see this turn in his disposition from the lighthearted talks that they had been engaged in.

"The gods did not bring me back to you. God did."

"I don't understand what you are saying."

Marcus took her hands in his. "This is very important that you understand. I have been both blessed and cursed with experiences and knowledge that most will never see or know."

Marcus spent the rest of the day telling the story of his star crossed path with Jesus of Nazareth. Their passing in the desert as infants, his search for his purpose in life, his conversion to what he was now calling a Christian religion, and his witnessing of the miracles of the one he now knew as the son of God.

Marcus told her of the many parables and teachings of Jesus. He said, "Think about this one simple commandment, do for others as you would have them do for you. Think of it Didyanna. If everyone followed that one simple commandment, think of what kind of a world we would be living in."

He told her of the lame boy whom he had seen made to walk by Jesus. Then there was the stormy night when Jesus had walked on top of a ragging sea to save his disciples. How the waters calmed at his command.

He had had tears in his eyes as he told her of the crucifixion. He described how Jesus had predicted his death but showed no hesitation in doing what he said that his father had willed even unto death.

Jesus had said that he would arise from the dead on the third day after his death. A woman by the name of Mary Magdalene who had followed Jesus in his ministry came to him and to another disciple, Peter, and told them that Jesus had fulfilled the prophecy. He had risen from the tomb.

Marcus went on with a certain excitement in his voice. "Peter and I ran to the tomb where Jesus had been placed. The tomb was carved out of the rocks and upon placing the body of Jesus in the tomb, a large stone had been rolled in front by several men so that no one would take the body.

When we arrived at the tomb, the body was gone. The cloth that had covered the body was there but Jesus was not. The stone had been rolled away.

I later spoke with a Roman soldier who had been placed nearby to guard the tomb. He said that there had been several after shocks from an earlier earthquake and that suddenly the stone had been moved away from the opening. He described a scene where a great light came from inside the tomb and a man dressed in white garments entered the tomb. Later he saw three women enter the tomb. Shortly, they ran out screaming that Jesus had risen from the dead. He said that this so terrified him and the other guards who were with him that they ran away for protection."

Marcus told her of the threats against all of the disciples including him by the Jewish governing council and the high priest. He decided to return to Rome. One night as he rode along the coast of the Great Sea, he saw Jesus, risen and reminding him that he had promised to put down in writing all that he had heard and seen.

Looking again at Didyanna, he asked, "Can you accept any of what I have told you?"

She put her arms around him and held him pressed tightly against her. "I accept all that you have said, Marcus. My love for you would not have allowed otherwise. But, I also believe in what you have said because I see the truth of your words in your eyes. They never deceive for you are truly a good man." She looked up at him and finished by saying, "And now, you are a man of God."

Their talks continued over the next several days. They talked much about Jesus as a man and as the son of God.

"Did he have the love of a woman as you have with me?" Didyanna asked.

Marcus thought about this. "He could have had such love. There was one of his followers, Mary, the sister of Martha, daughter of a man called Lazarus. Jesus seemed to have a special affection for her. He looked at her as I imagine I look at you. I have heard that she wanted to be his wife. But, he never asked for her hand in marriage. I think that he knew that his time in this world was short and that it would not be fair to her to ask that she sacrifice as he knew he would. I think his love for her was that great that he did not accept her love to a point that it would hurt her."

Didyanna eyes filled with tears as she listened to Marcus. "Men never understand that for a woman, even a day with the man that she truly loves is a lifetime of memories that she will forever hold dear in her heart."

Didyanna wiped a tear away and asked, "Do you believe that Jesus arose after his death?"

"I do believe this. I not only experienced this by the Sea but I see it in many things that happen each day. Jesus taught that man was made in God's image. Not just in appearance but in the working of his inner soul. When one man does some good for another, he is acting as Jesus has taught and as God has designed."

Didyanna asked, "How is it that not all men then act as God intended?"

Marcus shifted in his chair, "God gives man a choice. Man can do good deeds for which God will be pleased or he can decide to do things that are not good and suffer God's displeasure. Jesus teaches that if you follow the guidance which he has provided, then you will be rewarded, if not on earth then in heaven."

"How do you know that you have done well by God, if you have not learned all the lessons given by Jesus?"

"Didyanna, think of your own life. Have you ever had the experience where you have done something nice for someone else and in seeing the good that it has done, feel something radiating from inside yourself that makes you happy? That is the gift that God has given all of us. Jesus calls it our soul.

When we help those who are sick or give comfort to those who are less fortunate than we are, we have that feeling. We have done for them what we would hope that others would do for us if we were not as fortunate."

Marcus paused as his thoughts wandered for a moment. He then went on in a more subdued voice. "The sad part of all of this is that not all men saw Jesus as I saw him. Not all men heard what Jesus had to say as I did. If they had, he never would have been killed. A part of me died the day he was crucified. But, as our risen Lord, he showed to me that there is life after death. This is important for all of us. It gives us an eternal hope. It is also what makes it possible for us to go on even after we have lost someone who is close to us."

Realizing that he was sermonizing to her, he brightened the tone and direction of his conversation, "I wish that you could have met him, Didyanna. He was a man like no other. He had no formal schooling but was wise beyond anyone I have ever met. To see him stand before thousands of followers and show compassion for the very least among them is something that was a lesson for us all.

He was asked once why he wasted his time on sinners. He answered with but a few words that he was not sent to save the righteous. Think about that answer to a question any one of us might have asked. His answer was simple and yet profound. That was how he was.

He once told the parable of a son who squandered all of his father's money while another son honored his father and worked hard for his father. When at last the prodigal son came home, the father celebrated and gave to his wayward son the best food and drink that the father had. Jesus was asked how he could celebrate a son like that. Jesus said, 'I do not celebrate the prodigal son, I celebrate the forgiving father.'

He appeared as a simple peasant from a rural frontier province with no education other than as a carpenter's apprentice. A carpenter's apprentice does not think and speak this way. Jesus was taught by the divine inspiration of his Father, in Heaven. He was the son of God who came down to earth to bring us back to our Creator."

Didyanna asked one last question of Marcus. "How will his message be spread to others that all might know who he was and what he said?"

Marcus stood up and looked into the night time sky. "Jesus called twelve men to his side to follow him as his disciples. His thought was to train them in God's ways so that they in turn could go out and train and teach others. He asked them to travel to the ends of the earth with the good news that God had given to them.

For two years, the twelve that he had chosen traveled with him and saw the miracles and heard the lessons. There were many times when they did not understand what he was giving to them. Most of the twelve came from humble beginnings in and around Galilee. What he asked of them was monumental for them. They worked hard at trying to learn the lessons that he taught. They were devoted to him as their teacher. After he was gone, the holy spirit of God descended upon them and gave to them the knowledge and direction they will need to carry out their intended missions.

But there is one thing more. Jesus told me that I am his other disciple, his thirteenth disciple. He said that God had selected me long ago. To me would fall the responsibility of writing his gospel so that beyond the spoken word there would also be the written word to preserve and to proclaim the teachings and the will of God.

Jesus told me that that is my purpose in life. He directed that I do all that is in my power to survive and to complete the work that I was destined to do. I love you Didyanna...more than anything else in this world, but I must do what I am called to do by Jesus and by my Lord."

Didyanna stood and walked over to where Marcus was standing. She took his hand, squeezed it, and said, "If this is the direction that you want to follow in life then I will go there with you. I will do all that I can to help you and to support you and to love you."

They looked long at one another and as the night mist wrapped around them they kissed in the fading moonlight. Their bond and their pledge to one another sealed for eternity.

Chapter 69. "Confirmation"

Marcus and Didyanna were married and established their home on the outskirts of Xanthos. Over the next few years, Marcus spent his time writing all that he could remember of his time with Jesus and the stories that were told to him by the other disciples. Because most of the stories had been shared with him on separate occasions, he tried to put them into context with the three years of Jesus' ministry. He was not comfortable with this but he had no way of confirming the timeframe for many of the events.

There was also a lot of local interest in the things about which Marcus was writing. He began to give sermons to small groups in and around Xanthos. Gradually other city-states in the Lycian League began to invite him to speak to groups of citizens about his holy experiences.

He traveled to Patara, Myra, and Olympus and found that in each city the people hungered for the message that he brought to them. It was a message of forgiveness, love, and hope.

One night while coming back to Xanthos from Myra, Marcus had a dream that Jesus had joined with him in Myra and had asked him to baptize those who attended his sermon with water. In his dream, Jesus carried a jug of water while Marcus dipped his hands in the water and then baptized each of those present by placing his hand on their heads and giving them the grace of Jesus and his Father in Heaven.

Marcus awoke with a start. The dream was as real as if it had actually happened. Marcus was given the knowledge that he not only had to spread the word of God but that he was also being directed to give the forgiveness of God to those who accepted the way of the Lord.

The next day, he returned to Myra and was greeted by not only those who had heard him the day before but ten times that number. He told them of his dream and that Jesus had come to him and given him the authority to baptize. He explained what that was and all who heard declared their faith and received baptism.

When Marcus finally returned home to Xanthos, Didyanna and all who knew him well noticed a change in Marcus. He appeared older and wiser somehow and his writings took on a degree of certainty that he had not had before.

People in the town who had accepted Jesus as their Savior were always anxious to share any news brought to town about other Christians. One day, a follower of Marcus came to him with news that another disciple by the name of Matthew had been preaching in Antiochia and was on his way to the city of Tarsus.

Marcus went home immediately to talk with his wife.

"Didyanna!' He called out as he entered his home.

Didyanna recognized the excitement in her husband's voice. "What is it Marcus?"

He ran to her and smiling broadly said, "I have received word that Matthew, one of the disciples is going to Tarsus to preach."

Not knowing what else to say, Didyanna smiled and said, "Wonderful."

Marcus realized that his mind had been racing ahead of his words. He took her into their great room and sat down on the divan. "This means that finally I may be able to have one of the original twelve review my manuscript."

"But how?" She asked with a concerned look spreading over her face.

Marcus expected this reaction from Didyanna. She was always worried when he traveled even within the Lycian borders. Alex and he had discussed his safety and had concluded that he was all but forgotten in Rome. Sejanus had been put to death by Tiberius after Tiberius had discovered that Sejanus was plotting against him. No one had ever come to Lycia with an inquiry about Marcus. The citizens of Xanthos were now very protective of their holy man. Many had been converted to the faith in Jesus as the son of God. His teachings were a very natural progression for their basic beliefs.

Marcus answered her concern. "I will travel with a few of those who are interested in meeting one of Jesus' original twelve. There are many here who are interested in seeing the healing powers of the original disciples."

Didyanna smiled. "You are said to have those same healing powers!"

Marcus was aware of the many beliefs that were associated with his own ministry. "Didyanna, I have all but finished my gospel to Jesus. Matthew was one of the few that were literate among the disciples. He could read and write in Aramaic. He has the education and the experience to do what I need to have done. I think that he has been led in this direction to assist me in putting forth the true history of our faith."

"Marcus, you know that I support you in all that you do. It is just that I still worry about someone arresting you and taking you away. I have heard how they treat Christians in other parts of the Roman Empire. You will not even take up a sword to defend yourself. Cale tells me in private that he disagrees with you on that. He says the world is too dangerous a place to go about with no such self protection. He says that you, of all people, should carry a sword."

Marcus had discussed this before with Didyanna. It was an argument that had no resolution. He responded as he always did, "God will watch over me."

Didyanna knew that this was something that Marcus felt he must do to complete his writings. She also sensed that he needed the contact with another disciple to reassure himself of the expanded role he now had taken in this new faith.

She gave one last look at the floor and then facing him asked, "When will you be leaving?"

"A ship sails in two days that will take us to Selinus. The sooner I leave, the sooner I will return to you."

They both hoped that that would be true.

Two days later, Marcus and five of his followers sailed from the Lycian coastal city of Myra to Selinus and then traveled by land along a coastal road to Tarsus. It did not take the Lycians long to locate Matthew. There was a great gathering on a hillside and in the midst of all the people was Matthew.

As Marcus and those with him sat down to listen to Matthew, Marcus noticed that Matthew had changed. The former tax collector for Herod Antipas had been somewhat withdrawn and kind of a frail individual compared to the other disciples. Marcus had spent one evening talking with Matthew while he had accompanied Jesus through Judea.

Matthew had once owned a great house and had friends who enjoyed all that wealth had to offer. He told how he would keep some of the tax money to support his life style and to entertain his friends. One day, while Matthew was collecting taxes, Jesus happened upon Matthew in Capernaum. Jesus looked at Matthew and then approached saying to him, 'Tax collector, is your work satisfying?' Matthew had never been asked that before. He answered Jesus saying that it was a way to make a living. Jesus then said, 'Follow me and you will live a better life.'

Matthew told Marcus that there was something in the way Jesus spoke and in his words that had struck a cord inside of him. He had invited Jesus and those disciples who were with him to have dinner that night at his home. Jesus came with his followers and they talked most of the evening about discipleship. When the evening meal was completed, all who were there had asked to be blessed by the son of God. They all knew that Jesus was the prophesied Messiah. Matthew vowed his allegiance to Jesus. He gave up his wealth, his home, his work as a tax collector, and used the money that he had to further the work of Jesus in helping the poor.

Matthew told Marcus a story which he said would stay with him until the day that he died. The morning after Jesus had had dinner with Matthew and his friends, a Pharisee that knew Matthew asked Jesus, 'How is it that you eat and drink with tax collectors and sinners?' Matthew then laughed asking Marcus if he could guess at Jesus' response? Marcus continued to listen. Matthew said, 'Jesus looked the Pharisee in the eye and said to him, those who are whole have no need of a physician but those who are sick need the physician's attention.'

Marcus remembered them laughing together as they speculated about how the Pharisee received this undeniable truth.

He heard Matthew now saying to the multitudes who had gathered on this hillside, "Jesus came not to call the righteous for they already know the way of the Lord. Jesus came to show the sinners the error of their ways and to call upon them to repent.

Jesus has shown us that our Lord, God in Heaven, is a forgiving God. He has sent his son to us to tell us that if we are truly sorry for the wrongs that we have done; if we honestly and truly ask for God's forgiveness; then through Jesus, his son, we can still be saved.

Our reward will be in Heaven for on that day that we are called to leave this world, we will be welcomed into a better world in the kingdom of Heaven."

Marcus marveled at the power of Matthew's sermon. He also marveled at the response that Matthew elicited from the crowd. He saw it even on the faces of those who had come with him. He thought to himself, 'Truly the Holy Spirit is with Matthew.'

After his sermon, Matthew walked through the crowd touching those who sought his blessing. When he reached the place where Marcus was standing, Matthew stopped and a wide smile of recognition spread across his face. "Marcus! God be praised. It is good to see you."

Those who had been pressing Matthew now stepped back. Soon the news was spread that there was not one but two of the disciples of Jesus in their midst. The crowd fell silent. Slowly they began to get down on their knees, praying and asking to be blessed by the disciples.

Matthew said to Marcus, "My brother, help me to baptize those who wish to be freed of their sins through our Lord, Jesus Christ."

Marcus turned to one of his followers and asked that he get a jug of water. Two jugs were immediately brought forward and Marcus and Matthew proceeded to offer to those who requested it, the forgiveness of their sins in Jesus' name.

The two disciples and their followers then went to the encampment that Matthew had placed outside of Tarsus.

"What has brought you to Tarsus?" Matthew asked Marcus.

"You have brought me here."

"How did I bring you here?"

"Word of your ministry in Seleucia and your intention to carry that ministry into Cilicia and to Tarsus reached me in Lycia. I knew that this was the hand of God that was reaching out to me. I had a need and you are the instrument of our Lord in fulfilling that need."

Matthew did not understand what Marcus was saying. "You have to explain this to me Marcus. I am not understanding you."

"Our Lord, Jesus, directed me to set down in writing all that I have seen and all that I have learned in a gospel of our Lord. This I have worked upon for the past year or more. Much of my work has dealt with things that I did not personally witness but which others, including you, have told to me.

This work of mine, this gospel to our Lord, must be exact. It must be truthful in every way if it is to provide a testimony to Jesus and to our Father in Heaven. I believe that what is written will be the guide by which others will learn to follow.

Long after you and I and all of the others are gone, the gospel will live on and future generations will have the benefit of what each of us has discovered in our hearts.

I came here to Tarsus so that you might know what I have written and confirm for me that it is as I have written it."

Matthew looked at Marcus with a sense of awe and inspiration. "Marcus, you know that I will give you whatever assistance that I can. Jesus once told me of his charge to you. He said that you were literate in the universal language. You know that neither I nor any of the other disciples have that knowledge?"

Marcus nodded, "I do know that but I also know that you of all the disciples are literate in Aramaic. I propose that you and I review what I have written and that together we tell the story as it unfolded. You can then translate the gospel into your Aramaic language and I will also translate my Greek manuscript into Latin. In this way, the written word may be shared with all people."

Both men felt the power of this idea.

"Marcus, I agree with you that God's hand has brought both of us to this place and time. We will begin our work tomorrow.

Matthew and Marcus spent the next several weeks reviewing and revising the order of some of the events in the life of Jesus. Matthew had additional information and experiences to add to the gospel. Marcus was pleased with their final product. They both labored on the three translations. They called the work the gospel of Jesus Christ.

The five followers that had come from Lycia and nine of those who were with Matthew all were given an oral reading of the work. Some cried, others touched their hearts as they listened. In the end, each of their followers volunteered to be emissaries of the word and to carry the written word to other parts of the world.

It was decided that eleven of them would carry a translation to each of the other disciples. Matthew informed Marcus that Judas Iscariot had been replaced by a vote of the remaining disciples. His replacement was a constant follower of Jesus throughout his ministry by the name of Matthias.

Marcus accepted this appointment of Matthias by the other disciples recalling that Jesus had said that wherever one or more of you gather in my name, thereto shall I be. And, whatever two or more of you bind here on earth so shall that be bound in heaven.

Thinking about Judas Iscariot, Marcus commented that it must have been very hard on Jesus to have one of his own betray him and equally as hard on Judas to have to live with that betrayal.

Matthew nodded, "His betrayal of our Lord condemned him before man and God. He went back to the high priests and attempted to give back the thirty pieces of silver that they gave him for leading them to Jesus. They would not take it and scoffed at him as a traitor to his own kind. He was later found dead having hanged himself."

Marcus had known that Judas Iscariot had hung himself. He could only imagine the self inflicted suffering that one would have after betraying someone that you had followed for three years. "Judas will forever be judged as one of the most undesirable persons in history. Someone totally lacking in character and integrity."

Matthew agreed. "To this day, I do not believe that any of us understand how he was able to do what he did."

"My guess is that in the end, he was unable to justify what he did even to himself. His repentance even before those guilty priests was not accepted." Marcus concluded. He never again gave thought to Judas Iscariot.

Chapter 70. "Lycia"

Marcus traveled back to Lycia alone. He and Matthew had bid each other farewell not knowing if they would ever see one another again. Marcus had a strange feeling as he had watched Matthew walk away that he would not be able to see his fellow disciple again. Having worked with Matthew on the gospel, they had formed a bond through understanding and their mutual nurturing of their faith. He did not like the feeling that he now had as Matthew turned one last time to waive good bye. There was something very sad about him. Marcus felt a small part of himself disappear as Matthew too disappeared beyond the rise.

Didyanna ran to Marcus as he walked up the path from the Gate. They embraced, kissed, and as he took her hand and walked into the house he said, "It is done."

"You finished your work on the gospel?" She had stopped and pulled lightly on his hand.

"Yes. Matthew was the right person to help me finish the work. He gave me the right time frames and even shared some things which I had not known before. We rewrote portions of the script and even have translated the finished version into three languages."

She hugged him with joy. "Now, at last, you can have some peace. I know how heavy the responsibility of what you had to do weighed upon your mind."

He smiled. "It is true. Finishing the gospel to Jesus was a responsibility that I have lived with since my Lord gave me that charge." He looked at his beautiful wife and pulled her gently to him. "Now, I can devote the rest of my life to you."

Marcus continued to teach the ways of Christianity to the people of Lycia. Several times a year he would travel to the other city-states that were a part of the Lycian League and preach the gospel as he and Matthew had written it. Other men and women would come to him and ask to be granted authority to carry his message of the gospel of Jesus Christ to other villages and towns. Always, he could see something in them that reached out to him and gave him confidence that those who asked had a higher calling. These were not just followers, they were those who could carry the message and teach. The lessons that he taught to them, they now would be able to share with many others. He was certain that this was as God intended for his word to be spread.

As the years went by, Marcus was happy with how the gospel of Jesus had spread to most of Lycia. It had become a dominant religion for the people of this mountainous region.

Marcus and Didyanna were blessed with two children during this time, a boy that they named Mark and a girl that they named Alexandra. Marcus was elected to serve as a representative to the Lycian League. He would travel to Patara, the capital city of the Federation at least one week a month to discuss issues of common interest. His focus was always on the less fortunate in their society and on the education of the youth of the Federation.

Rome was beginning to exercise more interest in Lycia. In 45 AD, the Roman Emperor, Claudius sent an emissary to meet with the League's representatives to discuss the Federation becoming a Roman province. Marcus and others questioned the emissary on the need for such annexation by Rome. The emissary said that the Emperor was concerned about the safety of the territory that bordered the Great Sea. After weeks of negotiations, it was agreed that the Federation would continue to govern itself in all matters except for those that dealt with external security. A Roman Legion would be posted on the coast near Myra and would provide for coastal protection against pirates and others who would threaten Pax Romana, the Roman Peace.

It took another year for the treaties to be signed. In 46 AD, Lycia became a Roman province. A Roman fortress was built on the coast near Myra and a Roman Legion took up residence in the fortress.

When the fortress was completed in 47AD, Marcus and his fellow representatives were invited to meet the Primus Pilus, the senior Centurion of the Legion.

As they entered the fortress, Marcus and the other members of the Federation's governing body were welcomed by trumpets and by a cohort of more than a thousand soldiers, standing at attention in full battle dress. Marcus noticed that the legionnaires wore considerably more body armor than they had when he was a young boy in Rome. Their shields, helmets, and equipment were formidable. He realized that this show of strength was intentional. It was designed to impress the Federation's leaders that the Empire had a strong footing in its newest province.

The Federation members were led pass the cohort to the far end of the parade grounds. There they met the five centurions who commanded the Legion. As the Primus Pilus stepped forward removing his helmet, Marcus was shocked at the recognition of his old friend, Lucius Neros.

Lucius had not yet seen Marcus as he began his welcome. "On behalf of the Emperor Claudius, I wish to welcome you to our fortress. Rome has long enjoyed a bond of friendship with the city-states of Lycia. As you offered your assistance to Rome during the Third Macedonian War, Rome now offers its assistance to you as we maintain the great Peace of Rome throughout the civilized world. The security of your people and of the trade routes, over land and by sea, is our primary responsibilities. It is our hope that you will call upon us whenever you have need of our services."

Lucius then introduced the centurions who were his subordinates.

Alex Atoli was now the elected leader of the Federation's senate. He in turn introduced each of the representatives of the Federation and identified the city-state from which they came.

Alex finished his introductions with his own city-state of Xanthos. "Xanthos has three representatives. I am one, Thaddeus Larcos is the second, and my son-in-law, Marcus Titus is the third."

Lucius had only half been listening as Alex had run through more than thirty representatives from nineteen city-states. His head came up fast at the mention of Marcus' name.

Seeing Marcus for the first time in more than fourteen years, he walked directly to Marcus and extended his arm in Roman fashion. Marcus took it. To the amazement of Romans and Lycians alike the two men appeared to be genuinely happy to see one another.

"Marcus, I can not believe my eyes."

"Lucius, congratulations. Primus Pilus, first spear!"

"And you, a son-in-law! I never thought of you as a married man."

Alex Atoli interrupted the two old friends. "Perhaps this reunion would be better served off the parade ground."

Lucius looked at Alex and smiled. "You are quite right Senator Atoli. In the excitement of seeing my old friend from Rome, I have neglected my duties."

Lucius turned to his junior centurions, having purposefully identified Marcus as his friend from Rome, and asked them to divide their guests into smaller groups and give them a full tour of the fortress.

Turning back to Alex, Lucius said, "It would be my honor if you and your son-in-law would join me."

Alex looked from Lucius to Marcus and then answered, "Please take no offense at this but I think that it would be well if I let the two of you enjoy your reunion without the father-in-law in tow. I will join one of the other groups and let you both get reacquainted. Fourteen years is a long time!"

As Alex moved away, Lucius said to Marcus, "Your father-in-law is a wise man."

"Yes, he is. He has great insight and has done a lot of good for the people of Lycia."

"Come Marcus, let me show you my new quarters. I need to take off this body armor."

The two friends went inside the barracks and walked to where Lucius had his own private quarters.

"Lucius, I could not help but notice the heavy body armor that the Legion now employs."

"Yes, it is newly issued. There is a lot of complaining among the cohorts and the auxiliary about its weight and coverage but it does provide a lot more protection in battle. To be honest with you, I think we lose in maneuverability what we gain in protection."

Marcus thought about this for a moment, then said, "Roman Legions have always prevailed because they move as one and bring maximum force against their opponents. It is probably the reason why whoever it was that designed your heavy armor decided that maneuverability was not as important as protecting the total force."

Lucius had just removed his armor as he looked at Marcus and laughed. "The holy man has not lost his interest in military matters."

Marcus smiled. "Holy man?"

Lucius placed his helmet on a staff with the rest of his body armor. "Yes. I have heard that you put down in writing the history of the Rabbi, Jesus of Nazareth. Did you know that one of the other disciples translated your work into Aramaic?"

Marcus was amazed that Lucius had so much information about not only his work but that of Matthew's as well. "It is true that I have written a gospel of Jesus Christ. I also worked with Matthew to have the work reviewed by him and translated into Aramaic. But how did you learn of this?"

Lucius went to a cupboard and took down a jug and two glasses. As he poured some wine into the glasses, he said, "I have come to know one of the original twelve disciples fairly well." He offered a glass to Marcus. "John. He is an interesting person. Although a fisherman by trade before becoming a disciple, he has some wealth. Did you know that he has been caring for the Rabbi's mother since her son's death?"

Marcus nodded. "I was aware of that."

"Marcus, does it not amaze you that for fourteen years neither of us have seen nor spoken to one another and yet we both know of these things? The Empire has made this sharing of information possible." Lucius took a full drink from his glass. "The Empire also has made it possible for us to enjoy a good glass of wine. The barrel of wine that this comes from is from Gaul."

Marcus took a sip of wine and savored its taste. "It is true. The Roman Empire protects the Great Sea for trade and has built roads that will last a thousand years. Travel is much improved and the movement of products and ideas has benefited from the expansion of Roman influence."

Lucius raised his glass. "Let us drink to Roman influence."

Marcus raised his glass. "To Roman influence and justice for everyone."

Lucius hesitated, then tilted his glass toward Marcus and took another full drink of the wine from Gaul. Marcus did likewise.

Lucius walked over to a chair and sat down. Marcus followed and joined Lucius by a table.

"Marcus, justice has always been something that you have championed. We have talked about this in the past. About justice as you perceive it and the state of the world as it really is."

"Lucius, I know that you and I do not see things in the same way, but through the eyes of the one you call Rabbi, I have seen that even in this world good and just people are rewarded and find contentment in their souls."

"Finding that contentment may cause their death." Lucius looked at his friend with what Marcus perceived to be sadness.

Lucius continued, "Not all the news is good news Marcus. John has shared with me some of what has happened to the other disciples who followed the Rabbi.

As you know, the one who betrayed the Rabbi, hung himself shortly after the Rabbi's crucifixion. He left a note that was found on his body. He wrote that he prayed for forgiveness for betraying his Lord.

The one called James the greater, the son of Zebedee, John's brother, was beheaded upon the order of Herod Agrippa. The leader of the faith in Jerusalem, Peter, was thrown into prison and most likely would have also been beheaded but for his escape.

Bartholomew traveled west to Abanopolis and preached salvation to those who would hear. King Astyages took exception to the teachings of Bartholomew and had him beheaded.

Simon, the one known as the Zealot, went to Egypt to preach and to convert followers to the ways of Jesus, the Rabbi. He found that those to whom he preached did not accept his teachings so he left Egypt and went to Persia. John learned that he was killed in the city of Suanir. His captors beheaded him.

Just before leaving Judea to come to Lycia, John informed me that Thomas, too, had been killed in the western frontier. He was told that Thomas converted a ruler's wife and son to the faith. The ruler became so enraged by this that he had Thomas tied to a stake and put to death by spears.

Marcus, I tell you all this because I do not want you to suffer the same fate as the other disciples. Your writings are becoming the foundation of this new religion. Your gospel of Jesus Christ, puts you and your family at risk. Now, that we are here in Lycia, it will only be a matter of time before the pieces are put together and Rome learns who you are and what you have done.

Your identity will not come from my lips but it will come to light."

Marcus listened carefully to all the Lucius was saying to him. What he had done he had done in the belief that it was what God intended for him to do. He had no doubt that it was the right thing for him to accomplish. Now, Lucius had called his attention to that which he had always known but had not feared until now. Not only was he at risk but his family was at risk as well.

"Lucius, why do you think that we are at risk?"

"Emperor Claudius is concerned with the expansion of trade routes and as a result the expansion of the Empire. But there are many around him that long for his throne. They are trying to incite persecution of the Christian Jews by saying that it is that group that seeks to overthrow Roman rule. If the day comes when Claudius or his successor accepts these charges, no believer or disciple will be spared. You will be an obvious target."

"Lucius, once you advised me to leave Jerusalem. I took your advice and looking back, it was the right thing to do. What advice would you give me now?"

Lucius looked down at the floor. He took a deep breath and said, "It is strange that you are the scholar and yet I am the adviser. You need to become invisible. At some point in time, Marcus Titus must cease to exist. As long as you bear the name, Rome will know how to find you."

Marcus understood what Lucius was telling him. They discussed many options before Marcus took his leave from Lucius.

As they took each others arm to say good bye, Marcus said, "Thank you my friend, I will pray on what we have talked about and ask for God's guidance."

Chapter 71. "The Visitor"

Marcus spent much time in prayer asking for guidance to his future path of life. He hoped for an answer that would lead him to whatever the next phase of God's plan for his life would be. Gradually, his concern for the safety of his family lessened.

His son and daughter were growing up and both showed signs of having keen minds and athletic bodies. Lucius was a frequent visitor and would tell the children wild stories about Roman battles much to the displeasure of their mother. Lucius also would tell the story of how he and their father, Marcus Titus, met in the great stone Amphitheater of Statilius Taurus in Rome. How they defeated hundreds of combatants before reaching the final four contestants. With age, Lucius focus on the contest where Marcus had fractured his arm took on a new tone of respect. He always praised Marcus for his commitment to abide by the rules, even when it resulted in his injury.

Strangely, neither Marcus nor Lucius ever discussed Lucius' suggestion that Marcus must disappear if he and his family were to be safe. Marcus often wondered if Lucius had had second thoughts about his concerns. It seemed possible since Rome had experienced several changes in leadership over the past few years.

Lycia continued to function as a Federation of city-states under Roman provincial rule. Its coastal cities increased their trade and the inland and mountain cities and towns enjoyed peace and prosperity.

From time to time, early followers of Jesus would find their way to Xanthos and seek out Marcus. They would carry news of what was now referred to as the Christian Church and of the leaders who had taken up the calling and were preaching Jesus' message. Marcus had found that his written gospel was being used over a wide swath of the Roman Empire and out to the frontiers. He wondered how much of it was his original work and how much had been altered, added to, or deleted by those who used it.

One visitor by the name of Appollos informed Marcus that Peter had gone to Rome and had founded a Christian Church in the heart of the Roman Empire. Appollos also told Marcus of the many preachers who have been called from all walks of life and all backgrounds. He said that he was particularly impressed by one who was a citizen of Tarsus in Asia Minor. Appollos had traveled with the man and gained his own calling from his relationship with him.

"What is the name of this preacher?" Marcus asked.

"His name was Saul but he took on a Christian name when he converted to a believer in Christ as Savior and the son of God. Now, he goes by the name of Paul."

Marcus had not thought about his Christian name. Jesus had said that he would be known as Mark. He assumed that Mark and Marcus were one in the same and had not given the use of the Christian name much thought.

"What else can you tell me about Paul?" Marcus was intrigued by the thought that there were others now who preached the word but who had never actually witnessed Jesus' presence. He was not alone then in commissioning surrogates to go forth and spread the word of God.

"I know that he was raised in a Greek culture and speaks and writes in three languages, Greek, Latin, and Aramaic. He believes that one does not have to be Jewish to be a Christian. In fact, if it were not so, I would not be here." Apollos laughed easily at the humor he saw in what he said.

"Before becoming a Christian, Paul actually persecuted Jewish Christians as a citizen of and auxiliary fighter for Rome. He told me that on a trip to Damascus, he had a vision of Jesus, as the son of God. So powerful was this vision that Paul was blinded by it. He could see nothing else but Jesus. Jesus spoke to him and told him that he must do the work of the Lord.

When he regained his sight, he was so moved by what had happened that he turned back and went to Jerusalem. There, he met and stayed with Peter. They talked for fifteen days with little to eat but water and unleavened bread. On the fifteenth day, Peter asked John and James to join them and together they baptized Paul.

Paul was sent out by Peter to speak to Gentiles and to try to convert them to the Christian Church. Peter gave Paul a copy of your writings, the gospel of Jesus. He has studied it to the point where he can recite every passage without reading from it. Your writings have had a tremendous impact on his work."

Marcus felt a sense of accomplishment at hearing this. His charge had been to create a history that would live beyond the present. It was to preserve for the ages, the story and the teachings of Jesus of Nazareth. It was to be Jesus' connection to the entire world, Jew and Gentile alike. Marcus was satisfied that he had fulfilled the work that was intended for him.

Appollos was on his way to see Peter in Rome. When he and Marcus parted, he assured Marcus that he would carry Marcus' good wishes to Peter and would tell Peter of Marcus' work in Lycia.

Later, on the day that Appollos departed, Marcus was watching Didyanna tending to her garden of flowers. He thought to himself how strange were the pathways of life. Thirteen men were called by God to follow his son here on earth. Thirteen who received the Holy Spirit and were graced with the message of mankind's salvation. Yet how many of them had met a terrible death at the hands of those they hoped to save.

It seemed that martyrdom was the fate of all who followed Jesus. He wondered if Peter, John, Matthew and those who were still alive would also one day be martyred. Would he one day suffer that fate?

Didyanna saw him staring at her from the balcony. "Marcus, you are watching but you do not seem to be seeing. I have waved to you twice now. Have I gotten so old that you no longer are interested in me?" She laughed warmly knowing that this was not so.

Marcus went down the steps leading to the garden. "You will never grow old my love. No, I was actually thinking about how lucky I am to have you." He kissed her lightly on the lips. "I am fortunate that I can enjoy our life together and our family all these years."

Didyanna knew her husband well. "Our recent visitor, Appollos, has made you aware of how good God has been to you?"

"Yes, in a way Appollos has made me take time to appreciate how truly blessed I am. You have been my blessing ever since the day we first met. We have had a good life together. Our children are all that we could hope for. I pray that it will always be so."

With his last words, Didyanna detected his concern. She shared it every day of her life though she rarely spoke of it. She knew how close he had come to being arrested and perhaps killed when he fled Rome. She knew that his writings would be taken by some to be seditious and an attack on Rome. She understood that a day might come when all that they had might be lost. She knew these things but she refused to dwell on them. Her job was to care for her family and this was always foremost in her thoughts and deeds.

"Your prayers are answered!" She said as she handed him one of her garden tools. "Help me remove the weeds from my garden."

They both laughed as they tended to the soil.

Two months later, Marcus returned home from a three day journey to Phaselis. He had given a sermon that dealt with much of Jesus' message to the people in his Sermon on the Mount.

When he walked into his home he was startled to see a face from years long past. Peter was seated on a divan with Didyanna and her father, Alex Atolis. All three looked up from their conversation as Marcus entered the room.

"Marcus, it is good to see you. Forgive me for not letting you know that I was coming. I have been telling your wife and father-in-law that I had planned a trip to Cappadocia to see my brother, Andrew.

Before beginning my journey from Rome, a young man by the name of Appollos came seeking an audience with me. He is quite a remarkable young man. He is well spoken and has a good education. He reminded me of another young man I met years ago. With age, I have come to appreciate such men." Peter laughed knowingly. "Unfortunately, it was not always so.

Marcus, think of my surprise when I heard that you were here in Lycia. As I said, I was thinking of our first meeting while Appollos was speaking to me and then he mentioned having visited with you. It was as if God was directing me to you."

Marcus had recovered from his initial surprise at Peter being here in Lycia.

"Peter, it is great to see you, too! I never expected to find you here in Lycia." Turning to his wife and father-in-law, Marcus continued, "Peter was chosen by Jesus to be the head of his flock when the time came to pass that Jesus was no longer here on earth."

Turning again to Peter, Marcus said, "From all that I have heard, it has not been an easy path for you to follow."

Peter's eyes gave a hint of sadness. "It has not been an easy road for any of us. Already four of our brethren have met the same fate as did our Savior and Master, Jesus Christ." Peter touched his chest as he mentioned Jesus' name.

Peter put his hand on Marcus' shoulder and went on, "In part, that is the reason for my travels. Our Christian Church is growing. The Lord's message has reached the four corners of the world. The multitudes flock to our calling. The message of forgiveness, redemption and hope given by our Lord has found many more followers than even you and I could have imagined. But with its acceptance comes great risk.

The Romans fear the power of God's word. They fear that it will foster a rival kingdom to their own. Most of all, the imperial rulers fear the tenants of our faith will cause their demise.

They have already begun striking out at all who preach the faith. Many Christians have been imprisoned and many more have been killed, even crucified as was our Lord. These are dangerous times for we who believe and profess our faith.

I understand that you have become both a historian of the word as well as one of its spokesmen."

Marcus acknowledged his work. "My gospel of the life of Jesus has been completed and I do speak the word to many in Lycia."

Peter walked over to a pouch that had been laid on the floor. Picking it up and opening it, he took out a sheath of papers tied with a chord. "I have your gospel Marcus. It is a wonderful work! I have shared it with many who have come with a calling. In Rome, we have a group who do nothing else but reproduce your work."

Marcus reddened with Peter's praise.

Peter turned to face Alex and Didyanna. "Our Lord told us not to hide our light under a basket. Marcus' written work is the light of Christianity. He has captured for the ages the essence of our Master. The teachings, the miracles, the gifts from God are all here for those who but read and understand."

Peter walked over to Marcus. "You have done well Marcus. But you must now do more."

"More?" Marcus asked.

"Yes. You have captured pieces of Jesus' life and lessons. God wants you to write all that is known about his son.

I had a vision after my visit with Appollos. I saw a white dove flying high in the sky and then a voice spoke to me. I was told to go to my brother for his day was almost at hand. Then I was told to see you and let you know that your life's work is just that. You must continue to learn and to write as you have already done. I was told to tell you that your gospel is the never ending story about our Lord. It is to be a never ending work for you."

Marcus was completely at a loss by Peter's revelation. He had never considered his commitment as one that would continue for a life time. He had thought that once he had pieced together his narrative based upon what he had seen and heard, his work would be completed. Now, as he thought about what Peter said, it became obvious to him that the writing of the gospel would indeed be a continuing process.

Peter spoke as if reading his thoughts. "All of us, all of the disciples of Jesus have made a lifetime commitment to his teachings and to our calling. Marcus, you were called to set forth by the printed word his teachings and the lessons of his life. It was a purposeful calling. Your calling is the equal of the rest of us. We spread his word by our missionary work and our preaching in distant lands. Together, our preaching and your writing will prepare the way for generations of followers to come."

Marcus then thought of his discussions with Appollos on the night before he continued on to Rome. "Peter, there are others who are also writing about the life of Jesus and his teachings. Appollos told me of one such scholar by the name of Paul."

Peter knew Paul from Tarsus. "I know the one of whom you speak. He and I spent time together in Jerusalem. He will write as well but he has not had the personal relationship with our Lord that you were blessed to have. Jesus once called you Mark. Mark will be your Christian name. Write your next gospel by your given Christian name for it is in Christ that you were chosen to go forth."

"This is a mighty task that you have set before me. I am not sure where I would begin."

Peter smiled, "Begin as I did, with John. John brought me to Jesus. John became a believer almost at the inception of our Lord's ministry. He has God's authority as do you and I. He will help you with your continuing work on your gospel of Jesus."

Peter spent a week with the Titus family. Marcus could see that his time with the family had a profound effect on their commitment to Jesus and to the faith.

Toward the end of Peter's week long stay, Peter asked, "Marcus, have you administered baptism to your family?"

Marcus was embarrassed to think that after all these years and after all the baptisms that he had performed, he had never thought about administering baptism to his own family. "Sadly, I have not."

Peter then asked, "I would consider it an honor if you would allow me to baptize them."

"The honor would be ours, Peter."

That same day the Titus family, along with the Atolis family prayed with Peter in the Titus family's garden. Each member of the family asked God for forgiveness of their sins. Peter then took water from the fountain in the center of the garden and blessed it. Peter poured the water into a large earthen bowl that Marcus held. As he moved from one member of the family to the next, he dipped his hands in the water and then placed his hands on their heads baptizing Didyanna, young Mark, Alexandria, Cale and his new wife Cassandra, Alex Atolis and his wife Cecilia, in the name of Jesus Christ. When the baptismal ceremony was completed, they celebrated with a feast of roasted lamb, local fruit and vegetables. Marcus thanked God for the abundance of food, love and friendship that filled his home that day.

On the last day of Peter's stay, Lucius came to visit his friend and his friend's guest. Lucius had known Peter from the days when they both were residents of Jerusalem. Their relationship had bee strictly professional. Peter, as head of the Christian Jews in Jerusalem, had had many occasions to come into conflict with the high priests of the Temple. On more than one occasion, Lucius and his cohort had been called to quiet protests and stem any rioting.

One of the household servants announced Lucius to Marcus and Peter.

"Welcome Lucius. I am happy to see you." Marcus was sincerely happy that Lucius had come before Peter's departure. He now believed that it was again God's hand that had brought Peter to him and that it was in answer to his prayers concerning the warning and advice that Lucius had given to him.

As they greeted one another in Roman fashion, Marcus looked at Peter and said, "Lucius, I believe that you know Peter."

"Yes, we saw each other more often than either of us most likely would like to admit to."

Lucius let go of his friends arm and took a step toward Peter but stopping before he was within arms reach. "I heard that you were in Lycia. I thought that Marcus was probably the reason for your journey to this province."

Peter walked over to a chair and sat down. "Centurion Lucius." Peter smiled. "A loyal Legionnaire, loyal Roman, and loyal friend. Marcus, did you know that during my time in Jerusalem, the high priests of the Temple had me arrested and imprisoned. I have no doubt that their intention was to have me killed as well."

Marcus looked from Peter to Lucius for confirmation. Lucius continued to stare at Peter as Peter went on. "A miracle occurred the first night of my imprisonment. My jailer neglected to lock the cell that I was in after he had brought me my dinner. Even more miraculously, I made my way out of the Fortress of Antonia without encountering a single guard."

Marcus remembered how well fortified and guarded was the fortress. He also knew how well trained the legionnaires were. He again looked at Lucius but received no indication from his Roman friend that what Peter was saying was either to be dismissed or confirmed.

Peter concluded, "Later I was given to know that the Centurion from the first cohort was in command of the fortress guards that night. I am forever grateful to whoever was responsible for my deliverance from the hands of the Sadducees."

Lucius walked over to a chair near Peter and sat down. He said, "There are some myths which are best said in the confidence of friends or not at all."

Peter looked up at Marcus. "What I have just shared with you must be forgotten. It is an old story no longer of any consequence."

Marcus understood and offered to get some food and beverages for his guests. Neither were ready to eat or drink. Both had things to talk about with Marcus that could not be delayed any longer.

Lucius began, "Marcus, I have received word from Rome that the Emperor has ordered a crackdown on all Christian leaders and gatherings. I would guess that that may be one of the reasons that your guest is here."

Peter looked at Lucius. "You are of course correct. Our Church will be attacked throughout the Empire. Many innocent people will die. I fear that those who are disciples of Jesus Christ will be singled out for punishment and execution. The purpose of my travels is to reassure the followers of Christ that though they may perish in this life, God will reward them in the next life. I want to let them know that their faith in Jesus Christ will open the gates of Heaven to them and that they will have eternal happiness with our Lord."

Lucius looked Peter directly in the eyes. "Simon Peter, let me speak perfectly clearly. I came to my friend's home today alone. I knew that you were here. I also know that Rome has issued a warrant for your arrest. The next time that I come to where you are staying, I will come with an escort of legionnaires.

I also have come today because of the fact that you are a guest of Marcus, and that puts Marcus at great risk. Many already know of his gospel and his work for his faith. If he is found to be an apostle, he will be sentenced to be put to death. I do not believe that that is a sentence that either you or I wish to have on our conscience."

Peter stood up and looked at both men. "You are fortunate to have a friend such as this Marcus.

What the Centurion has said is true. Jesus once told me that I would be the rock upon which his church would be built. He also told me that though I would achieve great and wonderful things in his name, I and the others to whom he gave his charge would suffer as he would suffer.

The way of the cross is not an easy way. But, it is the right way. The more that I preach the lessons that I learned from our Lord, the more I understand the truth of his path to a better life."

Peter focused on Lucius. "You have a life that is more difficult than mine or your friend, Marcus. You serve two masters, Rome and your friendship with Marcus. Someday, you may have to choose between those masters. I will pray for you that God helps you to make the right choice."

Looking at Marcus, Peter went on, "I am going to visit with my brother, Andrew, because I believe that we both will not see each other again until we meet in heaven. We have chosen a path that leads to our death here on earth. Jesus knew this when he preached the word of God and all of us who follow know that we too may well face that same fate.

Marcus, you have said that Lucius has advised you to become invisible to Rome. I believe that this is good advice. I think that it would be wise for you to leave Lycia with your family and go to a place where Rome has little interest and take on a new life that will not carry with it the baggage of Marcus Titus. You will, in a sense, be reborn. Use the Christian name that Jesus gave to you.

Jesus told me once that it was God's plan that you would survive to write the word in all of its glory to the end of your time. You must go forth and do as he has commanded for you to do."

The three men talked through the day of plans, arrangements, and of many places in the known world where a person could live with a family and write the word of God in anonymity. By nightfall, Marcus realized that his days left on earth had been mapped out for him not by man but by God.

Peter said good-bye to the Titus family on the next morning. "I doubt that we shall see one another anytime soon. God be with you and your family, Mark."

Chapter 72. "Lost at Sea"

It took several months to accomplish what needed to be done for the wellbeing of Marcus and his family.

Quintus and Marcus had been in regular but guarded contact for many years. Quintus had overseen Marcus' estate in the northern province of Italia and was now well on in years. They both agreed that it was time to part with the land that had prospered so well and supported so many including the two of them.

The property was sold to an adjoining landowner and the profit was used to provide a pension for Quintus along with a home in Rome. A sizeable amount was also brought to Xanthos for use by the Titus family.

During this time, Peter met with Andrew in Cappadocia. They talked about the future of the Church, the teachings of their beloved Savior, and the need for inclusion of all people who accepted Jesus as their Savior.

The two brothers also spoke of family. Peter talked about his wife and children whom he had given up to follow in the Master's footsteps. He missed his family but had no doubt that he was doing what his God expected of him. He confided in Andrew that it was a lonely life with many, many challenges. He told Andrew that he prayed daily for guidance in making the correct choices.

Andrew talked about their father, Jonah. He had been a fisherman his entire life. He had often told his two sons that the greatest gifts that God had given to mankind were the sea, the sky, the moon and the stars by night and the warmth of the sun by day. Andrew remembered the many times the three of them would put out to sea together. How in the midst of hauling in a great quantity of fish, Jonah would tell his sons to pause, feel the spray of the ocean on the wind, feel the sun upon their cheeks, and give praise to the God above.

Andrew asked Peter, "What do you think our own father would say if he knew what we were about now?"

Peter looked at his brother and wisely said, "I believe he knows."

Both apostles nodded in agreement.

As planned, Peter met with Appollos, who was now working with Andrew.

"Appollos, I have a very important matter for you to handle for the Church." Peter explained what was required and why it was one of the most important assignments that Appollos could now undertake. Appollos did not hesitate to accept.

Lucius and three of his subordinate centurions were at the docks of Myra the day that Marcus set off on a merchant ship for the port in Caesarea on the coast of Judea.

Lucius made a point of introducing Marcus Titus to his fellow centurions.

"Where are you bound for?" Lucius asked of Marcus.

"Caesarea and then Jerusalem. I have some affairs of my father, Marcus Aurelius, to settle."

The centurions all had either heard of Marcus Aurelius or had served with him. It was appropriate that Marcus Titus take care of his father's affairs.

The passage to Caesarea was rougher than expected. Storms battered the ship and tossed it about for days. Then a terrible wind swept over the ship only a day out of port. Three men were washed overboard and never found. It was reported to the Roman Consul in Caesarea that one of the three was a Roman citizen, Marcus Titus.

Chapter 73. "The Risen Disciple"

Philip had left Jerusalem after the death of the Messiah and gone to Phrygia to preach the word of the Master. He gave testimony to having seen the many miracles of the Messiah, the greatest of which was the resurrection, a testament in and of itself to life everlasting.

Phillip was married at the time that he accepted Jesus as the Messiah. He had answered Jesus call to follow. He had been faithful to his calling and had witnessed all that Jesus had done during his ministry.

Now, as he grew older, he returned to Caesarea where his family was living. His four daughters were fully grown and had received the Holy Spirit in their hearts. He spent much of his time teaching the lessons of Jesus while his daughters evangelized throughout Samaria to the Sea of Galilee.

On one bright day, Philip went to the coast with several of his students and was teaching them about the great storm that Jesus had used as a lesson in faith. He was not surprised to see a familiar face appear among those who were listening.

"You have traveled far." He said to the stranger.

"I have traveled far. And I have many more miles to travel before I sleep."

Philip said to the man, "Come join us that together we may learn from our travels. What is your name?"

"My name is Mark."

"Do you believe in Jesus Christ as your Savior?" Philip asked.

As the man looked at the other expectant faces, he said, "I do."

He sat down beside the other students and listened to a story that he had not heard before.

Philip picked up his lesson where he had left off. "And Jesus said, 'I will show you a clear and perfect picture of my Father in Heaven.'" Philip paused to look at his students and then continued. "I was filled with anticipation and cried out to my Master, 'Lord, show us now that we may rejoice and be glad.'

Jesus looked at me and said, 'Philip, how long have I been with you and still you do not know me. If you have beheld me with your eyes and with your faith, then you have seen my Father also. I am in the Father, and the father is in me.'

The revelation was both startling and a statement of truth that I then knew in my soul.

I now bear witness to both the Father and to the Son. By God's grace, I witnessed what few men ever will. Having said this, how much greater is your faith, having never seen either the father or the Son and yet you believe."

Mark spent a month with Philip. During this time he remained unshaven. He gained much from his month at the side of the apostle. He learned of many things that he had not known before about Jesus of Nazareth. In the end, Mark was sorry that he had not gone to Judea sooner to be at the side of Jesus and share the many wonderful experiences that Philip had shared with the Messiah.

When the time was appropriate, Philip sent word to John in Jerusalem that the disciple, Mark, was staying with him and would like to arrange a meeting. A week later, the three disciples met in Scythopolis.

Scythopolis was chosen as the place for their meeting because of its mountainous location and the lack of any significant Roman presence. They met at an inn run by a Christian family who had been Gentiles and were brought to the faith by Philip. Their devotion to the Lord was the equal of any disciple.

Marcus was amazed when he first saw John. John had been the youngest of all the disciples even though he was among the very first that Jesus called to follow. Jesus had chosen John to oversee the care of his mother, Mary. Marcus had learned from Philip that John had taken this responsibility very seriously and in fact looked at no other woman out of a sense that it would be a shirking of his responsibility to the Holy Mother.

John greeted Marcus and Philip with his well known warm smile and friendly way. "Marcus and Philip, it is good to be with you both again. I pray to our Lord daily that you both are in good health and watched over by our Savior, the Lord, Jesus Christ." John touched his hand to his heart then his lips and said, "The peace of the Lord, I give to you."

The way in which he did this struck a deep response in Marcus. It was as if Jesus himself was there giving he and Philip his blessing. He was too moved to respond.

Philip had preached with John throughout Judea and knew the effect that John had on people. "John, it was good of you to join us. Marcus, whom we now call by his Christian name, Mark, has been sent to you by Peter. Peter has had a vision in which the Lord appeared to him and directed him to convey to Mark that he must continue with his work on the gospel."

John and Peter had worked closely in the years immediately after the crucifixion of Jesus. They preached together in Jerusalem until Peter's imprisonment and subsequent escape. When Peter went to Rome, John stayed behind in Jerusalem and continued to evangelize and administer to those in need. All who met him sensed the holiness of the man and were at once taken with him. Even the Romans and the Sadducees could harbor no ill will toward John. He preached love and charity to all. Many of the Romans and Sadducees, who had participated in the persecution of Jesus, later went to John repenting and asking for absolution. John graciously and with true compassion gave it to them saying that as Jesus gave his life so that those who sinned could be forgiven, as a disciple of He who John loved, he could do no less. This endeared him to those who now believed in Jesus. They had heard the thunder, saw the ground breaking apart, knew that the body of Jesus had mysteriously disappeared, and were told the story of his resurrection and ascendance to Heaven. John believed that the Holy Spirit had shown them the truth and that he now was the instrument of God's great forgiveness.

When John heard that Peter had sent Marcus to him, he said, "Peter is the Lord's pillar. If it has been given to him to know your direction here on earth then I will willingly do whatever it is that is necessary to help you with your mission."

Marcus replied, "John, Peter told me that of all the disciples, you know the Lord better than the rest. He told me that you above the rest are most like our Savior and therefore most understanding of his ways and his teachings. I would like to spend time with you improving upon my earlier gospel to Jesus. I know from talking with Philip this past month that there are many lessons that were not set forth in my narrative of the

Lord's history. I am certain that you also have many experiences that could further illuminate the time that our Lord was here on earth."

John nodded. "I am traveling to Damascus to ordain a bishop of the Church there. Travel with me, Mark, and I will share all that I can of our Lord. Perhaps we will both grow closer to his perfection and love for us and learn something greater than what you seek."

Marcus had heard that John, although having little formal education, was wise beyond his years and often confounded those who listened to him because his reference point was beyond their understanding. This was not so for Marcus. He understood immediately what John was saying. Marcus had sought experiences, facts about things that had actually taken place. John was offering more. He was offering an understanding of the reasons for what had taken place.

Marcus looked directly at John and both knew that each of them were of one mind. Marcus said, "I am glad that Peter sent me to you. You already have shown me that I should look beyond the horizons of my writings."

That evening, Marcus shared with John and Philip the concerns that Peter and his friend, Lucius, had for the safety of all the disciples. He told them of Peter's specific concern that Marcus continue his work for the future of the Christian Church.

Marcus described the plans that had been made for Marcus Titus, author of the gospel of Jesus Christ, 'to fade from history' and a new disciple to arise, one who's Christian name is Mark.

The next day, the two disciples bid good bye to Philip and began their journey north. Years later, both disciples would attest to their individual enlightenment from the three weeks that they spent together.

Chapter 74. "A New Life"

The death of Marcus Titus caused a week long period of mourning in Xanthos and many other parts of Lycia. His father-in-law presided at the funeral service. There was no body since Marcus had been lost at sea during a ragging storm but a small wooden cross was placed where the casket would normally have been during the funeral service.

Many citizens walked pass the cross, some kneeling to pray and others gently touching the wooden symbol of the man who led them to God. All knew him as either a disciple, an evangelist, author of the Gospel of Jesus Christ, or as a friend and member of their community.

Didyanna consoled her children impressing upon them the truth of the story that their father often told to them about the resurrection of Jesus Christ because of Jesus faith in God who was in Heaven.

Lucius represented Rome at the funeral of his friend and citizen of Rome. He presented a message from Emperor Nero to the representatives of the Lycian League expressing condolences for the loss of one of their members who he reminded them was also a member of a prominent Roman family.

Among the many Christians that attended the funeral, there was one from Asia Minor who was called Appollos. Arriving after the ceremony, he paid his respects to the family at their home.

A month later, while the Titus family was still in mourning, Alex Atolis let it be known that the family had decided that Xanthos held too many memories for Didyanna and the children. They would soon leave to start a new life away from all that reminded them of a beloved husband and father.

Two months later, a tall, muscular, dark skinned man who was heavily armed arrived at the Titus home. He was to be the escort and protector of the Titus family as they journeyed forth to their new life somewhere on the frontier. When asked, family members said that it was Didyanna's wish that their life and contacts with Lycia be completely severed. Otherwise, the memories would be more than she and her children could bear. People who knew the family understood. Marcus Titus had lived his life for two things, his family and his God.

When the day came for them to leave, the Titus family said good byc to their family and friends and turned north with their strange new companion. After about an hour's ride, Didyanna looked over at the dark man, smiled, and asked, "Metros, how many days is it to Germania and our new life?"

"Anna, you will need some patience for this journey. When it seems that we are almost arrived, you will see God's mountains rise up and disappear into the heavens. Crossing those mountains will be almost as long a period of time as it will take for us to get to them." Metros laughed. Then looking at the two children riding behind them, he went on, "Do his children know?"

"Yes, I told them last night. They hardly slept after that. They love their father." She looked back at her son and daughter with a smile. For the first day in weeks, her heart was happy. They smiled back at her.

Appollos had carried out his assignment from Peter. After leaving Rome, he had traveled north to the frontier city of Raetia. It was the last city within the Roman Empire before crossing over into what was known as Germania. Located on the northern most side of the Alps, Raetia was a city few in Rome had ever heard of and, but for a handful, would ever visit.

Appollos was able to purchase a mountainside piece of land and house less than a mile from the city. It had pastoral views and a gentle slope. The land was being used for raising cows and the owners were ready to retire and move into the city with their daughter and her husband. The older couple was pleased to receive the Roman silver that Marcus had provided for Appollos' use.

Appollos took one last look at the house, the beautiful mountains rising behind it, and then the pastures gently sloping down to the road in front. He pictured 'Marcus, no Mark,' in this setting writing about the life and lessons of their Lord and Savior. It seemed to Appollos that this new life for Marcus Titus, Mark, was what God must have intended.

Chapter 75. "The Reunion"

Appollos had met with Mark one last time. He provided Mark with all that Mark needed. He reported that Anna and the children were well and were soon to be on their way to Raetia. Metros had willingly agreed to safeguard them to their new home.

The people who sold the land and home to Appollos knew only that the family that was buying the property was moving here to enjoy the beauty and peace of the mountains and the lakes in this beautiful countryside. Having received the price they were asking, they needed to know no more than that.

It took Mark longer than he had thought that it would to reach his new home. As he walked the last mile from the city of Raetia up to the base of the mountain, he understood what Appollos had said to him, 'God's hand is upon the land.'

The mountains towered up into the heavens. The fields were a maze of green and gold as the mountain flowers grew wild amidst the grass and clover.

Every day, for more than a month, Anna and the children would stand watch in front of their home. They looked for signs that their beloved father and husband was on his way up the road that led from Raetia to their front door.

Alexandria was sitting on the steps of their home when she noticed the tall bearded man with a familiar walk. At first, she rose slowly to get a better view. The walk of the man was as she remembered. His now long brown hair was the right color. Sounding a little tentative, she called out, "Mother, someone is coming." Then as joy spread through her body and touched her soul, she shouted, "Mother, father is home."

Alexandria was off at a run. Young Mark had been cutting wood behind a barn when he heard his sister cry out. He, too, came at a run. As the two children ran down to their father, Anna came out of the house.

Seeing her husband, she recognized him immediately. She wrapped her shawl around her shoulders and hurried after the children.

The thirteenth disciple was home with his family and God's hand was upon him.

Epilogue

Mark and Anna would have another thirty-three years together. They were blessed with a third child, John. Their children would marry local Celtics and would work the land, raise dairy cattle and provide Mark and Anna with twelve grandchildren.

Mark brought forth two more gospels, the first under his own name and the second dedicated to his fellow disciple who helped him with his first gospel of Jesus Christ, Matthew.

Appollos would visit Mark and Anna periodically and would take the completed works of Mark back to the Church in Rome for dissemination to the worldwide Christian Church.

Simon Peter firmly established the Church of Rome. He continued to preach the divinity of Jesus Christ and gained many followers. He also formed the conference of Bishops and appointed many to lead the church in far and distant lands.

Emperor Nero took notice of Peter's work and commanded Peter to recognize the Emperor of Rome as a divine being. Peter refused. Nero had Peter crucified. To show his disdain for Peter, Nero ordered that Peter be crucified on a cross with his head down and his feet nailed to the top of the cross.

Andrew, Peter's brother was taken prisoner by the Roman Governor, Aegeates, of Achaia and was crucified by being tied to a cross to prolong his suffering.

Jude had gone to Persia to evangelize. He was killed by being shot to death with arrows while he was tied to a cross.

Matthew was apprehended by the Roman authorities in Ethiopia and beheaded.

Philip remained in Caesarea, preaching and offering absolution to all who repented of their sins. His four daughters followed in his path and preached throughout Judea and even into Syria. He died of natural causes at the age of ninety-three.

John lived into his nineties. He was widely traveled and in his advanced years retired to Ephesus where he decided to write the forth and final gospel of the New Testament. He was given to experiencing many visions which encouraged him to correct some of the passages of the gospels of Mark, Matthew, and Luke, all of which he spent many years studying before his own gospel was completed. He died at the age of ninety-two, having never married and maintaining a pure love for Jesus of Nazareth to the very end of his life.

Pontius Pilate continued to have problems with those under his authority. When he ordered a violent reprisal against a gathering of Samaritans, he sparked further unrest in Judea and Samaria. The Emperor was displeased with Pilate and had him recalled back to Rome. A hearing was held before the Emperor and Pilate was banished without compensation. He died a pauper.

Appollos continued to learn the faith and became a powerful preacher of the Christian faith. He founded the Church in Corinth. Later he preached throughout all of Asia establishing a permanent Christian presence.

Lucius Neros never saw his friend Marcus Titus again. In 70 AD, his Legion returned from Lycia to Jerusalem to join with two other Legions in putting down the revolt led by the Jewish Zealots against Rome. His commander was Emperor Vespasian's son. Ironically, the son's name was Titus. The Temple of Jerusalem was destroyed.

Centuries later, the Church would have to contend with many writings that conflicted with the original writings and their authors. Many of the early tenets of the Church were passed down by word of mouth and also conflicted with the early history and writings of those who witnessed the life and teachings of Jesus Christ. There came a time when the Church sought to unify its beliefs into one comprehensive testament that would be acceptable to all. The establishment of a cohesive theology was done with as much attention to the details as could be brought to bear at the Council of Nicea, more than three centuries after the birth of Jesus of Nazareth.

Some of the original historical writings were passed over and some of the witnesses to the truth of what took place were eliminated to satisfy the desire for simplicity and universal acceptance. But the words of faith, hope, forgiveness, and salvation have survived for more than two thousand years.

Two of the three gospels written by Mark were preserved in the New Testament. The gospel of Matthew and the gospel of Mark provide a foundation for the Christian faith and the window through which we have come to know and understand the life and teachings of Jesus Christ.

The work of the other disciple, the Thirteenth Disciple, is finally complete.

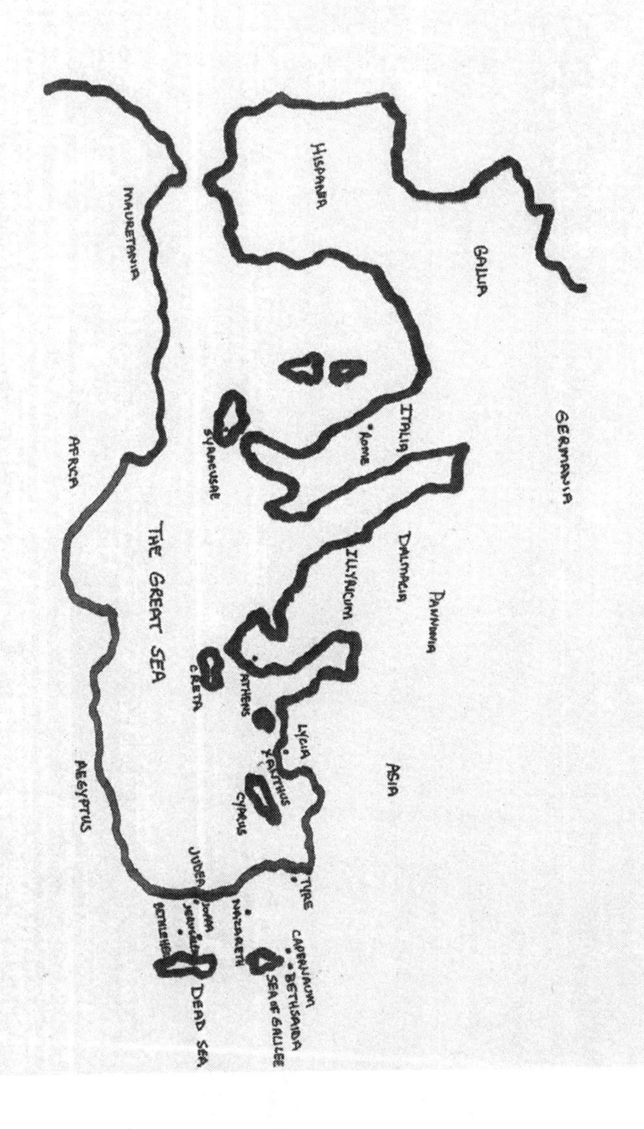

HISPANIA
GALLIA
GERMANIA
MAURETANIA
ITALIA
ROME
SYRACUSAE
AFRICA
THE GREAT SEA
DALMATIA
ILLYRICUM
PANNONIA
CRETA
ATHENS
LYCIA
ASIA
CYPRUS
AEGYPTUS
JUDEA
TYRE
NAZARETH
CAPERNAUM
BETHSAIDA
SEA OF GALILEE
DEAD SEA

About the Author

Jack Luchsinger is an attorney and active community leader in Upstate New York. He is the author of a political novel entitled "The Politician", published in 1996, as well as a short story entitled "A Holiday Message" published in 1989.

His parents were from different religious backgrounds, his mother being a Roman Catholic and his father being a Protestant. Jack likes to consider his religious background as ecumenical having been confirmed in both the Roman Catholic faith as well as in the Protestant faith.

"I have always been a student of religion." It was not surprising for Jack to take a special interest in a sermon delivered by a visiting priest from Canada one Sunday in 2005. The subject was 'the other disciple'. After years of research since that day, Jack has brought forth this historical novel dealing with the life of 'the other disciple' and his importance to the Christian faith. "I wanted to write something that would be interesting to today's readers. Something that will encourage readers to explore the great offerings that the Bible has for all of us."

A book based upon fact and inspiration, The Thirteenth Disciple is a must read for those who seek a new look at traditional beliefs.

CPSIA information can be obtained at www.ICGtesting.com
Printed in the USA
BVOW010051160911

271407BV00001B/25/P